PENGUIN BOOKS

Runner

Patrick Lee lives in Hudsonville, Michigan. He is the author of three previous novels: *The Breach* (a *New York Times* bestseller), *Ghost Country* and *Deep Sky*.

Runner

PATRICK LEE

PENGUIN BOOKS

PENGUIN BOOKS

Published by the Penguin Group
Penguin Books Ltd, 80 Strand, London WC2R ORL, England
Penguin Group (USA) Inc., 375 Hudson Street, New York, New York 10014, USA
Penguin Group (Canada), 90 Eglinton Avenue East, Suite 700, Toronto, Ontario, Canada M4P 2Y3
(a division of Pearson Penguin Canada Inc.)
Penguin Ireland, 25 St Stephen's Green, Dublin 2, Ireland (a division of Penguin Books Ltd)
Penguin Group (Australia), 707 Collins Street, Melbourne, Victoria 3008, Australia
(a division of Pearson Australia Group Pty Ltd)
Penguin Books India Pvt Ltd, 11 Community Centre, Panchsheel Park, New Delhi – 110 017, India
Penguin Group (NZ), 67 Apollo Drive, Rosedale, Auckland 0632, New Zealand
(a division of Pearson New Zealand Ltd)
Penguin Books (South Africa) (Pty) Ltd, Block D, Rosebank Office Park,
181 Jan Smuts Avenue, Parktown North, Gauteng 2193, South Africa

Penguin Books Ltd, Registered Offices: 80 Strand, London WC2R ORL, England

www.penguin.com

First published in the United States of America by Minotaur Books 2014
First published in Great Britain by Penguin Books 2014

001

Copyright © Patrick Lee, 2014

The moral right of the author has been asserted

*This is a work of fiction. All of the characters, organizations and events portrayed
in this novel are either products of the author's imagination or are used fictitiously*

Set in 12.5/14.75pt Garamond MT Std
Typeset by Jouve (UK), Milton Keynes
Printed in Great Britain by Clays Ltd, Elcograf S.p.A.

A CIP catalogue record for this book is available from the British Library

ISBN: 978-1-405-94049-8

www.greenpenguin.co.uk

In memory of William Sharp and Marge Toporek

PART ONE
Rachel

If there is a witness to my little life,
To my tiny throes and struggles,
He sees a fool;
And it is not fine for gods to menace fools.

Stephen Crane

Chapter One

Just after three in the morning, Sam Dryden surrendered the night to insomnia and went running on the boardwalk. Cool humidity clung to him and filtered the lights of El Sedero to his left, the town sliding past like a tanker in the fog. To his right was the Pacific, black and silent as the edge of the world tonight. His footfalls on the old wood came back to him from every part of the darkness.

It was just as well not to sleep. Sleep brought dreams of happier times, worse than nightmares in their own way.

Mercury lights over the boardwalk shone down into the mist. They snaked away in a chain to the south, the farthest all but lost in the gloom where the boardwalk terminated at the channel. Dryden passed the occasional campfire on the beach and caught fragments of conversations amplified in the fog. Soft voices, laughter, huddled silhouettes haloed by firelight. Shutter glimpses of what life could be. Dryden felt like an intruder, seeing them. Like a ghost passing them in the dark.

These night-time runs were a new thing, though he'd lived in El Sedero for years. He'd started taking them a few weeks before, at all hours of the night. They came on like fits – compulsions he wasn't sure he could fight. He hadn't tried to, so far. He found the exertion and the cold air refreshing, if not quite enjoyable. No doubt the exercise was good for him, too, though outwardly he didn't seem to need it. He was lean for his six-foot frame and looked at least no older than his thirty-six years. Maybe the jogs were just his mind's attempt to kick-start him from inertia.

Inertia. That was what a friend had called it, months ago. One of the few who still came around. Five years back, right after everything had happened, there had been lots of friends. They'd been supportive when they were supposed to be, and later they'd been insistent – they'd pushed him the way people did when they cared. Pushed him to start his life again. He'd said he appreciated it, said they were right – of course you had to move on after a while. He'd agreed and nodded, and watched the way their eyes got sad when they understood he was only saying those things to make them stop talking. He hadn't tried to explain his side of it. Hadn't told them that missing someone could feel like a watch you'd been assigned to stand. That it could feel like duty.

He passed the last of the fires. Here the beach beneath the walk became rocky and damp, the moisture catching the glow from each lamppost. The shore lay vacant for the next several hundred yards. A minute later, in the middle of the dead stretch, Dryden came to an intersection in the boardwalk; a second branch led away inland.

He slowed and stopped. He almost always did, at this spot. He wasn't sure what drew him to it – maybe just the emptiness of it. The junction lay in the darkness between lights, and there was never anyone around. Nights like this, with no moon and no surf, this place was the equivalent of a sensory deprivation chamber.

He leaned on the wooden rail with his elbows, facing the sea. As his breathing slowed, faint sounds finally came to him. The hiss of tires on the freeway, a mile inland beyond the dunes. Tiny animals moving in the beach grass behind the walk. Dryden had been standing there for over a minute when he heard another sound: running footsteps on the boardwalk's planking.

For a moment he thought it was another jogger. Then he knew otherwise – the cadence was too fast. This was someone sprinting full-out. In the saturated air, the sound's origin was hard to trace. He looked left and then right along the shoreline stretch of the walk, but against the light glow he did not see anybody coming. He was just stepping back from the rail, turning to look down the inland route, when the sprinting figure crashed into him from that direction.

He heard a gasp – the voice of a young girl. Instantly she was fighting, pushing back from him in a panic, already turning to bolt away along the shoreline course.

'Hey,' Dryden said. 'Are you alright?'

She stopped and faced him. Even in the faint light, Dryden could see that she was terrified of something. She regarded him with nothing but caution and kept herself balanced to sprint again, though she seemed too out of breath to go much farther. She wore jeans and a T-shirt but no shoes or socks. Her hair – dark brown, hanging below her shoulders – was clean but uncombed. The girl could not have been more than twelve. For the briefest moment her eyes intensified; Dryden could see the calculation going on behind them.

Just like that, her defensive posture changed. She remained afraid, but not of him. She turned her gaze inland instead, back the way she'd come from, and scrutinized the darkness there. Dryden looked, too, but saw nothing out of the ordinary. The inland run of the boardwalk led to the harbor road, across which lay the dune ridge, shrouded in the thick night. All appeared calm and quiet.

'You live near here?' the girl asked.

'Who's after you?'

She turned to him again and moved closer.

'I need somewhere to hide,' she said. 'I'll tell you everything, but please get me out of here first.'

'I'll take you to the police station, kid, but I can't—'

'Not the police,' she said, so abruptly that Dryden felt an impulse to turn and continue his jog. Whatever the girl was in trouble for, getting caught up in it was not going to improve his night.

Seeing his change of expression, she stepped forward fast and grabbed his hand, her eyes pleading. 'I'm not running from the police. It's not like that.'

Her gaze snapped to the side again, in the same moment that Dryden sensed movement in his peripheral vision. He followed her stare, and for a moment couldn't make sense of what he saw. Somehow he could discern the shapes of the dunes now, invisible in the gloom only moments earlier. They were rimmed with a faint, shifting light. The girl's breathing trembled.

'Yes or no,' she said. 'I can't wait any longer.'

Dryden knew the sound of real terror in a person's voice. This girl wasn't afraid of getting busted for some misdemeanor; she was afraid for her life.

The light around the dunes sharpened, and Dryden suddenly understood what he was seeing: People with flashlights were about to crest the ridge from the far side. The urge to distance himself from the girl was gone, replaced by a sense that something was very wrong here, and that she wasn't lying.

'Come on,' Dryden said.

Still holding her hand, he ran north along the boardwalk, back in the direction of his house. He had to slow his pace only slightly for her. As they ran, Dryden kept looking to the dunes. He and the girl had gone no more than fifty yards when the first sharp spike of light topped the ridge. Within seconds, three more appeared. He was surprised by how close they were; the night had been playing tricks on his sense of distance.

Directly ahead along the boardwalk, one of the overhead mercury lights was coming up fast. Dryden stopped, the girl almost pulling his arm off as she stopped with him.

'What are you doing?' she asked. She watched the pursuers as tensely as Dryden did.

He nodded to the cone of light on the boardwalk. 'They'll see us if we run through the light.'

'We can't stay here,' the girl said.

The men with flashlights – six of them now – were descending the face of the dune ridge at sprint speed.

Dryden looked over the rail on the ocean side of the boardwalk. The beach was only a few feet below. He gestured to it, and the girl understood. She slipped under the waist-high rail, and he followed, his feet touching down on the loose stones piled beneath the walk. Beyond the stones, the beach extended a hundred feet to the waterline, rocky but still mostly sand. Dryden knelt and touched the surface; it was smooth and flat, saturated by the mist, and bore not a footprint as far as he could see in the near-dark. If he and the girl made any move on the beach, the pursuers would easily spot their prints and follow.

He turned his attention to the space beneath the walk. It wasn't promising. The piled stones were volleyball sized; picking their way over them would be slow going, especially in the deep shadows there. Worse, support beams crisscrossed the space every few feet. They'd make little progress before the men arrived, and

8

certainly at least one of the six would drop to the beach to put some light under the boardwalk. As a hiding place, it was a dead giveaway.

Dryden looked up over the planking and saw the men reach the base of the dune. It was all happening too quickly. In the still night he heard their running footsteps on the asphalt of the harbor road, and then on the wood of the inland boardwalk stretch. In less than thirty seconds, they would reach the rail above this very spot.

Dryden looked at the cross bracing under the walk and saw the only solution available. He guided the girl underneath. She was shaking but seemed relieved to be getting out of sight. Below the surface planks, heavy beams ran lengthwise along the walkway. These were in turn supported by far thicker beams, running sideways like the planking. Above these lower beams were gaps, not big enough for a person to fit into, but big enough for a pair of feet or hands.

'Hold on to me,' Dryden said, and pulled the girl against his chest. She complied without hesitating; the footsteps of the approaching men began to shake the boardwalk.

With the girl hugging tight against him, Dryden reached up and grabbed one of the lower beams with his fingertips – it was far too big to get his hands around – and then swung his feet up and hooked them into the gap above the next beam, five feet away. He made a hammock of himself, with the girl atop him,

9

and pulled himself as tightly against the underside of the boardwalk as he could. It was like doing a push-up in reverse.

It was immediately clear he could not hold this position for long. Everything about it was wrong. His fingertips had no traction on the giant beam, requiring him to apply pressure to hang on. The muscles in his forearms were burning within seconds. At the same time, keeping his body straight involved contracting half of his muscles in ways they weren't meant to be used.

The girl seemed to understand, perhaps feeling his muscle tremors. As the footsteps thundered toward them, she put her mouth to his ear and whispered, 'They have guns. They'll kill us.'

A moment later, the gaps in the boardwalk above filled with flashlight glare. The men had reached the shoreline stretch of the walk and had begun to fan out along it.

One of them spoke, his voice ringing clear and strong. It sounded like a voice accustomed to giving orders.

'Search the beach. Search beneath the causeway.'

Boots scuffed the wood, then landed hard on the rocks nearby. The glow of the flashlights filled Dryden's peripheral vision, though for the moment the beams remained pointed toward the sea. The girl hugged him tighter; he thought he could feel her shutting her eyes as she buried her face in his shoulder. The pain in his muscles was beyond burning now, but pain wasn't the problem. There were ways to disregard agony – Dryden had learned them long ago – but at some point his muscles would simply fail. Willpower couldn't beat physics forever.

He managed to swivel his head a few degrees toward the beach. The flashlight beams finished sweeping the sand, and then one by one they turned to scour the space beneath the boardwalk. Dryden looked upward again, to prevent his eyes from shining. Staring at the planking above his face, he saw the diffused glow as beams passed directly beneath him. If even one of the searchers was clever or suspicious enough to raise his light by two feet, it would all be over. Dryden waited for the blinding glare that would signal that very thing.

It never came.

The vague wash of light subsided. Darkness. Dryden counted to ten and risked another glance at the beach. The searchers had moved on to the north, inspecting the boardwalk as they went. It was time to swing down and try for a quiet getaway, whatever the risk. Every moment he delayed increased the chance that he'd simply fall, which would be anything but quiet. He was starting to slide his feet out of the gap when a sound stopped him.

Footsteps. Heavy and slow, on the boardwalk above. They approached from the south, the direction the searchers had come from. Dryden remained frozen. The man on the boardwalk stopped directly above him; traces of sand fell in Dryden's face.

'Clay,' the man called out. It was the leader. The guy with the voice. He'd remained on the boardwalk while the others searched.

One of the men on the beach, Clay apparently, turned and approached, his flashlight playing haphazardly over the ground. He stopped at the edge of the boardwalk, looking up at the leader. Had he lowered his gaze and looked straight ahead, he would have locked eyes with Dryden, no more than eighteen inches away. Dryden dared not even turn his head upward again; the slightest movement could give him up. He hoped the shuddering of his muscles didn't show as intensely as it felt.

Of Clay's features, Dryden could see almost nothing. The man was barely a silhouette against the black ocean and sky. Only the backscatter glow from the flashlight beam offered any detail: medium-length hair, dark clothing, a weapon hanging at his side by a shoulder strap. A submachine gun – something like an MP-5 with a heavy sound suppressor.

Above, on the boardwalk, the leader said, 'This is out of hand already. Go back to the van, set up coverage of police channels in a twenty-mile radius. Call Chernin, get him working on personal cell phones of officers and whatever federal agents are based in the area. Gold-pan the audio for keywords like *girl* and *lost*. Try *psych ward* while you're at it.'

'You think if she talks to anybody,' Clay said, 'they'll think she walked out of a mental hospital?'

Dryden suddenly felt his fingertips slipping from their hold on the fog-dampened wood. No amount of exertion could stop it; he was going to lose his grip in a matter of seconds.

'Solid chance of it,' the leader said.

Dryden's fingertips held by a quarter inch. He felt that margin shrink by half in the span of a breath.

'And if we lose the trail anyway?' Clay asked.

For a second the leader didn't answer. Then he said, 'Either she gets buried in the gravel pits, or we do.'

Dryden tensed for the fall, trying to imagine any way he could get on his feet and escape with the girl.

At that instant he felt her move. Without a sound, she took her arms from around his chest, reached past his head to the beam, and clamped her hands as tightly as she could over his fingertips. The minor force she could apply was enough to make the difference; his grip held.

Above the clamor of thoughts demanding Dryden's attention, one briefly took precedence: *How the hell had she known?*

A second later Clay pocketed his flashlight, climbed onto the boardwalk, and ran off in the direction the group had come from. Dryden waited for the leader to move off as well, but for a moment he only stood there, his breath audible in the darkness. Then he turned and thudded away to the north, following the searchers. When his footsteps had grown faint, Dryden at last slipped his feet from the beam and swung down. Blood surged into his muscles like ice water. The girl got her balance on the rocks and leaned past him to look up the beach. Dryden looked, too: The searchers were a hundred yards away.

The girl sniffled. Dryden realized she was crying.

'Thank you,' she whispered. Her voice cracked on the first word. 'I'm sorry you had to do that for me.'

Dryden had a thousand questions. They could all wait a few minutes.

He turned and scanned inland for the best route away from here. There was a comforting span of darkness between the boardwalk and the harbor road. A block north along its length, the back streets of El Sedero branched deeper inland, into the cover of night. He and the girl could take the long way around and circle back to his house, half a mile north on the beach.

Taking a last look to make sure the searchers were still moving away, Dryden guided the girl under the boardwalk and into the long grass beyond.

Chapter Two

Neither of them spoke until they were three blocks in from the sea, moving north on the dark streets of the old part of town. Even there, Dryden kept watch for Clay, on the chance he'd gone this way en route to the van – the marine fog wasn't dense enough to provide them cover. For the moment, though, they seemed to have El Sedero to themselves.

Dryden spoke quietly. 'Who are they? What is this – are you a witness to something?'

He couldn't imagine what else it could be.

The girl shook her head. 'I don't think so. I don't really know.'

'You don't know if you witnessed something?'

'There's more to it than that,' she said.

Dryden could still hear a hitch in her breathing, though she'd stopped crying a few minutes earlier.

'It's not too late for you to keep yourself out of this,' she said. 'What you've already done is more than—'

'I'm not leaving you out here by yourself. I'm taking you somewhere safe. We can still go to the police, even if these guys can listen in.'

The girl shook her head again, more emphatically this time. 'We can't.'

'There are police stations that have a hundred officers in them,' Dryden said, 'even this time of night. You'd be protected, no matter who knows you're there.'

'You don't understand.'

'Then explain it to me.'

The girl was quiet again for a moment. She looked down at her bare feet, padding silently on the concrete.

Dryden said, 'My name's Sam. Sam Dryden.'

The girl looked up at him. 'Rachel.'

'Rachel, I'm not going to think you're crazy. I saw them. I heard what they said. Whatever this is, you can tell me.'

She kept her eyes on him as they walked. If Dryden had ever seen a kid look more lost, he didn't know when.

'Where would you be safe?' he asked. 'You must have family. You must have someone.'

'I don't know if I do or not,' she said. 'I don't remember.'

She seemed about to say more when an explosion of sound cut her off, ripping through the mist in front of them. Rachel jumped and grabbed Dryden's arm, but already they could both see the source of the noise. A cat had knocked a metal trash can lid to the sidewalk, seeking some unseen quarry among the garbage inside. Rachel calmed, but kept hold of Dryden's arm as they started forward again.

'All I can remember is the last two months,' she said. 'In that time, no, I don't have anyone.'

There was a worn-out quality to her speech that no kid's voice should have. It would've fit a soldier, months or years into combat deployment. The spoken counterpart to the thousand-yard stare.

'Where did you come from tonight?' Dryden asked. 'Where were they chasing you from?'

'From where they were keeping me. Where they had me the whole time I can remember. They were going to kill me tonight. I got away.'

They passed the cat in the trash can. It paused from its hunting to regard them warily, then went back to business. Dryden stepped over the lid in his path, and then a thought came to him. It skittered like fingertips down his spine. Even as the notion took shape, Rachel froze and stared at him with wide eyes, seeming to react to something in his body language.

Dryden looked at her, briefly distracted by her uncanny perception, then let it go. He turned his attention back on the fallen lid.

'We need to get off the sidewalk,' he said.

He was moving even before he finished saying it. He guided Rachel into the shadows beside the nearest house and around to the back side. Here, the adjoining rear yards of two rows of homes formed a channel that paralleled the street. Dryden picked up their pace, north through the channel, determined to get away from the trash can as quickly as possible.

'They'll come to that sound, won't they,' Rachel said.

'Yes.'

He'd no sooner said it than running footsteps thudded on concrete, somewhere nearby. He shoved Rachel behind a shrub and ducked in alongside her; they were sandwiched between tiny branches and the foundation wall of a house. Staring out through the gap between the shrub and the concrete, Dryden had a limited view to the south, back the way they'd come from. He saw a shape flash by, two houses away. Seconds later the searcher's boots stopped on the sidewalk Dryden and Rachel had abandoned a moment before. Silence. Then came the beep and hiss of a communication device. In the still, dense air, the man's voice reached Dryden with clarity.

'Three-six, north of three-four's position. No contact.'

A voice came back over the communicator, distorted but perceptible as Clay's. 'Copy, this is three-four, on my way back from the van.'

Now a third voice came in; Dryden recognized it as that of the leader. 'Three-six, continue the street search. We think the girl doubled back. Resweep of the beach picked up a lead.'

'Copy, what'd you find?' the nearby man asked.

'A man's wallet,' the leader said. 'Under the causeway, right where we lost the trail.'

Dryden shut his eyes and exhaled. He didn't even need to check; his ass against the foundation wall told him what was missing from his back pocket. He checked anyway. His wallet was gone.

Over the communicator, the leader said, 'Double set of tracks in the sand, inland from the wallet toward your position. The team's coming to you now. Coordinate with them and sweep the neighborhood. Three-four, meet me at the van; the wallet's owner lives just north of here.'

Chapter Three

Martin Gaul stood on the private balcony outside his office. He had his phone in his hand. He was holding it tightly enough that he could hear its glass display stressing.

The balcony faced south from the top floor of the building, overlooking Los Angeles from Sunset Boulevard. Gaul stared down on the night-time expanse of the city – a thousand square miles of lighted gridwork, crisscrossed with freeways like the fiber-optic veins of an electronic life form.

He shut his eyes and tried to steady his breathing. Tried to choke the anxiety that had arrived with a phone call three minutes earlier.

Curren's team had lost the girl.

Gaul turned from the rail. He paced to a table near the sliding door and set the phone on it, willing the damned thing to ring again, this time with news that everything was taken care of. He stared at it a moment longer and then went back to the view.

There was a taste in his mouth – a mix of low-burning fear and tension. He had experienced it before, thirty years back, the summer between college and the army, when he lived in Boston. He'd gone to a Sox game with friends and hit a bar outside Fenway afterward, and a lot of shots later he'd come out alone, vaguely aware that his friends had already gone. There'd been a girl he thought he was doing pretty well with, but then she left without saying good-bye, which put him in a rough mood. He remembered wandering outside and walking toward what he thought was the bus stop, and much later ending up down by the river, near Harvard Bridge. He was looking for a spot to take a piss when the trouble happened.

All this time later, he couldn't remember much of how it had started. There'd been a guy there. Maybe a homeless guy, he'd thought at the time. Maybe just another drunk coming from a bar. They had argued. Gaul might have started it – he could admit that to himself now. He'd been in that mood, after all. He'd started lots of arguments because of moods like that, and given people no choice but to argue back.

This time it had become more than an argument. There had been shoves and punches, and one of his had connected just right and dropped the guy at the edge of the river, and Gaul had gotten out of there. It'd only occurred to him later, ten minutes and ten blocks away, to wonder if the guy had landed with his head in the water. Something had splashed, but in the moment he'd ignored it. He got a bus home and lay awake for over an hour, convincing himself he'd imagined that splash – the mind could invent all kinds of things to color in its fears.

The story had led the local newscast, noon the following day. Grad student dead in the Charles, foul play suspected, police asking for tips. Gaul's mind had filled up with *what-if*s. How many outdoor security cameras had he stumbled past, going to and from the river? How many cabbies and bouncers and late-shift bus drivers had seen him out there, well enough to describe him to the police?

All summer long, that taste in his mouth, just like right now. Like your throat had some chemical it only made when you were in deep trouble – the kind of trouble that left you with nothing to do but wait.

The phone rang. He snapped it up as if it were prey.

'Tell me you got her,' he said.

'I left the bulk of the team searching,' Curren said. 'They'll report when they've got something. Clay and I are inside Sam Dryden's residence now. He's not here.'

'You haven't made your presence there obvious, have you? If he and the girl are still en route to the place—'

'They wouldn't see us. Drapes are closed. No lights on that weren't already on. I don't expect them to show, though. They should've been here by now if they were coming. Maybe Dryden noticed the wallet missing and got spooked.'

'If he's helping her, where does it put us?'

'In trouble, I would say.'

Gaul felt a vein behind his ear begin to throb against the band of his glasses. 'Let's hear it,' he said.

Curren recited a summary of Dryden's bio, no doubt

reading it off a handheld unit. 'Sam Dryden. Army right out of high school, Rangers, then Delta for three years. Generalized training along the way, multirole stuff: rotorcraft pilot certification, HALO jumps, like that. Then he resigns from Delta and the record goes black for the next six years.'

'There's no such thing as black,' Gaul said.

'That's above my pay scale. Officially, he disappears off the planet from age twenty-four to thirty. When he appears again, he's out of the military, living here in El Sedero. Marries at thirty-one, has a kid, goes to school to get a teaching certificate. He's a year into that when the wife and kid die in a car crash, at which point he gives up on the teaching thing. That's five years ago now. File's pretty thin since then. Some income from private security work, consulting for small companies. Nothing special.'

It took a moment for Gaul to reply. His free hand was gripping the balcony rail. The sodium-lit tundra of the city lay hard and clear in his vision. He hadn't blinked in all the time Curren had been talking.

'Sir?' Curren said.

The girl was gone, probably being assisted by a man whose training surpassed even Curren's. Gaul could make two calls and have access to the blacked-out portion of Sam Dryden's file within half an hour – he would do that as soon as he ended this conversation – but the details hardly mattered. The fact that Dryden had done anything worth blacking out meant he had a formidable skillset, even if it was outdated by a few years.

'Turn the house inside out,' Gaul said. 'Every name, every e-mail address, run everything through the system.'

'Clay's on it now.'

'Help him,' Gaul said, and hung up.

He made the calls to get his people working on Dryden's file, and then he made another call. The voice that answered sounded rough and cracked. Its owner had probably been awake already – it was after six in the morning in Washington, D.C. – but likely by no more than a few minutes.

'I'm sorry to disturb you,' Gaul said.

'What do you need?'

Gaul had long admired the man's directness. Late-night television comics had the guy all wrong, playing him as an affable buffoon. He was off balance in front of a microphone, that was all.

Gaul spent ninety seconds filling him in, sugarcoating none of it. When he was done the line stayed silent a long time. Then something sloshed in a glass. Not water, Gaul knew – not even at this hour.

'I need satellite coverage,' Gaul said. 'I need the Mirandas, the whole constellation. I need full control of them, I need Homeland and DoD locked out, and I need it to stay that way until I say otherwise.'

The man on the other end sighed. Something – maybe a couch – creaked and settled.

'I'll have to take that up the chain,' the man said.

Gaul didn't ask how long it would take. There wasn't a hell of a lot of chain above the guy.

'I'll call you back,' the man said. 'Fifteen minutes.'

Chapter Four

Dryden stared out through the boughs of a cedar at the edge of a small park. He and Rachel had traveled only three blocks from the yard they'd first hidden in. They were still deep inside the residential back streets of El Sedero, with Rachel's pursuers everywhere.

Within sixty seconds of the last radio transmission, the rest of the men had filtered into the neighborhood like shadows. When they wanted to be quiet, they were good at it. They'd also stowed their flashlights, making it much harder to pinpoint their locations. Each time Dryden had led Rachel from one piece of cover to the next, he'd studied the open ground for at least a minute first. Even at that, they'd been lucky to make it this far; these people had elite training in their backgrounds. Dryden could see it in the moves they made – and didn't make. No wasted motion. Nothing extraneous. He'd had the same principles drilled into him years before.

He studied the park. One side butted up against a row of backyards; another lay open to the street. As he watched, a silhouette passed through the space between the jungle gym and the swing set, forty yards away.

Dryden turned his attention toward the adjacent

homes. They lay east of where he and Rachel were hiding – inland, away from the sea. The plan, so far as he had one, was to move in that direction, into the broad commercial district across the interstate. If nothing else, that part of town was much larger, with storefronts and warehouses and industrial lots. Easier to hide in. Harder to seek in. The plan could evolve from there.

The man in the park slipped away to the street, crossed it, and vanished into the shadows between houses on the far side. Dryden turned the other way again, scrutinizing the open ground between the cedar shrub and the east-side row of homes. The distance he and Rachel would have to cross was seventy feet, give or take. It lay mostly in darkness, but there was no cover at all. Anyone watching might see them, once they went for it.

He gave the street and the yards beyond one last survey. No one moving. No one there at all, that he could see. He was already holding Rachel's hand; he turned to her and nodded in the direction they would run. She nodded back, scared but ready. Dryden was tensing to move when she squeezed his hand sharply, a convulsive action that could only be a warning. He didn't even look toward her. He didn't move at all. He held dead still and took quiet breaths through his mouth.

Three seconds later a man passed in front of the cedar shrub, less than ten feet from where they crouched. He'd come from behind and to the side, his approach hidden by the bush itself. His footsteps were entirely silent on the damp grass. Even now, watching each step, Dryden could hear nothing. How Rachel had detected him, he couldn't imagine. She was maybe three feet closer to where the guy had appeared from, and kids' ears tended to be better than those of grown-ups, but for all that, her senses had to be unreal.

Dryden waited. The man moved deeper into the park. He stopped there and turned a slow circle, briefly swinging his gaze past the place where Dryden and Rachel were hiding. It occurred to Dryden that only the sheer number of such shrubs – hundreds throughout the park and the surrounding blocks – prevented the searchers from systematically checking them all. They were watching open ground for movement instead.

The guy finished his sweep and moved on, following the same path as the man before him. When he'd gone, Dryden scanned the street again. Empty – at least as empty as it had seemed before. He looked at Rachel. She nodded, ready as ever. They ran.

They didn't stop running until nearly ten minutes later. When Rachel slowed, five minutes in, Dryden picked her up and kept going at almost full speed. He only stopped when they reached the top of an embankment high above the freeway.

He was winded and felt a vague headache at his temples: not quite pain, but a kind of chill. Whatever it was, it meant he'd slipped a bit since his prime. Back in his days in the unit, he'd routinely knocked out ten-mile runs hauling gear that weighed as much as Rachel.

He recovered enough to breathe quietly and listened to the night around them. Above the whisper of traffic, sparse at this hour, he strained for what he hoped he wouldn't hear: a helicopter. Someone who could assemble a team of men with silenced machine guns — and was brazen enough to deploy them on civilian streets — might be able to call in other resources. A chopper with a thermal camera would spot him and the girl as easily as if they were glowing.

Dryden listened for twenty seconds longer but heard nothing. It didn't mean they were in the clear.

He stared across the freeway toward the commercial and industrial parts of town. Chopper or no chopper, they still had to hide. He was about to start down the embankment when something stopped him — an instinctive impulse, deep in his mind, like the feel of the hair on his neck standing taut.

A response to a threat. But what threat?

He held still and listened again. There was no sound but the traffic. He scanned the darkness and saw nothing.

The fear hadn't come from anything he'd seen or heard — it had only been a thought, just below conscious awareness. Some sense of an extra wrinkle in the danger they faced. What was it?

He waited, but the idea stayed out of reach. All that came to him was a sudden conviction: Hiding in El Sedero was the wrong move.

Rachel watched him. Her eyes were full of concern, though she said nothing.

Dryden nodded across the interstate. Beyond the trees on the far side, a quarter mile away, the lights of a twenty-four-hour superstore shone in the humidity.

'Time to go,' he said.

The computer room, one level below Gaul's office, was lit only by the glow of its plasma monitors – nine in all. Gaul paced while his chief technical officer, Lowry, prepped them for the image streams from the Miranda satellites. There was no actual image data coming down yet, just blank screens configured and waiting. Gaul had yet to receive access to the birds, and every additional minute of delay made his pulse louder in his ears.

'Signatures locked,' Lowry said. 'Ready whenever we get the streams.'

The Mirandas were the most impressive machines humans had ever put into orbit. Their thermal imaging capability was ten years ahead of what even the most optimistic science journalists supposed it was. A Miranda could distinguish a fat man from a skinny man anywhere on earth, day or night, although that wasn't what made them special. Lots of spy birds could do that. The difference was that a Miranda could do it from an orbit fifteen times higher: 2,000 miles up instead of the standard 130 for most recon platforms. That meant each one of them had a very wide area in which to hunt.

The full constellation of Mirandas had overlapping coverage of the entire planet at all times, like the GPS network. The system could watch any spot on earth, at any moment, from at least three satellites, and often four or five. It could lock onto a moving target, whether it was a jogger or a cruise missile, and follow it with ease. There was nowhere to run from it, and sure as hell nowhere to hide.

Of course, you had to find your target before you could follow it. Gaul would only be able to spot Rachel and her new friend if they were still on foot in the countryside around El Sedero by the time he got access to the Mirandas, and every second he had to wait, that window of opportunity slipped closer to shut.

Suddenly message boxes bloomed on all nine of the monitors; Lowry snapped to attention. A second later, Gaul's phone rang. He answered.

'They're all yours,' the man on the line said.

Dryden and Rachel reached the edge of the superstore's lot at a run, and stopped to survey the scattered cars parked there. Most were clustered at the front of the building, probably belonging to the store's third-shift employees, but a handful were parked out at the periphery. Maybe they'd been left there by workers pulling a double shift, who'd arrived last evening when the lot was full.

Dryden led the way to the nearest of the outlying vehicles, a dark green Taurus. The more commonplace the model, the better; anything they took would be reported stolen within hours, and Rachel's pursuers had access to police communications. Blending in would be critical. Dryden gave the Taurus only a passing consideration, however, because it was new enough that it almost certainly had a smart key; it couldn't simply be hot-wired.

They moved on, skirting the rim of the lot toward the next group of vehicles, forty yards away.

Lowry muttered his thoughts aloud as he entered commands to target the satellites. 'Number twelve, frame at three by three kilometers. Number fifteen, slave to twelve, index outdoor biologics, human. Number four, slave to twelve, ditto command.'

Complementing the Mirandas' remarkable hardware was a software suite right out of a conspiracy theorist's worst nightmare. A Miranda could be instructed to canvass an area the size of a town, and isolate all human figures who were not inside man-made structures. One satellite could count the targets in a wide frame, while another two or three could set to work zooming in on each of them for close-up shots. Throughout the process the birds could communicate with one another so as to efficiently divide up the workload. The whole operation would take less than thirty seconds.

It was already underway.

On the first monitor was the wide frame of the town, the land and ocean showing up as cool black. Sharp points of bluish white light indicated homes and other heat sources.

On the next three monitors, still frames began to pop up: the tight snapshots of human targets, coming in from the other satellites. The first image showed a group of people encircling a superbright thermal source.

'Beach campfire,' Lowry said. 'Tell it to ignore?'

Gaul nodded. Lowry instructed the system to disregard that target.

Other snaps showed Curren's team rendezvousing with him at the van. Gaul had ordered them back to it moments earlier, so they could move on Rachel and Dryden as soon as their location was available.

As more still shots came in – a woman walking a dog, a tall man taking out the trash – it became apparent that the Mirandas were choosing their targets in a progression from west to east. In this case it meant they'd started at the shore and proceeded inland. Probably a default setting of the software. Gaul stared at the monitor showing the wide image of the town. It extended about a mile and a half in from the coast to some kind of shopping center on the far right. The Mirandas had now indexed all of the outdoor targets on the left half, and would have the right side finished in another ten to fifteen seconds.

*

There was only one vehicle in the outer reaches of the lot worth considering; Dryden settled on it even before getting close enough to know whether it was locked. It was a Ford F-150 pickup from the early nineties, possibly the eighties; it would have nothing in the ignition but copper wires and insulation. He found the driver's door locked – no surprise there – but, ducking to look through the cab, saw that the passenger side was not. Rachel, running ten feet behind him, understood; she diverted to the passenger side, got in, and reached across to open Dryden's door. He slid in behind the wheel.

Two thousand thirty-one miles above the Rockies, fleeing southeast toward the Gulf of Mexico at just under four miles per second, Miranda Fifteen kept its lens platform pointed at El Sedero and snapped rapid-fire shots of the human targets on its list. Target seven, captured and sent. Target eight, captured and sent. Target nine – the onboard computer faltered. There was no target nine at the stated location. Miranda Fifteen automatically communicated this error to Miranda Twelve, the satellite running the master frame and assigning targets. Miranda Twelve replied that target nine had vanished 2.315 seconds earlier; there was no longer a signature of two human beings outdoors at that location, but instead a signature of two human beings inside a vehicle, 99.103 percent likely to be a Ford model F-150 manufactured in 1988. The last command string

34

from the operator had specified only human targets outdoors; therefore target nine was no longer valid.

Miranda Fifteen considered this dilemma for 485 nanoseconds, the time required to run all three of its what-if algorithms, and determined that this was not a problem the human operator needed to be troubled with. It ignored target nine and moved on.

Dryden found a screwdriver in the truck's glove box. He used it to crack open the ignition housing; it took only a few seconds more to hot-wire the vehicle.

'Not stealing,' Dryden said. 'Borrowing.'

'It's pretty old,' Rachel said. 'How upset can they be?'

Dryden pulled out of the lot and turned left. Just ahead lay the southbound on-ramp to the 101. Rachel looked back at the town's lights, diffused in the mist, and exhaled deeply.

'Let's hear the rest of your story,' Dryden said.

Gaul stared at the completed batch of satellite snaps like a man staring at a slot machine on which he'd lost his last dollar. Fourteen human beings were outdoors in the target area. None of them were children.

She was gone.

Lowry was already retargeting a wider search frame, but Gaul had no hope for it. The first frame had covered as much area as anyone on foot could have gone in the time allowed. Their absence meant they'd found transportation.

Gaul sat in a chair and rested his forehead on his hands.

Rachel, out of his reach.

Out there in the world.

She couldn't remember anything important, but that was only temporary. With the drug out of her system, her memory would begin stitching itself back together within a week. Soon enough after that, she'd remember everything.

The taste in his mouth thickened. For a few seconds he was back in Boston, in that shitty little flat on West Ninth Street, waiting for the day the police would knock on his door.

'Sir?' Lowry said.

'What is it?'

'One of the Hail Mary processes might give us something.'

Gaul raised his head. On the first computer, Lowry had run an option – actually, he'd simply agreed to an option the program had recommended. The software suite had drawn the same conclusion as Gaul: Failure to locate someone on foot probably meant they'd found a vehicle.

'Part of the latest software bundle,' Lowry said. 'Sometimes there are heat trails on pavement if a vehicle has just left the search area. It'd be pretty faint, but the Mirandas can turn up their sensitivity and detect the heat for up to sixty seconds, depending on how fast the vehicle was going. If anyone drove out of the area recently, we might get lucky.'

The wide image of El Sedero remained motionless while the satellites carried out the new task. Suddenly the image reframed to tighten on the right side, a close-up of the shopping center. Faint, and fading even as Gaul watched, a twin set of dark blue lines snaked from the parking lot to the road, then to the freeway's on-ramp.

'Show me that parking lot sixty seconds ago,' Gaul said.

Chapter Five

Dryden changed lanes to pass a semi, keeping the pickup just above the speed limit to avoid drawing attention. Visibility on the 101 was better than it had been in town. As the freeway followed the coast, it also climbed above the fog.

For now, his goal was simply to put distance between themselves and El Sedero. He would decide on a destination after hearing the rest of Rachel's story. She'd been quiet for the past minute, contemplating how to tell it. Finally she turned to him.

'Before I say anything, I need to do something so you'll believe me,' she said.

'There are men with machine guns after you. Whatever's going on, you don't need to convince me it's real.'

'You might feel different after you've heard more of it.'

She looked down at her hands. They were drumming a pattern on her knees. Whatever she was about to do, it was making her nervous.

'This is going to weird you out,' she said. 'Just so you know.'

'More than what's already happened tonight?'

'Way more.'

She exhaled hard, and before Dryden could respond, she said, 'Think of a four-digit number. A random one, not part of your phone number or anything else someone might know. Don't say it out loud, just think of it. Clamp your lips together, too, so you don't accidentally mouth it.'

Dryden glanced at her, wondering if it was a joke. It wasn't. She was staring at him, anxiety running through her like an electric current.

Dryden focused on the road again and went with it. He closed his mouth. He ignored numbers that meant anything to him. He let his mind spin up one that was purely random: 6,724. The idea of it had hardly formed when Rachel spoke again.

'Six thousand seven hundred twenty-four.'

Dryden turned and stared at her. She stared back. The truck strayed onto the rumble strip, and he jerked the wheel back to the left and watched the road again. For a few seconds he couldn't think of what to say. Never before had he encountered something unbelievable and undeniable at the same time.

He glanced at her again. She was still watching him for his reaction.

He faced forward and thought, *Say antelope if you're hearing this.*

'Antelope,' Rachel said.

Curren accelerated to ninety, veering through the light traffic on the freeway.

'They're four and a half miles ahead,' Gaul said over the cell phone. 'They're doing just about exactly the speed limit, so you'll catch up to them in a matter of minutes. Next exit is more than twenty miles out.'

'Copy,' Curren said, though he could tell Gaul had already hung up.

Working for Gaul sometimes felt like working for God. The man's knowledge resources seemed to border on omnipotent, while remaining almost entirely shrouded. Also, you didn't want to piss him off. Curren wouldn't have been surprised to learn Gaul could turn people into salt pillars.

'You can just . . . read me?' Dryden asked.

He felt his mind trying to get a fix on all of it, and not quite managing.

'*Reading* might be the wrong word,' Rachel said. 'That makes it sound like I'm doing it on purpose. It's more like hearing. It just happens. I can't even shut it off.'

'And you hear everything. Every thought. Every idea.'

Rachel nodded. 'As far as I know. Sometimes it's confusing, if I can't tell my own thoughts from someone else's. If I find myself thinking, *It would suck to get shot right now*, it's hard to know if that's your thought or just mine. But most thoughts, yeah, I can tell they're yours.' Then, softer: 'I can tell you're a nice person, and that you like me, and that being with me reminds you of someone. And that makes you happy and sad at the same time.'

Tension crept into Dryden's mind: Would he have to censor his thoughts now? Every stupid, random thing that leapt into his head? Could he even do that?

'Don't worry about it,' Rachel said.

It took a second for him to realize what had just happened – that she'd replied to something he hadn't even said aloud.

'Sorry,' Rachel said. 'I can wait for you to actually say things, if you like.'

For a long moment Dryden said nothing. He watched the lines on the pavement sliding past.

'How do you do it?' he asked. 'How does it work?'

'I don't know.'

'You've always been able to?'

'For the past two months, at least. How long before that, I have no idea.'

In her own way, she sounded as confused as he felt. No doubt she was.

'I know it doesn't work over much distance,' she said. 'If you ever need some privacy, a short walk would do it.'

The strange chill at Dryden's temples was still there. It hadn't faded at all since he'd first noticed it, near the freeway. Now that he thought about it, he wondered if it had been there even before that – back in town, back on the boardwalk even, in the first moments after he'd encountered Rachel.

'The chill comes from me,' she said. 'Whatever it is my brain does, that's what it feels like to the other person.' The way she said it – quiet and vulnerable, apologetic – Dryden could almost read *her* thoughts. Don't think I'm a freak. Don't abandon me. Please.

'I barely feel it,' Dryden said. 'Don't worry.'

She nodded, then drew her knees against her on the seat and hugged them. She seemed tiny, sitting there like that.

Four minutes until they would overtake the pickup. Curren couldn't see its taillights yet, through the rises and turns of the coast highway, but he'd done the math in his head.

He looked over his shoulder at the van's middle bench seat, where three of his men sat with their weapons ready.

He saw no pleasure in their expressions, and felt none himself. The job needed doing; nothing more to it than that.

'Don't bother disabling the vehicle,' Curren said. 'Start with killshots. The girl first.'

'The place they had me in was like a hospital,' Rachel said. 'Except it was empty. There was just me, and the people keeping me there.'

'This was the place you were running from tonight?'

Rachel nodded.

Dryden tried to picture it. El Sedero was a pretty

42

small town; it was hard to envision anything like an abandoned hospital there. He thought of the district Rachel's pursuers had seemed to come from: the area just inland from the dune ridge. There was an office park over there – a hundred acres of well-kept grounds, with an array of sprawling one- and two-story buildings. The kind of structures you could drive past every day for twenty years and never so much as think about. You could work in one of them and not have a clue what went on in the place next door.

'Those were the buildings,' Rachel said. 'The one they had me in was off by itself, way in back.'

Dryden waited for her to go on. She still had her arms around her legs. She was staring ahead at the night rolling toward them.

'I woke up there, two months ago,' she said. 'I was strapped to a hospital bed. I didn't know where I was, or who I was. A doctor with blond hair would show up sometimes, either to hook an IV to my arm or take one away. Other times, different men would come in, the same ones who were chasing me tonight, and they'd untie my bed straps. Then they'd come in later and strap me down again. Nobody would ever speak to me, no matter how much I asked. Nobody would tell me what was happening to me, or why.'

Dryden felt his hands tighten on the steering wheel.

'Sometime in the first few days,' Rachel said, 'I noticed strange thoughts in my head. For a while I thought they were my memories coming back, but not for long – they were just too bizarre. They didn't seem like my own thoughts at all. Like, some of them were a man's thoughts about his wife, from his own point of view. These thoughts got a lot louder whenever the blond man or the others came into the room, and at some point I understood what I was really hearing.'

Dryden passed another semi. Ahead of it, the road lay empty and dark for a mile or more.

'Everything I know, I got from their thoughts,' Rachel said. 'The people in that building. It wasn't much; they hardly knew anything at all. They'd been assigned to keep me there, but they didn't know where I came from. They knew I could hear thoughts – they'd been warned about that – but no one had told them *how* I could do it, how I got this way. So I don't know, either.'

'They must have known other things. Who they worked for – the government, a company, something like that.'

'It was hard to get anything like that from them. Most of the time they weren't close enough for me to hear them thinking. Even when they were, it almost never helped. You'd be surprised how scattered people's thoughts are. You hear little chunks of an argument they had with someone, looping over and over. Probably stuff they wish they'd said. Sometimes you just hear a song in their head. You hardly ever hear important things about their lives: their name, their job, anything like that. Like, how often do you actually think of your own name?'

'I guess I can see that.'

'When people do focus their thoughts, they mostly think about what they *don't* know. What they're unsure of. So with these guys, a lot of their questions were the same ones I had. Like who I was. Where I came from. They didn't know. I did get the name of someone they work for, someone pretty powerful, I think – a man they thought of as Gaul.'

The name struck Dryden. He'd heard it before, though he couldn't quite place it. Someone at the top of one of the big defense contractors, he thought. Way up in the overlap between corporate America and the government. That wasn't a world Dryden swam in himself, but he'd learned more about it than he cared to, during his active years.

'The people in that building wondered about him a lot,' Rachel said. 'They were always nervous about him. Especially the blond man. He's the one I mostly learned things from. He had a room down the hall from me – his office, I guess. He was in there a lot. Maybe he thought it was out of my range, but it wasn't. Not quite.'

'What did you learn from him?'

Rachel shut her eyes. Dryden got the impression again that she was framing her thoughts, trying to put them in some order that would make sense.

'That they were supposed to get information from me. Things I know – things I *knew*, anyway, when I could remember.'

Dryden waited for her to continue.

'That's what the IV drugs were for. To make me talk – in my sleep. Only it was more than that. The drugs were supposed to make it so I could have conversations in my sleep. Someone could ask me questions, and I'd answer. Like if I was hypnotized, I think. My memory problems come from the drugs, too. The way the blond man understood it, that was a side effect that only kicked in while I was awake. When I was asleep – *talking* in my sleep – I could still remember what I knew.' She breathed out softly. Dryden heard emotion in the sound of it. An edge of fear, for some reason.

'Did you find out, after a while, what they'd gotten from you?' Dryden asked. 'Did you hear it in the blond guy's thoughts?'

Rachel shook her head. 'It was never them questioning me. What I heard in his thoughts was that he and the others always had to leave the building as soon as the drugs knocked me out, and that other people would be coming in to question me. Those people would always be gone before I woke up. The blond man and the others had no idea who they were – never even saw them. So I had no way of knowing what I'd said in my sleep.' She was quiet for a second. 'I guess that all sounds pretty strange to you.'

Dryden watched the highway. What Rachel had said didn't sound strange at all. Dryden could name three different narcotic agents that had the effects she'd described. He'd seen each of them used on people, time and again. All three carried the side effect Rachel now suffered: a roadblock in the memory, usually lodged right at the point when the drugs were first administered.

Rachel turned to him. He glanced at her and saw her eyebrows knit toward each other – confusion at what she'd just heard in his thoughts.

'There's a lot about me I'll have to explain to you sometime,' Dryden said. 'If you want to know.'

She nodded and faced forward again.

'This information they were trying to get from you,' Dryden said. 'It sounds like it scares you.'

Rachel nodded again, and Dryden heard the same tremor in her breath he'd heard before.

'Why are you afraid of it?' he asked.

'Because *they* were afraid. The blond man, and the others there, the soldiers. They didn't know anything themselves, but they knew other people who had some of the details. Other people who worked for Gaul, higher up. And whatever the information is that's in my head, those people are terrified of it. They're scared the way people get when it comes to really big things. Like diseases. Like wars. It's like there's ... something coming.'

The chill in the girl's voice seemed to radiate into Dryden's bones.

'That's it,' Rachel said. 'That's all I know about it. And I'm scared.'

Before Dryden could ask anything else, a new set of headlights appeared in the mirror, far back along the freeway. The newcomer changed lanes to pass another vehicle, moving fast.

Rachel reacted – either to Dryden's sudden alertness or to the thoughts beneath it. She turned and leaned forward and looked into the passenger side mirror.

Dryden kept his eyes on his own mirror, watching the road ahead only as much as he had to. The new arrival slipped through the headlights of the vehicle it'd passed, becoming a silhouette for a fleeting moment.

It looked like a van.

Gaul watched the F-150, its engine compartment and cab lit up in ghostly blue-white thermal, from three separate viewing angles. A fourth Miranda had a wider view, which included the van containing Curren and the team. The van was closing distance easily, and there was no sign that Sam Dryden had spotted the pursuers. The pickup maintained its speed.

Gaul's cell phone rang; it was Hollings, the man he'd assigned to dig into the classified part of Dryden's background. Gaul ignored the call; nothing in the world mattered right now as much as the drama about to unfold on these monitors, hopefully with brutal speed and efficiency. Dryden was a well-trained soldier, but all the training in the world couldn't counter the odds he faced. Curren and his team were six men with state-of-the-art weapons and training, and the element of surprise.

The van closed to within five hundred yards. There was no escape.

The cell phone quit ringing.

Dryden watched the van close in. It had slowed a bit after first appearing, maybe to keep from standing out, but had still halved its distance in the past sixty seconds.

'How did they find us?' Rachel asked.

Dryden thought of the unformed suspicion he'd felt earlier, when he was listening for a helicopter. Now it took shape fully in his mind. He'd overlooked the answer initially; he hadn't known that anyone as powerful as Gaul was involved.

'They're using a satellite,' he said. 'Maybe more than one.'

He sorted through the implications of that fact, trying to stay rational even as the van closed in. Depending on how good Gaul's birds were, he and his techs might be able to watch the entire conflict that was about to unfold. In that case, it would be no use stopping and fleeing on foot into the hills; thermal satellite cameras would easily follow them, and Gaul could direct his men on the ground accordingly. In fact, any kind of escape would be pointless as long as the pursuers were in any shape to follow. That left a limited range of options, none of them friendly.

Dryden felt old mental tricks coming back to him.

49

Ways of keeping his pulse down and his mind cold. The sensation was strangely pleasant, like the bass rhythm of a song not heard in years.

'I'm getting a reassuring vibe from you,' Rachel said, 'but I have to wonder why you're still going the speed limit.'

'It keeps them thinking surprise is on their side,' Dryden said. 'Which means it's really on ours.'

Ahead loomed yet another semi. There would be just enough time to pass it before the van caught up. And that was going to be critical, because Dryden suddenly understood what he had to do. The road was perfect for it: two lanes, bordered on the left by a concrete median divider, and on the right by a guardrail and then a 45-degree drop to the sea. No shoulder on either side. The freeway might as well have been the Lincoln Tunnel – exactly what he needed.

He glanced at Rachel. 'You already know my plan, don't you,' he said.

'I think so,' she said. She gripped the armrest on the passenger door, bracing for things to get rough.

Dryden risked a slight increase in speed to pass the semi, even using his turn signal when he changed lanes. Behind them, the van changed lanes, too, and began the final push to close the gap.

Gaul leaned in toward the nearest monitor. All the night's stress and anxiety would end within the minute, right there in a pixelated blaze.

At that moment, footsteps came sprinting down the corridor outside, and a technician appeared in the doorway with a cordless phone.

'Sir,' the man said, 'it's Hollings. He says it's critical.'

Keeping his eyes on the monitor, Gaul took the phone from the tech.

'Can it wait thirty seconds?' Gaul said into the phone.

'I'm not sure it can, sir,' Hollings said. 'I tried calling your cell, but I couldn't get through—'

'You're wasting seconds now. Just tell me,' Gaul said.

'I have part of Sam Dryden's restricted file. He is significantly more advanced than Delta. If Curren's men are still pursuing him, they need to be told.'

'What did Dryden do after Delta?' Gaul asked.

'A federal program called Ferret. It might've been under Homeland, I'm still trying to figure that out.'

'What sort of work did he do in Ferret?'

'The only thing Ferret does at all. Extraordinary rendition.'

The two words seeped into Gaul like winter drafts.

His eyes went to the monitors again. The pickup, cruising along at the speed limit. The man at the wheel carrying six years' experience in abducting people for the United States government. Six years honing a skill set that would include violent conflict in every possible civilian environment.

Gaul's focus went to the van, closing fast on the truck, and he saw the absurdity that had been right in front of him for minutes: There was essentially zero chance a man like Sam Dryden would fail to spot trouble on his tail.

Gaul dropped the cordless unit and grabbed his cell phone in the same movement.

Chapter Six

Curren watched the F-150 slip past the nose of the semi ahead. He could see Dryden and the girl in silhouette above the pickup's seatback.

'When he gets back in the right lane,' Curren said, 'I'll stay in the left and come up just shy of passing. Clear to fire when I say go.'

The three shooters on the bench seat took position. A fourth prepared to slide open the door.

Curren's cell rang – Gaul. He reached to answer it, then simply ignored it. Taking his attention off the action now would be the wrong move.

Ahead, Dryden merged back into the right lane. Curren accelerated along the length of the semi and beyond it. He would overtake the pickup in less than ten seconds. The man at the side door slid it open; wind roared into the vehicle. The shooters brought their MP-5s to the ready.

In the last moments before it would all go down, Curren found himself wondering how a man like Sam Dryden – a former Delta operator, not to mention whatever the hell he'd been for those six black years – could end up this naive.

Then Dryden did something strange.

He put the truck's turn signal back on and merged once more to the left, though there was nothing ahead of him to pass. The pickup was directly in front of the van again.

'What the fuck is this?' Curren said.

Dryden watched the van and the semi in his rearview mirror. The timing was going to come down to tenths of a second, though there was no way to be that exact in the execution. This was going to be messy as hell.

Beside him, Rachel pulled her seat belt tight.

The van was behind the pickup, a single car length from its tailgate. The semi was another two lengths behind the van, in the next lane.

'Close enough for government work,' Dryden said, and slammed his heel on the brake.

The effect was all he could have asked for.

At freeway speed, the van's driver had nowhere near the time or space he needed to react. There was no place for him to go but the open lane to the right, directly in front of the semi. The van swerved hard for it, missing the pickup's back end by inches.

In the same instant, Dryden took his foot off the brake; his speed had dropped to forty. When the van passed the pickup's back end, Dryden veered right as well, ramming the van's nose from the side and sending it into the guardrail at an angle.

At more than seventy miles per hour.

All that was left was the physics: mass, momentum,

friction, velocity, no forgiveness in any of it. The van's front end dug into the guardrail, and its tail swung outward. It spun more than 360 degrees, and then its tires got a grip on the pavement when the vehicle was more or less sideways, pitching it into a tumble along the freeway. In the mirror, Dryden saw at least two bodies thrown from the vehicle, from what looked like an open side door.

All of this had happened within three seconds of Dryden hitting the brakes. For those same three seconds, the driver of the semi had been trying to stop – unsuccessfully. The semi plowed into the tumbling van and partially rolled up over it, finally grinding both the van and the semi to a stop in a shower of sparks. The van, which had ruptured its fuel tank at some point during its acrobatics, was ablaze by the time it slid to a halt.

Dryden stopped the pickup fifty yards beyond the wreckage. He stepped out onto the freeway and looked back. He saw the semi driver open his door, drop to the pavement, and run like hell, no doubt expecting the van to go off like a bomb. But the van's fuel was mostly spread along the freeway, and what remained in the tank was already burning. Dryden squinted into the glare and saw the van's occupants trapped inside, fully engulfed. The two who'd been thrown lay far from the wreck, on the asphalt. It was possible they were alive. It was not possible they would be of any use to Gaul in the near future, if ever again.

Dryden got back in the truck. He found Rachel staring at him, scared, her eyes huge.

'I'm sorry that had to happen,' Dryden said.

He considered saying more in the way of justifying it, but didn't. She wasn't stupid, and in any case, it was time to get going. Without a doubt, Gaul was already sending whatever else he could mobilize – probably something with wings or rotors this time. The only way to survive the next hour was to lose the satellites, though at the moment Dryden had no idea how he was going to do that. Whatever he came up with, it would take time to do it, and there was no telling how long they really had. He put the truck in gear and got moving. He pushed it up to eighty this time, the fastest he could go without risking a blown cylinder.

He glanced at Rachel. She was staring straight ahead, her eyes rimmed with tears. She wiped at them and said, 'I don't mean to make you feel bad. You protected me, and there was no other way. I understand that. What I'm crying about is weird, and . . . stupid. It's just me.'

'If you want to talk about it, you can.'

For a moment she said nothing. Then: 'When you hit them from the side, in that little bit of time afterward, before they hit the guardrail, they were close enough that I could read them all. And right before they hit, they all knew they were going to die. Going that fast, and suddenly out of control like that, they just knew. It was every bad feeling at the same time. All the hardness about them was gone, all the training, everything. There was nothing but fear, and knowing they were dead.'

Dryden saw her turn to him.

'I loved it,' she said. 'I loved that it was that bad for them. I thought, *This is what you get, I hope it hurts.* I felt all that for about a second, and then it hit me – how bad it was to think something like that, and I just lost it.'

She wiped at her eyes again. She looked miserable.

'If anyone in this world has earned a little vindictive-ness,' Dryden said, 'it's you.'

'It still doesn't feel right.'

She rested her head on her knees.

'You need me to stop talking for a while,' she said. 'You need time to think.'

Dryden nodded. 'I need time to think.'

Chapter Seven

The computer room bustled. Gaul had summoned four techs, in addition to Lowry, to pore over maps of the cities that lay ahead of Sam Dryden on the 101. Predicting his next move, or at least narrowing the possibilities, was critical. It would be stupid now to assume any amount of naiveté on Dryden's part. Certainly he knew he was being watched by satellites, even after his disposal of Curren's team. Obviously Dryden's primary goal now was finding a way to throw the birds off his trail.

The one advantage Gaul could exploit was the degree to which satellites had improved in the years since Dryden had been familiar with them in Ferret. The Mirandas were orders of magnitude more powerful, and adaptable, than anything in the skies during Dryden's service. He probably had a dodging move in mind, and it would probably be clever enough to fool any of the satellites he'd ever worked with. It would almost certainly not fool the Mirandas.

It was only necessary to keep Dryden in sight for another half hour at most, and then it would all be over. Gaul had already made the calls – he'd been on the phone before Curren's van had even stopped tumbling – to get his second play off the ground, literally. Within minutes, an AH-6 Little Bird had lifted off from a pad in Los Alamitos. It was now speeding north across L.A. at 150 miles per hour, almost head-on toward Dryden, who was north of the city and coming south.

Gaul paced and silently berated himself for not sending the chopper earlier, when the girl had first gotten away. Had he done so, the damn thing could have been on-site above the pickup by the time things had gone bad on the freeway. But there had been no reason to think Curren could fail, once the Mirandas had located Rachel and her new friend. With all the stress over simply finding her, it hadn't occurred to Gaul that the team might be defeated.

He sank into a chair before the bank of monitors running the Miranda feeds. One had a wide angle on the AH-6, crossing over Century City now. Three others were locked onto the speeding pickup containing Dryden and the girl. The truck was within a mile of its first chance to exit the freeway since El Sedero. Gaul's techs looked up from their maps as the pickup closed in on it. They had compiled a list of possible places toward which Dryden might be headed, in order to ditch the satellites. The consensus was that Dryden would have to get underground somehow, into the basement of a large building, or even into a sewer tunnel. If he chose a large enough building, or a complex enough tunnel network, he would have his choice of dozens of possible exits, some of them separated by hundreds of yards. This was exactly the kind of move Gaul hoped he would make: overwhelming for a satellite from a few years ago, a cakewalk for the Mirandas.

On the monitors, the F-150 passed the exit without taking it. The techs immediately discarded two pages of material and focused on the exits farther ahead.

The software was continually updating the distance between Dryden and the AH-6, the two closing toward one another at a combined 230 miles per hour. If Dryden kept going south on the freeway, the chopper would intercept him that much sooner. Unfortunately, he'd reached a densely populated area, with half a dozen exits available in the next few miles.

Gaul stood and paced again. His own confidence unnerved him; he'd been confident that Curren would finish the job, after all, and as a result he'd been slow to make his next move. While it was close to impossible for Dryden to evade the Mirandas, prudence called for having a backup plan anyway. Gaul stepped into the corridor and called the D.C. number again. It was answered on the second ring.

'If Dryden gets free of these birds,' Gaul said, 'he will vanish off the face of the earth. It won't be worth the time to stake out the houses of old friends and relatives; he won't make a mistake like that. He won't make any mistake at all, and there'll be no loose end for us to grab.'

'What's your point?' the man asked. He sounded more awake. Limbered up by the alcohol, maybe.

'If we lose him, it's going to take something extreme to get him back. We would have to turn the eyes of the civilized world on him. Do something guaranteed to command headlines for days.'

There was a silence on the other end. Gaul pictured the man moving away from listening ears.

'Do you have something in mind?' the man asked.

Gaul thought about it. 'Roughly. Yes.'

'Tell me.'

Gaul explained it to him. He covered it in broad strokes in thirty seconds.

'If we do this and it goes badly,' the man said, 'we're in a lot of trouble.'

'We're in more trouble if she gets away from us.'

Silence on the line. Gaul heard the man breathing.

'I'll talk to Marsh at Homeland,' the man said. 'Let me know when this goes from the back burner to the front.' He hung up before Gaul could reply.

Gaul returned to the computer room. The techs were animated, sending a flurry of command strings to the available Mirandas, all four of which were now targeted on the F-150.

'He's off the freeway,' Lowry said. 'Moving toward a cluster of five candidate locations. Highest probability is a four-story hospital, half a mile away.'

One of the Mirandas had already been tasked on

the hospital; the software had pulled up the building's schematics from a database. There were twelve exits, including one into an underground tunnel connecting to a second hospital across the street, which itself had seven exits. Between the two buildings, there were five access points into service tunnels below street level.

The other candidate buildings were almost as complex, and there would be no telling which Dryden would choose until the last moment. The very fact that he was moving toward them was a good sign, though. So far, he was doing as the techs had predicted.

'Come on, asshole,' Gaul said. 'Step into the trap.'

Dryden coasted through the nearly empty streets. The sky was still ink black, the first hint of dawn probably an hour away. Ahead, the shapes of a few office midrises stood above a sprawl of low-slung buildings – shops, restaurants, warehouses.

He could feel the eyes of the satellites on him like crosshairs. Since leaving the wreck site, he'd thought of little else but the various spy platforms he'd worked with in Ferret – and the performance improvements he'd witnessed during those six years. Several more years had passed since then.

Rachel remained quiet. She sat with her hands in her lap, no doubt nervous but containing it well.

Just ahead, a green light went yellow. Dryden slowed and stopped.

'We'll be where we're going in less than a minute,' he said.

Rachel nodded. 'I like your plan. It's . . . different.'

'It has to be.'

Rachel stared forward through the windshield, looking for the destination.

'How do you know about this place?' she asked.

'My wife and I met there, when we were kids.'

'Is this going to be dangerous? I mean, for the people inside?'

Dryden shook his head. 'They practice for this all the time, in case the real thing ever happens. It'll be just another drill.'

'It's going to make them really mad, though.'

'I'll send them a donation when it's all over.'

'Let's hope.'

On the monitors, the pickup got moving again, rolling through the intersection. It coasted along for another thirty seconds, then slowed and pulled to the curb. It was three blocks shy of the hospital, and no closer to any other building the techs had predicted. Instantly they started shuffling their handwritten notes while Lowry pulled up database programs, frantically trying to identify the building Dryden had stopped in front of.

The pickup's doors opened; Dryden and the girl emerged, already running. They sprinted up the long walkway toward the building's main entrance. Gaul stared at the monitor showing the widest image of the place. Its layout and profile suggested a single-story hotel: long hallways lined with small rooms. The satellites could roughly image the shapes of bodies inside, reading the infrared right through the roof. The clarity was starkly reduced, to something like a view through pebbled glass, but was still good enough to establish the size and outline of each figure.

All appeared to be asleep, understandably at this hour.

Gaul leaned closer to the nearest monitor. Something about the sleepers bothered him, but he couldn't put his finger on it.

'Got it,' Lowry said. 'It's a boarding school.'

The techs traded looks. What the hell kind of place was that to dodge the satellites?

Gaul suddenly understood what had caught his attention about the sleepers: They were small. They were all kids.

'Oh shit,' Gaul said.

The doors would all be locked, of course. It didn't matter. Getting in quietly was not the point, and in fact couldn't have been further from it. Midsprint, Dryden stooped and picked up a heavy landscaping rock from beside the walkway. As he and Rachel reached the entrance, he heaved it through the glass-block window beside the left door. The suddenly empty frame was too narrow for Dryden to slip through, but Rachel made it easily. A second later she opened the door from inside.

They ran to the nearest hallway intersection, and then Dryden stopped, turning to her.

'You know what to do?' he asked.

Rachel nodded.

'Alright,' Dryden said. 'When you get outside, run in the direction we were driving – that's east. I'll meet you five blocks from here. But even then, we're going to keep distance between us for a while.'

'I understand,' she said.

He patted her on the shoulder. 'Let's make some noise.'

They split up down the divergent corridors. Dryden spotted a fire alarm handle twenty yards ahead, but even before he could reach it, the calm was shredded by the hundred-decibel bass drone of the alarm system. Rachel had beaten him to it.

Gaul didn't need audio to know what was happening. Every sleeper in the building jolted awake in perfect unison. It was a surreal thing to watch from an overhead view. Within seconds they flooded into the hallways.

Just like that, the Rachel shape was lost in a sea of similar shapes. Dryden should have been easier to distinguish, being taller than the kids, but with enough people in a confined space, the hallways became solid rivers of blue-white thermal glow. Worse, the shapes of other adults – teachers or whoever the hell lived there full-time – were now converging from various wings of the school, seeking to manage the chaos. There would be no way to distinguish them from Dryden when the crowd exited the building.

Dryden moved among the flood of kids making their way to the nearest exits. As he did, he heard the message that was spreading through the crowd far faster than anyone could walk. Spreading from person to person like a blast wave from its point of origin – wherever Rachel had begun saying it: *It's not a fire. It's a gas leak. Get as far from the building as you can.*

Gaul stood back and watched it all come apart. People were leaving the school en masse and running away. Had they stopped at a distance of a block or two, the Mirandas could have probably kept track of them as a group and noted any stragglers leaving its outskirts. That would have enabled them to spot Rachel and Dryden.

The fleeing kids and teachers weren't stopping after a block or two, though, or even five. And secondary effects were kicking in now: People in other buildings, seeing the evacuation in progress – third-shift workers, early arrivals – were joining in the flight.

The search area was simply too large, and too busy. It was information overload, for the satellites and for the techs.

'This is fucked,' Lowry said. His hands flew over the keyboard, commanding the birds to widen their frames.

'Aren't kids supposed to just line up outside when there's a fire drill? That's how we did it at my school.'

'Dryden thought of that,' Gaul said.

'How would he know he *had to*? He didn't know what these satellites can do.'

'He didn't know,' Gaul said. 'But he knew he didn't know. Get it?'

'No,' Lowry said. He returned his attention to the monitors. To the nearest tech he said, 'Set twenty-six to two-by-two kilometers. Slave the others to it. We can get him.'

'No you can't,' Gaul said. He took out his cell phone and left the room again.

Chapter Eight

The Mojave lay in meditative calm beneath the pink sky, waiting for dawn. Dryden kept the Jeep Cherokee at a pace to match the sparse traffic around him, running north out of Palmdale into the desert.

He and Rachel had taken the Jeep from a parking lot more than a mile away from the boarding school. Ten miles farther on they'd switched its license plate with that of another vehicle. Then they'd gone east across Simi Valley and the northern part of the San Fernando, and up through the canyons to the desert. Dryden had chosen the busiest roads available, as an extra precaution against being reacquired by the satellites.

For all that, he was only just now relaxing. Having no way of knowing the satellites' capabilities, he hadn't assumed the boarding school trick had fooled them. He'd prepared himself for every oncoming vehicle to suddenly spin out, automatic weapons blazing. For the entire drive he'd kept his mind strictly focused on response scenarios, if/then procedures he would use if needed, based on every form of attack he could anticipate – including from above. These plans had to be revised to fit each passing street.

At last confident that trouble would have arrived by now if it were coming, he allowed the scenarios to fade.

Rachel reacted visibly to the change, as if Dryden had turned down a blaring radio.

'How do you make yourself do that?' she asked. 'How do you focus that much?'

'It's an old trick. It comes with practice.'

They rode in silence for a minute. The desert and highway were still deep in gloom, but the San Gabriel Mountains ahead and to the left had begun to catch the sunrise – a skin of light sliding down over the peaks.

'The drugs they were using on you,' Dryden said. 'Did you happen to catch what they were called?'

Rachel shook her head. 'The blond man never really thought about the name. Like with his own name – it was already familiar to him.'

'Was it just one certain drug?'

Rachel nodded.

'And he gave it to you in a drip bag?'

Another nod.

'What color was it? The liquid.'

Rachel thought about it. 'Mostly clear, but kind of blue, I guess. You could just barely see the color.'

'When they gave it to you, it put you to sleep within two or three minutes, right?'

'Yes.'

'And just before you fell asleep, your hands would start shaking, and you'd get a taste in your mouth, like mustard, for no obvious reason.'

She stared at him. 'Yes.'

Dryden nodded. 'There are a handful of drugs they use for sleep interrogation. That's the most common one.' He looked at her. 'Your memories will come back, but not right away. It'll take a week, give or take a day, maybe.'

Her reaction to the news was complex. There was relief in her eyes, but it was replaced almost immediately by something close to fear. Anxiety, at least. Dryden thought he knew why.

They stopped at a Burger King in Rosamond. There was a mess of loose change in the Jeep's console, including a few crumpled singles. It felt strangely wrong to take it, even from a vehicle they'd already stolen, but this would be the only time it was necessary. Soon enough they'd be done borrowing or stealing anything.

They ordered burgers and fries and took them to a seating area outside. In the sun's glare, every piece of chrome in the parking lot gleamed like a blade.

Dryden realized he was seeing Rachel in the light for the first time. Her eyes were darker than he'd first thought – deep brown, like her hair. Other details stood out, unnoticeable before now: The girl was skin and bones. Her arms were covered with bruises of varying age – the telltale markings of the things she'd told him about: restraining straps, a swollen scar where the IV connector had been.

He thought of the boardwalk – the way she'd crashed

into him at the junction. If he hadn't been there, what would've happened? She might've gone north along the walk; she'd have seen for herself that south was a dead end. Maybe she'd have dropped to the beach and run north there. Either way they'd have caught her inside of two minutes.

She looked down at her tray. The wind whipped her hair around.

'I'm sorry,' she said softly.

'For what?'

'This. You being caught up in all of it. I'm sorry.'

'Don't be. It's okay.'

'How can it be okay?' she asked. 'You can't go home. Anywhere you go, they'll—'

'Hey.' He said it as gently as he could.

She stopped talking and held his gaze.

'You can hear what I'm thinking,' he said. 'If I could go back to last night and not be there, would I?'

Her forehead furrowed. She looked down into the table again and spoke in a whisper. 'Thank you.'

Desert birds wheeled and turned above the restaurant. They alighted and hopped around a few yards from the table.

Rachel watched them, managing the first smile Dryden had seen from her. It lit up her eyes. She threw the birds the last few fries from her carton; she'd inhaled the rest of her meal in a couple of minutes. Greasy fast food, but no doubt the best thing she'd eaten in two

71

months. A minute later the birds were gone, sweeping away in high arcs over the parking lot and the scrubland. Rachel watched them, her eyes taking in the wide open space all around, the flat pan of the desert reaching away to the mountains. Dryden wondered what it must look like after two months stuck in a room.

'How did you escape?' he asked.

Rachel bit her lower lip. 'I did something pretty bad. I mean, it was all I could think of, and if I said I regretted it, that wouldn't be true, but . . . it was bad.'

Dryden waited.

'Last night the blond man gave me the drug at seven o'clock, like every night. I woke up a little before three in the morning – also like every night. But this time, after I woke up, he came in with another drug bag. That had never happened before. And it wasn't the usual drug. *This* one he was thinking about. It was something called a barbiturate. There was enough of it in the bag to stop my heart. Which was the idea, I guess.'

'Christ.'

'I told him I knew what it was. He got flustered, but he didn't stop what he was doing. So then I told him something else. Something I'd heard in the soldiers' thoughts when they strapped me down for the night. The fact that it was true must've helped me sound convincing.' She was quiet a beat. 'They had orders to restrain him and put him in a van with my body, and drive us both to a gravel pit thirty miles north of El Sedero. Along the way they were going to wrap his head in cling wrap to suffocate him, and then bury him right on top of me.'

Dryden imagined it. The guy standing there, hearing that, knowing it was true. Knowing the kind of man he worked for.

'What happened then?' he asked.

'I asked if he knew how the building's security system worked. He said he didn't. I told him I knew as much as the soldiers knew about it – which was everything. I said I'd help him escape if he'd let me go, once we were out. He agreed. He even meant it; I guess he knew he couldn't lie to me. So we went. We got as far as the building's back door. I gave him the code to disarm the door alarm. I didn't tell him there were motion detectors behind the building, and that there was no way to shut them off.'

Dryden thought he knew what was coming. If she really didn't feel good about it, he was prepared to feel good about it on her behalf.

'I told him we had to run,' she said. 'We opened the door and counted to three, and then he went. He got about twenty feet before the lights came on and everything started blaring – around the time he realized I hadn't followed him. He turned around and saw me still standing in the doorway, and he understood. But by then there was nothing he could do about it. He had no choice but to keep running. I stepped out and hid in a shrub beside the wall, and right after that the soldiers came out and went after him. I waited until they were out of sight before I made my own run, in the other direction, and I heard the gunshots about ten seconds later. I don't know how much of a lead I got by doing all that. A minute, maybe. I saw their flashlights behind me pretty soon after the shots.'

Her voice had dropped to nearly a breath by the time she finished.

'I know he deserved it,' she said. 'I just don't like telling myself people deserve it.'

They got back on the road. They came to Highway 58 and took it west toward the San Gabriels. Toward Bakersfield. Climbing into the foothills, Dryden glanced in the rearview mirror. The outlying sprawl of the Mojave glittered in the sun like a spill of broken glass. Like the shattered ruin of a city.

Whatever the information is that's in my head, those people are terrified of it. They're scared the way people get when it comes to really big things. Like diseases. Like wars. It's like there's . . . something coming.

In the passenger seat, Rachel shivered. She glanced at Dryden.

'It's scary waiting a week to find out what I know,' she said. 'Whatever it is, maybe I could warn people about it, if I could remember.'

Dryden thought of the drug they'd given her. Thought of the places he'd seen it used – little cinder-block rooms in Cairo and Tikrit, the holds of ships anchored at Diego Garcia. For a few seconds his background seemed almost to be another passenger in the Jeep, leaning forward into the space between himself and Rachel. He ignored the feeling and focused on the drug again. Focused on the specifics he knew about it.

'There might be a faster way to get to your memories,' he said.

Chapter Nine

Bloom where you're planted.

The saying had become a kind of mantra for Gaul, over the years. The moral equivalent of a shoehorn, he supposed, though he preferred not to think of it that way. It was an assessment of reality, that was all. An organizing principle.

He'd gotten the phrase from a college buddy who'd gone on to be a successful defense attorney. This old buddy had once cross-examined a fifteen-year-old girl who'd been raped at a fraternity party. The girl was poor southern white trash, and the defendants were Tulane students from wealthy families – one had a federal judge for an aunt. Gaul's buddy had explained to him over drinks, years after the fact, the mindset it took to put a teenaged girl on the stand and rip her to pieces in front of her family. There was a meticulous strategy to it. There was no question she'd end up crying in front of the jury, but that was okay, as long as you made her look like a liar before that happened. Yes, the jury was going to feel protective of her, and yes, those feelings would kick into higher gear when the tears came, but as long as you tripped her with her own story first, as long as you did it *just right*, then it wouldn't look like you'd bullied the poor little thing. If you played it perfectly, put a little English on it, as they say, then the crying would actually work against her. It would lend weakness to her testimony. There was all that to consider, while in the back of your head, humming like an old fridge, was the knowledge that your clients had actually done it. Had held her down in a hallway off the frat house's kitchen, the music so loud she could feel the bass in her shoulders and hips where they were pressed to the floor, so loud that people in the next room couldn't hear her screaming when all three of the defendants fucked her. It wasn't your job to wonder why they'd done it. Heat of the moment, too much alcohol, alphas being alphas and all that. Neither was it your job to find it fake as all hell when they looked contrite in your office a week later, their eyes full of nothing but fear for their own futures. No, your job was to help them salvage those futures. And if that meant shredding a little girl on the witness stand – violating her again, your conscience would say if you let it – well, what of it? You had to do your job. You had to bloom where you were planted.

Gaul had found the notion as useful as a machete in jungle foliage whenever life had put him somewhere tricky. In career terms, there were all kinds of problems you could hack your way out of – and opportunities you could hack your way toward – if you had that idea in your grip. It even helped him bury old guilts, like that ugly splash in the water under Harvard Bridge, which sometimes came to him in the darkness before sleep.

Gaul had the saying in his head now, as he stood under the palms near the overlook, three hundred feet above Topanga Beach. The Pacific Coast Highway curved past, far below. Beyond, the ocean lay soft blue in the late morning haze. Gaul watched a black SUV swing off the highway onto the canyon road. It made its way up through the switchbacks and took the turn onto Overlook Drive, and came to a stop next to Gaul's BMW. There were no other vehicles or people around.

The SUV's back door opened, and a man named Dennis Marsh stepped out. He was fifty, trim, his hair just going thin. The wind coming off the ocean set his tie and the legs of his dress pants flapping. Marsh crossed to where Gaul stood, put his palms to the wooden top of the railing, and stared at the sea. No handshake.

Gaul didn't ask how his flight from D.C. had been. Marsh had gotten here in the backseat of an F-16 trainer, the needle pegged at Mach 2, in order to have this conversation in person. There were things you shouldn't talk about even on secure phone lines.

Gaul studied the man's face. He'd known Dennis Marsh for more than twenty years. The guy was a realist when he had to be – he wouldn't have become the secretary of Homeland Security otherwise – but he was very far from being a subscriber to the *bloom where you're planted* philosophy. A fact that made Gaul just a little nervous, given the man's stature.

If small people created problems, they could be dealt with easily enough. Like the idiot doctor who'd been overseeing Rachel in El Sedero. The man had taken a lunch meeting with a guy from the *L. A. Times* a week ago. Audio recordings of the conversation had picked up nothing damning, and it had turned out the reporter was the doctor's cousin, but all the same, Gaul had opted to play it safe. Why leave a troubling door open even a crack? But such easy solutions weren't on the table when you were dealing with someone at Marsh's level.

'I heard from our friend,' Marsh said. His gaze stayed fixed on the ocean. 'He explained what you want me to do.'

Gaul said nothing.

'There's not a chance I'm doing this blind,' Marsh said. 'You know that. You need to tell me what I'm dealing with here. I want to know everything.'

'I can't tell you everything. I don't know everything myself.'

'If I do what you're asking, I'm risking a lot more than prison,' Marsh said. 'I'm risking household-name status as a bad guy. Tell me.'

Gaul wanted to tell him to relax. Wanted to remind him that there were very large political boulders rolling and grinding around over this thing, and that among the men who wanted to see it resolved was Marsh's boss, the one with the rose garden outside his house. Wanted to tell him, in short, that his cooperation was in no sense a fucking favor he could call in later on. Instead Gaul kept his voice respectful and said, 'I appreciate the position I'm putting you in, Dennis. I'll owe you for this.'

Marsh finally turned to face him. Zero tolerance for friendly bullshit in his expression. 'Tell me.'

Gaul rested his elbows on the rail and looked down at the highway. How much to really give him? Where to start?

'I know parts of it already,' Marsh said. 'I know it's not really Sam Dryden you're after. I know there's a girl, and I know you had her in your custody for two months, and I know this is tied to research at Fort Detrick, more than a decade ago.' Marsh's voice went quieter, as if the specks of people on the beach below might hear him. 'I came out of military intel, Martin. All kinds of interesting watercooler talk in that field. I know about the animal testing at Detrick, way back. The gibbons. I'm aware there were human trials later, trying to get the same effect, and I've heard from more than one good source that it worked. Have I got all of it right so far?'

Gaul nodded without looking at him. He heard a little hiss of breath from the man in response.

'Christ,' Marsh whispered. Then: 'Is she one of them? Is she a mind reader?'

Gaul kept his reaction hidden. Kept his jaw set and his eyes on the sweep of the ocean.

If you think all she can do is read minds, then your sources aren't half as good as you imagine. Hearing thoughts is the least damn thing Rachel can do, when she gets in your head.

'Yes,' Gaul said. 'She can hear thoughts.'

In its own temporary way, he supposed, that was the whole truth. Until her memory came back, Rachel *would* be limited to mind reading. That was a passive ability, like hearing, or feeling pain. The rest of her capabilities were active, focus-intensive skills. With her memory blocked, she didn't even know she had them.

'So lay it out for me,' Marsh said. 'What exactly is happening? What are you asking me to step into?'

For a moment Gaul didn't respond. A bright yellow open-top Humvee went by, down on the highway. As it passed below the overlook, the three girls inside screamed laughter, the sound of it immediately washed away in the same wind that blew their long hair around. Gaul watched the vehicle slip away down the coast toward Santa Monica. What would it feel like to be that carefree? To not know how much the world was about to change.

'Martin?'

Gaul blinked. He turned back to Marsh and stood up from the rail.

'I won't go into the details of what happened at Detrick,' Gaul said. 'Except to say the research there ended five years ago, and the work was taken up by private interests instead. Defense contractors.'

'Plural?'

Gaul nodded. 'Two of us. My company, Belding-Milner, along with Western Dynamics.'

Something flickered through Marsh's expression at that. He looked like a chess player assessing some new arrangement of pieces on the board. Easy enough to guess what had struck him: Belding-Milner and Western Dynamics had been rivals forever. Bitter ones. Everybody knew that. Marsh's eyes narrowed for a tenth of a second as he filed the news away.

'You both took over the research,' he said.

'We *each* took it over,' Gaul said. He watched Marsh pick up the subtle point of the wording.

'Each company working independent of the other, you mean. No sharing.'

'No sharing,' Gaul said. 'I'm sure the government was happy enough to run it that way. In spite of what you hear, they're okay with a little competition now and then.'

'So who won?'

Gaul looked down. He felt his jaw tighten. Bullshit for the sake of saving face had never much appealed to him. 'The other guys. In five years our research has yielded almost nothing. Western Dynamics had success right from the start.'

Marsh waited for him to go on.

'As of now, they're beyond just doing research. They've got a finished product in final trials.'

'What kind of product?' Marsh asked.

'People. I don't mean test subjects – actual operatives. Loyal personnel.'

'And these operatives are . . . also mind readers.'

Gaul nodded.

Mind readers, among other things.

The operatives at Western Dynamics could technically do all the same things as Rachel, though that was like comparing junior high chess club kids to Gary Kasparov. Rachel was almost a god next to them.

'So where do you come into this?' Marsh asked.

'I came into it a few months ago, with a phone call from a good friend at Detrick. Head of a small working group following up on the old research there. He had information about a test subject from back then – a girl. The events that ended the research at Detrick were . . . traumatic. But this girl had not only survived them, she'd escaped. She'd been free all this time since then, five years, but there was a chance to . . . reacquire her. My friend wondered if Belding-Milner wanted to head up that effort.'

'And gain something you could use against your competition.'

'All's fair.'

'She's a kid, Martin. What were your people going to do with her?'

Bloom where we were planted.

'Nothing harsher than necessary. Most of the tests we had in mind could be done with a few drops of her blood, or functional MRI scans. But our first move was to set up narcotic interrogations. Her knowledge alone had to be worth looking into.'

'And?'

Gaul sighed. 'She knew something, alright.'

'What did she know?'

Gaul was quiet a long time. Far to the southeast, a big yacht slid out of Marina del Rey, turning away into the haze.

'What did the girl know?' Marsh repeated.

Gaul told him. By the time he'd finished, three minutes later, Marsh's face had paled a shade or two. A sheen of sweat sharpened the lines on his forehead.

'This is real?' Marsh asked. 'This isn't just some tech proposal someone worked up—'

'I'm told it's standing by to go active anytime. Do you understand, then, why the girl can't be left alive? Under the wrong circumstances, she could interfere with it. There would be serious problems. This is bigger than a pissing match between defense contractors, Dennis. My orders to kill her came down from on high. I have to follow them.'

Marsh nodded weakly. His mouth worked, his tongue trying to wet his lips.

'Are you on board with this?' Gaul asked. 'Are you going to help me?'

Another nod, just perceptible. Marsh was staring past Gaul, his gaze taking in the spread of Los Angeles. Maybe he was seeing it in the light of what was coming.

'Then we're done here,' Gaul said. 'You know what to do.'

He didn't wait for Marsh to nod again. He turned and crossed to his BMW, got in, and started it. He backed around in a semicircle, pointing the car's nose downhill, then craned his head to look at Marsh again. The man was still standing there at the rail, lost in what he'd just learned. For a moment Gaul felt the same tinge of nervousness he'd had when Marsh first got out of the SUV. Just how much of a realist was the guy? How willing to play along? Then Marsh turned, his expression set with acceptance, and strode back to his vehicle.

That'll have to do, Gaul thought. He took his foot off the brake and coasted down toward the canyon road.

Chapter Ten

The man behind the counter in the sporting goods store was looking at a magazine with naked women in it. Rachel couldn't actually see the magazine – the man had it down behind the countertop, out of view – but she could more or less see the pictures in his head. There were lots of tattoos in the images. There were metal rings and spikes stuck through skin. Now and again the man would turn his attention on a woman in the store. Rachel could feel his eyes tracking over the the smooth lines of girls' legs, following them up to the hems of their shorts. Over these mental pictures came his thoughts, crude and simple. They seemed almost like animal noises. *Nice nice nice, fuck yeah . . .*

Rachel tried to keep herself out of his sight as best she could. She stuck close to Sam as he pushed the shopping cart around. The sporting goods store was in Bakersfield. It was just past ten in the morning, and through the big glass wall up front, Rachel could see the parking lot and the city beyond, everything blazing in the sunlight.

Right there, parked at the near edge of the lot, was the used car they'd bought down the street. A Toyota something, a RAV4, she thought Sam had called it. It was old, but he was satisfied with how it ran. They'd left the stolen Jeep in a long-term parking lot at the airport and walked to the dealership from there – after first hitting a Payless to get Rachel a pair of sneakers. But before they'd done any of that, before they'd even reached Bakersfield, they'd driven up a dirt road in the mountains southeast of town. At the base of a pine tree in the middle of the woods, Sam had dug up a plastic box with three things inside it. First was an envelope containing ten thousand dollars in fifties and twenties. Next was a handgun and a box of bullets. Last was a cardboard sleeve with three sets of fake identities inside it. All of these had Sam's picture but different names.

It helps to have friends in dark places, he had said.

Rachel had asked him why he had this stuff hidden up here. He'd explained that with his old job, he'd sometimes worked against very powerful people. In a perfect world, those people would never learn his name, but in the real world, stuff happened – *shit happened* was how he'd phrased it in his thoughts.

What I mean is, this isn't the first time I've had to think about vanishing, he'd said.

Which had made her wonder about something: Was it strange that she'd run into someone – she had literally run into him – who was this good at keeping her safe from Gaul and his people? Wasn't that a doozy of a coincidence?

On the heels of that thought came another, this one from somewhere deep in her mind: *Had* it been a coincidence?

She couldn't imagine what else it could've been, but the question unsettled her.

They were standing in front of a shelf full of something called freeze-dried meals: foil packets with pictures of hikers on the fronts, labeled with dish names like *Lasagna with Meat Sauce* and *Chicken Teriyaki with Rice*.

'Fair warning,' Sam said. 'This stuff's all going to taste terrible. Very light to carry, though.'

He filled half the cart with them. The other half was already full of clothing, his size and hers. Atop the clothing were two items: a propane cookstove the size of a CD spindle, and a hand-pumped water purifier. Tucked into the space beneath the cart were two backpacks, two sleeping bags, and two pair of hiking boots. Everything they would need to stay in the woods for a week or more. By the time they emerged again, she would know who she really was – if they didn't find out sooner.

A middle-aged woman walked by. Rachel caught the fragmented spill of her thoughts: *Still like the gray one, but . . . what's over here? No, those are men's.*

Way in the background, like a radio turned down but endlessly droning, the man at the checkout was still staring at the dirty magazine.

Sam pushed the cart to the next aisle. Rachel followed. She'd found she didn't like getting too far away from him. Compared to everyone else she'd been near today – even people in other cars on the highway – Sam's thoughts were unique. No matter what he was thinking at any one moment, there was a feeling that was always there, a feeling that seemed to be pointed right at her. It made her think of the warmth near a fireplace. That was how Sam's thoughts felt. Like protective heat. Like arms around her.

They were heading north through the city, ten minutes later, when it happened. They had two more stops to make: an electronics store here in Bakersfield, to buy an audio recorder, and a specialty shop in the city of Visalia, an hour away. What they needed in Visalia were two unusual items – Sam had spent ten minutes on a pay phone, calling places to ask about them. These items would be for emergency use only; Rachel hoped like crazy they wouldn't need them.

Sam made a left toward a Best Buy half a mile down a cross street. The moment he'd completed the turn, Rachel felt her breath catch. It was like someone had driven an elbow hard into her chest. A choked little sound came out of her mouth.

Sam turned to her. Concern flared in his thoughts.

'What's wrong? Rachel?'

She forced out a breath, sucked in another.

'I'm fine,' she said. She heard how she sounded, though. She didn't sound fine. She didn't really feel fine, either. For another second she had no idea what she *did* feel. Fear, it seemed like, but why? What was she afraid of?

Then her eyes locked onto it. Just north of the Best Buy, rising out of the city sprawl: a cell phone tower. There was nothing special about it. It was just standing there, its red beacon lights hardly visible in the sun. Yet she could barely make herself look at the thing. It was like staring at a close-up picture of an insect face. Everything about it made her skin prickle.

'Rachel, what is it?'

'I don't know,' she said.

She didn't want to tell him. He'd think she was crazy.

Sam put the Toyota's blinker on and pulled off the road into a strip mall. He put it in park.

'Hey,' he said. His voice was soft. The fireplace feeling was stronger than ever. She looked away from the tower and let that sensation drive the fear away.

'You can tell me,' Sam said. 'Whatever it is.'

Rachel nodded. She took a deep breath and explained it the best she could. She expected to hear judgment in his mind when she finished, but there was none there. All he did was stare at the tower and try to make sense of what she'd described.

'Maybe the drugs just made me paranoid,' Rachel said.

Sam was still looking ahead through the windshield.

'I don't think so,' he said.

'What else is there? Why would I be afraid of something like that?'

Now that she'd kept her eyes off of it this long, she found herself unwilling to even glance at it again.

'It sounds like a conditioned response,' Sam said.

'What's that?'

'It means if there was something you were afraid of before you lost your memory – something you were *really* afraid of – you'd still be scared of it now, even if you couldn't remember why.'

The word *Pavlov* flickered through his thoughts.

'But even before I lost my memory,' Rachel said, 'why would I have been scared of cell phone towers?'

'Maybe we'll know soon enough.'

Chapter Eleven

The last good time Owen Carter could remember having, before the Gravel Man started talking in his head, was a day last year when he took his grandfather's pickup out into the desert and found a turtle, and drew sketches of it all afternoon while it sunned itself. There was peace in drawing. He'd known that since high school, ten years back. He liked the simplicity of the task: Make the drawing look as much like the real thing as you could. Make it *feel* like the real thing even, the way it felt to be looking at it in person. It was work he could escape into when other things in his life got too hard to get his head around. Which happened all the time.

He's not stupid, he had heard his grandfather say once, years back. Owen had been coming in from the pole barn, his hands greasy from changing out the gearbox on an old Suburban, and he'd caught the end of the conversation from outside the screen door. Grandpa was talking to his friend Carl, who ran the grocery store in Cold Spring, a few miles down the road. That was where Owen always bought his sketch pads and his pencils.

He just needs things explained a certain way, Grandpa said, *and nothing distracting him. He can fix anything under a hood as good as I can.*

What's gonna happen to him if you kick it tomorrow, Roger? Carl asked. *I mean you're only sixty-eight, but shit happens. Is he gonna run the shop by himself? Is he gonna handle the money, and the overhead, and upkeep on the equipment? Is he gonna handle these dumbshit rich pricks that have a breakdown on the highway and get towed in, and piss and moan about the labor costs because they're having a bad day and they need someone to bitch at? And that's a moot point, anyway, 'cause you need state certification to run the shop, and I don't see how he's going to have that.* Carl's voice got a little nicer then. *I'm just saying someone's gonna have to look after him. And it ain't gonna be me and Tonya. We're going down to the Gulf Coast after I retire. Look, I get that you don't want to think about this, but you're running blindfolded on what happens to him when you're gone. You need to have a plan.*

Owen had stood there outside the door, waiting to hear what Grandpa would say back to all that, but Grandpa hadn't said anything. The man only let out a long breath and then Owen heard his chair creak, the way it did when he leaned it back and put his hands through his hair.

Now and again that conversation would come back to Owen, when he was having his cereal in the morning, or cleaning up the tools in the shop.

What happens to him when you're gone?

Memories like that were just the sort of thing that made him want to draw something.

That day in the desert, with the turtle, had ended with the kind of sunset you sometimes saw in magazines. Against the red sky there had been a few high, feathery clouds, and an old jet trail flattening out and unshaping itself in the wind way up there. Owen had made a few quick sketches of that, and then gotten in the pickup to head back to the house, but before he could turn the ignition he heard a voice in his head say, *I think I've got one.*

He stopped. His hand fell away from the key. He turned in his seat and looked into the truck bed, as if the voice had come from there, though he already knew it hadn't.

Mark it, the voice said. *Off-axis three seven . . . two? Mod track's pretty strong, but try to dial it in.*

It was a man's voice, coming to him as if from far away, and it was rough and broken, like the man was speaking through a mouthful of gravel.

That's a little better, the voice said. It sounded much closer now.

Okay, good, yeah. Now just step out. Yeah, leave the room, I've got it.

Owen felt his heart banging against his rib cage. Was he going crazy? Was this how it started?

The voice spoke again, as loud as if the man were in the truck's cab with him, though still garbled and pebbly.

Tell me your name.

'What?' Owen found himself saying aloud.

94

Tell me your name. Don't be afraid.

Sweating now. His breathing kicked up into high gear, trying to keep pace with his heartbeat.

You're not crazy, the gravel voice said. *I promise. Please tell me your name.*

In a single convulsive move, Owen grabbed the ignition key again and turned it. When the old pickup's engine rolled over, he goosed it hard, dumped it into drive, and floored it. The truck fishtailed a little and then the tires bit into the desert two-track and Owen was racing along.

You can't ignore me. You can't get away from me, either.

Owen stabbed the ON button for the radio and cranked the volume high. The gospel station out of Cold Spring washed out at him. He punched one of the presets and got Ozzy Osbourne singing 'Flying High Again,' and turned the volume dial as far up as it would go.

But even over the music, and the scream of the engine and the rattle of the old truck's suspension, the voice was still there.

You don't have to be scared of me.

There was maybe a minute or two when Owen almost believed he could make it go away. It wasn't the music or any other noise that helped; it was the hard concentration it took to drive this fast in the desert. The quick thinking he had to do when little turns and cross-ruts would come sliding into his headlights, and he'd have only half a second to brake or veer. It was the kind of thinking that normally wore him out in no time at all. It was wearing him out right now, too, but it also seemed to push the voice away, if only a little.

Then he saw his grandfather's house, a mile ahead. A single pool of light in the wide open desert. Owen couldn't come racing into the dooryard at this speed, with the radio going loud. How would he explain that behavior? It'd been years since he'd really gotten in trouble for anything, but sometimes he'd do something dumb and he could tell Grandpa was disappointed in him. Even with those things, though, Grandpa always understood that he hadn't meant to do wrong. That helped. But driving like crazy for no reason at all – no reason he could talk about, anyway – would be a different kind of deal. He wasn't sure what Grandpa would say about that.

A quarter mile out, Owen dropped his speed to twenty and killed the radio. He'd no sooner done it than the voice came back as strong as ever.

Tell me your name and I'll leave you alone for a while. I promise.

Owen could see Grandpa in the pole barn, the big sodium lights turned on inside. Grandpa was working on the tractor Mr Seward had brought over last Friday.

Tell me your name. That's all I want for now.

'Owen,' he said. It came out of him like a cry of pain.

The rest of it, too. Your whole name.

This time he didn't even get as far as saying it. All he did was think it – his whole name like it appeared when he signed up for a fishing license – and just like that the voice repeated it back to him.

Owen Carter. Thank you, Owen Carter.

The voice stayed away all that evening, through dinner and through the TV shows Owen watched, while Grandpa read and checked the computer for e-mails from customers. Owen went to bed at eleven thirty. He turned the light off right away; he'd found himself holding tight to the idea that if he could get to sleep quickly, everything would be fine in the morning. A good sleep could make a lot of troubles go away.

He'd been lying in the dark no more than thirty seconds when that hope came to an end.

Hello, Owen.

No Ozzy Osbourne to distract him here. No wheel ruts or turns to grab his attention either.

'Stop,' Owen whispered. 'Please.'

He was sure he was only talking to himself, but pleading felt like the thing to do, all the same.

This doesn't have to be bad for you, you know. It can be good, if you don't fight me. Here, I'll show you.

Owen was breathing fast again. He wasn't sure he'd ever felt fear like this. Confusion, yes. There had been lots of confusion in his life, and it was always a little scary, but this—

All at once, something happened. Some change of his mood. It came over him so quickly, he didn't recognize what it was right away. And then he did.

'What in hell?' he whispered.

Go with it, the gravelly voice said. *There's nothing wrong with feeling good.*

Owen had felt this way many times in his life, though in recent years the intensity of it had faded a bit. When was the last time it'd felt this strong? Maybe when he was twenty or so.

Beneath his underpants, he felt his erection swelling.

It's good, right?

Owen only nodded. His mind was filling up with pictures of girls now. He'd never been with one for real, had never even seen one with her clothes off in person, but he'd seen pictures and videos. Back in high school his friend Bobby Campbell had shown him his father's stash of magazines and DVDs. Bobby was a good guy, and had made Owen copies of three of those discs, and all these years later Owen still had them hidden behind the loose paneling board inside his closet. How long had it been since he'd watched one of those? A couple years, he thought, but the images came back to him now, and so did the feelings those movies had given him.

Go with it. Go on.

It felt real. Not like watching a movie now, but like the real thing – at least like the dreams he'd had a few times in his teens. Like there was a girl here with him.

Sliding around on top of him, warm and soft and smooth. Tearing her clothes off, and – oh Lord—

He was still breathing fast, but fear no longer had any part in it. He had his shorts down and his hand around himself in one quick move, and he finished in no more than twenty seconds. He lay there panting afterward, the images in his head still there but fading, every other thought a distant wisp in the dark.

Good for you. You can have that every night if you don't fight me.

Almost in spite of himself, Owen felt the question rise in his thoughts: What if he did fight? What then?

We'll see about that tomorrow, the voice said.

The next day they saw about it. Grandpa went into town for groceries, and when Owen was still watching the dust from his tires settle in the yard, the voice spoke up.

Think of something your grandfather cares about. Some object of his, there in the house.

'What?'

Do it.

Owen wanted to resist, but even the suggestion was hard to ignore. The answer popped into his mind a second later. He thought of the porcelain cat statue on Grandpa's nightstand. The one Grandpa had bought for Grandma Lilly when they were just kids themselves, way back.

That's perfect. Go into his room.

'I never go in there,' Owen said.

Go. Trust me.

Owen felt uneasy but did as he was told. He crossed the living room to the threshold of his grandfather's bedroom. He could see the cat statue already. A slender little thing, standing upright, the cat frozen in the middle of licking a raised paw.

Knock it over. Shatter it on the floor.

'What are you talking about? I'm not doing that.'

You are. You will.

Owen turned his back on the bedroom and went to the front door. Enough of this. Maybe he was crazy, but he wasn't about to be a bad person because of it. If he was going to have a voice in his head the rest of his life, well, he'd get through it. He'd gotten through plenty of other things.

He shoved open the screen door and had taken three steps into the yard when the feeling hit. It came on fast again, like the good feeling the night before, but that was all the two feelings had in common.

This one seemed to grab his stomach and twist it. It wasn't quite pain – not physical pain like from a cut. It was deeper than that. Harder to understand. Not hard to feel, though.

He saw Grandpa standing next to Grandma's coffin at the funeral, ten years ago. Standing there wiping at his eyes while people came and went, putting a hand on his shoulder and trying to say nice things. He saw Grandpa later that same day, in his bedroom with the curtains pulled, lying there curled on his side, the sunlight filtered ugly blue through the heavy fabric. *I'll come out and fix you dinner in a bit,* he had said. His voice sounded awful, like he was sick. *Just give me some time, alright? Go out and take a walk or something.* Lying in there trying not to full-out cry, and only partway succeeding.

It happened because of you, the gravel voice said.

'What?'

Her heart giving out like that. It was because of you. Because of how hard it was living with you.

That was bullshit.

Still the feeling inside him, deeper than pain and somehow worse, held its grip. It tightened. Twisted harder.

She died because of you. And he was crying because of you. Because how was he going to go on after that, without her and yet still having to put up with you?

'Shut up,' Owen said. 'You're lying.'

His whole life after that was going to be miserable. Nothing to look forward to anymore, and still all the work and drudgery of looking after you. And the fear, too. The fear of what would become of you when he was gone.

'It's not true,' Owen said. He was gritting his teeth. Spitting the words. 'You're only me. You're my own head screwing with me.'

Afraid not, the voice said, and a second later the feeling in his gut seemed to blossom and spread. Like a balloon full of poison had just burst in his blood. The images became more real, the way the naked girl on top of him had become more real. There was Grandpa at the graveside. Grandpa in his bedroom in the ugly light, making whimpering noises like a sick dog.

All because of you, Owen.

It didn't seem to matter anymore that it was bullshit. He felt it anyway. Felt it all being his fault, all the pain Grandpa had inside him that he could never talk about. All the things that made his shoulders hunch down like he was hauling weight.

Go back in and break the statue. I promise this will all go away.

'He got it for her. He keeps it because of her.'

He can glue it back together. It'll be fine.

'Why do you want me to break it?'

So I know you'll do what I say.

'Give me something else to do.'

No. Go break it. You can tell him you just bumped into it.

'I never go in there. I won't be able to explain what I was doing.'

You'll have to make something up. That's your business. Just go in there now and break it.

Owen made no move to do so. He stood there, his back to the screen door, the dirt yard blurring in his tears.

You want to feel this way all day? All night, too? You want to feel it so bad you don't even get to sleep? I can make that happen. You know I can.

He knew. You didn't have to be smart to know that much. His tears overran his eyes and spilled.

Go, Owen. The voice was soft now. Talking to him like a friend who cared. *You'll feel better as soon as you've done it. It'll only take you a second.*

Nodding now. Feeling his resistance let go. He wiped at his eyes, turned, and went back to the door.

In the weeks that followed, there were other tests. Most weren't as bad as the one with the cat statue, but some were scarier, because they made one thing clear: He wasn't going crazy. Whoever – or whatever – the Gravel Man was, Owen's brain wasn't making it up.

He knew it for sure two weeks after breaking the statue. It was another time when his grandfather had gone into town. The voice sent Owen into the desert on foot, with a hand shovel, to a place three hundred yards due south of the pole barn. There was a spot where three Joshua trees made a triangle, ten feet apart from each other. The voice told him to dig right in the center of the shape, and within thirty seconds he hit something hard that sounded like plastic.

It turned out to be a long rectangular case, and though he knew what it was even before he opened it, Owen took a sharp breath when he saw what was inside.

Have you ever held a gun before, Owen?

'I'm not allowed.'

You can hold this one. It's called an MP-5. It's already loaded and ready to shoot. The safety isn't even on. Pick it up.

It was heavier than he'd imagined. His arms shook a

little. Maybe that was just his nerves. He brought it to his shoulder the way people did on TV.

Fire it. Shoot at the dirt twenty feet away. No one will hear.

He hesitated.

You're not going to fight me on something this easy, are you, Owen?

He took a breath and pulled the trigger. The gun kicked hard against his grip – he almost dropped it.

You have to hold it tight. That's why we're practicing. Don't worry, I'll tell you all about how to use it.

The worst test of all came four months later. This time Grandpa was up in Cedarville looking for a new chainfall. He would be gone for hours.

Get on the quad and take it across the road, the Gravel Man said. *Go straight north into the desert. We'll talk while you ride.*

Owen got the four-wheeler out of the pole barn and headed north. It was state land up here, this side of the road, no houses or two-tracks, not even Jeep trails. Just empty desert with a few hills and canyons and a lot of wide open nothing. Owen rode, topping one rise after another, his grandfather's house falling farther and farther behind.

I need to tell you about something important. A basic rule of life that you probably don't understand yet.

'What is it?'

The way most people deal with pain. The way they pass it off onto others.

Owen had no idea what that meant.

I know you don't. It's okay. I'll explain. You must have had bullies in school, right?

'Yes.'

I'll bet most of them were getting their asses kicked at home by their fathers. That was how the pain came to them. And maybe they could've just taken it in, absorbed it, dealt with it somehow. But they didn't. They went to school and passed the pain off to you. That's what people do. Not just bullies, either. There was a girl you liked, right? The summer before ninth grade. Carrie?

Owen had long since stopped being surprised the Gravel Man knew these things. You couldn't keep secrets from someone who could get inside your head.

'Yes,' he said.

She liked you, too, didn't she? Isn't that why you still remember her? Because for those two months you had fun together. She liked working on cars, the same as you, and you weren't so nervous around her, the way you were with everyone else.

Yes, he supposed Carrie had really liked him. So what, though. What could've really become of it, over time? How much chance had it had?

You got back to school that fall and you hung out with her for one day, and that was all it took for her to see what everyone else thought of it. How the girls with the nice clothes laughed at her for being with you. How everyone laughed. And the next morning you went to her locker to say hi, and her friends were there with her, and she looked at you and made that deadpan face. Remember what she said back to you, instead of hi?

Yes, he remembered. He was never going to forget that.

She said yep. You said hi and she said yep, with that face that really said, What are you doing here? Why do you think you're good enough for me? And she walked away with her friends, and that was that.

'Why are you talking about this?'

Because she passed the pain off to you, like a bully. The pain she would've felt if she'd stayed with you and endured all their teasing. Or the pain she'd have felt if she tried to sit you down and explain the whole thing, how shallow that would've made her feel. The easiest thing for her was to make that face and say yep and walk away. No pain for her then. All of it landed on you instead. That's what people do, Owen. That's the axis the world spins on, and you need to understand it.

'Why?'

Because you're going to do it, too. You're going to pass your pain off onto someone else. You're going to learn how, today.

A mile later he topped a final rise and saw a lime green convertible out ahead on the plain. As he closed in on it, he saw a low, dark shape tucked down behind the car's back end. All at once the shape jumped, and Owen saw that it was a man sitting there, hunched on the ground. The man's head turned toward the sound of the quad, and then he sprang up – not entirely up, though. There was something wrong with the man. He couldn't seem to stand up straight.

In the last fifty yards Owen saw what the problem was. The man's wrists were tied together and bound by a chain to the car's bumper. His ankles were bound together, too, though they were free of the car. He moved like a fish on a line, his whole body jerking around in big arcing jolts. He had his feet on the ground and he was bent over at the waist, watching as Owen stopped ten feet away and killed the four-wheeler's engine.

'Jesus, you're a lifesaver,' the man said. He nodded at the quad. 'You got tools on that thing? Something to take this bumper off with?'

Up close, the man was barely a man at all. He looked like a college kid. He had dark hair, and he wore shorts and a tight T-shirt. There was a little barbed-wire tattoo going around his upper arm.

You don't have to say anything to him, the Gravel Man said. *You're not going to help him.*

'Did you hear me?' the kid asked.

Owen nodded. 'I don't have any tools.'

'Well, just call the cops, then.' His voice was full of fear. 'The guys that did this might come back. Tell me you got a phone.'

Owen only stared. This was another moment that didn't take a smart person to understand. He knew this much: Like the buried gun had been left just for him, this young man tied to the car had been left here. Just for him.

'Hey!' the kid said. 'Are you listening?'

'What is this?' Owen whispered. He heard a shake in his own voice.

Go around the front of the car to the passenger side. On the floor in front of the seat there's a claw hammer.

Owen understood what he was meant to do. A wave of fear ran up his back, making him flinch.

'I can't do this,' he said.

You can start with his head. The screaming won't last very long that way.

Owen's knees threatened to give. The kid was screaming something at him, red-faced angry now, but the meaning of the words didn't come through. Owen's own pulse was thudding in his ears, and his own voice in his head was muttering *No, no, no, no.*

The Gravel Man's voice was louder, though.

You've seen that I can make you hurt, but I can make it worse than it was before. Worse than anything you ever felt.

'I can't do it.'

Get the hammer and beat him to death with it.

'I can't!' Owen screamed.

The young man fell silent at that. He looked confused. That was the last thing Owen saw before the feeling dropped on him like an engine block.

He saw his grandmother's grave again, but this time Grandpa wasn't there. There was no one there but himself, and the ground before the headstone was torn open in a deep gouge that exposed the coffin. Down there, framed by dirt and clay, the coffin lid creaked.

Your fault, Owen. Your fault, your fault, your fault—

'I can't do it, no matter what you make me feel.'

I can make it hurt. So much hurt you'll have to pass it off onto him. You won't have any choice.

'I can't.'

You will.

Before Owen could say any more, the coffin lid swung open, and in the same awful moment he found himself pitching forward and down, off balance, into the pit. He could hear himself screaming, but the sound wasn't enough to block out the Gravel Man's voice.

Do you know the word putrefaction, *Owen? Do you know it, dummy?*

He saw her bones, dirty white in the sun, half a second before he landed on her ribs and snapped them like pretzel sticks. His hands and knees splashed down in the bottom of the coffin, two inches deep in something wet. Wet but thick like gravy.

Putrefaction is what happens after you die, even if they embalm you. Putrefaction means you turn to soup.

Screaming louder now. He reared up, and his hands came up to cover his eyes, but they were thick and dripping with—

Soup. People turn to soup. Your grandmother is soup because it killed her to have to raise you—

How he got back onto the quad, he didn't know. He was aware of the young man screaming again and rattling the chain, no longer mad but simply terrified. Owen saw all that and then his hand was on the ignition and the four-wheeler was roaring, and a second later he was off. He saw the desert blurring past. He felt the wind searing his face. The young man and the lime green car were far behind him, and—

And what was this? The Gravel Man's voice had lost

some of its hold on him. It was only faint now, barely getting to him. Hadn't that happened once before? That first night in the desert, driving fast in the pickup, concentrating hard on the ground rolling through his headlights. Wasn't that all it took? He gave the quad everything. He couldn't even see his speed through the vibration and the tears. He didn't care. Faster. Just go faster. He felt his control of the machine slipping away. Felt it want to flip out from under him with every little jarring dip in the ground. That didn't matter. The distraction was working, that was what mattered. The Gravel Man was speaking, but Owen couldn't make out the words.

In the next instant he crested a rise and found himself airborne. His stomach heaved upward and his shoulders clenched. Then the wheels came down and the shocks compressed and the chassis slammed against the undercarriage, and his hands took over and killed the throttle and worked the brakes.

He was atop the next rise by the time he stopped. His breath was ragged, and the engine was growling low and guttural.

He turned and looked back the way he'd come from. Over the swells of the land he could see the convertible half a mile back. The young man had twisted around to stare at him. His face was a tiny white circle in the sun.

You can't get away from me. It's not even worth trying.

'Please,' Owen said.

You know what I want. You know what I'll do to you if I don't get it. I can still make it worse. I can keep you in the soup as long as I want to. Take a few minutes to think about it. Our friend isn't going anywhere.

The voice went silent.

There was no sound but the low rumble of the quad's engine and the ringing of blood in Owen's ears.

When he breathed in, he could still taste the air inside the coffin. Like the smell when a rat died in a wall somewhere in the house, and there was no way to find it to get rid of it. He looked at his hands. They were clean and dry, but he could still feel the thick liquid coating them, dripping through the gaps between his fingers.

He slid off the quad and sank to the ground next to it. He crossed his arms and gripped his own shoulders and began rocking forward and back at the waist. He hadn't done that since he was very young – kids at school had teased him to death for it – but here it was, back again. He didn't fight it.

When he rolled the quad back up to the convertible and cut the engine, the kid didn't say anything. He only stared at Owen, his eyes wary.

Owen went around to the passenger door. The claw hammer was there in front of the seat. He leaned down and got it, and when the kid saw it, a kind of nervous hope seemed to fill his face. Like Owen had found a tool to help him with after all. Then the kid met his eyes and saw what was there, and he drew away like a chained-up animal. He made sounds that weren't quite words – or if they were words, they might have been *please* and *no*. His bound-together feet slipped out from under him and he thrashed his body around.

Owen stood above him with the hammer down at his side.

'I don't mean it,' he said.

He rode back up to the spot two days later, when Grandpa went into town for brake pads. The convertible was gone, and where the young man had bled, there was only a scoured patch of ground. A good bit of the desert topsoil had been raked up and taken away.

Three months had passed since then. Every night at bedtime, the Gravel Man visited and made the girls in Owen's memory come to life. It was always good – there was no denying that – but whenever the nice feelings faded and he was alone again, the same thoughts always came to him. They circled like ghosts in the dark of his bedroom.

Where was all this going?

What was it for?

To those questions, the Gravel Man never offered any answers.

PART TWO
Beta

This world nys but a thurghfare ful of wo,
And we been pilgrymes, passynge to and fro.

Geoffrey Chaucer

Chapter Twelve

It was raining when Holly Ferrel arrived at Amarillo Children's Medical Center. The car pulled under the overhang at the entrance, and two of the three men with her – the two seated on the passenger side, front and back – got out fast. From her position in back, Holly couldn't see their heads, but she knew they were sweeping their gazes over the geography surrounding the hospital's entry. She could see their hands ready to go under their suit coats for the sidearms holstered there. She could see their posture, tense and wired, the embodiment of her own anxiety.

One of them gave the roof a double pat with his fingertips; only then did the driver put the car in park.

'Clear,' the driver said to her. He said it the way a ticket taker at a movie theater might say 'Enjoy the show.' Every step in the process was routine – to him and to her. It'd been going on for weeks.

One of the others came around and opened the door for her. The two of them followed her as far as the entrance, then took up positions outside as she went in. She liked to tell herself the fear stayed outside with them. That it was like an overcoat she could hang up at the door and not think about again until it was time to go home. Some days it almost worked.

Sixty seconds later, and five stories up, Holly passed through another door. An engraved steel sign beside it read ONCOLOGY.

She didn't go straight to her office. She nodded hello to the nurses on duty at the station, crossed to the north-wing hallway, and went to the third doorway on the right. The door was wide open. Even before reaching it, she saw the dim room inside strobing with familiar light. She came to it, leaned in, and knocked on the frame.

Ten feet away, Laney Miller looked up from the video game on her laptop. Her eyes brightened.

'Hi, Holly.'

Laney's voice, soft and raspy, reminded Holly of a teenaged girl who'd just spent a week singing lead in the high school musical. For a second the awful math swam into Holly's thoughts: the odds against Laney ever doing that. The odds against her becoming a teenager at all. Holly buried the notion before her face could register it.

She crossed to the bed, leaned down, and kissed Laney's forehead beneath the pink knit cap that kept her scalp warm.

'How do you feel today?' Holly asked.

Laney managed half a smile. 'Same.'

So many things going on in that face, in that tone. *I*

don't want to lie to you, but I also don't want to make you feel bad. I know you're doing everything you can.

Holly returned the smile. 'Same is better than worse, right?'

One of her professors at NYU had told her doctors weren't supposed to get attached. Not *very* attached, anyway. That was better left to nurses. Her attending physician during her residency at Anne Arundel, in Annapolis, had said something similar. In the decade since, Holly had never taken the advice.

Laney was playing the video game again. Its name slipped Holly's mind, but she was familiar with how it worked: The player existed in a 3-D world made up of small, discrete cubes – cubes of grassy earth, exposed dirt, sand, and rock. You could dig shafts deep into the ground or into the sides of cliffs, and use the freed material – also in the form of cubes – to build things with. For three days now, Laney had been creating a replica of Egypt's Giza Plateau in the game. The three largest pyramids and the Sphinx. It was absorbing work. Which qualified it as a godsend.

'I found a new Neil deGrasse Tyson video on You-Tube,' Laney said. 'He was talking about Europa – that's one of Jupiter's moons. He said the whole thing is covered with ice, but under the ice there's an ocean of liquid water, and there might be life down there.'

Before her time here, Laney had been about as serious an astronomer as a sixth grader could be. She had shown Holly pictures from her blog, of herself and her little sister at the Hayden Planetarium in New York. Once Laney had even been to the Kitt Peak Observatory in Arizona. What she'd liked most of all, though, was just lying on the rooftop deck of her home, in farm country north of Tulsa. *It's a long way from city lights,* she had told Holly. *It's dark enough that you can see satellites going over, if you watch long enough. They don't blink or anything. They look just like stars, except they move. They slide right across the sky in a minute or so.*

Holly's phone beeped with a text message. She took it out and looked at it.

Karen Simonyi: Lab just sent the new numbers for Laney. Not what we hoped for.

Holly kept her expression blank. From Laney's point of view, it might've been a text about dinner plans. Still, when Holly met the girl's eyes, it was possible to imagine she knew otherwise – to imagine Laney could tell what she was thinking.

Holly almost shivered at that idea.

That all too familiar idea.

Laney looked puzzled. 'Are you okay?'

'Yeah. Sorry, just spacing out.'

The girl offered another smile, this one a little closer to full. 'Doctors aren't allowed to space out. Too many responsibilities.'

'That's *why* we space out.'

Holly kissed her forehead again and left the room.

Two minutes later she was standing at her office

window, looking out over the Texas flatlands in the rain. The numbers for Laney were on her computer screen. She'd looked them over twice. She leaned her head against the windowpane. Far below, one of her bodyguards walked out under the entry overhang. He turned and surveyed the road in both directions, then headed back to the door. He did this several times per hour.

Holly went to her desk chair and sank into it. She shut her eyes. In the silence were all the memories that always came to her. Like old acquaintances. These days, just about anything could trigger them. Could send her back to when everything had gone wrong – to when it could've gone right if she'd done things differently. If she'd been stronger.

She squeezed her eyes more tightly shut. Felt the pressure against her eyeballs. Saw little pops and flashes of light in the black. She'd found long ago that this helped her deal with the other feeling – the sense that regret could be a physical thing. That it could stand behind you with its hand on your back, and that sometimes it could reach inside you and clutch your heart in its grip.

'Rachel,' she whispered. She braced her elbows on the desk and put her face into her palms, and the name echoed in her thoughts as if she'd spoken it in a catacomb.

Chapter Thirteen

Evening came to the forest and brought with it a change of soundtrack, from chaotic birdsong to the sedate rhythm of a billion insects. Dryden sat on the small porch of the cabin and watched the shadows deepen among the sequoias. Through the open door he could hear Rachel breathing softly in her sleep. If she began speaking, it would take only seconds to step inside and switch on the audio recorder next to her.

The cabin, a simple one-room structure, was an old Fish and Game Department outpost Dryden had found while backpacking, years earlier. Department field workers probably stayed in it a few nights a year; the rest of the time it was left unlocked for the use of any backcountry hiker that happened by. No harm in that – there was nothing of value kept inside. Dryden sat with his back against the exterior wall, waiting for answers to emerge from Rachel's dreams.

For the first hour that she'd slept, Dryden had sat on the floor next to her sleeping bag, though for reasons that had little to do with listening in on her. He was concerned with keeping her from hurting herself: The drug they'd used on her worked by inhibiting something called REM atonia, a kind of natural sleep paralysis – the body's own countermeasure against sleepwalking. Under the drug, that paralysis was blocked. Subjects would act out their dreams: moving their limbs, which wasn't helpful for interrogators, and moving their lips, which was.

Sleep interrogation wasn't especially new. Dryden had heard firsthand accounts of the practice going back forty years or more, with older and less sophisticated narcotics. The principle had always been the same, though: Get the subject dreaming, get him talking, and then interact with him. Try to influence the dream by suggestion. Dryden had seen interrogators sit at bedsides and whisper in Farsi or Arabic, pretending to be a subject's brother or father or son. Subtlety was everything. Dreams were fragile, evanescent things; the surest way to end one was to let the subject *realize* he was dreaming.

Rachel had less than the normal dose of the drug in her system right now, but there was no question she still had some of it left in her. It took forever for the kidneys to filter the stuff out of the blood. The subjects Dryden had seen during his years with Ferret had always been tied to their beds for at least one more night after their last interrogation session. In almost all cases they moved and talked that extra night, if only a little. Sometimes the interrogator would try to get a bit more out of them on those occasions; why not?

Dryden turned and looked in on Rachel. She lay on one side with the sleeping bag pulled up around her chin.

So many questions. Who was she, really? Where had she come from, before her time in that building in El Sedero? Did she have a family somewhere? Did she have anyone? Rachel herself had rattled these questions off before lying down, and then she'd surprised Dryden.

Don't ask me any of those things in my sleep. Like you said, if this works at all, it'll be just barely. You might only have time for a question or two. I can wait a week to find out who I am. Just ask about the other stuff.

When she'd said it, the fear beneath her expression had been palpable. Above the edge of her sleeping bag, her face was relaxed now. Soft features, untroubled. The face of a child, at last. Part of Dryden hoped she'd just sleep through the night. She sure as hell deserved to.

Less than a hundred yards from the cabin, a jay scolded and flew from a low branch. Dryden turned fast and studied the place it had flown from. He watched for movement, more out of instinct than any real fear that Gaul could have tracked them here. Dryden's precautions had been a few degrees beyond paranoid, even under these circumstances.

For starters, there was nothing to link him to this location. His hiking trips had always been personal outings, never related to his military service – wilderness training or anything else on record. Of all the documents in Dryden's past for Gaul to dig up, there could be nothing to indicate he'd ever been to Sequoia National Park, much less to this nameless little structure more than a mile from any marked trail. There was simply no way anyone could know he and Rachel were here.

Yet Dryden kept his eyes on the spot from which the jay had fled.

A fern swayed.

It wasn't the wind; the weeds around it were still.

The pistol, a SIG SAUER P-226, was two feet from Dryden's hand, on a shelf inside the door.

The fern shook harder, and then a fox kit sprang from it, tackled a second later by its sibling. They wrestled in the clear patch for a few seconds, then tumbled into brush on the far side.

Dryden let his nerves rest. It felt nice, if only for a minute, to see the forest the way he might have seen it as a kid. Or as a father. Erin would have been six years old this month, maybe a little young to come out here backpacking overnight, but not by much.

His mind sometimes made a picture of her, the way she might look now. He imagined her standing here under the sequoias, staring up with her eyes wide, feeling six inches tall.

He'd learned years before not to let those kinds of thoughts last. He'd learned how to let them fade – how to let everything fade, really. How to go through the day in logical steps: sleeping, breathing, buying groceries, taking the trash to the curb. Life as a mechanical process. As limbo. As inertia.

That it could all change – that there was anything for

it to change *to* – had not crossed his mind in years. Not until today.

He looked into the cabin again. Rachel had eased onto her back. For a minute or two he watched her sleep. Then he faced the woods again and watched the dark come down.

Chapter Fourteen

Long after night had claimed the valley, after the moon had risen through low clouds, sending wraiths of pale light playing over the forest floor, Rachel began to murmur in her sleep. Dryden entered the cabin, moving carefully so as not to wake her. His adjusted eyes found the audio device, and he pressed RECORD.

For the first minute or two, her sounds were indecipherable, even from a foot away.

Then her body stiffened. Her right arm jerked. Dryden knelt beside her, ready to take hold of her if it looked like she could injure herself.

Her arm spasmed again. The other did the same. Both started to move away from her sides but stopped after traveling less than two inches, held fast as if by invisible straps. She tried to sit up, but her shoulders also met unseen resistance. With a chill, Dryden understood. After two months of sleeping in restraints, Rachel's body had become conditioned to the limits. Dryden took a moment to reflect with satisfaction upon the revenge she'd dealt the blond man, even if she hadn't meant it as such.

Her murmurs fell silent for thirty seconds, and then she said, 'It's so pretty from this window at night.'

Her eyes were still closed. The cabin had no windows, regardless. Rachel was describing something in her dream.

'From up here,' she whispered, 'all the lights . . .'

She trailed off.

Dryden sat down on the plank floor beside her. He steadied himself. This would either work or it wouldn't. All he could do was try.

Making his voice as soft as he could, he said, 'Hello, Rachel.'

She didn't quite startle. The reaction was more reserved than that. A twitch of her eyebrows in the faint light. Tension in her features that hadn't been there a few seconds earlier.

'Hello,' she said. Her tone was devoid of emotion.

'Can I ask you some questions?'

Rachel exhaled slowly. When she spoke, she sounded like she was reading from a note card.

'Rachel Grant. Molecular Biology Working Group, Fort Detrick, Maryland, RNA-Interference Cohort, Knockout One One.'

Dryden took in the words. Took in their meaning, at least in the abstract – the rough implication of where Rachel had come from. Of what she was.

But more than the words themselves, what struck him was the way she'd said them, and the way her jaw clamped shut when she was finished. The mix of determined and scared shitless that etched itself across her face.

It was a look Dryden had seen on other faces. Many others.

As carefully as he'd first spoken, he said, 'Do you recognize my voice?'

She appeared to think about it. Her eyes, already shut, tightened as if narrowing.

Then the scared resolve fell back over her like a shadow, and she replied in the same flat tone as before.

'Rachel Grant. Molecular Biology Working Group, Fort Detrick, Maryland, RNA-Interference Cohort, Knockout One One.'

An old, familiar phrase surfaced in Dryden's mind. One that was known to soldiers the world over.

Name, rank, and serial number.

Rachel's stock reply was the equivalent. She held it in front of herself like a shield, because in her head she was back in that little room in El Sedero. Whatever pretty dream she'd been having a minute ago, the very act of questioning her had changed it, and now her mind was stuck in the phantom restraints as surely as her arms were.

Dryden rubbed his eyes. Christ, how to explain it to her – that he wasn't one of those people? How to explain it without telling her too much and waking her up?

Rachel's head turned a few degrees toward him, though her eyes remained shut.

'Waking who up?' she asked.

Dryden stared at her. Because he'd been with her all

day, because he'd gotten used to having her respond to things before he actually said them, he almost missed what'd just happened – that she'd heard his thoughts, even from inside the dream.

'Inside what dream?' she asked.

Shit. *Shit.*

Dryden felt it all getting away from him. Like a stack of dinner plates atop his hand, unbalancing, pitching outward—

He made his voice as stern and cold as he could manage, and said the words as quickly as they formed in his head: 'The thing everyone's scared of – tell us about it again. Right now. You've already given us that much, there's no harm in repeating it.'

For a moment Rachel seemed to continue looking at him through her closed eyelids, as if still hung up on the question of who was dreaming. Then the strained resolve settled back into place.

'Why do you need to hear it again?' she asked. 'I told you.'

'Just do it,' Dryden said. 'Tell us what it is.'

'I told you *where* it is. Go see it for yourself if you want to know about it. You can walk right up to it. No one's going to stop you.'

Before Dryden could respond to that, Rachel's forehead furrowed, and she turned her head toward the cabin's nearest wall.

'Who's in the next room?' she asked.

Dryden ignored the question – that she was referring

to someone in her dream was obvious, but to dwell on that for even a second would only further break the spell.

'Alright then,' Dryden said. 'Tell us again *where* this thing is.'

Rachel stared at the wall a moment longer, her face still full of concern.

'Stop stalling, Rachel. Tell us.'

'Elias Dry Lake, in Utah.' She gave up on the wall and sank back onto the fabric of her sleeping bag. 'It's right there. You can't miss it.'

'Keep talking,' Dryden said. 'Tell us what's there.'

A strange little smile turned up the corners of her mouth. If anything, it made her look more scared.

'What's the point of threatening me now?' she whispered. 'I already know what Gaul's going to do to me. So do you guys.'

Dryden could see tremors running through her body. It was all he could do to keep from putting a hand on her shoulder.

'It must burn him up, though, right?' Rachel said. 'He gets something as useful as me in his hands, and he doesn't get to keep me? Someone else builds a new toy for themselves, and Gaul has to kill me because . . .' Rachel laughed; the sound of it crept under Dryden's skin. How many times had he heard a prisoner laugh that same way, in the deep end of despair, holding on to bravado as if it were a punctured raft? 'Because any time now they're going to stop test driving that new toy and really give it the gas . . . and if I'm still alive when that happens . . . talk about a wrench in the gears—'

She cut herself off. All at once she looked confused. For a second Dryden expected her to open her eyes.

Then she said, 'Who are you? Wait . . . Sam?'

Dryden spoke softly again. 'Yeah, it's me.'

'Who's with you? Who's in the next room?'

'There is no other room, Rachel.'

She started to reply, then stopped herself. She looked thoughtful. 'I'm dreaming, right?'

'You're dreaming,' Dryden said. No point trying to fool her now. 'You're dreaming there's someone in the next room.'

Rachel shook her head. 'I can hear a man thinking, but he's not in my dream. He's there with you. He's right on the other side of that wall.'

Chapter Fifteen

In the fraction of a second it took Dryden to understand, everything changed.

Outside the cabin, feet scraped the dry ground as the intruder reacted to what Rachel had said, and then footsteps sprinted hard along the exterior wall. Sprinted toward the front of the structure, and its still-wide-open door.

Dryden came up from his sitting position beside Rachel, threw his body at the shelf next to the door, and had the SIG SAUER in his hand an instant later. He braced a palm on the door frame and shoved himself backward, dropping to a shooter's stance in the middle of the floor.

In the next second a man appeared in the doorway.

A big man, silhouetted against the moonlit forest.

Holding a shotgun.

Dryden fired.

Three shots in rapid succession, into the figure's chest from less than ten feet away.

Rachel woke, screaming.

The intruder dropped the shotgun and staggered backward. One foot went off the edge of the porch platform, and he fell on his back in the dirt.

Rachel called out Dryden's name, groping around in the darkness, disoriented. Keeping the SIG and most of his attention on the fallen man outside, Dryden found Rachel's flailing hand and held it.

'It's okay,' he said. 'I'm right here.'

He could hear her hyperventilating, trying to get control of herself. Waking up to gunshots was a hell of an alarm clock for anyone; he couldn't imagine how it felt to a kid.

In his peripheral vision he saw Rachel sit up and look out through the doorway. The man was just visible outside. Dryden gave her hand a squeeze and then let go. He moved toward the dying man, ready to put another few shots into him at the first sign of movement. When he reached the door and got a full view past the lip of the rough platform, the SIG immediately felt heavier in his grip.

The man on the ground was a uniformed cop.

Implications flared in Dryden's mind like muzzle flashes. Dots and connections, stitching together in rapid fire. He heard Rachel take a sharp breath in the dark behind him, picking up on what he'd seen.

He crossed the porch, stepped to the ground, and knelt over the officer. The man was still breathing, but Dryden could tell from the sound that his lungs were shredded. They were filling with blood. The guy had a minute at most.

There was a 9 mm on the cop's hip. Dryden popped

the holster strap, pulled the gun out, and slid it far from the man's reach. As he did, he saw the guy's head move. Dryden met his eyes just as they opened and fixed on him.

He thought to ask the man if he was alone, then decided it was a waste of fading seconds; if there was another cop within a hundred yards, there'd be bullets coming out of the woods already.

The officer struggled to take a breath. When he let it out, his body was racked with a violent coughing fit. Blood came out of his mouth; it looked black in the moonlight.

'How did you find us?' Dryden asked.

'Hiker saw your car . . . trailhead. You stupid fuck.'

'How would a hiker know to look for it?'

The cop's voice grew fainter on each word. 'Whole world's looking for it. You were on TV all day.'

Dryden sat back on his knees, as if pushed by the force of the strange information.

'On TV for what?'

'You know for what,' the cop said. Another coughing fit seized him, worse than the first. When it ended, his breathing went fast and shallow. Then it stopped. The man convulsed once and went still. Gone.

Dryden stood and turned toward the cabin. Rachel was standing in the doorway, shaking; she couldn't take her eyes off the body.

'Rachel—'

Dryden stopped himself.

He turned and listened.

The sound was right at the edge of his hearing. Rising and falling against the night wind. Then it solidified, and there was no doubting it.

Rotors. Far away but coming in. The drumming reverberated off the mountains on both sides of the valley, masking its direction and even its distance. It didn't matter. It was already too close. Dryden went to Rachel and turned her face away from the dead man. He spoke softly but urgently.

'They're coming,' he said. 'We need to go.'

She nodded, still looking dazed. Dryden stepped past her into the cabin, put the SIG in its holster, and clipped it around his waist. Then he picked up the duffel bag containing the two emergency items from Visalia. The last thing he took was the audio recorder; he put it in his front pocket and left the sleeping bags and other gear behind.

Rachel, already following his lead and putting on her shoes, indicated the duffel bag in his hand. 'Shouldn't we get those out now?'

'Not yet,' Dryden said. He went to the doorway and listened to the drumbeat of the incoming chopper, so much louder already. 'Not just yet.'

Rachel finished tying her shoes, and they left the cabin at a run.

Gaul was ready to put a chair through a window. He went so far as to pick one up, then slammed it back down, his hands gripping the armrests hard enough to whiten his knuckles.

He was in the computer lab again. The window, spared for the moment, looked out on the same L. A. nightscape as his private balcony upstairs.

Lowry and the others were at their stations. They sat transfixed by what the Mirandas were showing from four separate angles. Dryden and the girl were sprinting through trackless backcountry in Sequoia National Park while the body of the officer cooled in the dirt far behind them.

Gaul's people had been explicit in their instructions to local authorities, from the moment the hiker's tip had come in: They were not to interfere. Apparently this one hadn't been able to resist getting his name on Fox News. Well, mission accomplished.

The element of surprise was gone. Granted, it wouldn't have lasted much longer anyway; Dryden still would have heard the chopper coming. But he wouldn't have known it was hostile and would have lost precious minutes weighing the choice of whether to run for it. In truth, though, none of that mattered. There was no possible exit for Dryden and the girl this time.

There were only seven roads within a twenty-mile radius of the cabin they'd been holed up in. All of those roads were now blocked by local and federal authorities whom Gaul had control of, in a roundabout way, but those personnel were a redundancy; Dryden had no chance of reaching even the nearest road. The helicopter, a Black Hawk, carried ten specialists who answered directly to Gaul. They were his new sword point, promoted to fill the vacuum left by Curren's group. The Black Hawk's pilot had been instructed not to risk getting close to Dryden; there was no telling what sort of weaponry he was packing right now, having been free and unaccounted for all day. Instead, the pilot would circle Dryden and the girl at a distance of half a mile, guided by the techs watching the Miranda feeds, and deploy the ten-man specialist team into the forest at different points along the circle. They would form a mile-wide ring around the prey. Then it was just a matter of tightening in on them.

The helicopter was close now – closer than either of the ridges from which its echoes rebounded, to the east and west. Because of that, Dryden could finally determine the chopper's location by sound, even though its lights were predictably blacked out. The aircraft was less than a mile to the south, and in the last minute it had halted its advance to take up a stationary hover.

That, too, was predictable.

There was a big difference between this conflict and those of the previous night: Dryden had had all day to contemplate this one. From the moment he'd settled on the cabin as a destination, he'd been aware that its primary asset was also its greatest vulnerability. The secluded forest made a perfect hideout, but failing in that function, it made a terrible place from which to flee. In a game of cat-and-mouse against satellites, desolation was a fatal disadvantage.

Usually.

That had to be what Gaul was thinking now, in any case. He would also be thinking of Dryden's background and skill set; he would've taken both into account in planning this assault.

It was no surprise, then, that the chopper had gone stationary at a distance, rather than coming in for a sniper kill. Gaul would have to play it safe and assume Dryden had the means to take down any chopper close enough for that; a good .50 caliber with a nightscope would have done the trick, if aimed well enough. Dryden had in fact considered getting one. He'd decided against it on practical grounds: Taking down the helicopter in this scenario would not be a winning play.

As he and Rachel ran, he heard the chopper begin to move again, having hovered in place for maybe twenty seconds. Its new course was neither toward them nor away; it seemed to orbit their position counterclockwise, maintaining its safe distance, and after traveling a few hundred yards it halted again. Obviously men were fast-roping down out of it, probably one to three of them each time it stopped to hover. It would either deposit them in a straight-line pattern, in which they would comb across the wilderness like hunters driving game, or it would off-load them in a giant, constricting circle.

Either way, the fast-roping was also something

Dryden had expected. He was counting on it, in fact, though the plan would be far from risk-free. As the chopper resumed movement after its second stop, Dryden considered the fact that there were now at least two soldiers on the ground within half a mile, running straight toward them with satellite techs speaking through their headsets.

Catching his thought, Rachel said, 'I think it's time to open the duffel bag.'

'I think you're right.'

On-screen, the third specialist was roping down into the forest. Gaul watched. It was hard to make out the details, looking at the scene from such a high angle, with a heat source as bright as a chopper right above the action—

'What the fuck?' Lowry said.

Gaul turned toward Lowry's workstation. Lowry was tapping the monitor as if it were glitching.

'What?' Gaul asked.

'Dryden and the girl,' Lowry said. 'They just disappeared right in front of me.' He keyed the handset through which he communicated with the soldiers on the ground. 'Continue on vector, but be advised we've temporarily lost the targets.'

'Bullshit,' Gaul said. 'There's gotta be a tree in the way. They're fucking redwoods.'

'We had four birds on them,' Lowry said. 'They can't all be blocked. Not for this long.'

On the monitor displaying the widest frame, the Black Hawk was moving again, arcing toward its fourth drop point. The three men on the ground continued their sprints inward toward an objective that appeared to have vanished. Gaul's sense of calm had vanished with it.

The specialty shop in Visalia sold gear for firefighters, including the two remarkable items Dryden had purchased, one large and one small – the smallest in stock, anyway. They were called proximity suits, or more commonly kiln suits. Surprisingly lightweight, at least considering their capability, they were made of several insulating layers, with an outer skin of aluminized fabric to reflect radiant heat. This kind of suit was standard issue for fire crews aboard aircraft carriers or at oil refineries, people whose jobs might at times require them to actually walk into the flames. The material was that good at blocking heat.

The suits Dryden and Rachel had just donned were rated to keep out temperatures up to 1,500 degrees Fahrenheit. With any luck they'd keep 98.6 degrees *in* – at least for a while.

They were wearing the suits inside-out, for whatever good it might do. Even the hoods – made of the same fabric as the body, and sporting a flexible plastic face screen – could be reversed. Dryden supposed the suits might've hidden them whichever way they'd worn them, but there was a good reason to have flipped them, regardless: Full-body reflective clothing was bad camouflage on a moonlit night. Reversed, the suits were simple black fabric on the outside.

They were also damned uncomfortable to run in. The moment he and Rachel had put them on, they'd turned and sprinted into the trees on a course perpendicular to the one they'd been on. Anyone watching on satellites, no longer able to see them, might assume they were still moving forward on their original path or had doubled back. Any other direction would be a guess.

As it happened, they were running almost straight north, toward a terrain feature Dryden had chosen earlier using a detailed map. The only way out, even if it was a long shot.

Chapter Sixteen

Gaul sat slumped in the chair he'd nearly thrown through the window. The full team was on the ground now. They'd converged on the spot where Dryden and the girl had vanished, and where Gaul had been certain they would find a mine shaft or natural tunnel of some kind; no other explanation made sense. Yet they had turned up nothing except the same hard ground – too rocky to hold a footprint – that covered the valley for miles in all directions.

'So, okay, let's work through it,' Lowry said. 'They fool the satellites, however the hell that's possible, and they run. They disappeared twelve minutes ago, figure ten minutes to cover a mile—'

'Figure seven,' Gaul said. 'They're motivated.'

'That puts them almost two miles from where the team is, in which direction, we don't know. We have a round search area growing in diameter by one mile every three or four minutes—'

Gaul stood, crossed to Lowry's workstation, grabbed the communicator, and keyed it.

'Put the chopper on the deck,' he said. 'Right now. Pick up the team and get airborne. Stow the fucking thermal vision; if the satellites can't see them, neither will you. I want every man aboard wearing a standard amplified night-vision headset – there's plenty of moonlight for that. I want all eyes scouring the woods from five hundred feet up.'

He set the communicator down and paced away. When he turned back, he found Lowry staring at him like an idiot.

'I don't know where the chopper should start its search, sir,' Lowry said. 'Which direction to send it.'

'Figure it out!' Gaul said. 'People used to do that, before they had computers.'

Lowry knew better than to reply to that. He looked at his feet until Gaul turned away, then faced his monitor and brought up the widest Miranda image of the forest. He broadened it further still, to a width of five miles, and added a topographic map overlay.

'Let's assume a man like Sam Dryden knows the terrain,' Lowry said.

'Let's,' Gaul said.

'He's also going to know we have the local roads blocked. But here's Highway 198, about thirty miles away. He could figure we're not expecting him to get that far, so maybe we're not blocking it. Plus it's busy; better chance to stop a vehicle and commandeer it.'

Lowry highlighted the path of a narrow waterway on the map.

'This stream bed transits the valley right down to the highway,' he said. 'Straight shot, the whole thirty miles downhill. Dryden and the girl could probably make double time if they followed that. To reach the stream, their shortest path would be straight north from where we lost them. They wouldn't have reached it yet, and right now they'd be right about . . .' He did the math in his head, then tapped the screen with his finger. 'Here.'

He picked up the communicator and relayed the instructions to the Black Hawk's pilot.

'Copy that,' the pilot said. 'I'm setting her down now. There's a clearing half a klick north of the team's position, the only one big enough to land in. All boots rendezvous there.'

Captain Walt Larsen took the Black Hawk down into the clearing carefully; descending among sequoias was a first for him. They were about three times the height of any wilderness cover he'd ever landed in.

At twenty feet from the deck he saw that the clearing floor was a mess of ferns and scrub, two or three feet deep everywhere. Probably no risk of snagging a wheel, but he'd be careful on takeoff all the same. The Black Hawk set down as firmly as she would have on a tarmac.

'If you gotta step out for a piss, you got time,' Larsen said to his copilot, Bowles. 'Team's one to two minutes out.'

He'd no sooner said it than he heard one of the

soldiers clamber into the troop compartment behind them. He turned.

It wasn't one of the soldiers.

Dryden and Rachel had been sitting concealed among the brush from the moment they'd reached the clearing, ten minutes earlier. Waiting for the chopper had been the hardest part. Though Dryden had been confident it would land here, there was always the chance things could go wrong.

Then it had thundered in above them, silhouetted like a giant insect against the near-black sky, and set down only a few yards away. Dryden had been up and running before it had even settled on its wheel shocks.

Now he vaulted into the bay, tearing off the hood of his proximity suit with one hand, leveling the SIG at the flight deck with the other. The pilot turned to him with what started as a casual expression, and then paled.

'Sidearms on the console, right now,' Dryden said. 'I'd rather not kill you.'

Both pilots were now staring at him, too surprised to comply. Dryden stepped forward and smashed the barrel of the SIG against the copilot's nose. Blood burst from it in a gush.

'I shoot on three,' Dryden said. 'One, two—'

He didn't get any further. Both pilots carefully withdrew their .45 sidearms and placed them on a flat portion of the console.

Behind Dryden, Rachel climbed into the troop bay.

'Both of you, out,' Dryden said to the pilots.

That surprised them, but they didn't argue. They opened their doors, dropped to the undergrowth, and ran.

Dryden climbed forward into the pilot's seat, and Rachel followed, discarding her own hood as she squeezed past him into the copilot's chair. By habit he grabbed the pilot's headset and put it on, even as he sat; the heavy ear protectors cut out most of the chopper's noise. Rachel donned her own pair. Dryden reached to the comm selector switch near the headset jacks and set it to cockpit only – the chopper would no longer transmit audio from the headsets to any outside listener.

'You really would have shot them on three,' Rachel said, not asking, knowing. 'That wasn't a bluff.'

'That's why it worked,' Dryden said.

His eyes roamed the instrument panel. He'd trained in a standard UH-60 Black Hawk; this was the MH-60K special ops variant, but the panel was nearly identical. It had a few extra bells and whistles, notably an all-purpose display that was currently showing what looked like a satellite feed of the forest – a pretty damn impressive satellite feed compared to the ones Dryden had seen in his day. In the image, the chopper was centered and two bluish white spots of light – the pilot and copilot – were visible at the edges of the clearing, where they'd retreated to. A few hundred yards to the south, the gathered team could be seen, coming north toward the

Black Hawk. Fast. Without a doubt, they'd been told what was happening.

Dryden took the controls. He increased the power and felt the Black Hawk shift beneath him. Rachel grabbed the sides of her seat. The rotors reached a scream, and the forest floor dropped away. Dryden hit the master switch for the exterior lights; the encircling wall of sequoias appeared from the darkness as if he'd waved a magic wand. From the cockpit of the helicopter, the clearing suddenly looked a lot smaller than it had from outside. With the trees topping out above two hundred feet, it felt more like a deep well than a clearing. Climbing out of it was going to be the most dangerous part of the escape.

Compounding the risk was the fact that he had to do it quickly. On the satellite feed, the team on the ground had cut their distance from the clearing by half, in less than a minute. They'd be right beneath the Black Hawk in another fifty seconds or so, firing at it with everything they had.

Dryden divided his attention between the trees and the satellite image. He pushed the climb rate to the maximum that he felt comfortable with – then pushed it 10 percent higher. It was a reasonable gamble: risk crashing by going too fast, or guarantee being shot down by going too slow.

He leaned forward and tried to see the treetops. It was hard to judge, but he guessed he had seventy feet to go. On the display, the team was now perhaps fifty yards from the clearing.

Dryden noticed a data tag in the lower left corner of the satellite feed: SAT-ALPHA-MIRANDA 21.

Miranda. He'd heard whispers of a project by that name, just hitting the drawing boards around the time he'd gotten out of the business.

At that moment the satellite display went black.

'I guess we weren't supposed to see that,' Rachel said.

'Be glad they can't shut off the engines. That'll be on next year's model.'

The tops of the trees were dropping past them now. Their highest boughs fell away, and suddenly the Black Hawk was in the clear above the forest. The sequoia canopy planed away to the base of the mountains, like a rough carpet in the moonlight. Dryden pushed the stick forward and felt the bird tilt in response. That was when the first bullets hit.

It sounded like a hailstorm against the armored underside of the craft. Multiple firestreams raking the metal at once. Rachel screamed. One of the lights shattered, and something near the tail rotor gave off a shriek, but the caution advisory panel remained silent.

After what felt like ten seconds but was probably no more than two, the chopper lumbered forward in response to the tilt. In the last moment before it left the airspace above the clearing, the front-right nose window imploded, and Rachel gasped sharply – an involuntary sound that had nothing to do with fear. Dryden had heard men make that sound before.

Leaving just enough of his attention on the controls to keep the Black Hawk climbing away over the forest, he switched on the cabin lights and turned to Rachel. Her eyes were huge, and she was holding her left arm to her side with the other hand. Where the arm met her chest, there was blood everywhere.

Chapter Seventeen

They were over open country now, ten minutes west of where they'd taken off. The overspeed indicator was screaming. Dryden ignored it. He ignored everything he could afford to and kept the rest of his attention on Rachel.

There was no way to assess the extent of her injury. He needed both hands – both feet, too – on the controls, and she couldn't remove the top half of the kiln suit by herself. With the suit still on, Dryden could get only the roughest visual sense of where she'd been hit. The arm, at least; he could see the exit hole the bullet had made near her triceps. He guessed it'd entered on the inward part of the arm, lower down. Whether it'd hit anything else before that – leg, abdomen, upper torso – he couldn't tell.

'Keep pressure on the arm,' he said. 'I know it's hard, but you have to.'

Rachel nodded, frantic and exhausted at the same time. Losing strength.

'Take another deep breath for me,' Dryden said. 'Slow in, slow out.'

She complied. Over the headset, he listened to the sound as she exhaled.

No rattle. No wheeze. Good signs, so far.

'Any pressure?' he asked. 'Anything feel like it's stopping you from expanding your lungs?'

She shook her head.

Also good – but no reason to relax. Damage to the chest could be tricky, as well as deceptive. A bullet could miss the heart and lungs but still cause internal bleeding, slowly building pressure against the lungs until one or both collapsed. In shock, as Rachel certainly was, it was possible to miss the signs.

Dryden had the Black Hawk as low as he felt comfortable flying – two hundred feet off the deck. Out ahead was Fresno, maybe another ten minutes away, though outlying districts of the city were closer.

He looked at Rachel's arm again. She had her right hand clamped around it above the exit wound – a far cry from a tourniquet, but the best option available for now. There was some blood visible around the hole in the suit, but there was no way to tell how fast she was bleeding. Anything coming out of her was running down her arm inside the sleeve.

So far, she hadn't cried. Dryden wished he could chalk it up to heroism on her part, but life had taught him better. It was the shock – she simply hadn't begun feeling the pain yet.

It was coming though. Coming on right now, he guessed, given her body language.

'It's starting,' he said.

She nodded, moved her hand to reposition her grip on her arm, and winced hard.

A second airspeed alarm sounded, this one telling him he'd descended too low for this rate of speed. He climbed until it went silent again. Beside him Rachel shuddered, fighting the tears but losing.

Gaul paced, his cheeks and forehead flushed darker than any of the techs had seen them before.

The satellites kept up with the chopper easily. Three feeds were dedicated to it, at varying frame widths. A fourth frame was scaled wide enough to take in all of Fresno, along with forty miles of open country to the north and west. There was a reason for that. There were other airborne objects being monitored. Fast-moving ones.

'How's the math stacking up?' Gaul asked.

'It's going to be tight,' Lowry said.

Gaul said nothing more. He continued pacing.

Watching Fresno rise to meet them, Dryden scanned the outlying grid for a place that met his requirements. It had to be open enough to land the chopper in, but it also had to be crowded with people. The parking lot of a mall might do. He watched for one – then saw something better.

'You like football?' Dryden asked.

'I might,' Rachel said. 'I don't remember.'

The stadium – for a high school, by the look of it – lay a quarter mile ahead, lit up with a night game in progress. The stands looked to be a third full. Dryden pulled back on the stick, slowing the Black Hawk's forward speed.

Fifteen seconds later they were directly above the field, hovering stationary. Every face below, in the stands and on the turf, was turned up toward the chopper. Dryden dumped it into a breakneck descent, and the players scattered like leaves in the rotor wash.

'I'm going to carry you,' Dryden said, 'and it's going to hurt like hell. But no matter what, you're going to keep pressure on that arm.'

Forty feet above the deck now. Thirty. Twenty.

'I don't know how much more it can hurt than this,' Rachel said.

'You will. And if you need to scream, scream.'

He gave it power at the last second to soften the touchdown, and the instant he felt the wheels hit, he was out and moving, rounding the nose to Rachel's side, opening her door.

'Lean against me when I lift you. I'm going to carry you with one arm.'

'What are you going to do with the other one?' she said, and then she understood – not by mind reading but simply by seeing. 'Oh wow.'

'Try to see the humor in it,' he said.

She tilted her body into his own, sucking in a deep

breath as she did. He got his arm beneath her knees and lifted her.

She screamed.

Behind Dryden, a few dozen gawkers were running from the sidelines toward the Black Hawk. He turned to them, raised the SIG SAUER in his free hand, and opened fire into the dirt far shy of them.

Panic hit the crowd like a rogue wave, turning it, propelling it back. Even those in the stands reacted, surging for the big exit tunnels at each level. As Dryden had seen from the air, the tunnels were huge relative to the crowd that would flow through them. No risk of the kind of dangerous bottlenecks that sometimes happened with stampedes. Just a couple of hundred people hauling ass for the parking lot.

Carrying Rachel, Dryden sprinted to follow the crowd, making for the nearest field-level tunnel.

He was halfway there when the ground came to life with a bass vibration and a pair of F-18 Hornets screamed over the stadium, missing the top seating section by no more than a hundred feet. A heartbeat later the trailing sonic boom shattered the field lights, plunging everything into near-darkness.

Dryden wondered how much closer he could have cut it. He had no doubt the fighters would have turned the Black Hawk into a fireball if it had still been airborne.

He kept moving with the crowd. The darkness and

confusion were to his advantage, if anything. He kept the SIG low at his side, ready to raise it and deter any potential heroes, but it turned out to be unnecessary. In the chaos of the tunnel, nobody recognized him as the shooter.

Passing a pay phone at the outer end of the tunnel, he grabbed a directory and yanked it free of its flimsy chain.

A minute later he and Rachel were in the lot, which was clearing out rapidly. He broke the window of an early-nineties model Honda, unlocked it, and set her carefully in the backseat. Her face had lost a lot of color, even since they'd left the chopper.

He got behind the wheel, smashed the ignition with the grip of the SIG, and hot-wired it. Then he handed the phone book to Rachel.

'Look for the letters MD after someone's name,' he said.

All around them, the lot was mayhem. People were driving over the curbs just to get the hell away from the stadium. He put the Honda in gear and headed out, just another cow in the herd.

Wind scoured Gaul's computer room, at times whistling between the shards that still clung to the huge window frame. When it gusted, papers flew, but nobody dared move from his workstation to gather them.

Chapter Eighteen

Dena Sobel was skimming her pool when the Hornets made their second pass over Fresno, this time a few thousand feet up, and not dragging a damn shock wave behind them. Whatever hurry they'd been in the first time, it seemed to have passed. They were heading back in the direction they'd come from earlier, probably going home to Travis Air Force Base, Dena supposed.

Across the golf course, a few of her neighbors were outside their homes, tending to lights and windows that had been damaged by the sonic boom. Dena, a surgeon aboard the USS *Carl Vinson* for three tours, was familiar with the effects of supersonic flybys, and the one that had shaken her house minutes earlier had been louder than any she'd ever heard. The fighters must have been traveling a lot faster than the speed of sound.

A breeze stirred the white oaks that overhung the pool, bringing with it the sound of sirens from the direction of downtown. Within half a minute there were more, mostly police but a few ambulances as well. They sounded like they were everywhere.

Dena set the skimmer in its clip on the wall and headed inside to call the ER desk. Whatever was happening in town, if there were injuries, word would have reached there by now. As she picked up the phone, headlights washed the front windows, and brakes chirped on the driveway. Not five seconds later, someone pounded on the front door.

Dryden saw a shadow approach, through the windows that framed the entry. Assuming Dr Sobel would look out through them before opening the door, he recalled the dying police officer's words.

Dryden stepped back out of the light and turned toward the Honda to make his features less visible. A woman's face appeared in one of the small windows, and Dryden waved her out frantically. If there was any recognition in her eyes, it didn't show.

'Please help me!' Dryden yelled, indicating the car. 'It's my daughter!'

His desperation, every ounce of it sincere, apparently came across. The door swung inward, and a woman in her fifties emerged.

'Are you Dena Sobel?' Dryden asked.

She nodded, eyeing the Honda. Dryden was already running to it, opening the back door.

'She's hurt,' Dryden said.

In the backseat, Rachel sat holding her now-exposed arm. Dryden had pulled into a parking lot en route from the high school, gotten in back, and helped Rachel remove the top half of the kiln suit. He'd verified at last that the arm was her only injury, but how badly hurt it was, he still couldn't tell. He doubted the artery had

been fully severed – if it had, Rachel would be unconscious or dead by now – but there was some chance it
had at least been nicked, or that some different but still
significant damage had happened.

Dena was beside him at the door now. She pushed
past him, leaned into the backseat, and got her first
look at the injury.

'This is a gunshot wound,' she said. 'Why the hell did
you bring her here? She needs to go to the ER—'

She'd turned back to look at Dryden as she spoke.
Now she cut herself off, seeing the SIG in his hand.

He wasn't pointing it. He held it low at his side,
aimed down, his finger outside the trigger guard.

'I need you to help her here,' Dryden said. 'In the
house. No hospital. No police report.'

'I'm not doing that.'

'You have to. If there's any official report of where
this girl is, she'll be dead within the hour.'

Dena stared at him. Her eyes went to the gun once
more, then returned to his face and stayed there.

'You're the guy on TV,' she said.

'I'm the guy on TV. But whatever they're saying is
bullshit. We can tell you the truth – we can even prove
it – but right now you need to take care of her. Please.'

'Why should I believe you?'

Rachel leaned toward the open door from inside the
back of the car. 'Think of a four-digit number,' she said.

Chapter Nineteen

'Sources in law enforcement are confirming, just in the past few minutes, that the events in Fresno are tied to the Homeland alert we've been reporting on since early today.'

The CNN anchor looked appropriately grave delivering the lines. The thrum of excitement behind her practiced expression was only just discernible.

Dryden was standing in Dena's living room, watching the coverage on the wall-mounted television. On-screen was a live aerial feed of the high school football field, the Black Hawk centered in the shot. It was sitting right where he'd landed it, angled across the 50-yard line. Flasher-equipped vehicles from what looked like half a dozen state and federal agencies were parked around it on the field.

For the first ten minutes after bringing Rachel inside – and parking the stolen car in a strip mall four blocks away – Dryden had stood in the spare bedroom where Dena was tending to Rachel. Dena had given her 800 milligrams of ibuprofen, then set to work examining the arm. The key points she'd been able to assess immediately. 'The bone's intact. No damage to the brachial artery or the deep brachial. Exit wound's consistent with a solid bullet coming out – no fragmentation inside.' Each word had fallen over Dryden like the answer to a separate prayer.

'I can clean it up and start antibiotics now,' Dena had said. 'Another thirty minutes, the meds will have the pain knocked down a bit – not a lot – and I'll give her stitches.' She'd given Rachel a long all-over glance then. The two halves of the girl's kiln suit lay on the carpet, and her clothing was all but pasted to her skin by half-dried blood. The heavy suit had contained nearly all of it, keeping it inside where it could saturate her shirt and pants.

'While we're waiting on the painkillers, I'll clean you up,' Dena said. Her tone was softer than it had been. 'My daughters kept a lot of their old outfits. I'll find something that'll fit you.'

Dryden had taken this as a cue to step out of the room. Now, half an hour later, he'd seen enough of CNN and Fox to understand what'd been airing all day.

It was bad.

Very bad.

The bullet points, repeated every few minutes, were straightforward enough: Based on solid but still-undisclosed evidence, Homeland Security believed there was a man inside the United States with a working radiological bomb – a dirty bomb. This man had all the knowledge and tools necessary to arm and detonate the weapon, and there was credible intelligence that he intended to do so. The money quote had come from the Homeland secretary himself: *We are working in a time frame of perhaps hours. We need everyone looking for this man.*

There was no official name for the suspect, but there was a picture. A digital composite, they called it – purportedly a high-tech version of a police sketch, computer generated based on surveillance images that weren't being released to the public.

The picture was no composite, though; Dryden recognized it at once. Gaul's people had gotten it from the hard drive of his home computer in El Sedero. It was a picture that had originally contained his wife, Trisha; the two of them had taken a trip to San Francisco, a few months before Erin was born, and had asked a passerby to snap the shot of them standing together on the Embarcadero. Someone had now erased everything in the image except Dryden's head, reshaped his mouth to turn his smile deadpan, and filtered the whole picture to make it look less like a photo and more like something compiled by software.

For all that, it was a dead-on image of him. It was no wonder Dena had recognized him so quickly.

Others had recognized him, too, it seemed. The salesman he'd bought the used car from in Bakersfield. A clerk at the sporting goods store. The image had gone into rotation on the news probably just a couple of hours after they'd left that city. The car dealership had contacted authorities early in the afternoon, and the vehicle's description had gone into the news mix immediately. Once the hiker had found the car at the trailhead, it would've been an obvious move for police to check the few human-made structures in the surrounding miles.

As Dryden watched, the dead cop's face appeared on-screen. He'd seen it there a few times now, accompanied by the man's name and a slug for a bio: *Glen Carlton, 47 years old, 23-year veteran of Kern County Sheriff's Department.*

'Is that part true?'

Dryden turned. Dena was standing at the near end of the hallway, watching him.

Dryden nodded. 'That part's true.' He looked at the screen again. Looked at the man's face. A guy who'd done nothing worse than risk – and lose – his life for what he'd believed was a valid reason. 'In the moment I couldn't see what he was.'

He could think of nothing else to say about it. He stared until the image had left the screen again.

'She's resting,' Dena said, nodding back down the hall. In her hands she held a spool of surgical thread and the needle she'd used for the stitching. 'I want to know everything. You, her – everything.'

She crossed to the open kitchen, set the needle and thread down, and rinsed the blood from her hands.

Earlier, after Rachel had demonstrated her ability in the driveway, they'd told Dena a few of the basics. The fact that the manhunt was really for Rachel. The memory loss.

Dena dried her hands with a towel, came around the

island that divided the kitchen from the living room, and leaned back against it, facing Dryden.

'Everything,' she said.

He told her. It took twenty minutes. He finished by taking the digital recorder from his pocket and playing back the audio from the cabin.

Until arriving at Dena's house, Dryden hadn't spent even a minute thinking of what Rachel had said in her sleep. There hadn't been a minute he could spare. Once Dena had begun tending to Rachel's injury, and Dryden had gone to the living room to watch the news, he'd revisited the girl's words. He did it again now as the recording played. He watched Dena's reactions to the key passages.

Rachel Grant. Molecular Biology Working Group, Fort Detrick, Maryland, RNA-Interference Cohort, Knockout One One.

I told you where it is.

Elias Dry Lake, in Utah.

Any time now they're going to stop test driving that new toy and really give it the gas . . . and if I'm still alive when that happens . . . talk about a wrench in the gears . . .

When it was over, neither of them spoke for thirty seconds. Dryden could see Dena taking it all in, or trying to.

Finally she said, 'What the hell could it be? I don't assume it's really a vehicle – that sounded like a figure of speech, but . . . Jesus.'

'If Gaul didn't build it,' Dryden said, 'then the government or some other company did. Maybe another defense contractor. It sounds like a weapon system of some kind, doesn't it?'

Dena nodded. 'Something related to what Rachel can do.'

'And they're afraid to crank up the juice to it while she's alive.'

As to the reason for that, Dryden couldn't even guess. The gaps remaining in their knowledge were maddening.

'I don't think you'll get another shot at questioning her,' Dena said. 'She's resting now, but I wouldn't expect her to sleep again for some time, after what she's been through. And if this drug you described is making its way out of her system—'

'No, the cabin was the only chance,' Dryden said. 'We were lucky to get that much.'

They were quiet another long while. Then Dryden said, 'Do you have a computer?'

Dena nodded. She crossed to the end table beside the couch, opened a drawer and took out a touch-screen tablet. She turned it on, brought it to the island, and set it in front of Dryden.

It occurred to him that any use of the Internet could be a serious risk. Even back when he'd been with Ferret, technology had existed that could monitor local ISPs for search-engine queries. Certain keywords typed into Google within a specified area – a city, maybe a county – would trigger flags and give up the computer's location.

There was a lot he could learn without doing a text search, though. He opened the tablet's default Web browser, went to Google Maps, and switched to the photographic overhead view. He dragged and zoomed the image until Utah filled the frame.

Elias Dry Lake.

If he'd ever heard of it, he couldn't remember it now. He zoomed the map in until terrain features with labeled names were visible – small rivers, lakes, mountains – and began methodically dragging it left and right in narrow search bands, working his way down from the state's northern edge.

He found it three minutes later. The arid lake bed lay toward the southern end of a huge desert region west of the Rockies. U.S. 50 passed by five miles to the north; a single narrow two-lane led south from the highway to the lake's northern rim and simply ended there. Even in a wide frame of the entire lake bed – it measured maybe three miles by three – it was clear that no buildings stood anywhere near it. The whole expanse lay glaring white and vacant, empty even by the standards of a desert.

'What's that?' Dena asked.

She pointed to a single pixel in the middle of the screen, just dark enough to stand out from the background. Whatever it was, it stood almost centered in the lake bed. Dryden had missed it at first glance.

He zoomed in until the thing took up half the screen, though he'd known what it would be even before it resolved.

It was a cell phone tower. The structure itself was nearly invisible from overhead; only its shadow on the sand gave it away.

'False alarm,' Dena said.

'I don't think so.'

Dryden told her about Rachel's panic attack in Bakersfield, at the sight of an ordinary cell tower there. Then for good measure he dragged the map to show the freeway again, and the small town clustered around the nearest interchange. It took less than a minute to find the cell tower that served it; it was located right at the north edge of town, near the off-ramp. Dryden scanned the freeway itself for several miles in each direction and found additional towers that served traffic along its route. All were within a few hundred yards of the road.

'The tower on the lake bed doesn't serve U.S. 50 or the nearest town,' Dryden said, 'and there's no other town of any kind for twenty miles. There's no reason to put a real cell tower in that spot. It would make no sense at all.'

'What do you think it is, then?'

He had no answer to that. He centered the lake bed again, stared at it for thirty seconds, and then straightened up and paced away from the island.

'Most of what Rachel said in the recording is lost on me,' Dena said. 'But one word rang a bell. *Knockout.*'

165

'You know what it means?' Dryden asked.

'I know one meaning of it. I'd almost bet my life it's the relevant one.'

Dryden waited for her to go on.

'It's not in my field of expertise,' Dena said, 'but lots of people in medicine have heard the term. Usually it refers to mice. Knockout mice. It means they've been genetically modified – that a specific gene has been switched off. Knocked out.'

Dryden considered what that implied. It fit well enough with the rest of what Rachel had said. Molecular biology. RNA interference. Dryden had no serious background in science, but clearly those terms came from the world of genetic research.

'Why would turning *off* genes give someone a new ability?' he asked.

Dena shrugged. 'Because DNA is a mess. People call it a blueprint, but it's more like a recipe – one that nature's been tinkering with for a few billion years. That's how a professor of mine described it: an old recipe, where outdated instructions get lined out instead of erased. When an animal evolves away from having a certain trait, like when we lost our tails or most of our fur, the genes for that trait wouldn't have been deleted. Instead, what usually happens is that a new gene is created that blocks those genes. Those new genes are like the pen lines crossing out older parts of the recipe. So if you knock out *those* genes, the new ones, then the old instructions won't be crossed out anymore. They come back into the mix. Does that all make sense?'

Dryden went back over it in his head. He nodded. 'More or less.'

He paced to the sliding glass door at the back of the room. He stared over the pool and the golf course beyond.

'Mind reading,' he said.

Sprinklers were wetting down the fairway. The grass glistened in the glow of landscaping lights.

'I go to conferences a few times a year,' Dena said. 'You should see some of the PowerPoint talks people give. There are animals that can naturally regrow limbs – newts can do it. Amputate a foreleg just below the shoulder, the newt grows the whole thing back. The elbow joint, the humerus, all the bones and muscles and nerves in the hand. All the skin. Everything. They've always been able to do it. There are researchers who think all vertebrates have it in their DNA to do that, too, including us. There are just other genes suppressing the ability. The trick would be to identify them and knock them out.'

Dryden turned from the sliding door. 'That doesn't make sense. Why would we have evolved *away* from being able to do something that important?'

'Best guess I've heard is that it's better to just take the loss. A new limb is weak for a long time; the skin is raw, vulnerable to infection. Survival odds probably go up if you just scab over the stump and get by with three limbs instead. What's that old line? Mother Nature's a bitch but you gotta love her?' She shrugged. 'But why evolution would ditch something like mind reading, I can't begin to guess.'

On TV, a few emergency vehicles were still clustered around the Black Hawk. Dryden went back to the computer and stared at the image on its screen: the dry lake and the tiny speck of the tower's shadow.

'You're planning to go there,' Dena said. It wasn't a question.

Dryden nodded.

'Why not just wait for her memory to come back?' Dena asked. 'You can both stay here as long as you need to.'

'Can she stay here without me for the next day or two?'

'Of course. But why risk going to that place?'

Dryden's eyes were still on the display.

'Because I don't like flying blind. I don't like spending the next week with these people knowing everything, and us knowing almost nothing. Rachel said herself the answers are there.'

'You'd only have to wait six or seven days—'

'And Gaul knows that. He knows that once she remembers, she'll have a whole range of options, maybe something as simple as going public with her information – but Gaul has a full week to plan for every move Rachel can make, before she even knows what they'll be. What he might not be prepared for is her making a move sooner than that.'

Dena indicated the tower. 'Gaul knows about that place. Rachel told him. I wouldn't think he'd expect her to show up there again, but how hard would it be for him to keep watch on it, just in case?'

Dryden thought of the satellites. 'Not hard at all. But I'm going.'

'Not without me.'

Dryden and Dena both turned. Rachel stood at the mouth of the hallway. Dryden saw the bandage Dena had applied to her wound: heavy gauze pads on the front and back of her arm, wrapped together with white tape. Her new clothes, a pair of jeans and a purple T-shirt, were only a little too big on her.

Dena went to her. 'Honey, you need to be lying down—'

'I'll sit,' Rachel said. 'This is important.'

Dena started to respond but held back. She could see the same thing in Rachel's eyes that Dryden could: The girl was determined to make her point.

'I want you to take it easy,' Dena said.

Rachel nodded and followed her back to the island. Dena pulled out a chair, and the girl sat carefully in it.

'Did you hear the recording playback?' Dryden asked. 'In your thoughts, when you both listened to it.'

Dryden glanced at Dena. Despite her earlier exposure to Rachel's ability, she still appeared shoved off-balance by it.

When Dryden looked back at Rachel, he saw her eyes fixed on the computer. She put her fingertips tentatively to the screen and zoomed in until the cell tower filled it.

'You know I can't take you there,' Dryden said. 'It's one thing to risk my own life. Yours, no way.'

'We can get within a few miles of it without any risk,' Rachel said. 'If you want to look closer then, by yourself, I'll understand, but you can't leave me a thousand miles behind. Besides, there are good reasons to take me along. There might be things there that jump out at me that wouldn't stick out to you at all. That place might jog a memory.'

For a long time Dryden didn't respond. He looked at Rachel, then the computer screen, then nothing at all.

'I think there's a lot more at stake here than us,' Rachel said softly. 'Don't you? I think we should go. Right now.'

Dryden rubbed his eyes.

'Christ,' he said.

Silence drew out. It was Dena who broke it. 'You both know what I think, but I won't try to change your minds. I've got a second car that my daughter uses when she's home from school. It's old, but it's reliable. There'll be roadblocks set up all around Fresno, I imagine, but . . . I could get you past those. You can hide in the trunk, and I'll drive you north to Modesto and take a train home. If you're caught, you'll have to say you broke in and stole the car while I was gone.'

Dryden traded a glance with Rachel, then looked at Dena again.

'I don't know how we could ever thank you,' he said.

'Don't die,' Dena said. 'That would do it.'

Dryden kept the unpleasant reply to himself: For almost any outcome he could imagine, Dena would never find out what became of him and Rachel. The girl said nothing in response to that thought, but she shivered as if a chill had crossed her skin.

Chapter Twenty

They left five minutes later.

The car was a Honda Accord, ten or twelve years old. Its backseats could be folded down to open up the trunk space to the passenger compartment, but for the moment there was no reason to do that. Dryden lay curled on one side of the trunk, Rachel on the other. Three minutes and five turns after leaving the house, Dena called back to them, her voice muffled by the foam of the seatbacks. 'They're stopping drivers at the on-ramp. Stay quiet until I say it's clear.'

The car braked thirty seconds later, then crept forward, start-and-stop. Dryden pictured a long line of clotted traffic, all of it washed in the LED flare of police lights. A moment later he heard the crackle of two-way radios. In the darkness, Rachel found his hand and held it tightly. Footsteps clicked on asphalt. Dena's window buzzed down, and the sounds of the city came through.

A man said, 'Evening.' Sharp voice, a practiced balance between hard and polite.

'Hi,' Dena said. 'Is this about that thing on TV?'

'Yes, ma'am. Can you show me your ID?'

Seconds of silence. Then white light shone at the seam where the seatback met the trunk. It darted and roamed. The officer was shining a flashlight beam around the car's interior.

'Can I ask where you're headed tonight?' the man said.

'Just getting out of here for a couple days. If that guy's here in town with that thing – you know – I'd rather not be here.'

It sounded like something Dena had been rehearsing in her head for the past several minutes. No doubt it was. Her delivery of the line was dramatic – too much so. Dryden tensed.

Another five seconds passed, and then the officer said, 'Do me a favor and pop your trunk for me.'

Rachel's hand convulsed around Dryden's.

'Is that really necessary?' Dena asked.

'It won't take long. Go ahead and open it.'

Dena said nothing.

Dryden had the SIG SAUER in his rear waistband, but he made no move to draw it. There was simply nothing he could do with it that would make any difference. There would be a dozen or more officers within twenty yards of the car, all of them prepared to encounter trouble tonight. There would be multiple choppers, local and federal, stationed above the city. There was no possibility of escape.

'Ma'am?' the officer said.

No response. In his mind, Dryden saw Dena at the wheel, her mouth working to speak, but nothing coming out. Everything falling apart right in front of her.

'*Ma'am.*'

'I have personal things in the trunk,' Dena said. 'I'd prefer not to have someone going through it. Can I please just go?' Her voice was high and stretched. Everything about it would be a big red flag to a cop.

'Ma'am, I need you to open your trunk. Now.'

'Don't you need a warrant for that?'

'I can have one on my phone screen in about thirty seconds. Would you like me to do so?'

'I just want to get out of Fresno,' Dena said. 'I'm just scared out of my fucking mind being here, and none of this is helping me.'

'Ma'am, I'm not going to say it again—'

All at once the cop cut himself off. For an awful second Dryden imagined Dena had done something to make him do that – like reach for the gear selector to dump the car back into drive.

But there was no sudden lurch of the vehicle. No sound or movement at all. Just silence playing out. Dryden could feel Rachel shaking, the sensation traveling through her hand into his own.

The silence held. Like fingers gripping a cliff edge.

Then the officer spoke again. 'Alright, it's fine. You can go on through. Have a good night.'

For another moment Dena said nothing. Maybe she thought the guy was kidding. Then his footsteps moved off along the pavement, right past the trunk to the next car in line.

Dryden heard Dena exhale shakily, and a second

later the Honda was moving, weaving through the blockade and picking up speed. It crept through one last turn and then accelerated rapidly, and even over the revving engine Dryden could hear Dena up front, breathing.

'Okay, it's safe,' she called.

Dryden pulled the handle that released the seatback from its hold and shoved it forward and down. Air and light from the passenger compartment flooded the trunk. He saw Rachel next to him, looking pale and almost sick.

'You okay?' he asked.

She managed a nod. She was still shaking badly.

'Come on,' Dryden said. He guided her forward onto the folded-down seats. Outside, the edges of Fresno were sliding by at seventy miles an hour.

Dena looked back at the two of them. She was as badly rattled as Rachel.

'I don't get it,' Dena said. 'I don't know why he let me go. He just . . . did, all of a sudden.'

Dryden's mind went to bad explanations first – old habit. Maybe it was a trap. Maybe someone with a thermal camera had seen that there were warm bodies in the trunk. Maybe there'd been standing orders to let anyone like that go through, to be followed, and someone had given word to the cop at the last second.

'Did the officer have an earpiece in?' Dryden asked. 'Did he touch his ear like someone had told him something?'

Dena shook her head. 'Nothing like that. He was right in my face, I would've seen it.'

'What about someone giving him a hand signal? Did he look away at another cop before he let you past?'

'No. I was watching him the whole time. He was staring right at me and then . . . he just changed his mind. I still can't believe it.'

Dryden couldn't believe it, either. *Didn't* believe it. Not quite, anyway. He turned and stared through the back window. He could see the glow of flashers half a mile behind, pulsing against street signs and buildings near the interchange.

Dena seemed to pick up on his tension.

'What is it?' she asked. 'Is there something I should know?'

Dryden watched the road behind them a few seconds longer, then turned forward again.

'I don't know,' he said.

They reached Modesto just after two in the morning. Dena stopped first at a Walmart on the edge of town.

'There are things you'll need,' she said, 'and you'll want to minimize the time you spend in public places like stores.'

Dryden and Rachel stayed in the car while Dena went in. She came back out twenty minutes later with several bags full of non-perishable food, plus a flashlight, batteries, and fresh bandages and antibiotic gel for Rachel's arm. She'd also bought a baseball cap and a pair of wrap-around Oakleys for Dryden. 'Better than nothing,' she said.

They were at the train station ten minutes later. Dena parked and left the engine running, and for a moment no one spoke.

'When I wake up tomorrow morning,' Dena said, 'I'm going to lie there for thirty seconds and wonder if I dreamed this.'

Rachel leaned forward between the seats and hugged her. Dena held on for a long time, her eyes closed.

'Thank you,' Dryden said. It was probably the fifth time he'd said it.

Dena opened her eyes over Rachel's shoulder and looked at him.

'Protect her,' she said.

Dryden nodded. 'With my life.'

He hoped like hell it would be enough.

A minute later he and Rachel were on the freeway, accelerating into the sparse middle-of-the-night traffic. In his mind Dryden went back over the route he'd eye-balled on Dena's computer. For a few seconds he couldn't recall the name of the town right at the end – the one at the U.S. 50 interchange, where the two-lane led south to Elias Dry Lake. Then he remembered: The town was called Cold Spring.

Chapter Twenty-one

Cobb woke an hour before sunrise, took a long steam shower, and went out on the balcony off his bedroom suite to have a smoke. The bedroom overlooked the valley, its mountain walls thick with snow. Every bit of it glittered in the sharp air, and overhead the brightest stars stood out in the predawn twilight.

He heard the patio door slide open right beneath him. The twins came out and crossed the pavers to the edge of the pool. While they waited for its thermal cover to retract, they peeled each other's clothes off, taking their time with it, kissing, whispering to each other in whatever language it was they spoke. They weren't really twins; Cobb had simply thought of them that way since the day he'd met them. They looked like each other, that was all – same skinny little bodies, same big dark eyes and pert little tits, same pouty expressions when the whiskey or the vodka or the pot ran out, though there was always someone by to restock it inside of an hour. Cobb didn't even know the girls' names. In his head he called them Callie and Iola, for shits.

He watched as the steam from the uncovered pool filled the air around them – the girls insisted on keeping the damned thing at 100 degrees, and Cobb didn't argue; he sure as hell wasn't paying the energy bill for this place. Before the steam cloud obscured them, Callie slipped into the pool and Iola seated herself at its edge, her feet dangling in the water. Callie went under the surface and came up again right in front of Iola, her face between her thighs. The girls were only shapes in the steam now; Cobb watched as Callie's face dipped forward and Iola leaned back on the pavers, her breathing turning into cute little moans. Cobb glanced over his shoulder at the nightstand clock in the bedroom. Thirty minutes until his shift started. Plenty of time to go down to the pool and join them.

It was the damnedest thing, the turns life could take. A year and a half earlier he'd been a logistics specialist – which was to say a warehouse worker – stocking shelves at a supply depot in Ramadi. In addition to killing camel spiders the size of his Christ-loving hands, that life had consisted of squaring away pallets of toilet paper and potato chips and coffee for the private American army in Iraq – about the same size as the real army that'd withdrawn a few years before. Cobb had woken up every morning there in his shitty little particleboard housing unit, his twenty-third birthday just behind him, his framed diploma from Ohio State six thousand miles away at his folks' place in Rochester, and he'd thought the same thing he so often thought now: *How the hell did I end up here?* Hadn't that always been the million-dollar question, though? Yes indeedy. Seth Cobb, the directionless wonder. Where will the wind take him next?

Where it had taken him about fifteen months ago was to a hiring office out at the edge of the company grounds, there in Ramadi, after someone had stuffed a bright green flyer under his door in the middle of the night. The flyer had been both vague and right to the point.

GENEROUS PAY / EXCELLENT LIVING CONDITIONS (NON MIDDLE-EAST LOCATION) / MUST BE WILLING TO CUT OFF CONTACT WITH FAMILY, LOVED ONES FOR FIVE YEARS / EXTENSIVE PHYSICAL AND PSYCH TESTING REQUIRED

Cobb had family and loved ones, but he was more than willing to miss out on their company for five years, and he was quite sure the feeling was mutual. So just like that, he'd found himself sitting at a little desk in the run-down building the flyer had directed him to. It was a disused hangar of some kind; he could see fuel stains on the concrete floor. There was a door to a back room, and every time someone opened it Cobb got a glimpse of bulky, high-end medical equipment inside. One of the machines was an MRI, he thought.

Before he got any closer to that room, there were written tests to complete. These would turn out to be the strangest part of the whole process. None of the questions were difficult, exactly. There weren't even right and wrong answers, only judgment calls, like *Your house is on fire and your dog is trapped inside; do you risk your life to save him?* Or *Would you play a single round of Russian roulette to save a loved one from certain death?* After two days' worth of that stuff, the written tests had culminated in something that deeply puzzled Cobb – at the time, at least. He had been made to sit off in a corner of the big room, away from any other applicant, and a man in his thirties had sat down directly behind him, saying nothing. The man just sat there while Cobb paged through one final test packet. This last test, he saw, contained no questions. There were just instructions, like *For the next five minutes, think in detail about the worst things you've ever done and gotten away with* or *Have you ever deeply hurt someone you cared about? Think about it, in specifics, for the next five minutes.*

What the hell was the point of this, he wondered. He could sit here running Pink Floyd lyrics through his head and they wouldn't know the difference. But for the hell of it, he went ahead and obeyed the instructions. He found it oddly stressful, after a while; it even seemed to give him a headache, or at least a funny chill at his temples.

That test lasted an hour, and when it was over, the man behind him stood up and left, taking out a phone as he went. Twenty minutes later Cobb had been ushered into the back room at last, and he spent the next four hours getting poked and scanned and being buzzed into the claustrophobic tunnels of diagnostic equipment. That day had ended in a little office outside the hangar, with Cobb seated across from two men he'd never seen before. Both were fortyish and hard and leathery. He never learned their names.

'If you accept this job offer, you'll be working for a company called Western Dynamics. You know it?'

Cobb nodded. 'Big defense contractor.'

'You'll be required to take three doses of a drug, a simple pill, the first one tonight if you're on board.'

'Is this a drug trial?'

'Not at all.'

'What does the drug do?'

'Nothing dangerous. You won't know what it's for until later. That's part of the deal. And the flyer wasn't bullshitting about losing contact with your kin. You won't have a phone. You won't have Internet access or mail service either.'

'What's the generous pay?'

'Two hundred thousand a year, all of which you can bank, because room and board will be provided for you.'

Cobb whistled and sat back in his chair. He asked if he'd have a stack of non-disclosure forms to sign if he took the job. No, the men told him. When it came to that, the situation was very simple: If he ever shared the details of this job with any outsider, he would be killed, and no one would ever be prosecuted for killing him. Cobb looked into their eyes and saw that it wasn't a joke. Which made him believe the rest of it, too.

'Let's have the first pill,' he said.

A funny thing had happened that same night, back at

his housing unit on the other side of Ramadi. A messenger came by with a thick three-ring binder, and Cobb laughed, because here was the paperwork after all. Of course. Only it wasn't paperwork. Inside the folder were detailed profiles of over one hundred women; no names for any of them, just reference codes. All of the women were between the ages of eighteen and twenty, and every last one was a heartbreaker. The profiles included high-res face photos as well as nude shots. Tucked inside the folder's front flap was a handwritten note: *Pick any two, and submit your choices to the hiring office tomorrow at 0800.*

Less than twenty-four hours later, Cobb had been in the air aboard a C-17 transport. He'd dozed en route, waking when the plane touched down here at the compound – the place he'd called home ever since. Even now he had no idea where it was located. Somewhere in northern Canada, he guessed. There were mountains, and it was cold as hell year-round, and there were no roads connecting the compound to anything else. Nothing surrounding the place but northern wilderness as far as you could see. The compound itself consisted of the airport, with its array of buildings and hangars, and then a single road looping out into the woods, skirting the rim of the valley and accessing the dozen houses that stood there overlooking the drop-off. Each house was a hundred yards from the next, every one of them screened from its neighbors by the intervening forest.

The wind shifted and partly blew the steam cloud away from the patio. Cobb took in what it revealed, then smiled around his cigarette.

Callie was still at it, her eyes closed, lost in the moment; Cobb couldn't see her mouth, but he could tell she was smiling. All at once she opened her eyes and looked up at him. She raised one hand from Iola's thigh and beckoned him with it. Cobb nodded and took another deep drag.

The two girls had arrived here the day after he had. By then he'd all but forgotten having picked them from among the profiles; he'd mostly figured that was just another psych test. That first day here, on his own, he'd simply marveled at the house; he had it all to himself. It was brand-new – you could still smell the carpet and the paint – and it looked like something you'd see on *MTV Cribs*.

EXCELLENT LIVING CONDITIONS.

No shit. There was the heated pool, with a hot tub at one end; the patio itself was heated by electrical coils under the paver bricks. There was a home theater with 7.1 surround sound. There was a sauna. There was a Sub-Zero fridge in the giant kitchen, and on the granite counter there was a tablet computer dedicated solely to a list of food and drinks. You could scroll down that list and tap two dozen items – or just one, if you had a craving for it – and the groceries would show up at the door thirty or forty minutes later, no charge. Cobb had been soaking it all up, wondering what in the name of hell he was supposed to do here, when the doorbell rang and he met Callie and Iola for the first time.

Those first few weeks, it remained unclear what exactly the job would be. An older guy named Hager stopped by a few times, early on, to explain some of the ropes. There were two more scheduled dosages of the drug, he said, which would be brought to the house at the necessary times. It was fine if Cobb used the available alcohol and marijuana, within reason; those substances would not conflict with the drug, either now or later on when his work began.

'What sort of work?' Cobb had asked.

'That'll come later. Another few weeks. For now, just settle in. Enjoy yourself. There are marked hiking trails that go up on some of the ridges close by. Take the girls out for a walk, if they feel like it. If you ever encounter any of your neighbors, it's fine if you want to say hello, exchange pleasantries, but keep it to a minimum. They'll all be doing the same work as you, but you're not to discuss it. I've had this same talk with them, so it'll be fine.' Hager had ended the conversation somewhat cryptically. 'There's a landline phone in the basement. I'm sure you saw it. It connects to my office here at the compound, and nowhere else – you just push the red button. In time there'll be something you want to ask me about. When it happens, give me a ring.'

That was all.

In the weeks that followed – very, very nice weeks – Cobb did as Hager had said. He settled in. It was clear from the start that communication was never really going to happen between him and the girls; he didn't know what language they spoke, but he thought it was something from Eastern Europe. Maybe they were Romanian – they reminded him of the cute little gymnasts from there that he'd always tuned in for when the Olympics were on. In any case, how much talking did you really need? You could share an emotional connection well enough without words. Some nights the three of them would get bombed out of their minds and load up a foreign film from the theater's digital library, something in French or German so that none of them could understand it. They'd try to follow along and end up laughing so hard it actually hurt, and then the clothes would come off and for the next few hours Cobb's whole world would just be smooth skin and moisture and heat, clenching little hands and sighs and screams, and before he finally passed out in a tangle of their limbs, he'd think, *I feel sorry for every last person on earth right now, stuck living their lives and not this one.*

When it finally happened – the thing that would make him pick up the phone downstairs – he didn't immediately recognize what was going on. This was a month or so after he'd taken the last of the three pills, and in fact he hadn't thought about those pills in days. He was high when the effect started, and his first thought on the matter was that he was hallucinating.

True, pot had never made him do that before, but there had to be a first time for everything. Anyway, this wasn't a full-on hallucination. Not a visual one, at least. Just an auditory thing – Callie's and Iola's voices in his head, chattering away in the same language they spoke. It was about six hours before he put it together, enough time for the high to be long gone and for his thinking to crystalize. It was early evening, and he was standing in the kitchen with Callie. By then he'd realized he was getting images in his mind alongside the girls' voices. One of these images suddenly stood out vividly: a can of Pepsi being popped open. Not three seconds later, Callie turned and crossed to the fridge and took out a can of Pepsi. A minute after that, Cobb was in the basement pushing the red button.

Hager walked him through it as if he were talking to a man on a ledge. Yes, he said, those were the girls' thoughts he was getting in his head. Like stray radio stations. Yes, the pills had done that to him. Yes, the condition was permanent. There was more to it, though, than hearing thoughts. The pills had given Cobb other capabilities, but these were active skills that would have to be trained up. Hager would send a man over in the morning to begin said training.

'What other capabilities?' Cobb asked.

'Think of it as sending instead of just receiving. Ship to shore, shore to ship, that sort of thing.'

'You mean putting thoughts in other people's heads, not just hearing theirs.'

'Thoughts, but more importantly feelings, deep emotional impulses, like guilt or disgust, or even elation. Forcing people to feel those things.'

'What the hell for?' Cobb asked.

'For lots of reasons. It's useful in all kinds of ways.'

Cobb had grasped the meaning of it then, like something sharp and jagged in his hands. A sculpture made of broken glass.

'I'm a weapon,' he said into the phone. 'You're going to send me all over the world to fuck with people's heads.'

'You're going to fuck with people's heads,' Hager said, 'but we won't need to send you anywhere.'

Leaning on the balcony rail now, finishing the cigarette, Cobb thought of how the weeks after that day had played out. The early training. The understanding of what he could really do. The abilities were limited, of course – while mind reading seemed to work on everyone, the more advanced skills only worked on certain people. Then there was the technology, all of it spooky as hell. Even Hager had confided he had no idea how it worked; the company had little teams of genius engineers squirreled away in places – maybe compounds just like this one, with their own Callies and Iolas – designing the stuff. It was easy enough to see what the equipment did, though even now, more than a year into the work, the whole project was still in testing. Still in beta, as the techs said. But it was growing fast, taking on momentum, and Cobb often felt there were angles to it that he was still being kept in the dark about. Things to come.

He shivered. Just the cold air, he told himself. Nothing more to it. His nerves were fine with all this stuff. He and Hager had settled the morality angle way back when, in that first phone call.

'You want to take your time and think hard about this,' Hager had said. 'Right now you're surprised by it all, you're rattled, and that's only human. What I want you to do is go back upstairs and take a good look at your situation. The house. The girls. You'd have to agree we've been good to you. Haven't we, Cobb?'

'Yes. Yes, sir. Everything here is amazing.' Cobb found the words coming out fast; he was tripping over them like a kid. All at once it occurred to him that he'd never thanked Hager – never thanked *any* of these people. Jesus, how had he overlooked that? 'Sir, I just want to say how much all this means to me, and I'm sorry I haven't—'

'Don't worry about that, Cobb. Just listen to me. This work you'll be doing for us, it's going to be hard sometimes. You're going to do things to people – bad things, that they don't deserve. You'll have to do it, though. It's just going to be that way. You have to help us out, like we've helped you out, alright?'

'Yes, sir.'

'When it gets tough, you're going to think about that house, and those girls, and you're going to do whatever it takes to keep them.'

'I will, sir.'

'And you want to remember something: The bad stuff that's coming, it's not your fault, 'cause if you weren't doing it, we'd just have someone else in your place. It would happen either way, so you might as well be the one to benefit. Does that make sense?'

'Perfect sense.'

'Alright, Cobb. Go on back upstairs now. Everything's going to be fine.'

Cobb stubbed the cigarette out on the balcony rail. Down on the patio, Iola's moans had turned into soft, ragged cries. She'd drawn her feet up out of the water, her toes gripping the pool's edge and her knees bouncing rhythmically. She reached down and laced her fingers into Callie's hair, then sucked in one deep breath and screamed. The sound rolled across the pool and out into the darkness over the valley. A few seconds later, her body spent like a wrung sponge, Iola sagged flat on the bricks. Callie took her hands, helped her sit up, eased her into the water, and hugged her.

Cobb dropped the cigarette at his feet. Yeah, his nerves were just fine with the work. He crossed the balcony to the steps leading down, pulling his shirt off as he went.

Chapter Twenty-two

It was a quarter past noon when Dryden and Rachel arrived in Cold Spring, Utah. The off-ramp T-boned into the town's main drag, a strip of chain stores and gas stations and fast-food places, all of it weathered and faded. There was high country half a mile east – a line of hills marching away south at a diagonal, their tops crowned with pine forests and scrub. Otherwise the landscape was low-rolling desert as far as Dryden could see.

He took a side street off the strip and crossed to the east edge of town and saw what he was looking for almost at once: a dirt lane running out toward the hills. Three minutes later he and Rachel were parked at an overlook halfway up the nearest incline, maybe two hundred feet above the desert floor and the town. U.S. 50 was visible for twenty miles or more, stretching away into the shimmer, back toward Nevada and California. Just as visible was the two-lane that formed Cold Spring's central strip, leading south out of town into the wastes. Five miles off in that direction, vast and stark and nearly blinding white, lay Elias Dry Lake. Dryden squinted but couldn't make out the tower at its center.

He leaned into the car and took a pen from the console tray.

'Give me your hand,' he said.

Rachel held it out, and Dryden wrote a phone number on the back. Above it he wrote the name Cole Harris.

'Who's that?' Rachel asked.

'A friend of mine. One of the only people in the world I trust. I was in the army with him, and we stayed friends afterward.'

He turned and studied the hillside above the overlook. It rose another two hundred feet to the crest of the ridge, the whole climb shallow and forested. There were no roads above this point. No houses or other structures, either.

'I want you to wait here,' he said. 'Go about halfway up the slope between this spot and the top. Stay in the trees, out of view and out of the sun, but keep an eye on the lake bed. After I'm there, if you see anything happening, a line of cars heading down there, a helicopter landing, then you go into town and call that number. Walk into a store and say you have to call your parents. No one will give you a problem with it.'

All the way from Modesto they'd tuned in to the news wherever they could get a signal. The manhunt was almost the only story being covered, and at no point had there been any mention of a young girl travelling with the suspect. Dryden supposed Gaul had his reasons for keeping it that way; if the plan was to kill Rachel, it wouldn't help to have the whole country praying for her safety while the search played out.

'Cole Harris lives in San Jose, California,' Dryden said. 'You call him and tell him your name, and tell him Sam Dryden wants him to come here and get you. And say this word: *goldenrod*. Okay? Remember it. Say *goldenrod* and he'll understand.'

'What does it mean?'

'It's called a non-duress code. We used them in the army. It means *This isn't a trick, nobody has a gun to my head*. Or more generally, *This isn't BS*. It's a word he and I agreed on, and no one else knows about it. If you say it, then he knows the message is coming from me.'

Rachel was staring at the number on her hand. Dryden hoped like hell she wouldn't need to call it.

'I think this is one of those moments when I can't tell your thoughts from mine,' Rachel said.

Up close, it was hard to tell exactly where the desert ended and the lake bed began. Whatever shoreline there'd once been had long since been smoothed out by the wind. All that gave away the transition was that the ground suddenly got a lot flatter under the Honda's tires, and the sage and desert grass all but vanished.

Out ahead, the cell tower was visible now, a standard steel lattice mast with guy wires stabilizing it. Hard to tell its height with no trees or buildings for reference, but it had to be two hundred feet tall at least. From this distance, still a mile or more away, nothing about the thing struck Dryden as unusual.

That perception had changed by the time he parked and got out of the car. In his years in the service, especially later on with Ferret, Dryden had encountered transmitter towers a handful of times. Once or twice he'd installed eavesdropping equipment on them, piggybacking it into cables at the base. In those cases he'd worked from instructions provided by a technician; he himself had no real expertise with industrial comm stuff like this. He had wondered, right up until getting within thirty feet of this thing, whether he would even know if something about it was strange. He wasn't wondering anymore.

He stopped within arm's length of the structure's nearest corner. The steel frame of the tower itself looked like all the rest he'd ever seen: triangular cross-bracing, the welded joints infused with copper connectors to help with conductivity. And like other towers, it had a metal tube bolted to one of its legs, running up inside the corner, protecting sensitive cables from the elements and from tampering. In most cases Dryden had seen, these tubes were made of steel or even aluminum – they usually escaped notice. This one had caught his eye right away; it was made of neither of those metals. He stepped closer to it. In the desert sunlight, the tube's surface gleamed a dull silver. The last time he'd seen this kind of material, there'd also been desert sun shining on it. A different desert, far away from here.

He rapped on the tube with his knuckles. It was like knocking on a thick slab of granite – the same way it'd felt that other time, tapping on the side of an M-1A1 Abrams where a bomb blast had stripped away the paint. The cell tower's cables were protected by a thick sleeve of depleted uranium. Tank armor.

Dryden stepped back again, getting a better angle on the higher portions of the tower. The uranium tube climbed to about half the structure's height and then connected to a large black cylinder; the thing had the shape of a beer keg but was maybe five times the size of one. Dryden couldn't remember seeing anything like it on a radio tower before. Whatever it was, he could hear it humming in the still air like a transformer.

There was nothing else attached to the tower. No cellular transceiver. No microwave relays. Nothing but the heavy tube and the strange black drum. As Dryden listened, the thing's bass hum seemed to come not only from overhead but from the tower itself, the steel lattice vibrating like a tuning fork. Even the hardpan beneath his feet seemed to throb.

Was there any reason to bring Rachel down to see this thing? What could she learn from it? He thought of her reaction to the tower in Bakersfield. If a random one could provoke that response in her, would the details of this one do more?

She would insist on coming. He could refuse – but what was the plan after that? Well, that was simple: There wasn't one.

Dryden cursed under his breath.

He went back to the car but didn't get in. If he was bringing Rachel here, there were safety measures to take first. These, too, were simple.

He tilted his face skyward and turned very slowly in a complete circle. He wasn't looking for aircraft. He wasn't looking for anything at all.

He pictured the satellite feeds he'd seen during his active years. Even that technology – outdated compared to what Gaul was using – had been able to resolve human faces in bright daylight. The resulting detail might not be wedding-picture sharp, but it would be more than enough to identify someone.

For good measure, Dryden made another slow circle, taking a minute or more to do it. If it had occurred to Gaul to keep watch on this place, then one of his computer rooms would suddenly be buzzing with activity.

Dryden opened the driver's door of the Honda, got behind the wheel, and settled in to wait.

Chapter Twenty-three

An hour passed.

Nothing happened.

Dryden opened the door and stood again. He made a visor of his hand and swept his gaze over the horizon on all sides. No choppers coming in. No vehicles coming down the two-lane from Cold Spring.

There were good-sized cities, sure to have at least one police helicopter, within half an hour's flight time of this location. Those aircraft would've scrambled within a few minutes, if one of Gaul's satellites had spotted Dryden here.

Gaul couldn't have known this was a trick – that Rachel wasn't in the car. At night, a satellite using thermal vision could've seen that she wasn't in the vehicle, but in sunlight, with the roof of the car hotter than any person who might be inside, there was no chance of that.

If Gaul had been watching this place, the response would've already come down. Fast and hard.

Dryden waited another minute, then got back in the car and started it.

When he pulled up to the overlook, Rachel practically sprinted out of the trees. He wasn't sure he'd ever seen relief so vivid in a pair of eyes before. She climbed into the passenger seat and took hold of his arm – it was like she needed to be sure he was real.

'Anything?' she asked.

'Nothing I could make sense of.'

She opened her mouth to respond, but he beat her to it.

'Yes, I'll take you there. We'll look at it for exactly one minute, and then we're getting the hell out of here.'

For the first three or four miles of the drive, right up until the tower came into view, Rachel felt only exhilaration. She guessed part of it was excitement at maybe learning something in the next few minutes, but there was no denying what was mostly behind the feeling: She was no longer up in the woods, all by herself.

She had no intention of telling Sam how that had felt. Being scared – for him, more than for herself – had been one thing, but above all, what she'd felt was . . .

Cold.

That was all she could think of to describe it. Being alone felt cold, after all this time spent with him. All this time spent close to that fireplace feeling that seemed to roll off of him and encircle her. She was pretty sure she knew what that feeling was, though she didn't plan to talk about that either. No doubt it would be awkward for both of them. No matter, though. It was enough just to feel it again.

She was thinking about that, and smiling, when her

eyes picked out the faint line of the tower, way out ahead against the desert sky.

The smile went away. The same irrational fear she'd felt in Bakersfield, as if she were looking at a giant bug, stole back over her.

Sam noticed.

'We can turn back,' he said.

Rachel shook her head. She tried to push the fear out of her voice before speaking. 'I'll be okay.'

She felt the vibration in the ground as soon as she got out of the car. It hummed through the soles of her shoes, into her feet and her bones.

'Are you alright?' Sam asked.

She nodded.

Her eyes had fixed on the large black pop-can-shaped thing, a hundred feet up. The whole tower scared her, but that thing was the worst somehow. She made herself take a deep breath – her breathing seemed to go shallow if she wasn't careful.

She let go of the car door and moved toward the base of the tower. One step after another. Easy does it. At the edge of her vision she saw Sam turning and scanning the road behind them. She kept going.

She knew what she had to do. She wasn't sure *how* she knew – maybe it was another conditioned response. She also knew it was just about the last thing in the world she felt like doing, but that really wasn't a reason to back down, was it? She was tired of looking scared.

Tired of *being* scared. She crossed the last few feet to the tower's base and grabbed hold of the nearest corner with both hands.

If the vibration in the ground had made her bones hum, this contact made them scream. It made the bones themselves feel hollow. Hollow and full of buzzing flies.

She heard herself making a noise. Whimpering. Crying out. Heard Sam somewhere behind her, calling her name, running toward her. She caught the intention in his thoughts: grab her by the shoulders and pull her away from the damned thing.

'No!' she said.

She heard him stop right at her back. He came around to the side, his hand closing on one of her arms.

'Rachel—'

This is how it works. I have to hold on until it happens.

The thoughts had formed on their own. She had no idea what they meant. What was supposed to happen?

'Rachel?'

Have to hold on. Any second now—

'Don't stop me,' she said. 'It's okay.'

He said something else, but she missed it. The sunlit desert fell away, and all at once she was lost in a world of voices and mental pictures.

Pictures of everything. People, dogs, cars, but in almost all of them there was—

The town. The place they'd driven through when they got off the freeway, north of here. These were mind pictures of the town, the stores she'd seen, the gas station, the hills to the east. And the voices were thoughts. Like a thousand people's thoughts at the same time, as if she were standing in the middle of a huge crowd, close enough to read them all.

Sam was still in the background saying her name. Asking if she was okay. She wanted to answer, but—

Something else was happening now. Beneath all the pictures and the voices, beneath her own feet even, there was—

A tunnel. Opening up like a trapdoor below her. She couldn't see it but she could feel it. A tunnel made of wires, crackling and humming like the big black thing halfway up the tower. The tunnel led down and away – far, far away. Her mind reached down into it, screaming along its length at dizzying speed, and she felt—

Someone else. Someone at the far end.

– another mind there. A man's mind, it seemed like. She felt his thoughts seeping into her. An image of a swimming pool with mountains behind it. Two women with dark hair, in the water, naked. Then a room full of strange machines and computers.

Mod signal on number two just got a little screwy, what's that about – whoa, hey, HEY.

Panic soaking the man's thoughts now.

What the fuck just happened? Get Hager, someone fucking get Hager!

Yet even these sounds and pictures were fading away from her, the crackling tunnel and all the rest of it, dimming and quieting, because suddenly she had a sense of—

What was it?

Some place inside her own mind. Like a room for storing things, only she couldn't see into it. There was something blocking the way, like a fabric stretched across the entry. A membrane. The things inside the room were pressing at it, their shapes pushing it outward, stretching it.

My memories. These are my memories trying to get free.

It seemed to her that the tower itself was shaking them up. The vibration in her bones, in her mind, jarring everything.

She could feel Sam's hand gripping her arm tighter now. Any moment he'd pull her away, but—

Something in the memory room was breaking through. Something important to her, its edges sharp and white hot, cutting through the membrane.

She saw a picture in her mind. A woman stooping to smile at her. She had kind brown eyes. She was beautiful.

Hello, Rachel. How are you feeling today?

What was her name? That's what was trying to cut through the barrier. The woman's name. She was sure of it.

Sam was talking louder now. Fear in his voice. Telling her to let go.

The membrane was stretched to the breaking point, the burning edge of the name almost through—

Holly. Her name is Holly.

Holly what?

The mental picture was still there. Holly's eyes, so pretty when she smiled—

What was the rest of her name?

Hadn't she heard that name somewhere else? Hadn't someone had it in their thoughts? Not so long ago?

Holly. Holly, Holly, Holly—

Sam's hands took hold of her fingertips and pulled them free of the metal. The terrible vibration cut out as if an OFF button had been pressed. She reeled backward and lost her balance, but by then his arms were around her. He was holding her and speaking softly.

'Are you alright? Rachel.'

She opened her eyes and looked at him. 'Holly Ferrel,' she whispered.

'What?'

For a long moment she couldn't reply. She was sorting it all out in her mind. Lining the ideas up, like toy cars on a track. Because she knew where she'd come across that name recently – and it was the worst place of all to hear it.

Chapter Twenty-four

Leland Hager had been in a good mood until thirty seconds before. He had been standing in his office, at the inward-facing window, looking down over the work floor. A few years earlier, when this compound was still being carved out of the wilderness, engineers had used this building as a garage for earthmovers. Now the earth movers were long gone, and the vast floor space was full of glass-walled rooms, twelve in all. From this window, Hager could look down on all of them in a single glance.

The rooms were arranged in three clusters of four. The three clusters corresponded to the three test sites in the continental United States.

Red City, Wyoming. Cold Spring, Utah. Cook Valley, North Dakota.

The three antennas.

In the eighteen months he'd been in charge of the compound, Hager had found he was at his happiest when he was standing there looking over the glass rooms – the stations, as everyone called them. In each occupied station lay a controller, flat on his back, electrodes stuck to his forehead with conductive gel. The stations were lit with dim red light, like darkrooms – *like wombs*, Hager sometimes thought.

It was quite the feeling, staring at all that through his own reflection in the office window – the reflection of a paunchy little bald man who'd come out of Dartmouth three decades earlier with a degree in finance. A hedge-maze of rational career choices later, here he was, like Oppenheimer out in the desert at Alamogordo with his tinted goggles on. Maybe his own name would end up in metaphors, decades down the road.

The work Western Dynamics was doing, at this place and others just like it, was exciting to the point of being scary. There were the antennas, and the controllers, and then there was the other thing – the thing that unnerved everyone who heard about it. Hager had to admit, at least to himself, that the other thing even unnerved him, a little. When it was finally rolled out and put to use – which could be any time now – there would be no putting the genie back in the bottle. Yeah, no question about it, it was scary as hell. All big things were scary, though. If you let that kind of fear get in your way, what would you ever amount to?

Hager had been in the middle of that thought when the commotion started, down in Cluster Two. The only controller on duty in that section, Seth Cobb, had suddenly sat upright as if someone had jolted him, and started yelling about something wrong at the antenna site.

Now, thirty seconds later, Hager was standing in Cobb's station, trying to calm him. The kid had pulled the paddles off his forehead; one of them had smeared gel into his eyebrow.

'What happened?' Hager asked.

'I don't know. It just felt like ... somebody was reaching for me.'

'What are you talking about?'

'Like there was somebody on the other end of the line – at Cold Spring. Like they were ... coming right through the connection toward me.'

That didn't make any sense, a fact Cobb seemed well aware of. The guy could only shrug, though, looking rattled. Whatever had happened, he wasn't making it up.

Hager was about to speak when he stopped himself.

For a couple of months now, there'd been word coming down from those above him, in Washington and elsewhere, about a potential threat to the project. These conversations had been vague, in ways Hager had gotten used to during his time with Western Dynamics. The whole shady arrangement – two rival companies working with the government, each with its own friends in high places – had been a mess from the beginning. Some of those high-up friends had connections to one another that complicated the game. There were loyalties and there was bad blood, there were favors and paybacks owed, and most of those connections lay hidden in the murk. SHB, Hager called it. Standard human bullshit. He'd run into it his whole career, in one form or another. It didn't matter how lofty your goals, how precise your planning or your actions. Every organization in the world was infested with the mildew of standard human bullshit. At times, the whole deal – the two companies and Washington – felt like a warped love triangle, operating by the rules of a damned Victorian courtship. Certain things were implied but never outright said. The risk of offending the wrong person was always there, hovering over everything. These warnings in the past two months were a prime example. As far as Hager could understand it, the danger was this: Somewhere out there, there was a loose end from the original research at Detrick, years back. A living subject who'd gotten away – a young girl, if the rumors were right. The girl may or may not have ended up in the custody of Martin Gaul's people at Belding-Milner, down in California, but regardless, she posed a potential hazard to the testing going on at the three antenna sites. There was a *risk of interference*. That was as far from vague as the warnings had gotten.

'Describe what you felt,' Hager said. 'As clearly as you can.'

'There was someone there,' Cobb said. 'Right at the antenna.'

'It's not the first time that's happened,' Hager said. A handful of times, high school kids had shown up at each of the towers and tried to climb them, usually late on Friday or Saturday nights.

'This was different,' Cobb said. 'I don't know how, it just was. There was somebody there. Who shouldn't have been there.'

Hager thought about it.

Risk of interference.

There were no security cameras at the antenna. No immediate way of seeing what was going on there in the desert. Hager had a friend in D.C. who could probably get access to satellite data, but it would take time; an hour, maybe. Now that he thought about it, he recalled that Gaul had especially close ties with that whole community, the kind of intel people who had spy sats at their fingertips – but he'd be damned if he'd involve Gaul or anyone else from Belding-Milner in this thing.

What to do, then?

He looked past Cobb to the reclined workstation chair behind him. The two gel-covered electrodes were lying across it where they'd fallen. Hager nodded to them.

'Put those back on.'

Dryden and Rachel were back in the car, heading north, within a minute of her letting go of the tower. The farther they got from it, the better Rachel appeared to feel. For an awful second or two, Dryden had believed the thing was electrocuting her.

She'd described in detail what she'd experienced. A sensation that she was hearing the thoughts of people up in Cold Spring, six or more miles from where the tower stood. Then the feeling of racing through a tunnel, of encountering somebody at the other end. Last, the visual sense of her own trapped memories trying to get free.

'It felt like the memory about Holly Ferrel was the most important,' Rachel said. 'Like I was desperate to get it back. And then when I did, I recognized it. I'd heard it someplace.'

'Where?' Dryden said.

'El Sedero. The building with the blond man and the soldiers. A handful of times, I heard the name Holly Ferrel, or sometimes *Dr F*errel, in their heads. Dr Ferrel . . . in Amarillo, Texas. I remember one of them thinking he might have to go visit her, sooner or later. At the time I barely thought about it – someone going to visit a doctor, that just sounds like a medical problem. But looking back at it now . . .'

She trailed off, but Dryden saw what she meant. If people working for Gaul had been contemplating paying Holly Ferrel a visit, it could mean something very bad for her.

'You don't remember anything else about her?' Dryden asked. 'What kind of doctor she was? Was she a researcher who . . . worked on you?'

'I don't know. There was nothing like that in the memory. Just the fact that she was nice. That she cared about me. A person can't fake something like that. Not with me, anyway.'

Dryden took her point.

'I don't know what her connection to Gaul is,' Rachel said, 'but she knows me. She might know everything we're trying to figure out. And if she's in danger, we need to get to her—' She cut herself off. 'Can we just call her? Look her up online in a library and—'

Dryden was already shaking his head. 'If she's really at risk from Gaul and his people, her phone's already compromised.'

If she's even still alive.

The thought was out before he could stop it. In his peripheral vision, he saw Rachel shudder.

'Sorry,' Dryden said.

'It's okay. I'm thinking it, too.'

'We can still look her up on a library computer, but we'd have to contact her in person, one way or another. There are ways to do that without exposing ourselves to much risk, even if she's being watched.' He considered the geography. Did the math in his head. 'Amarillo's probably ten or twelve hours from here.'

Rachel nodded. Her hands were fidgeting in her lap. Nervous energy.

For the next few minutes, neither of them spoke. At last the southern outskirts of Cold Spring emerged out of the heat shimmer. Dryden reached behind him and took the Oakleys and baseball cap from the backseat. He was just putting them on when Rachel screamed.

The pickup came out of nowhere, thirty feet ahead of the Honda. The road had been empty a second earlier, and suddenly the truck was there, lunging in from the side, from behind a shallow rise that had hidden its approach. Some local idiot out two-tracking in the desert – that was the impression Dryden's mind instantly formed, based on the truck and the guy at the wheel. He got a tenth-of-a-second glimpse of overalls on top of a stained shirt, and a stubble-covered face the word *yokel* might've been coined especially for.

Dryden locked up the Honda's brakes, and for an absurd second the truck actually veered toward the car instead of away, as if the driver in his panic had made exactly the wrong move. By then, though, the truck's momentum had carried it right across the road, missing the Honda by a foot or two, spinning out sideways on the hardscrabble beyond.

On flat ground the truck probably would've just skidded to a stop, but the desert surface at that spot was sloped down at 10 degrees or more. The vehicle slid sideways another sixty or seventy feet, and then its wheels caught a rut and flipped it through a neat half-roll. The pickup came down on its roof, the cab pancaking almost flat with the hood and the truck bed.

Dryden brought the Honda to a stop and put it in park. He and Rachel stared at the crippled truck, a hundred feet away, its rear wheels still spinning under power. The door visible on this side – the passenger door – had been blown open by the crash, but against the desert glare Dryden could see only darkness in the crushed compartment beyond.

They had no cell phone in the car. They could tell someone in town to call an ambulance, if need be, but they themselves would have to be long gone before the authorities arrived.

Either way, they couldn't leave here without checking on the guy. He could be choking on blood in there.

'Stay here,' Dryden said. 'I'm coming right back.'

He opened the door and got out, then stooped and reached under the driver's seat for the SIG. It was that last-minute swerve the truck had made toward the car – probably just a mistake, but damned strange all the same – that made him take the gun. He stuffed it into his rear waistband and stepped off the pavement into the desert.

Kill them, Owen. Crawl the fuck out of there and kill them. Right now.

Owen was hurting. Holy God, was he hurting. The pain was almost enough to distract him from the Gravel Man's voice in his head. Almost.

You're losing the advantage. What are you waiting for?

Owen twisted himself around; something in his shoulder popped, and it was all he could do not to scream.

At least that was his left arm. He used his right for the MP-5. He turned his head and saw it lying in a stir of dust, two feet away from his hand.

Outside, some distance off, a man called to him, 'Are you hurt?'

Lucky you. He's making it easy for you. Get the weapon and take care of him.

Owen reached for the gun with his right hand, but even that movement contorted the sore shoulder; he coughed at the pain and went still again.

You want me to hurt you? I thought we were past all that, Owen.

Then, muted almost to nothing, as if he were speaking to someone else, the Gravel Man said, *He's goddamn useless. Who else has a live asset near Site Two? Better get them in here.*

Owen could make no sense of that. Then again, this whole thing had baffled him, starting a few minutes ago when the Gravel Man had spoken up out of the blue. Owen had been helping his grandfather swap out a radiator when it happened. It was the first time, in all these awful months, that the Gravel Man had troubled him while Grandpa was around. Owen had come to trust that it would never happen, that he would never be made to do anything crazy in front of his grandfather.

Owen, this is important, the Gravel Man had said. There was something in his voice Owen hadn't heard there before. A kind of urgency. Maybe even fear. What did that mean? *Get the machine gun from under your mattress,* the voice said. *Then get in the pickup and go to the old Lake Road south of town. Right now.*

Grandpa had been staring at him by then, his head cocked. 'What's wrong?' he asked.

Owen could only shake his head. He'd never even considered what he would say if a moment like this came along.

Owen, you motherfucker, go! GO!

'Gotta use the bathroom,' Owen muttered, and ran from the pole barn. He was in the truck half a minute later, with the gun beside him, rolling fast out of the dooryard. By then the Gravel Man was talking to him again.

Get on the Lake Road near the bottom end of town and head south on it. You're going to find someone down at the radio tower, or maybe they'll be coming north away from there. Whoever it is, stop them and kill them.

As it'd happened, he'd damn near done that in the moment he reached the road. He'd even swerved a bit there, thinking to hit the car once he saw it – a shitload of good that'd done him.

He looked at the MP-5 again. Right there within his reach. He got a fold of his shirt between his teeth, bit down hard against the pain, and made another move for the gun.

Dryden was thirty feet from the truck, about to call out again, when he saw movement in the dim interior. A second later a man's foot eased out, followed by the other. The man was up on all fours and crawling out backward.

'You alright?' Dryden asked.

No answer.

'Can you hear me?'

When it happened, it happened fast – faster than he would have guessed it could. He supposed it was the strangeness of the situation that caught him off guard. The man eased fully out of the truck, his face still pointed inward at the crushed cab. His left collarbone looked broken, and he seemed to be cradling that arm in front of him with his right. All at once he heaved himself upward into a raised kneeling position, cried out in pain, and collapsed, spinning his body. And just like that he was sitting slumped with his back against the truck bed's wall, with an MP-5 submachine gun pointed up at Dryden.

Dryden heard a gasp, far behind him. He turned to look – Rachel was standing at the open passenger door of the Honda.

'Rachel, stay there!' he shouted. 'Get behind the car. Right now.'

For a moment she remained frozen, eyes huge and scared.

'Go!' he yelled.

She nodded and slipped around behind the trunk to the far side.

Dryden turned his attention back on the gunman. The weapon was shaking in his hand, but not enough that it would miss if the guy pulled the trigger.

Judging by the way his fingertip was flattened against

it, the trigger was already under a few ounces of pressure.

There was simply no chance of drawing the SIG without the man opening fire.

'Who are you?' Dryden asked him.

The man said nothing. His eyes kept going back and forth from Dryden to the Honda. The guy was injured, but not so badly that he couldn't get on his feet. If he killed Dryden, it would be a simple matter for him to get up and go after Rachel. She might be faster, but he had the gun, and there was nothing around but a mile of empty land.

'Take it easy,' Dryden said.

The guy's expression hardened. His finger flattened a little more on the trigger.

Do it. Owen, do it!

Owen watched the man who was standing nearby, but he found his eyes kept wanting to go back to the car on the road. He had crawled out of the wreck all set to do his job, to quiet the Gravel Man for better or worse, but then—

The little girl. Lord in heaven, what could she be, ten or twelve?

The Gravel Man had sent him to kill a pretty little thing like that?

I will hurt you. I will make it hurt like you've never imagined. I won't stop no matter how hard you beg.

'Please,' Owen whispered.

You know what to do. So do it.

Owen took a deep breath and let it ease back out. He felt the familiar – awful, but familiar – calm sink over him. What was the big word for that? *Acceptance*, he thought.

Dryden thought about going for the SIG anyway. He would be shot if he did it, no doubt about that, but he would probably have time, even after taking his hits, to bring the pistol around and get in at least a torso shot of his own. Enough to leave the guy right there, bleeding out where he sat, instead of chasing Rachel. It would probably work.

Probably.

Unless the MP-5 was set to full auto. Then a dozen rounds would leave its barrel within the first second. If even one of those caught Dryden in the head, then forget the whole plan. Rachel would be left defenseless.

Dryden watched the machine gun's barrel. Watched it sway through tiny arcs in the man's shaking hand. Waited for it to sway just far enough—

'I don't got a choice,' the man said softly. 'It ain't that I mean it.'

There was a trace of pity in the guy's eyes, though it seemed to Dryden the man was mostly feeling it about himself. But that was the least of what Dryden noticed about him. What struck him the most was that his early impression – even in that first glimpse as the pickup slid across the road – had been dead on. This man's intelligence could hardly be above that of a child. Even taking into account that he might've been dazed by the crash, there was no mistaking the signs.

It was, in its own way, the strangest thing about the situation: Why would Gaul – or whoever had sent the man – trust critical work to a guy like this?

Dryden had found himself at gunpoint before, and many more times he'd faced adversaries who at least had weapons close at hand. Every one of those men, no matter his ideology or his coldness or his rank in whatever pecking order, had been smart. Not just smart – animal sharp and quick. You could always see it in the eyes. Hired guns lived a Darwinian life. You didn't meet many stupid ones; they didn't last.

'I don't mean it,' the man in the overalls said again.

'You've got the safety on,' Dryden said.

The man didn't exactly fall for it. His reaction was nothing as dramatic as turning the gun sideways and peering at the thing. All that happened was a twitch of his wrist. A reflexive move, so-called muscle memory, in the instant before he caught himself. The MP-5's barrel turned maybe five degrees aside from Dryden, aiming itself at the desert floor ten feet behind him, but almost at once it began to pivot right back to where it had been. The whole flinch opened up no more than a third-of-a-second window of opportunity.

That was enough.

Dryden's hand moved. The action was as practiced and unconscious as flipping the light switch in his own kitchen. He drew the SIG from his rear waistband, leveled it, and fired twice.

Both shots took the man in the forehead. The first was centered, and the second was an inch to the left. The double exit wound blew the back of the guy's head open, the explosive force of it actually causing the head to jerk forward toward Dryden, as if the guy were trying to head-butt the space in front of him. He flopped face-first onto his own shins and lay still.

Dryden fell back two steps, then turned and sprinted for the Honda as fast as he could.

Chapter Twenty-five

Some impulse, maybe just good old-fashioned paranoia, told Dryden to steer clear of the town. He took the Honda off-road over the hard scrubland and went east for two miles until they came to a county two-lane running north; it had signs for an on-ramp to U.S. 50. Five minutes after that they were on the freeway again, eastbound. They'd said almost nothing since the moment they left the pickup behind.

'I don't know,' Dryden said at last. 'I don't have the first clue what that was.'

He didn't start to relax for another hour or more. By then they were on I-70, on the east side of the state. They came to a small town called Sumner; from the freeway it looked just big enough to have a library somewhere in it. When they found it, on Main Street across from a school, its parking lot was close to empty. That boded well for the place not being full of potential eyewitnesses. All the same, Dryden wondered just how effective the Oakleys and baseball hat really were.

The thought of sending Rachel in by herself went against all his instincts, but sometimes instinct was wrong. If someone spotted him, if they simply picked up a phone and dialed 911—

'A girl my age by herself might raise eyebrows, too,' Rachel said. Then, softer: 'I don't want to be alone again.'

There was a single librarian at the checkout desk, just inside the entry. She offered a professional but friendly greeting. Dryden answered with a nod, keeping his face in profile to her. Rachel gave her an energetic wave and a smile; it drew the woman's attention like a magnet.

Pretty smart, Dryden thought.

'Thanks,' Rachel said, when they'd gone by.

'Anything in her thoughts like *Is that the guy on TV*?'

Rachel shook her head.

They found a counter with three computer terminals in the back corner, all of them deserted. So far as Dryden could see, the only other visitor in the library was a kid of maybe fourteen, sitting alone in a sunlit reading area at the opposite corner of the huge room.

They pulled up two chairs and woke one of the computers from its sleep mode.

The obvious first move was a Yellow Pages search for Holly Ferrel in Amarillo, Texas.

No results.

Dryden tried the same search for all of Texas; maybe Holly lived outside of town and commuted.

No results.

He opened a Google map, zoomed in on Amarillo, and searched for hospitals. There were three large ones and a number of smaller practices, almost all of those simply named for a doctor working privately. None of the private doctors was Holly Ferrel.

Dryden checked the websites for each of the three big hospitals and navigated to the staff pages. The third one yielded an interesting result: a doctor named Holly Reese, whose bio was conspicuously missing a photograph. Every other doctor working in that hospital had included a face shot.

For the sake of being thorough, Dryden navigated through every page on the hospital's site that might contain photos of its staff, promotional stills of doctors at patients' bedsides or working in labs. He was on the next-to-last such page, about to click the BACK button, when Rachel's hand shot out and stopped him from touching the mouse.

'What?' he asked.

Her finger went to the screen. In a photo at the bottom, an EMT crew and a few ER docs were rolling a stretcher in off a rooftop helipad. The chopper was visible in the background, bright red and filling most of the frame.

Rachel was pointing to a woman standing just inside the corridor, half turned away from the camera. Because the camera's aperture had adjusted to deal with the sun-washed helipad, the hallway in the foreground appeared very dark. It would've been easy to look right at this photo and not even see the woman.

'Is it her?' Dryden asked.

Rachel leaned closer to the screen. She narrowed her eyes.

'I'm sure of it,' she said.

Dryden stared at the woman's face a second longer, running the implications through his head. It wasn't unheard-of for a relocated person to hold on to a first name; the risk was minimal, and it made the transition easier, psychologically.

Holly Ferrel.

Holly Reese.

Different last name, and no photo on her bio page. She wasn't just in danger. She was hiding from it. At least she believed she was hiding.

Dryden went back to the Yellow Pages and searched for Holly Reese in Amarillo.

One entry. Complete with address.

Dryden found it on the Google map ten seconds later, the photographic overlay showing a marker right above the house.

Holly lived close to downtown, on a street of narrow homes jammed together. Dryden opened Street View and got a look at the place from eye level, out front. It was the Texas equivalent of a town house like you might see in Brooklyn or Georgetown. Others of the same size lined the street on both sides, most of them adjoining their neighbors, a few with narrow alleys in between.

'If she's still alive, you think Gaul's people are watching her,' Rachel said. Not asking.

Dryden nodded. 'Have to assume it.'

'So how do we contact her?'

'I want to know more about her before we do that,' Dryden said. 'I believe you when you say she's someone who cared about you, but that doesn't mean I'm ready to go introduce ourselves.'

He studied the layout of the street, his thoughts going to the eavesdropping equipment he'd used so often in his time with Ferret. A good laser microphone would be useful; it could be pointed at one of Holly's windows from down the block and pick up sound from inside by measuring vibrations on the glass. It was decades-old technology, very reliable.

Very hard to come by, too. You couldn't get it at RadioShack or Best Buy.

Rachel put her hand to the screen again. She pointed to the narrow homes on either side of Holly's. 'Do you think we could get inside one of those? Maybe if no one was home?'

'I don't know. It's possible. A lot of buildings like that are broken up into apartments. If we got lucky, there might be a vacant one.' He turned to her. 'What are you thinking?'

'How wide are those houses?'

Dryden shrugged. 'Twenty-five, thirty feet.'

Rachel turned and stared on a diagonal across the library, to the young boy reading alone. 'How far away do you think he is?'

Dryden considered the distance. 'Sixty feet, maybe a little more.'

Rachel faced forward again and shut her eyes. She took on the expression of someone trying to make out a just-audible voice over a bad phone line. Then she spoke as if she were reading from a page. 'Well, he's dead now hisself. He knows the long and short on it now. And if ever a rough hand come to port, it was Billy. Right you are, said Silver. Rough and ready. But mark you here, I'm an easy man. I'm quite the gentleman, says you. But this time it's serious. Duty is duty, mates. I give my vote. Death.'

She seemed about to continue, then let it go. She opened her eyes and met Dryden's.

'Treasure Island,' Dryden said.

He stared at the distance for another moment, then looked at the houses on the screen again. Rachel wouldn't need to be in the one right next to Holly's to get in her head. She could do it from two or even three houses away. Maybe even from across the street.

'Interesting,' he said.

Rachel managed a smile.

Dryden opened a real estate site, entered Amarillo, selected the rental tab, and pulled up a map. Within thirty seconds he was staring at Holly's house.

There were three apartments available within the

necessary range. The best was a second-floor walk-up, two doors down. That would put Holly's entire residence in a zone between thirty and sixty feet from Rachel.

'When can we be there?' Rachel asked.

Dryden looked at the clock in the corner of the screen. He did the math. 'Midnight local time, give or take.'

Chapter Twenty-six

He kept to five above the limit the whole way. They stopped twice for gas, and once at a hardware store to buy a metal file. Dryden burned another ten minutes using the tool on one of the house keys that hung from Dena Sobel's key ring.

They pulled off I-40 into Amarillo at 12:35 Central Time. Dryden found a quiet parking lot a block and a half from Holly's home. The night was cool and full of the smells of restaurant food and vehicle exhaust.

'Don't look around for anyone watching,' Dryden said. 'We're two people walking home with groceries. Nothing more than that.'

They were on Holly's street now, a hundred yards from the place they wanted. Dryden had the shopping bags Dena had bought in Modesto. The sidewalk was deserted and mostly dark. No sound in the night except the background hum of the city. The diesel groan of a bus trundling by, a few blocks over.

The building's entry was locked, as expected. Dryden already had the modified key in his hand. A bump key, to use the common term. He had notched its blade into five equal-sized teeth, like little shark fins. With skill, a person could use one of these to bypass most of the standard door locks in the world. Dryden had used them in a dozen or more countries, at times when quiet entry into a structure was critical. In the years since his service, he'd never used anything less than a disc-tumbler lock for his own door. Those were immune to bump keys. They were also rare as hell.

The house two doors down from Holly's had a standard lock. Dryden got through it about as quickly as he would've with the correct key. The apartment door, on the second-floor landing, was no more difficult.

The unit was bare of furniture. They left the lights off and locked the door behind them. The interior was like most empty apartments Dryden had seen: new paint on the walls, the air scented by carpet shampoo.

The moment they were inside with the door shut, Rachel went to the east wall – the closest she could get to Holly's home – and shut her eyes. She stood there, leaning with her fingers splayed on the plaster, and said nothing for over a minute.

Dryden's vision began adjusting to the gloom. The only light came from the glow of streetlamps against the closed window blinds and the blue LED display of the stove.

'You must be hearing fifty people from here,' Dryden said.

Rachel nodded. 'It's like trying to find one voice in a crowd.'

'It's late. Maybe she's sleeping.'

'I don't think so. I can read people even when they're asleep. Right now I'm getting a bunch of people in the building right beside us, and a few that are a lot farther away, in that direction. But in between, there's a big space where there's nobody. I think that's Holly's house. I think it's empty.'

Rachel continued listening, waiting.

'Doctors keep strange hours,' Dryden said. 'Don't worry too much just yet.'

Rachel nodded again.

'You hearing anyone else?' Dryden asked. 'Anyone Gaul might have sent?'

For a long time Rachel didn't reply. Dryden saw her face tighten in concentration.

'Not that I can tell,' she said. 'Even bad people's thoughts are pretty normal, most of the time.'

She gave it another minute, then opened her eyes and turned from the wall.

Dryden went to the living room window; it faced out over the street in front of the building. He left the blinds closed but put his eye to the crack at their edge. From just the right angle he could see Holly's front porch. A single newspaper lay atop the steps, in a plastic sleeve.

Dryden returned to the door, where he'd set down the groceries. He opened the bag with the gauze pads and disinfectant.

'Let's have a look at your arm,' he said.

*

It was a quarter past two in the morning. Rachel had been asleep for an hour, curled on the floor near the wall. She'd made no sounds or sudden moves; that effect of the drug, at least, was long gone.

Dryden thought he could tell when she was dreaming, though: At times the chill at his temples seemed to intensify, doubling or tripling in strength. He'd gotten used to the steady background feel of it – it was there even when Rachel was asleep – but these swells and ebbs were something new. Some artifact of dream sleep, he guessed – uncontrolled activity, like rapid eye movement or night tremors.

He watched the blinds for the glow of headlights and listened for vehicles stopping or footsteps tapping on the sidewalk. Every time it happened he checked the window. So far, no arrivals at Holly Ferrel's house. The paper lay right where it had been.

He'd familiarized himself with the apartment; it hadn't taken long. There were five rooms: the kitchen, the living room, a bathroom, and two bedrooms. The second bedroom had a sliding door to a small balcony off the building's rear. In the murky light outside, Dryden saw a narrow alley running east to west, paralleling the street in front. On the far side of the alley were a few more town houses, but mostly there were nondescript little buildings that could've been anything. Real estate offices. Travel agencies. Coffee shops. There were broad alleys between them, leading out to the next street over.

He was sitting now, his back to the wall beside the living room window. From this position he could check Holly's porch just by turning his head.

He rubbed his eyes. He hadn't slept in well over forty-eight hours. He dropped his hands to his sides and opened his eyes. If he kept them closed for any length of time he'd only get more tired.

He listened to the sounds of the building. The HVAC system humming. The dull bass of speakers somewhere upstairs. Laughter – drunk friends, men and women.

Life being lived.

'Do you ever think about trying again?'

He turned.

Rachel was lying with her head on her good arm, her eyes open. Regarding him.

'Having a family again, I mean,' she said.

'I don't know. I guess I don't. I haven't, at least.'

He'd told her almost nothing about Trish and Erin – not by speaking, anyway.

'I'm sorry,' Rachel said. 'There's no way to keep from hearing it in your head, but I can shut up about it, if you want.'

He shook his head. 'Don't worry.'

The song upstairs ended and another started. Dryden thought he recognized the bass rhythm – 'Undercover of the Night,' by the Rolling Stones.

'You should be someone's dad again,' Rachel said. 'You'd be good at it. You are good at it.'

She got up and crossed to the window and sat down beside him. She leaned her head against his shoulder. A minute later she was asleep again.

It was twenty to four. The party upstairs had ended. There was no sound but Rachel's breathing.

In Dryden's peripheral vision, faint light rimmed the window blinds. A vehicle slowed and stopped close by.

Dryden turned and put his eye to the gap.

A dark sedan. Right in front of Holly's house.

Two men got out fast; the driver stayed at the wheel. The two outside scanned the street up and down.

'Rachel,' Dryden said.

He nudged her gently with his elbow.

She came awake, disoriented. Looked around in the darkness. Then she understood. She cocked her head as if listening, though not with her ears.

'Two men in front of her house,' Dryden whispered. 'Another inside a car. Can you read them?'

She nodded.

'Anyone else in the car?' Dryden asked.

Rachel shook her head.

Dryden was still watching them. The two men finished surveying the street. They went up the front walk, unlocked Holly's door, and went in. Dryden could almost see Rachel's attention swinging to follow them, her head tilting, turning by tiny degrees.

'Their thoughts are like a checklist,' she said. 'Kitchen clear. Front bath clear. Hallway clear.'

'Sounds like a security sweep,' Dryden said. 'Making sure the place is empty before the owner comes home.'

Holly had bodyguards working for her. Interesting.

Rachel continued listening. Dryden pictured the two men checking the place, room by room, proceeding methodically upward through its stories.

They came back out five minutes later and stood sentry on the porch. One of them picked up the paper and set it inside. The sedan pulled away, and for a long time after that nothing happened.

At 4:05 by the clock on the stove, the sedan came back. One of the men on the porch went down the walk to meet it. He opened the vehicle's back door, and a woman emerged. Forty years old, give or take. Small frame, delicate features. Though the light wasn't great, Dryden could see it was the woman from the hospital website photo.

Rachel was already locked onto her.

Dryden watched the security officer escort Holly to the front door. She went in alone, and the man took up his position again.

Dryden thought of what Rachel had said the other night: how tricky it was to get useful information from a person's thoughts. How often were thoughts even arranged into coherent sentences? How often were they just fragments of recent conversations, random images?

For five minutes Rachel said nothing. Sometimes she closed her eyes and seemed to concentrate harder.

'She's writing an e-mail,' Rachel said. 'It's medical

stuff about someone named Laney. I don't know what half the words mean. I think some of them are the names of drugs.'

Dryden felt the cool sensation at his temples spike again. No doubt a result of Rachel's intense focus. He said nothing about it – hardly thought about it, even. All his attention went to wondering what the next hour might tell them.

'Sent,' Rachel said.

She was quiet for another minute. Her concentration seemed almost to put her in a trance. Her eyelids slipped halfway shut.

Then they opened wide. She startled as if someone had prodded her.

Dryden didn't ask. He waited.

Rachel got her feet under her and stood. She went to the east wall as if pulled there by whatever she was hearing in Holly Ferrel's head.

'What the hell?' Rachel whispered.

Dryden stood, too. He was about to step away from the wall when he heard a sound: creaking wood.

Floorboards.

Someone was outside the apartment's door.

Chapter Twenty-seven

Rachel heard it, too. Her fix on Holly's thoughts broke. She spun fast and stared at the door, then at Dryden.

Dryden stooped and took the SIG SAUER from where he'd set it on the floor. He moved out from the wall, putting himself diagonal to the door, ten feet away. Rachel came to his side.

Dryden's eyes went to the gap where the door met the threshold. The dim stairwell light, just visible through the crack, was interrupted in two places.

Shadows of feet. Someone standing there. Not proceeding to higher floors or descending to the exit. Just standing right there on the landing, trying to be quiet.

For less than half a second Dryden considered the possibilities. Then he pushed all the questions away. No time.

He thought, *Rachel, go to the back bedroom. Open the slider. I'm right behind you.*

She didn't hesitate. She turned and vanished into the darkness of the hall. Dryden followed, walking backward, keeping his eyes and the SIG trained on the door.

He heard the slider drag open as he entered the bedroom. Behind him, Rachel's shoes padded onto the metal surface of the balcony – it was more like a fire escape without a ladder.

Dryden reached behind himself, felt the edge of the slider's door frame, and backed through it. Across the bedroom and down the length of the hall, he could still see the apartment's front door. Could still see the double shadow in the gap.

The doorknob rattled. Rachel flinched at the sound.

Dryden swung his head around and took in the space behind the row of town houses, the layout he'd studied earlier. He considered the buildings on the opposite side, and the offshoot alleys leading away between them. One alley was darker than the rest: a narrow passage between a four-story house and a two-story brick building. Dryden liked the look of it as an escape route. He'd liked it when he'd first seen it, hours before, and by force of habit had considered it repeatedly since then.

Forty feet away through the depth of the apartment, the knob rattled again.

Dryden put a leg over the rail and planted his foot at the balcony's edge, pointed inward between the balusters. He followed with the other leg, then gestured for Rachel to do the same. He held her good arm with his free hand as she swung herself over.

Something – a shoulder or a foot – thudded hard against the apartment's front door.

Dryden looked down: flat, empty pavement beneath the balcony, ten feet below them.

He stuffed the SIG in his rear waistband and took hold of Rachel's wrist.

'Know what I'm doing?' he whispered.

She nodded, nervous but ready.

He lifted her clear of the balcony by the wrist, his other hand gripping the rail. He crouched fast, bringing his seat down onto his ankles, his arm extending as far down as he could reach, until Rachel's feet were no more than eighteen inches above the pavement. He let go and heard her land lightly; her balance faltered and then she regained it and stepped back, clearing his way. He rose, pushed off the edge with his feet, swung down, and dropped to the ground.

Rachel was already moving, heading for the narrow channel Dryden had visualized. He drew the SIG again and caught up with her, nearly sprinting. They'd just rounded the corner of the brick building, into the alley beside it, when he heard the apartment's door crash inward far behind them. He looked back over his shoulder toward the sound, and in the same instant he heard another, much closer:

The action of a pump shotgun being cycled, ten feet away in the pitch black of the alley.

A woman's voice. 'Don't move. You swing the sidearm toward me, I'm going to shoot you.'

No hint of a bluff in her tone.

Dryden kept still.

Rachel was standing right up against him. Any

shotgun blast that hit him would hit her, too, if the weapon was loaded with buckshot.

'Eject the magazine,' the woman said. 'Then eject the chambered round. Then drop the gun.'

Out in the broader space between the rows of buildings, boot soles came down hard on the concrete. Someone had just dropped off the apartment balcony.

'Do it,' the woman said.

Dryden ejected the magazine. Then the chambered round. In the darkness beside him, he heard Rachel's breath escape. Like hope. He let the SIG fall to the pavement.

Footsteps crept toward the alley from beyond its mouth. They came to a stop just out of sight, the newcomer staying clear of the shotgun's line of fire.

Something metallic jingled behind Dryden.

'Turn toward me,' the woman with the shotgun said.

Dryden turned. In the dull light he saw the glint of handcuffs. The woman threw them; he caught them out of the air.

'Cuff yourself. Behind the back.'

Dryden still couldn't see the woman's face. In the bleed of light from the wider alley he could just make out Rachel. Beyond the fear in the girl's eyes he saw deep confusion, though at what, he couldn't tell.

'Behind the back,' the woman said again. 'Do it.'

Dryden put the cuffs behind his back and closed them around his wrists. A second later a flashlight came on, probably mounted to the shotgun's barrel. Its beam played over Dryden's lower back.

'He's secure,' the woman said.

The newcomer stepped into view at the front of the alley. Another woman. Dryden got only a sense of her in the shifting beam of the flashlight.

Rachel was turning back and forth, her gaze going from one woman to the other.

'I can't hear your thoughts,' Rachel said. 'Either of you.'

'Of course not, sweetie,' the newcomer said.

She grabbed Dryden by the shirt and pulled him forward off balance, tripping him and shoving him down hard, chest-first onto the concrete. She sat astride his back, and he heard something plastic click open – some small container, it sounded like.

'What are you doing to him?' Panic saturated Rachel's voice.

'Relax,' the woman said.

Rachel didn't relax. She screamed, *'What are you doing?'*

The last word got cut off to a muffle; the other woman had clamped a hand over Rachel's mouth.

An instant later Dryden felt a needle penetrate his neck. Heard the plunger slide down. Felt the rush of heat beneath his skin.

'Stop it!' Rachel screamed, pulling away the woman's hand. *'What are you doing to him?'*

The second woman was already clambering off of

him. Getting to her feet. Helping the first woman restrain Rachel back there in the dark. Dryden heard it all receding away as if into a fog. A place where all sounds were hollow and sourceless. He felt the heat spread up through his neck, across his scalp. Felt the pavement beneath him draw open into a kind of darkness. Rachel's muffled screams followed him down into it.

Chapter Twenty-eight

At times he felt almost awake. Up near the surface of sleep, where he could hear. Where he could feel.

He was inside some kind of container. The lining felt like smooth cardboard against his cheek. Someone was carrying it, saying, *Lift with your legs, easy, easy.*

Something was whining. A steady droning sound. Jet engines, it sounded like. Small ones. A moment later there was movement, the container seeming to slide while his body wanted to hold still. *Inertia,* he thought, and the word seemed funny to him, though he couldn't say why. He slid a few inches on the cardboard until his feet thudded up against the container's end. A few seconds later the world seemed to pitch and tilt sickeningly, and something thumped dully beneath the floor. Landing gear folding up, he guessed, and then he was out again.

He'll be fine. He's coming out of it. Give him another thirty minutes.

Are you sure?

I'm sure, honey.

*

His throat felt like he'd been eating dryer lint. His head pounded like hell. He ran his tongue over his lips. It scraped.

'Drink this.'

Rachel's voice.

He opened his eyes and saw a juice box six inches from his face, a little pink bendy straw stuck in it and aimed at him. Rachel pushed it forward, and he got his mouth closed around it. He pursed his lips and drank. High fructose corn syrup and artificial flavoring. Same way they'd made it when he was a kid. He sucked down the entire box, saw its sides cave in, let it go, and rolled onto his back.

He still had the cuffs on, but he was out of the container. He was lying on a couch somewhere. A little study. No windows. Bright, pale light washed in through the door, but from his angle he couldn't see the room beyond.

'Where are we?' Dryden asked.

'Home,' Rachel said.

'Your home?'

She nodded, her eyes excited in a way he hadn't seen them before.

Under the headache, Dryden felt the familiar cool pulse at his temples. It felt like it had at times the night before – double or triple the intensity he'd been used to in recent days.

He thought of the woman waiting in the dark alley. Waiting along the escape route he'd been considering for hours before that.

242

'They can hear my thoughts, too,' he said.

Rachel nodded again. 'They came from Fort Detrick, like me. They said the three of us got away from there, about five years ago, and we've been in hiding since then. They told me a lot about it, and I told them about the last few days. They believe me, but they still want to talk to you. They want to know for sure they can trust you, and then they'll take the cuffs off. Is that okay?'

Dryden shut his eyes hard. Compressed them repeatedly. It was the next best thing to rubbing them.

'Send them in,' he said.

'Thank you.' She got up to go.

'Wait,' Dryden said.

Rachel stopped. Turned back to him.

'Holly Ferrel,' Dryden said. 'You heard something in her thoughts, right at the end. Right before we had to run for it.'

The happiness receded from Rachel's eyes.

'What was it?' Dryden asked.

'She was thinking about a phone call she had to make. An important one. She was rehearsing the first part of it, over and over, the way people do.'

'What was she saying?'

'This is Holly Ferrel. I need to speak with Martin Gaul.'

Dryden stared. First at Rachel and then at nothing, trying to get a grasp on what it might mean.

A minute later the two women came into the room. Dryden saw them in detail for the first time. Both were in their thirties, lean, medium framed, medium height. Dryden got himself seated upright on the couch and faced them. One was blond, the other somewhere between blond and brunette. Their appearance was oddly unremarkable – it was, at least, far less remarkable than it could've been. Dryden got the impression they took great care to make themselves forgettable.

There was a second couch facing him across the small room. The two women sat on it.

'I'm Audrey,' the blonde said. 'This is Sandra.'

The hostility they'd shown in the alley was long gone. They seemed sympathetic, if not quite regretful. Which was fine – it was stupid to regret things that had seemed necessary at the time.

Sandra nodded at the thought. 'We just didn't know who you were,' she said. 'We'd been monitoring the area around Holly Ferrel's house, and when the two of you showed up it was pretty hard to miss.'

'We can't hear Rachel's thoughts,' Audrey said, 'any more than she can hear ours. But we could hear your thoughts, and most of the time you were thinking about her. We could tell she was there with you, and that you seemed to be helping her, though we weren't sure why. We decided to just get her the hell out of there and get the details afterward.'

'Our questions won't take long,' Sandra said. 'Answer

ours and then we'll answer yours. Most of them, anyway, for the time being. Fair enough?'

Dryden nodded.

It took half an hour. They walked him through the same story they'd no doubt heard from Rachel. Everything from the boardwalk to the town house. Then they asked him about his past. His career. He saw no reason to hold anything back.

When they'd finished, Sandra took a key from her pocket and removed the cuffs. Dryden worked his shoulders in slow circles, easing out the cramps.

'You're probably starving,' Sandra said. 'We'll tell you our side over lunch. While we get it ready, Rachel wants to show you around the place.'

Dryden had guessed the residence was a house, to the extent he'd thought about it. It hadn't crossed his mind to think otherwise. The moment he stepped to the den's doorway, he saw he'd been wrong.

Beyond the den was a broad living room with a wall of windows. Beyond the windows was Chicago, seen from what had to be eighty stories up. The view faced south across the tops of skyscrapers from a position near the north end of downtown. It was early afternoon, and the city gleamed in sunlight under a rich blue sky.

'We're in the Hancock Center,' Rachel said. 'This apartment takes up the entire eighty-third floor.'

Dryden looked at her, then at Audrey and Sandra, still standing just inside the den.

'This place is a hideout?' he asked.

'You'd be surprised how well it works,' Sandra said. 'Rich people have shaped the law to suit their privacy needs. In some ways it's easier to anonymously own a place like this than a split-level ranch in the suburbs.'

'There's one other reason to live here,' Audrey said, 'but if you're lucky you won't have to find out what it is.'

Rachel tugged Dryden's arm, anxious to show him around. He turned to follow her—

'Wait,' Sandra said.

Dryden turned back.

Sandra was holding his SIG SAUER out to him. The magazine had been reloaded into the grip.

'All you've done for Rachel,' she said, 'we can't tell you what it means to us. The least we can do is trust you.'

Dryden took the pistol, checked the safety, and stuffed it in his waistband.

The apartment's size and layout were surreal. The living room opened to the kitchen and dining room, merging into a vast space that extended to the southwest corner of the level.

The rest of the floorplan formed a giant rectangular doughnut, centered on the building's core. Among the other rooms were a library that spanned most of the northern stretch, and three bedrooms filling out the east end. The bedrooms were more or less equal in size, which was to say that each was huge. The room at the southeast corner was Rachel's. She led Dryden inside. He was briefly surprised by the casual state it was in – it looked as if it had seen regular use up until this very moment.

'The whole apartment was like this when we got here this morning,' Rachel said. 'Cups on the counter, left sitting there for two months. Audrey and Sandra were afraid to stay here while Gaul had me captive. In case he got this location from me.'

She went to the bed, its covers lying askew. A stuffed blue triceratops lay on its side there, half obscured by the comforter.

'I keep thinking some of this stuff might help me remember,' Rachel said.

She pulled the dinosaur free and hugged it to her chest.

'Sandra told me it has a name,' she said. 'I can almost feel it wanting to come back to me.'

She stared at the thing, and for a moment something rose in her eyes. Some fragile hope. Then her shoulders sagged. She set the dinosaur back on the bed.

'Give it time,' Dryden said.

Rachel nodded but looked unsettled about something.

'What is it?' Dryden said.

Rachel exhaled softly. 'You'll see.'

*

'When I was twenty-two,' Sandra said, 'I went to prison. I'm not going to say what for.'

The four of them were seated at the dining room table, near the southwest corner of the residence. Outside, the day had become cloudy. Ragged knots of mist slipped among the tops of the towers. Whenever one enveloped the Hancock, the city briefly vanished into a whiteout.

'In part because of priors, my sentence was sixteen years. I could be paroled in twelve if I was lucky. I'd been in for a month when a man visited me. Not in the room with the glass partition and the phones. Right in my cell, in the middle of the night. The chief of the guards came in and stood with him, and looked very pissed, but didn't say anything. The visitor said I could leave the prison that night, if I wanted. I could leave with him, right then, and live in a much nicer place, and I'd only have to serve two years there. Then I'd be free to go. This other place was a kind of dormitory, he said, where the army did medical trials. Like the FDA, but the military version of it. The deal was simple: I'd be given three injections of a new drug – an RNA-interference drug, he called it – in the first two weeks. After that, nothing. I could just relax, live there, watch TV, do anything I wanted. They would monitor me to see if the drug had any effect, but whatever it did, I'd be free after the two years were up. Free to start my life over, and not screw it up this time. I'd only be twenty-four years old when I got out. Or I could stay there in prison until my midthirties. That first month inside, I'd already been sexually assaulted twice. It was going to keep happening, too. No question about it. 'Think it over,' the guy said, but I'll be honest – I didn't really have to. I thought even if the medical trial killed me, that might be better than another twelve years in that place.'

'My experience was more or less the same,' Audrey said. 'My decision process *was* the same.'

They took turns telling the story, handing it back and forth. The place where they ended up, a living facility at Fort Detrick, really did seem like a dorm on the inside – the dorms they'd seen in movies, at least. Neither had ever set foot inside a real one. The only difference was that they couldn't leave. They were two of just ten women living there, all of whom got along well enough. The atmosphere was relaxed, relatively speaking. It sure as hell wasn't prison.

They got their first injections on day one. Nothing much to it – no worse than tetanus shots. The medical technicians said they might experience fever or chills, but they didn't. Not even after all three shots had been administered. There were no ill effects at all, and for the next two months it stayed like that. One of the girls in the dorm had done pretty well in science in high school, and remembered reading about something called a control group. Sometimes in an experiment, one group of subjects would get a certain drug, say, and another group would *think* they were getting the drug but instead just got sugar pills or shots of some neutral solution. Maybe that had happened here. Maybe they were just the control. That was a nice thought, and it lasted until about the middle of month three.

When the effect started, it came on slowly. Little bouts of it, at first. Even when it got stronger, it was hard to notice, because it didn't work among the women themselves. It only seemed to work on outsiders, like the medical techs, or people who drove past the building within a certain distance. For probably a week or better, each woman in the dorm kept the phenomenon to herself, afraid she was imagining it. Afraid she was going crazy.

Then the strangest thing happened: One of the techs, during a routine physical – they performed them twice a week – asked one of the girls a question he'd never asked before.

Are you hearing things in your head that seem unfamiliar? Thoughts that don't seem to be your own?

The girl's eyes went wide. *Yes*, she said. *Yes, what the hell is it?* Other girls overheard. They crowded around and spoke up, relieved to know they weren't alone with their symptoms. In the midst of it all, the tech took out a phone and dialed, and that was the end of life in the dorm.

Within the hour, the ten of them were in a different building – not so much like a dorm, very much like a prison, in fact. Each had her own barred cell. Different researchers came to look at them. Most of these were older men, some of them in military uniforms. They spoke among themselves, talking about the women as if they weren't standing right there, in their cages. As if the women couldn't hear them. Which was strange, really, since the women could do much more than hear them.

'They knew we weren't leaving that place,' Sandra said. 'Not in two years. Not ever. They didn't care that we could hear it in their thoughts, either. It didn't matter what we knew. They had us.'

'For a while we thought they might use us to spy on people,' Audrey said. 'Put us in hotel rooms next door to important guests – VIP types from other countries, something like that – find out what they were thinking. Sounds plausible, right? For the rest of our lives we'd just be glorified listening devices.'

She looked away into the glare of sunlight off the nearest towers. The highest floors gleamed wet where clouds had touched them.

'It turned out we weren't even going to be that, though,' she said.

Dryden looked at them, one and then the other. 'What did they want you to be?'

'White mice,' Sandra said. 'We were going to stay locked up the rest of our lives, so they could watch us and see what happened long-term. See if the effect changed over time – got stronger or weaker, anything like that. See if we all got cancer in three years, or seven, or ten. See if we got Alzheimer's in our thirties.'

'They *did* want human listening devices,' Audrey said, 'but they were going to choose those people very carefully. People who were just right for the job.'

'So that was going to be it for us,' Sandra said. 'Except our ages, nothing in that building was going to change for the rest of our lives. And then something happened. A physical exam of one of the women – her name was Rebecca Grant – turned up a result no one had even been looking for. Rebecca was pregnant. She'd conceived right before going to prison.'

Both Sandra and Audrey looked at Rachel.

Though she'd already heard the story, the girl's emotional response was evident. Dryden saw her throat tighten.

'Rachel was born on May 1, 2001,' Audrey said. 'They allowed Rebecca to raise her, right there in the living facility with the rest of us. The researchers were very interested in how she would turn out – whether she'd have the same capability as her mother. Even though Rachel was conceived *before* Rebecca had the RNA treatment, the drug would've still affected her as a developing fetus. You already know it worked on her, but as it turned out, it didn't work exactly the same way it had with everyone else. Rachel was different from her mother. Different from all of us, in one very important way.'

'Which was what?' Dryden asked.

Rachel turned to him. 'They won't tell me,' she said.

Chapter Twenty-nine

For a few seconds the room stayed quiet. Then Audrey spoke. She addressed Dryden; it was clear Rachel had already heard this part.

'There are things we just don't know how to explain to Rachel right now. Things that would be very hard for her to hear. Not just what makes her different. Other things, too. About what happened to her mother. About how we ended up free. About Holly Ferrel.'

'We *will* tell you,' Sandra said. 'Both of you. All we're saying is that we want Rachel to remember it for herself first.' Her eyes went to the girl. 'Honey, if we tried to tell you now . . . we're not sure you'd believe us. You sure as hell wouldn't *want* to believe us. You can imagine they're not happy stories.'

'You've kept a journal for the past few years,' Audrey said. 'We debated showing it to you, letting you learn everything that way. But we really think your own memories would make it easiest on you . . . that when you remember the things you've been through, you'll also remember that you've recovered from them. That's the best we can do. We've given it all the thought in the world.'

'Gaul knows where Holly Ferrel lives,' Rachel said.

'If she's in danger, I don't want to wait however long it takes—'

'Holly *is* in danger,' Sandra said. 'Grave danger, but not immediate danger. I know that doesn't make sense to you now, but I can say it with certainty. For the time being, this week for sure, nobody's going to hurt her.'

'But *how* do you know?' Rachel asked.

'I know. I promise.'

Rachel looked as frustrated as Dryden had ever seen her. He couldn't blame her. His own frustration was simmering.

'How did Gaul get to me?' Rachel asked. 'Two months ago.'

'That's tied into the rest of it,' Audrey said. 'In a way, it's all just one story – the things we're holding back.' Her eyes went to Rachel and softened. 'You don't want to hear it right now, sweetie.'

Against his will, Dryden thought, *Maybe you just don't want to tell it right now.*

He couldn't call it back any more than he could've kept it in. He saw all three of them react as if he'd said it aloud.

'I'm sorry,' he said.

'Not your fault,' Audrey said. She added, 'You're not entirely wrong, either.'

'What about the cell tower in the desert?' Dryden asked. 'Whatever it relates to . . . whatever so many people are afraid of.'

'It's not really the towers they're scared of,' Audrey said. 'Or what the towers are being used for right now. It's something else – and they're right to be afraid of it.' Her eyes went back and forth between Dryden and Rachel. 'The answers are coming soon enough, I promise. Bear with us, okay? When you know the rest, you'll probably wish you didn't.'

Darkness had slid down over Santa Monica Bay. Gaul stared at it from his patio, a mile inland and five hundred feet up. To the west, the Point Dume Headlands shone dull in the moonlight. To the east, twenty miles out in the night haze, lay LAX and the orange glow of the city beyond.

Gaul sank into a chair beside the pool. In the blue light rippling up through its surface, he looked at the bound document in his hands. In the months since he'd first read it, the block of text on its cover had come to embody stress itself.

U.S. ARMY BIOWARFARE RESEARCH INSTITUTE (USABRI)
LIVING WEAPONS INITIATIVE – COHORT 23.3
ACCIDENT INVESTIGATION REPORT – 'SNAPDRAGON'

Gaul shut his eyes and sank back into the seat cushion. His phone rang in his pocket. Lowry's ringtone. Gaul took it out and answered without opening his eyes.

'The Chicago option is up and running, sir,' Lowry said.

Gaul acknowledged him, hung up, and set the phone on the paver bricks.

Two months before, in the days after Rachel had been captured, chemical analysis of her skin and hair had yielded a pollutant profile consistent with greater Chicago. That wasn't where Gaul's people had grabbed her, but it seemed to be where she'd spent much of her recent time. It seemed to be her home.

She likely wouldn't remember her way back there for days yet, but in the name of caution the Chicago option was running now.

The thing was, it didn't speak of caution. It spoke of desperation. It was as ridiculous as it was clever. That he was grasping for it only heightened the feeling that he was drowning.

'So you're sleeping in the living room?' Rachel asked.

Dryden nodded. He stood in the doorway of her bedroom; she stood facing him from just inside, holding under her arm the triceratops whose name she couldn't remember.

'I know I'm safe here,' Rachel said. 'I just wish you were going to be closer.'

'Downside of owning a whole floor of a skyscraper,' Dryden said.

Rachel managed a smile. Dryden had seen precious few of them from her in the long hours since lunch.

Even this one slipped away in a second or two. She looked down at her feet.

'Scary,' she said. 'All this stuff. I wanted so much to remember. And now . . . I still want it, but in a different way. Like something bad I just want to get behind me.' She looked up at him. 'But bad things can take forever to get behind you, can't they.'

'They can.'

She nodded. Then she stepped forward and hugged him tightly. She held on for a long time, then said good night and closed her door.

Gaul flipped through the report, coming at last to the section he always stopped at. The one titled RACHEL GRANT. His fingertips traced over the page, passing slowly across the two words, as if they might cut him.

Audrey waited until Dryden had left the east hallway and gone to the living room. She stepped out of her bedroom and went to Sandra's, slipping in and closing the door behind her.

In the darkness, Sandra stood in silhouette at the window, against the shimmer of pier lights on Lake Michigan. Audrey went to her.

'It hurts, not leveling with her,' Sandra said.

'It won't be this way for long. A few more days.'

'What do you think it'll be like? When she starts to get it all back?'

Audrey breathed a laugh. The sound was hard and

cold, but not without amusement. 'Interesting. To say the least.'

Gaul turned the pages slowly, making his way through the section about Rachel. Rachel and all that she'd done in her short life. Color photos filled some of the sheets. Gaul had a strong stomach for images of this sort, but these tested its limits. Still he stared at each in turn. He felt obligated to do so – to remind himself what the stakes were.

At last he let the report fall shut. He set it on the bricks beside the phone. As always, his hand came away shaking.

PART THREE
Lucero

Let us alone. What is it that will last?
All things are taken from us, and become
Portions and parcels of the dreadful past.

Alfred, Lord Tennyson

Chapter Thirty

Deep in the night, Dryden woke. For a moment he felt sure something had roused him, a sound or a flash of light, but as the seconds drew out, the impression faded.

He rose from the couch, took the SIG SAUER from the end table, and made a quick, silent orbit of the living room, dining room, and kitchen. A quarter past four in the morning and all was well.

He went to the south windows. Here was the city at its most sedate, its streets as bare as they would ever be, its towers all but darkened, their rooftop beacons blinking a slow cadence.

The only thing in view that seemed awake was an intense white light fixed to a radio mast atop the tallest skyscraper – the Willis Tower, they were calling it these days. Against the sleepy backdrop of the city, this single point of light, the highest thing in the skyline, stabbed the darkness in a rapid and intermittent frenzy. It was as if its control board were shorting out. Something about this light drew Dryden's attention, like a face in a crowd to which he couldn't quite put a name. The more he studied it, the more out of place the thing seemed; it was easily three times brighter than any other light in Chicago.

Dryden turned and looked at the wall and couch behind him, bathed in the glow of the city. The flashing white light was bright enough to stand out within that glow, casting the shapes of the window frames across the room with each pulse.

This light had woken him.

He stared at it again. Logic told him he was obsessing over something meaningless; he'd woken up disoriented, and his judgment was off balance. Still he stared. Then he became aware of the strangest thing: Letters and words were forming in his mind, unbidden. He pictured them as if he were jotting them on a notepad, the vision he'd always used when deciphering Morse code—

Understanding hit him like ice water.

'How the fuck?' The words came out in a whisper, involuntarily.

The light atop the radio mast was transmitting a message. Not Morse code, but an encrypted variant of it that Dryden and his men had developed for themselves in Ferret. In situations where signal transmission was too risky, they'd used handheld infrared units to flash this code to one another. As an added layer of precaution, they had never officially documented the code's existence.

Only someone from his unit could have supplied it to whoever had programmed that light.

Now, as Dryden began to consciously process the message, all other thought fell aside. The words materialized, one every few seconds.

```
SEEN - THE - EVIDENCE - GET - AWAY - FROM - THEM -
AND - COME - TO - GAULS - PEOPLE - AT - WILLIS -
TOWER - SECURITY - OFFICE - OR - CALL - THEM - 062-
585-0184 - HIS - PEOPLE - WILL - NOT - KILL - YOU -
PLEASE - DO - THIS - THERE - ARE - MORE - LIVES -
AT - STAKE - HELLO - SAM - THIS - IS - COLE - HARRIS -
GOLDENROD - I - AM - HELPING - GAULS - PEOPLE -
CONTACT - YOU - THE - GIRL - DOES - NOT - KNOW -
WHO - SHE - REALLY - IS - SHE - HAS - A - CAPABILITY -
GREATER - THAN - MIND - READING - SHE - HAS - USED -
IT - TO - KILL - INNOCENT - PEOPLE - THE - TWO
-WOMEN - HAVE - MADE - HER - DO - THIS - I - HAVE -
SEEN - THE - EVIDENCE - GET - AWAY - FROM - THEM -
AND - COME - TO - GAULS - PEOPLE - AT - WILLIS -
TOWER - SECURITY - OFFICE - OR - CALL
```

Dryden stood staring as the message looped again. He felt his mind trying to get a handle on it . . . and trying not to.

Denial wanted to assert itself. He wanted to let it. Wanted to believe it was a trap, or a trick, one that Cole Harris had simply been fooled into going along with. Cole was a smart guy, but anything was possible. Gaul was a smart guy, too.

The message cycled again. Dryden put his hand

to the windowpane to steady himself. He shut his eyes. Through his closed lids he could still see the flashing.

THE – GIRL – DOES – NOT – KNOW – WHO – SHE – REALLY – IS

In his mind Dryden saw Audrey and Sandra at the dining table.

All we're saying is that we want Rachel to remember it for herself first. Honey, if we tried to tell you now . . . we're not sure you'd believe us. You sure as hell wouldn't want *to believe us.*

SHE – HAS – A – CAPABILITY – GREATER – THAN – MIND – READING

Rachel was different from her mother. Different from all of us, in one very important way.

SHE – HAS – USED – IT – TO – KILL – INNOCENT – PEOPLE – THE – TWO – WOMEN – HAVE – MADE – HER – DO – THIS

What the hell did that mean? How would any amount of coercion have made Rachel murder people?

I – HAVE – SEEN – THE – EVIDENCE

Dryden opened his eyes and pushed off from the glass.

Enough trying to make sense of what he couldn't

know. Life had taught him, by hard lessons, to act on what he *did* know.

He couldn't just leave here without Rachel.

He knew that.

Irrational options spun up in his thoughts. Get her out of this place. Acquire a supply of the drug – any of the kinds used for sleep interrogation would do – and keep her on low doses forever. Keep the memory roadblock in place. Maybe the flashed message was bullshit, maybe it wasn't, but with enough of the drug, he and Rachel would never need to find out. She'd understand. Hell, she'd insist.

Cooperating with Gaul was no option. Whatever he might do to Dryden, he would have Rachel killed on sight.

Only one move made any sense.

The SIG's balanced weight felt reassuring in his hand. He left the windows, crossed the living room, and entered the hallway toward the east end of the apartment.

Rachel willed the triceratops to reveal its name. It returned her stare with its plastic eyes gleaming in the half-light and surrendered nothing.

'Fine,' she said.

She rolled onto her back and watched the glow of the city shimmer on the wall. Sleep had been fitful, more off than on. She missed Sam's thoughts. Four times during the night, she'd stood and gotten halfway to her bedroom door, blanket and pillow in hand, meaning to go commandeer the second couch in the living room. All that had stopped her was embarrassment. It wasn't that Sam would think less of her – nothing would make him do that – but that she would think far less of herself. If she couldn't stand up to her own fears now, how would she handle whatever was coming? The things Audrey and Sandra couldn't bring themselves to tell her.

She grabbed the triceratops again, pulled it tightly against her, and closed her eyes. Forget about looking at it; most of her memories of this thing probably involved hugging it. The soft fabric felt good against her arms. It felt . . . familiar.

What was its name?

A word swam up toward the surface of her consciousness, flashed below the waves, and vanished again. So close her mouth had nearly blurted it out – but it was already gone, back into the deep.

Damn.

The dinosaur's name was the first domino; of that she was certain. This one detail from her past would unlock all the rest. Open it up like a blister, so she could just deal with whatever came out. It could happen any minute now. Any second. She hugged the triceratops to her chest as hard as she could.

Movement below the waves again. Here it came. Her lips strained to form the word.

It started with—

Her concentration suddenly broke like a thread. She sat up fast, the dinosaur falling away forgotten.

Sam was in the hallway.

His thoughts came to her like a voice from far away, fading in and out through gusting wind. She couldn't catch the words – not yet – but the nature of his thinking was unmistakable: hyperalert, and saturated with tension.

The windowless hallway on the east end, running north and south past the three bedrooms, was the darkest place in the apartment. Dryden's eyes were still adjusted to the bright skyline; he waited for details of the hallway to resolve. Rachel's door emerged twenty feet ahead. Somewhere in the gloom farther along was Audrey's door, and then Sandra's.

He could feel the cool pulse at his temples, growing as he moved toward Rachel's room. He supposed he was feeling a bit of it from the other two as well, even if all three were asleep.

If.

Dryden had led sneak incursions into a handful of intimidating places: container ships in which the crew knew every inch of the layout while he and his men did not; cave complexes that called to mind giant anthills. This place was worse. Beyond their built-in abilities, Audrey and Sandra were sure to have more conventional power at their disposal. Given the apartment's defensive setup – the door leading in from the elevator was inch-thick steel – it would be naive to think there weren't offensive measures, too.

He could rush both of their rooms and kill them right now. The first of the two would have only the briefest warning, and the second would have only the time between the gunshots and his arrival at her door, five seconds at most. He could do that.

Except he couldn't. Killing anyone because of the flashed message would require certainty he didn't have. Getting Rachel the hell out of here wouldn't.

He went to her door, opened it as quickly as silence permitted, and found her sitting wide-awake, waiting for him. She looked like she'd been up for a while already. He stepped through the door, closed it quietly behind him, and crossed to her. No doubt she'd picked up on his fear even in the hallway, but now, as she got the details behind it from his thoughts, understanding twisted her expression into dread.

'No,' she whispered. 'No, that can't be right.' She was shaking her head, too rattled to cry yet. 'Don't even think things like that.'

He put a hand on her shoulder.

'We'll sort it out later,' he whispered. 'Right now we're just going to get out of here. Come on.'

She didn't seem to hear him. She was still processing all the things he wasn't saying out loud. Her voice finally cracked as the heaviest of the ideas came through.

'You're not sure I'm real?' she asked. 'You think I'm someone bad?'

He knelt before her and looked into her eyes.

'You're the girl who saved my life,' he said. 'You knew that, didn't you? I was the walking dead before you came along. You changed that. How could a girl do that if she wasn't real? Do you trust me?'

She nodded quickly.

'Then trust me on this,' he said. 'This is you, who you are right now, and we'll find a way to keep it like that. But we have to get out of this place first. Okay?'

She nodded again, took his hand, and swung her feet to the floor.

The two of them had gone only a few steps when Dryden felt the chill at his temples intensify.

One or both of the others had just moved closer to this room.

Chapter Thirty-one

Dryden stopped fast. Rachel collided with him and nearly lost her balance. He steadied her with one hand; with the other he leveled the SIG SAUER on her closed bedroom door.

Within seconds the cool sensation stepped up again. He pictured both Audrey and Sandra in the hall, not far away. Rachel put her hand on his gun arm, not pushing it down but begging him to reconsider.

'What if it's not true?' she asked. 'Let's just talk to them. Maybe we can figure it out.'

Then came Audrey's voice, right outside the door. 'It's *not* true, Sam. Think about it. Is there anything Gaul wouldn't do to get to us?'

'We know you're confused,' Sandra said. 'Anyone would be, in your position. That's why Gaul's doing this; the trick is designed to force you into doubt.'

'Think of it this way,' Audrey said. 'We have all the guns in the world here; I'm sure you know that. If we were bad, wouldn't we have killed you long before this?'

Dryden thought about it. Their reasoning didn't quite hold. Of course they could have killed him, but until now there'd been no reason to. He'd been no threat to them, and as mind readers, they would've had plenty of warning if he ever *did* become a threat. They would've always had the option of killing him before he could make a move against them.

He started to voice the objection, then stopped – they'd heard it loud and clear already.

'Sam . . .' Sandra said. Her voice was soft, sympathetic. That tone, more than any words she might say with it, eroded the edges of his caution. He kept the pistol steady on the door; God knew what they might be pointing at it from the other side.

The germ of an idea came to him.

Before it could crystallize into words, before the two women could capture it and react, Dryden threw himself forward, put his shoulder to Rachel's dresser, and shoved it over. It hit the floor sliding, and he took advantage of its momentum, pushing it across the carpet until it lodged with a gratifying thud against the door.

Now they'd never come through fast enough to get the drop on him, and they obviously couldn't risk firing through the wall with Rachel in here.

'If you're telling us the truth,' Dryden said, 'then prove it. Give us Rachel's journal. Slide it under the door past the dresser. If I'm wrong, I'll apologize a hundred times.'

Beside him, Rachel tensed, waiting for the answer.

It came: the sound of a rifle's action being worked.

The girl reacted as if pierced. She sat down hard, looping an arm around Dryden's leg for support. With his free hand he took hers and held it tightly.

He hoped his hate for the other two was transmitting through the door with razor-wire edges.

'This is temporary, Rachel,' Sandra said. Gone was every trace of kindness in that voice. 'When you remember who you really are, you'll laugh at this.'

Rachel suddenly lunged to her feet. Taking Dryden by surprise, she grabbed the SIG from his hand, trained it chest-level on the door, and opened fire. She put a row of three shots through the door and the wall beside it before Dryden could get it back from her. He heard someone land on her ass out in the hall, cursing, and the rifle clattered against the baseboard. A second later the icy feeling at his temples faded just perceptibly; the women had retreated some distance down the hallway.

'Why don't you shoot back?' Rachel screamed at them. 'You might even hit *me*!'

Dryden put an arm around her shoulders. 'It's okay,' he said.

She turned into him and pressed her face to his shirt, her body shaking hard.

'Wow, they didn't see that coming,' he said.

She heard the smile in his voice and looked up at him, managing one of her own, through the tears.

'What are we going to do?' she asked.

Dryden looked around the room. Two solid walls, and two made of windows – with nothing on the other side but a three-football-field drop. There was a private bathroom, but it offered no better options than the bedroom did. Crazy solutions came and went: shoot out a window, rappel on Rachel's bedsheet to the apartment below and shoot their way into it. It didn't matter that their odds of surviving that were one in a thousand. What mattered was that Audrey and Sandra would read his planning of it and have a wide-open chance to rush the room.

'What about me?' Rachel asked. 'They can't read *my* plans.'

'Do you have a plan?'

She hesitated, her expression flickering between thoughtful and terrified.

'Yes,' she said.

Audrey felt Dryden's thought pattern flare with stress at what Rachel had just suggested. He trusted her, cared about her more than himself – but the idea of blindly following a plan of hers threw him, like a pilot asked to cede control to a passenger.

Then his logic came in, hard grid lines bisecting the discord of his emotions. Soldier logic. Fast and clear. Audrey had read this kind of thinking before in men and women tempered by combat. Dryden made his decision so quickly she almost couldn't follow the steps. The man saw nothing but futility in using his own plans, given their transparency. Therefore any plan of Rachel's was better.

He told her to do it, whatever it was, and then returned his full attention to watching the door.

No further knowledge would come out of that room.

In the darkness beside Audrey, Sandra's breath rushed out. 'Are you shitting me?'

Audrey heard fear in her voice. Felt it in herself, too. In the years since escaping confinement, she'd never once faced an enemy whose thoughts were hidden from her. She could not think of the last time she'd been reduced to guessing in a moment like this, and realized wearily that she didn't even know how to do it. Her grip tightened on the heavy rifle in her hands.

She turned to Sandra and tried to be steady. 'Someone upstairs or down will have called security about the gunshots. They'll be in the anteroom any minute, so we won't be leaving by elevator.'

'I'll get the parachutes,' Sandra said.

'Bring the tandem harness for me.'

Sandra understood. She sprinted off down the dark hallway.

Rachel crossed the bedroom to the attached bathroom. She stopped in the doorway and looked back at Sam, standing with his back to her and the gun steady on the barricaded door. She wished she could tell him what it meant to her that he trusted her this completely – trusted her not to do something stupid.

She hoped she wasn't about to.

Quietly taking the cordless phone from its cradle on her study desk, she stepped inside the bathroom and closed the door. In the silence, she stifled her own thoughts and focused on Sam's. The message from the flashing light on the Willis Tower, visible to him even now as it pulsed on the walls of her bedroom, ran unbroken in the background of his mind.

COME - TO - GAULS - PEOPLE - AT - WILLIS - TOWER - SECURITY - OFFICE - OR - CALL - THEM - 062-585-0184 - HIS - PEOPLE - WILL - NOT - KILL - YOU

The message was for Sam, and no one else. Her, they would kill. No question of that.

She stared at her dark reflection above the vanity. 'Whoever you are,' she whispered, 'you're not coming back.'

She pressed the TALK button, and the phone's key-pad lit up. This was the only solution. It offered at least some chance Sam would live, and all but guaranteed Audrey and Sandra would die.

Rachel dialed the number. A man answered on the first ring. She set the phone on the counter with the line open, and slid down the door to sit on the cold stone tiles.

Chapter Thirty-two

Dryden waited for it to happen, whatever it might be. There was no reason to even wonder what Rachel was doing – in fact, there was every reason not to.

The bathroom door opened, and she emerged, having been inside for perhaps three minutes. She came to him and for a moment said nothing.

'I won't ask,' Dryden said.

'It won't be much longer.'

Her tone chilled him like a night breeze in a cemetery.

Gaul finished pulling on his shirt as he entered his den. The telepresence screens were already up and running, showing him the computer room at his office in Santa Monica. The techs there were too busy to sit; they darted like bees among the workstations, configuring them for incoming data. The Mirandas were tasked and running feeds of Chicago, with the software drawing on street cameras to fill in the gaps – the deep steel canyons among the towers, where satellites couldn't see.

The master frame was five miles wide, rendering the city as a thermal spiderweb against the cool span of Lake Michigan. Gaul could see both of the AH-6 Little

Bird helicopters that had been staged on rooftops. The first had just lifted off, and the second, white hot on its pad, would rise any moment.

Lowry paced along the computer room's south wall, near the heavy-gauge plastic sheet that had been stretched in place of the old window. Through his headset he fed instructions to both chopper pilots.

'The highest row of windows is the hundredth floor,' Lowry said. 'Count down from there to the eighty-third. You're weapons-free to engage any warm body on that entire level.'

'Thank you,' Rachel said.

She took Dryden's hand, and he felt hers tremble in the moment before she tightened her hold.

'For what?'

'You love me,' she said. 'It's all you think, when you think about me. Even right now, you're thinking how it'll be okay if you can get me out of here, even if you die. You just . . . love me. Thank you.'

Against all instinct Dryden took his attention from the bedroom door. He turned to meet her eyes. He saw fear in them, but alongside it was something worse: resignation.

'Honey, what is it?' he asked. 'What did you do?'

'I'm so sorry.' She put her arms around him and held on.

Over her shoulder, Dryden saw the lights of an aircraft cresting the skyline less than a mile to the south, coming in fast. Just audible, the blade rate faded in, familiar to him as an old ringtone. It was an AH-6 or a close variant; Dryden could picture the snipers belted in above its skids as easily as if the chopper were just outside the windows. Which it would be in forty seconds.

Through the open bathroom door he saw the cordless phone, its display glowing green, and understood.

Audrey's fingers halted on the final clasp of the tandem parachute harness. She locked eyes with Sandra, who had also gone still, picking up the same thought from Dryden.

'She couldn't,' Sandra said.

'She did,' Audrey said. 'Watch the door.' She grabbed the rifle, threw it to Sandra, and left at a dead run.

Past Rachel's bedroom she took the hallway corner and crossed the sitting room to the southern windows, slamming to a stop with her palms against the glass.

The helicopter was already north of the river, following a line up Michigan Avenue. Behind it, a second chopper lifted off from the rooftop of the RMC Plaza.

A soft *ding* announced the arrival of the elevator car, no doubt full of security and police. Beyond blocking the easy way out, they were meaningless; they could no more open the heavy door than they could morph through it.

The helicopters, however, would have to be dealt with. Audrey ran to the nearest closet, opened it, and pushed hard on the shelving unit inside, swinging it inward to reveal the cavity beyond the closet's back wall.

Dryden had never felt this immobilized. For ten seconds, a stack of eternities under these conditions, he simply held on to Rachel and had no idea what to do. He kept the gun leveled on the door, and his eyes on the incoming helicopters – executioners to the scaffold.

'I'm sorry,' Rachel whispered again.

Dryden regained his composure and turned the girl's face up toward his.

'You can't do this,' he said. 'You can't give up. You'd be giving up for both of us, do you understand that?'

'If we get away,' Rachel said, 'and if I turn into the other me . . . you might wish you had this moment back. That you hadn't saved me.'

'Not a chance.'

He held her gaze a moment longer, hoping to see a glimmer of resolve there. She took a deep breath and nodded, looking stronger, if only by degrees.

'Let's get the hell out of here,' Dryden said.

The lead chopper was twenty seconds out.

In the hall, one of the two women was still standing guard – Dryden had heard the other run past to verify the helicopters for herself. Whoever was in the hall would make a move on this room in the final seconds before the Little Birds reached sniper range. She would have no choice, by then, if she intended to keep Rachel alive.

That move would come any moment now.

Dryden's eyes took in a long vertical split in the bedroom door, from the impact of the dresser. It followed the wood grain from the bottom of the door all the way to the top.

Don't think. Do it. Now.

He turned his eyes on the south windows. He visualized himself shooting out the glass and plunging into open space.

Rachel jerked as if stung, reacting to the thought. By reflex she reached to stop him from doing it.

Dryden pushed her away and, keeping his mind focused on the plan to exit through the window, turned and sprinted for the cracked door instead. There was just enough room to get up to speed. He vaulted the dresser, brought his leg up, and pistoned it forward to exploit his body's momentum. His foot connected with the door and broke it like a sheet of ice as he went through. The movement was awkward as hell. He ignored his balance – ignored everything but the SIG and the direction it had to be pointed.

The corridor was pitch black. He fired, even as he fell, and in the instant of the muzzle flash he saw Sandra ten feet away holding the rifle – a G-36. She wasn't aiming it. She looked deeply confused. The distraction, rough as it had been, must've worked – she'd gotten the image of him diving out the window, the same as Rachel had.

Dryden landed in a crouch, retargeted on the darkness where Sandra's face had been, and squeezed off three shots as fast as he could.

It was death by strobe light. Three snapshots within the deep black, Sandra taking the bullets to the neck, cheekbone, forehead. Crumpling like a dropped marionette.

Dryden heard screaming, somewhere. Not Rachel. Audrey. Along the south side of the apartment. Dryden scrambled for the heavy machine gun, groped for it in the darkness, and took it from Sandra's hands. He raised it to a firing position facing the south end of the hall, where enough city light bled past the corner to show that there was no one there.

Rachel appeared at her doorway. Dryden took a step toward her and stopped – something metal had rattled at his feet. He realized he'd heard the same sound when Sandra had fallen, but had missed it for more pressing details. He felt a barrel-mounted flashlight on the G-36 and switched it on.

Sandra was wearing a parachute.

He killed the light beam and checked the south corner again. Still clear. Audrey apparently knew better than to approach from that way; she didn't have to read his mind to know he had the machine gun now. With vague amusement, Dryden realized Audrey's mind reading gave him a small tactical advantage: For the moment he felt only Rachel prodding his thoughts, and he would sense the change as soon as Audrey got close enough to round the corner.

He turned the other way, toward the north end of the hall. Skyline glow shone there as well, from the library's windows. It was likely Audrey would circle the apartment to attack from that direction, but that would take her a minute or more. Her scream had placed her at the south side only seconds ago.

Rachel's bedroom windows began to hum as the nearer of the two choppers closed in. Dryden glanced through the doorway and saw the lead aircraft pass over the roof of the white marble building one block to the south.

'Take this,' Dryden said, handing Rachel the SIG. It had two shots left in it. He nodded over his shoulder at the north end of the hall. 'You see anything move up there, shoot at it.'

She nodded and raised the weapon. Dryden crouched over Sandra, keeping both the G-36 and his eyes on the south corner. By touch, he set to work removing the parachute harness from Sandra's body.

Two monitors in the computer room showed helmet camera feeds from the snipers on Sparrow-Four-One, the first inbound chopper, which had just gone stationary near the south face of the tower. Gaul watched the viewpoints pan across the glass and steel edifice.

The pilot's voice came over a speaker. 'No movement on the target level.'

Above and below eighty-three, the occupants of nearly every residence were at their windows, woken by the hovering chopper. The pilot directed a spotlight into the seemingly deserted floor, sweeping most of the southern stretch in a few seconds. Nobody there.

'Sparrow-Four-One, make a slow orbit of the building,' Lowry said. 'They're in there somewhere. Neighbors called in gunshots. Sparrow-Four-Two, deploy your men.'

'Acknowledged, out.'

On a tightened Miranda frame, the second chopper arrived on-site. Gaul watched it settle into position above the southwest corner of the roof. The Little Bird didn't need a proper landing pad; it was designed to off-load men onto rooftops in parts of the world where building codes weren't exactly strict.

In the satellite image, it was impossible to tell exactly when the chopper touched down, but suddenly the four-man specialist team bailed from the troop bay and sprinted across the building's roof. They reached a stairwell access and halted for a moment. Bright light flared as they torched out a lock, and then they were in.

Dryden released the final clasp and pulled the harness free from Sandra. Rising, he kept the machine gun trained on the near corner. Still no sign of Audrey, in his view or in his head.

He could hear both choppers now. The first was circling the building clockwise, moving up the west face. The second, having settled onto the rooftop moments earlier – its turbines sending vibrations down through the building's core – now powered up and lifted off again. The team it must've put on the roof would be inside this apartment in no more than four minutes. They would cut through the ceiling from upstairs if need be.

They'd be three and a half minutes late.

Dryden slipped the chute harness on with automatic ease, adjusting for the tightness. He nodded to Rachel; reluctantly, she lowered the pistol and stepped into the bedroom. Dryden followed.

'All you have to do is hold on,' he said. 'You're going to put your arms around my neck and grab your wrists with your hands as tight as you can. Don't focus on anything but holding on, okay?'

She nodded, already scared to death.

At that moment intense cold pressed at Dryden's temples, like the touch of icicles. Audrey. Close now, coming fast. Determined and reckless.

Rachel understood. She threw her arms around him, lifting her feet off the floor. Dryden raised the G-36, thumbed the selector switch to autofire, and raked the south windows. The panes disintegrated into a curtain of shards, raining out of the frames even as Dryden sprinted toward them. Wind surged in like water, plastering Rachel's hair across his face and spraying glass against them both. Two steps from the window he let go of the gun, locked his arms around Rachel, and dove.

Chapter Thirty-three

The city. Out in it, above it. Lights and windows and streets spinning in a wind-tunnel scream of night air. The tower filling up the world beside him. The choppers pounding the darkness with their rotors.

Dryden's senses stabilized. He turned his head to correct for the spin of his body and locked his eyes on the tower for reference. He and Rachel had fallen maybe ten stories, with seventy yet beneath them. He freed one arm from Rachel, pulled the release for the pilot chute, and had the arm tightly around her again before he felt the line go taut and rip the main chute from the pack.

A second later the straps of the harness wrenched his shoulders back, and the rush of air ceased. The night became silent except for the helicopters circling the tower high above.

Drifting now. The moment was deceptively peaceful. Dryden looked up at the canopy of the chute and saw the wind's influence at a glance. It was pushing them toward the tower.

'Can you hold on if I let go of you?' he asked.

Rachel nodded, her forehead against the side of his jaw, and tightened her arms over the back of his neck.

Dryden let go of her and grabbed the chute's steering lines, Velcroed to the straps above his shoulders. He pulled the left line and felt the canopy respond, turning hard counterclockwise, swinging him and Rachel outward like a pendulum. Within seconds they were facing away from the building and gliding just fast enough to beat the wind.

In the relative calm, Dryden considered their situation. It would take ninety seconds or more to reach the street. By then the choppers would spot the chute and report it to whatever ground units Gaul had dispatched along with them. Dryden had no sooner formed the thought than a trio of vehicles appeared to the south, veering fast through the sparse traffic on Michigan Avenue. It wasn't even necessary to hazard a guess: Those units would be parked below the Hancock long before he and Rachel touched down.

Dryden sought other options. The white marble tower across the street, directly to the south, rose from a base structure wider than itself – a building that occupied its entire block and stood perhaps ten stories tall. The roof of the base building offered a broad and easy landing zone and, more importantly, the tactical advantage of the building itself. Within the labyrinth of its interior, he and Rachel would have at least a fighting chance to evade Gaul's people. The layout almost certainly extended two or three levels beneath the street, with egress points into service tunnels through which neither satellites nor helicopters could track them.

The parachute's glide angle was already taking them toward that rooftop. They were a minute above it – they would land on it around the time Gaul's ground units arrived, or maybe sooner. This could work.

At that moment the parachute's canopy flared bright, and in the street far below, the circle of a spotlight shone, with the chute's rectangular shadow eclipsing its center. One of the choppers had spotted them.

The remaining sixty seconds it would take to reach the broad rooftop suddenly felt like an hour. It was enough time for the chopper to do a lot more than report them – it could attack them.

Already Dryden heard its turbines changing pitch and saw the spotlight angle swing: The chopper was coming down to their level.

A minute wouldn't do. Dryden reached above his head, coiled his hand around three of the chute's lines, and pulled hard. The effect was immediate. The canopy partially collapsed, dumping air, and he and Rachel began to plummet at twice the chute's normal descent rate, spinning wildly as they did.

Spinning – and no longer gliding. No longer heading south, toward the rooftop of the white building far below. While in this spin, they were once again at the mercy of the wind; it was shoving them north, back toward the cliff face of the Hancock.

There was a judgment call to make: How long to drop like this before filling the chute again and trying to glide for the white building's roof? Before Dryden could make the decision, the wind gusted. With each rotation he got another glimpse of the Hancock, and with each glimpse it was closer. A lot closer. They were going to hit it. He let go of the lines and held on to Rachel as tightly as he could. The chute reinflated and stopped spinning just a few yards from the tower's face, but they were still closing distance with the building at something like twenty miles an hour. Dryden had just enough time to consider that this was about as fast as he could sprint on the ground. Which meant that this impact would be like running full speed into a wall. He spun to take the collision with his own body instead of Rachel's, and tensed for it.

It felt like being hit by a bus. Every joint screamed. Rachel lost her hold around his neck, and for an instant – the instant that counted – momentum turned her eighty pounds into five hundred, and her body was wrenched from his arms. All pain vanished from Dryden's mind under a flash of adrenaline. His hands shot out for her, felt one of her sleeves – for a horrible second he imagined getting only her shirt as she fell free of it – and then locked around her wrist.

They were sliding down the glass wall now, her eyes looking up at his, wide and intense. Below her was the abyss, easily forty stories of open space.

There was something else below her as well, rushing up to meet them: a horizontal stretch of the tower's famous exterior bracing. There were diagonal beams that crossed to form X shapes, and there were lateral beams running sideways through them. One of these flat beams, forming a ledge maybe eighteen inches deep, lay thirty feet below their position. Thirty feet and coming on fast. Dryden looked up and saw the reason for their speed: The chute had partly caved against the building, losing over half of its drag.

Twenty feet to the ledge now.

Ten.

Dryden pulled Rachel up to his level and got his arms around her, once again meaning to take the collision himself first, though in this case there was no reason to think it would help.

They hit.

It was worse than he'd imagined. Once, in a training accident, Dryden had fallen three stories onto concrete. This impact on the ledge was at least that hard. He and Rachel were slammed downward into a tangled mass, his body cushioning her impact only slightly. He heard her breath rush out along with his own. He locked his arms around her before she could roll off him into open space.

She opened her eyes but took several seconds to focus on him, even though his face was nearly touching hers. She held on to consciousness for a moment, then lost it.

The dead chute fell past them, flapping uselessly against the tower in the straight-on wind. Seconds later it began shuddering violently in a different sort of wind, coming from above. Rotor wash.

Dryden looked past Rachel and saw the AH-6 directly overhead. It descended into a hover thirty feet to the side, filling all his senses. Even the taste of its exhaust reached him. It pivoted to give the sniper on its left skid a clear line. The man was close enough for Dryden to look into his eyes just before he raised his weapon.

Assuming Rachel would be the first target, and not willing to spend the last few seconds of his life soaked with her blood, Dryden cradled her against himself and turned inward. He put his back to the chopper, visually shielding her. It wouldn't save her, but they would at least have to shoot him first. He studied her face, absorbing the details one last time. Even with her eyes closed, she was as beautiful a thing as he'd seen in his life. He kissed the top of her head. Reflected in the windowpane behind her was the chopper, and the man with the rifle. The scope lens gleamed.

Then, from high above, something screamed down out of the night on a vapor trail. It turned the chopper into an inferno, pounding it downward like a sledgehammer striking a child's toy. Debris rained against the building, lit by the ghostly fire of the now-falling helicopter.

'What the fuck just happened?' Gaul shouted.

The pilot of Sparrow-Four-Two was yelling about a missile, and on the Miranda image, his chopper pulled hard to the west and sped away from the building.

The pilot of Sparrow-Four-One was not responding, probably because Sparrow-Four-One had become a flaming ball of metal. Gaul watched it hit the street with a bright puff of heat on all sides.

Audrey leaned as far out of the empty window frame as she could afford to, with the second FGM-148 Javelin resting in its launcher on her shoulder. The first launcher lay steaming on the carpet behind her.

No good. The other chopper was long gone; pilots were survivor types. She dropped the second launcher as well, held on to the window frame, and leaned farther out into the wind. Dryden's parachute hung against the building far below.

Audrey retreated ten steps into the bedroom, came forward at a sprint, and leapt.

Dryden took his eyes off the wreckage and set his mind to the only thing that mattered now: getting into the building. The window beside him looked into a darkened office, visible only when he cupped his hand to his eye against the glass.

He had no gun, and nothing heavy with which to shatter the pane. His search for a solution was interrupted by the ruffle and snap of a parachute opening, and not his own. He turned to see a slim figure – it could only be Audrey – hanging from the lines of a second chute. It had opened less than a hundred feet above, and sixty feet out from the tower. Audrey was turning and coming around now, not fighting the wind but seizing it.

It was clear within seconds that Audrey's control of the parachute was that of a master. While Dryden had made over two hundred jumps in his life, and could land on ground targets with the best of them, Audrey's movements spoke of a specialized skill level, an acrobatic ability that came from years of narrowly focused training.

There's one other reason to live here, Audrey had told him, *but if you're lucky you won't have to find out what it is.*

He understood. What other type of residence offered such a dynamic and unexpected escape route? All three of them – Audrey and Sandra, at the very least – had probably made a hundred aircraft jumps or more, in every kind of wind, until the controls of a chute were like extensions of their own bodies.

This was about to go bad.

He looked at Rachel again and found her eyes fluttering open, fixing on him. He could tell she'd read the danger in his mind.

'It's not too late,' she whispered. 'You can let me go.'

Her gaze went past him for a moment, beyond his shoulder to the wide-open drop.

Dryden pulled her face against his own, cheek to cheek, and just held on. He felt her tears spilling onto his temple, exactly where the chill always touched it.

A second later he heard the chute ruffle again. He looked up. Audrey had put herself into a dive; she stayed in it until she was almost lateral to their position, then pulled up and swung directly toward them. Twenty feet out and coming in fast.

Dryden readied himself. He'd killed with his hands before, but never while lying on a narrow ledge, forty stories up, with a child in his arms.

Audrey brought her feet up in the final seconds, coming toward Dryden like a battering ram. He raised his arm to block, knowing it would have almost no effect. Audrey's left boot came into his viewpoint, connecting with his cheekbone hard enough to make the world flash white. Then she was atop him, kneeling right on Rachel, raining blows against Dryden's face with some heavy steel tool in her hand. Blood everywhere now, in his mouth, his eyes.

With his left arm he blocked one of Audrey's blows and blindly got hold of her wrist. He sent his other fist into her face; with deep satisfaction he felt her nose disintegrate beneath it in a shower of blood. She screamed. Then she took the tool into her other hand and landed the heaviest blow yet, right behind his ear. His muscles failed almost instantly; he felt like he was buried in sand and trying to move. It was all he could do to stay conscious.

He felt Rachel's limp weight torn away from him, and then she was gone, along with Audrey.

He blinked, raised one lead-filled arm, and palmed the blood away from his eyes. Audrey had pushed off from the building and was gliding away. She held Rachel in one arm and with the other fastened a strap around the girl and locked her in place. Then she took to the controls again, spilling air out of the canopy and making what looked like a suicidal dive for the street.

Gaul's three ground vehicles covered the last block on Michigan Avenue and swung around the corner, only to be confronted by the blazing roadblock of the downed AH-6. The vehicles made no attempt to look for survivors in the wreck; they tried to nose around it instead, but the strewn metal covered the entire path, from the base of one building to the other, with pooled fuel burning under all of it. The vehicles could not get through.

Audrey reached the street in less than twenty seconds, pulling up from the dive and flaring the chute for a soft landing. She released the harness the moment her feet touched, and the freed canopy drifted away down the street like a ghost. As Dryden watched, she set Rachel on the pavement, then used the steel tool to pry up a manhole cover. She lowered Rachel inside, followed her down, and replaced the lid behind her. Obviously, she would be prepared. She would have the tunnel system memorized, and a vehicle staged somewhere, ready to go.

Gaul's vehicles didn't reach the manhole until nearly a minute after Audrey had entered it. She and Rachel were gone.

Chapter Thirty-four

The team that had landed on the building's roof got to Dryden first. They entered the office, broke the window, and hauled him in. They zip-tied his wrists and ankles. As they did, he got a look at their weaponry: 9 mm Berettas holstered on their hips, but tranquilizer rifles slung on their shoulders. Looking back, he thought the sniper on the helicopter had been aiming the same kind of rifle.

They took him down to the SUVs and shoved him into the back of one. He asked them nothing and they volunteered nothing. He expected the vehicles to swing back south onto Michigan Avenue and return to the Willis Tower, but they didn't. They went north instead, finally turning west on a street called Division. Three minutes later they got onto I-94 heading northwest out of the city, toward the glow of O'Hare on the horizon.

'Blink S-O-S for me.'

The medic – the man who seemed to be a medic, anyway – was leaning toward him, carefully watching his responses.

Dryden blinked S-O-S.

'Touch the tip of your tongue to the center of your front teeth.'

Dryden did.

'Are you having any double vision?'

Dryden shook his head.

'Are the lights in here causing any pain in your eyes?'

Dryden shook his head again.

He was seated in the cabin of a large private jet. It was pushing back from its hangar now, its turbofans whining. The predawn sprawl of the giant airport rotated past the nearest window.

His wrists and ankles were still zip-tied. He was secured to the seat as well, by a strap encircling his torso and the backrest. Across the aisle, ahead of and behind him, the men with the dart guns sat watching.

'Look directly into the overhead lights for me and count to three,' the medic said.

Dryden did. He squinted against the glare. Everything about it felt normal.

'No likely concussion,' the medic said, mostly to himself.

One of the gunmen took out a phone and dialed. He waited. Then he said, 'We're a minute from wheels up, sir.' Five seconds passed. 'Copy that. We'll have him ready when you get there.'

There turned out to be Andrews Air Force Base outside Washington, D.C. The jet touched down and taxied for a long time, winding its way among hangars and maintenance buildings. The structure it finally stopped near, Dryden couldn't identify. It was single-story but sprawling. It had poured concrete walls and no windows. The men unbound his ankles, left his wrists tied, and led him off the plane into the early sunlight. They walked him into the building through the only door he could see in its wall; it opened on a sterile white corridor with a few doorways on either side. They guided him through the first one on the left, into a room the size of a basketball court. There were long metal tables here and there, folding chairs clustered around a few of them. There were aluminum-and-canvas cots stowed against a wall. The men grabbed one and locked its legs into position. They set Dryden down on it and zipped his ankles again.

'Sleep if you can,' one of them said.

Two stayed behind to guard him. They took chairs from the tables and sat next to the door. The others left and closed the door behind them.

Dryden shut his eyes.

Footsteps in the corridor. Dryden came awake in time to see the two men stand from their chairs. A second later the door swung inward, and a man in his fifties walked into the room. Athletic build. Black windbreaker over khaki slacks and an oxford shirt. Dryden got the impression the guy had been a soldier once but had been something else for a long time since.

'Martin Gaul,' Dryden said.

The man nodded. Behind him, half a dozen men entered the room. Some of them carried computer equipment: a ruggedized tower case, a keyboard, a big flat-panel display. They got to work setting it up on the nearest of the metal tables.

Last through the door was a man who reacted to the sight of Dryden's bruised face.

'Christ, Sam.'

Cole Harris crossed to the cot and crouched beside it. He looked the same as he had the last time Dryden had seen him, a few months before. Six foot three, built like a tree trunk, the same haircut he'd had since basic training.

'Fuckers could've cleaned you up, at least,' Harris said.

'They checked me for a concussion. Nice of them, I guess.'

'Do me a favor,' Harris said.

'What?'

'Tell these guys everything. Every detail, the last three days. Everything you know.'

'I'd like to know what *you* know,' Dryden said.

'You will. They're going to tell you.'

At the table, Gaul's men had the display turned on. It showed a blank blue screen while they set up the computer.

Gaul came over to the cot.

'Why don't you get these off him?' Harris said, indicating the zip-ties. 'I don't think he's going to go next door and steal *Air Force One*.'

Gaul nodded. He gestured to one of the men at the door.

It took an hour to detail the three days. Dryden left out Dena Sobel's name, along with anything that could allow her to be identified, but otherwise withheld nothing. While he spoke, Harris stepped out and came back with paper towels and a bottle of rubbing alcohol. He dabbed at the cuts and the swelling and cleared off the congealed blood.

When Dryden had finished, Gaul sat staring at nothing for a long time. He seemed to be marshaling his thoughts, preparing what he had to say.

'Why were your men armed with tranquilizer guns in Chicago?' Dryden asked. 'Up until then you'd been trying to kill Rachel.'

'And you along with her,' Gaul said.

If there was any apology in the man's tone, Dryden missed it.

'Let me just run through it in order,' Gaul said. 'It's best for me if you're up to speed, and' – he glanced at Harris – 'in any case, your friend insisted on it.'

Harris nodded.

'So here are the bullet points,' Gaul said. 'I'm the head of a defense contractor, Belding-Milner. Our major rival is a company called Western Dynamics, and in the field of genetic R&D, they've been ahead of us for years. Two months ago I got Rachel in my custody; she was a remnant of the original military research, years back, that both of our companies had based their work on. Rachel was a valuable object to study. It wasn't just about what she was; it also mattered what she knew. She and her two friends – I guess you met them – had been shadowing our two companies for years, keeping up on our progress. Easy enough for mind readers to do that, and they had good reason to: We might have developed things we could use against them, for one. In any case, when my people interrogated Rachel, she had no reason to hold back what she knew about our rival. She didn't care if we learned that stuff. She told us all about them, including something new they had in development. Not just the antenna sites, and the current testing being done with them. Something else.'

'Something everyone's afraid of,' Dryden said.

Gaul nodded. 'You'll understand why, when I get to it. You'll also know why Rachel's friends didn't want to tell her about it. It's tied pretty tightly to her own past. The people behind it – the thing everyone's scared of – are actually afraid to use it while Rachel is alive. They think she might be able to affect it in some way, and I think they're probably right. That was why the government ordered me to kill her. I wasn't thrilled about it, but it wasn't my call.'

'Just following orders,' Dryden said. 'Nice defense.'

Harris chuckled. Gaul showed no reaction at all.

'I do what I do,' Gaul said. 'After you and Rachel escaped El Sedero, I brought the head of Homeland Security on board, because I needed his help. I hoped he'd see the situation my way. And he did. For a while.'

'What do you mean?' Dryden asked.

Harris spoke up. 'Head of Homeland's a guy named Dennis Marsh. Turned out he had a little bit of conscience still sloshing in the tank. He went along with the bullshit, setting up the manhunt for you, Sam, but he also looked into your background. He got in touch with me and a few others from the unit. He got in touch with Holly Ferrel, too. The guy was right on the fence, with what was happening to you and Rachel. Like he just needed a good push to do the right thing. Maybe some backup, too. We obliged. All of us, including Holly and Marsh himself, contacted Gaul and told him the game was going to change. This was the night before last.'

Dryden thought about it. That would've been the night he and Rachel had waited in the empty apartment near Holly's place. The night Rachel had heard Holly rehearsing a phone call to Martin Gaul.

'What's Holly's role in all this?' Dryden asked.

'You can ask her yourself soon enough,' Gaul said.

Dryden caught something in his voice. Petulance, it sounded like – that sharp little fragment of childhood some people held on to forever.

'We're prepared to go public with every inch of this mess,' Harris said. He was speaking to Dryden, but the hard edge in his voice seemed to be for Gaul's benefit. 'We're not stupid; we don't expect to prevent the roll-out of this technology, but we damn well mean to stop it from squashing one of our friends.'

The childish look stayed in Gaul's eyes a second longer, and then he shoved it away and looked at Dryden. 'So there it is. The game change is that you don't die, and neither does Rachel, or else I get a world of attention I'd rather avoid. Okay. I can bloom where I'm planted.'

Gaul went to the table where the techs had set up the computer. On-screen, the Windows desktop was strewn with shortcut icons. He clicked one, and a photo slideshow player filled the screen. The first image was a simple white background with black text. It read FT. DETRICK – 08 JUNE 2008.

For the moment Gaul made no move to advance to the next picture.

'There's a lot you'd better know about Rachel,' Gaul said, 'if we're going to do what your friends have in mind. So here we go.'

Gaul stood there thinking a moment longer.

At last he said, 'She's a knockout. Your assumption about what it means is exactly right. The research goes back to long before Rachel was born. It started with gibbons in the biowarfare lab at Detrick, in 1990. They'd been doing sensory deprivation tests on these animals, keeping them in enclosures that were perfectly sound-proof, lightproof, everything. Lab workers noticed that some of them – about five percent – somehow reacted to agitation of other gibbons in nearby labs. They reacted even while shut up in these sensory boxes, which should've made it impossible for them to be *aware* of the agitation in the first place.'

Gaul paced away from the computer. 'Well, you already know how they were aware of it. At Detrick they didn't know for another five or six years – not until genome sequencing got cheap enough to be widely applied. They found that the special gibbons, the ones that could react from inside sensory chambers, were naturally missing a gene called NP20. That gene suppresses a much older complex of genes: genes that we think allowed ancient, precursor animals to read each other's alpha waves – brain activity.'

'The same thing an EEG machine reads,' Dryden said.

Gaul nodded. 'If the gibbon is born without NP20, or has it knocked out with a drug, then those older genes are no longer suppressed. They become active genes, and they start altering synaptic patterns in the brain, creating structures that act like natural receivers and transmitters. They let primates read one another's neural activity. Those same genes, the ones that code for mind reading in gibbons, exist in all the higher primates, too. Chimps. Gorillas. Human beings. We also have NP20 to block them, but where gibbons have *only* NP20, we have three extra genes that do the same job it does. Like redundant safeties on a bomb. Our evolution seems to have made a point of keeping us out of each other's heads.'

'But why?' Dryden said. 'Why would we evolve *away* from something like that?'

'We can only guess,' Gaul said, 'but I think our guesses are pretty good. Alpha-wave reading probably started tens of millions of years ago, among the ancestors of modern primates. Maybe it was a kind of predator alarm, a way to spread a warning through the group without the risk of making noise. Easy to see the benefit in that. The running guess, though, is that mind reading carried a downside later on, when these animals started getting smarter. Fast-forward to gibbons, with social hierarchies and long-term memory, complex rivalries and emotions, and maybe it's not a great idea to hear each other's thoughts. In humans, capable of things like holding grudges for life, it might be a disaster.' Gaul's face took on a kind of weariness. 'Rachel's a beautiful example.'

'What are you talking about?' Dryden asked.

'You need to know, first, what sets Rachel apart. Why she's different than Audrey or Sandra, or anyone else they ever had at Detrick. Rachel can do a lot more than just read minds.' Gaul was looking at his hands. Now he looked up and met Dryden's eyes. 'You may already know about her other ability, without realizing it. Going by what you told us a few minutes ago, you've seen it in action yourself.'

Chapter Thirty-five

Both Gaul and Harris were watching him now, waiting for his response. He didn't have one. He had no idea what Gaul was talking about.

'You said someone gave you two a ride out of Fresno,' Gaul said. 'You and Rachel were in the trunk. A police officer demanded to search it, and then for no obvious reason he just gave up and waved the driver through.'

'I thought it was strange,' Dryden said. 'What does it have to do with Rachel?'

'Everything,' Gaul said.

Harris leaned forward and spoke softly. 'She doesn't just *read* minds, Sam. She can influence them, too. Right now she doesn't remember that she can do it, but she can.'

'The mind reading is passive,' Gaul said. 'Like seeing and hearing. It just happens. But the other part, influencing other people's minds, is different. It takes concentration and focus, and complicated mental routines. Same as playing chess or balancing a spreadsheet. Rachel spent years building up the ability, and at the moment she can't recall any of it.'

'Based on observations of Rachel in captivity, in El

Sedero,' Harris said, 'these guys think she can exert a small amount of control even now, but only subconsciously. The effect would be minor, and it would only happen if she was emotionally stressed. She wouldn't even realize she was doing it.'

Dryden thought of the checkpoint in Fresno: Dena trying to talk her way past the cop, digging the hole deeper by the second; Rachel beside him in the dark, gripping his hand, her body shaking.

Then the cop had just let them go.

I don't get it, Dena had said. *He was staring right at me and then . . . he just changed his mind.*

'Jesus,' Dryden said.

'What you saw there is almost nothing,' Gaul said. 'When she has real control of it, you can't imagine what she can do. There's a distinction I need to explain here. Those female prisoners at Detrick twelve years ago, including Rachel's mom, were given the earliest generation of the knockout drug. It was primitive stuff; administered to adults, all it did was give them the capacity to hear thoughts. That's all Audrey and Sandra could ever do. Twelve years on, now, Western Dynamics has a greatly improved version of that drug. They've given it to hired operatives of their own, and it allows them to read minds and exert a certain amount of control over people. Simple things, like putting a voice into someone's head, or forcing certain emotional states, like guilt or disgust, cranked up to a level you'd never feel in regular life. Positive emotions, too – euphoria, erotic sensations, that kind of thing. It all adds up to sticks and carrots to make people follow commands. The total effect is powerful, if it's used just right, and those antenna sites, like the one you found in Utah, are used to amplify the effect over a wide area, a radius of twenty or thirty miles from the tower.'

Dryden thought of the pickup almost crashing into him and Rachel, south of Cold Spring. The man with the MP-5.

'The guy in the desert—' he said, and saw Harris already nodding.

'Unwitting participant,' Harris said. 'He'd probably endured months of conditioning by one of the people from Western Dynamics, by the time he attacked you.'

Dryden remembered the pity in the man's eyes. Pity for himself, maybe, but that was understandable in its own way.

'The controllers at Western Dynamics are powerful,' Gaul said, 'but they don't hold a candle to what Rachel can do. Her skill set is that formidable.'

'But you said Rachel only got the first version of the drug,' Dryden said. 'She got it when her mother got it.'

'That's right. Rachel got it as a fetus at two months' development. Which makes all the difference.'

Dryden began to understand. Seeing him grasp the idea, Gaul nodded.

'It matters,' Gaul said. 'You better believe it matters. Adults are already formed. There's only so much the drug can change in them. But Rachel had all her development still ahead of her. All the circuitry of the brain yet to be formed.'

Gaul glanced at the slideshow player on the computer again. The text frame was still there. FT. DETRICK — 08 JUNE 2008. He made no move to click anything yet.

'You knew Rachel was born and raised in holding at Detrick,' Gaul said. 'Staff there noted her ability to hear thoughts, like the other prisoners. Those symptoms presented at around eighteen months. In hindsight, we know the other ability showed up when she was about four, though no one at Detrick knew it at the time. They knew nothing about it until she was seven years old, and then they learned an awful lot, very quickly. But most of the details I'm giving you now, we only learned later – two months ago when we got to interrogate her. Some of it, I honestly think she *wanted* to tell us. It wasn't quite bragging. It was mostly meant to intimidate us, I believe. Prisoners do that sometimes, don't they?'

Dryden said nothing.

'In any case,' Gaul said, 'Rachel described her ability in some detail. She has her own word for it: *locking*. Early on, at Detrick, she demonstrated it for her mother by making a lab tech scratch his head, across the room. By Rachel's account, her mother had a fit. Grabbed the little girl and just about pulled her arms off, and told her she was never to show the doctors what she could do. Rebecca knew if anybody found out, she'd never see

Rachel again. The kid would've been taken someplace else for separate testing, would've become some other team's project. Probably still right there at Detrick somewhere, but to Rachel's mother it would've been a million miles away.'

A cell phone rang close by. It belonged to one of Gaul's men. The guy took it out and answered, spoke quietly for a few seconds, and hung up. He nodded to Gaul. 'Landed five minutes ago. En route now.'

Gaul acknowledged with a wave of his hand, then turned back to Dryden.

'Rachel listened to her mom. She never told the researchers what she could do. But she practiced it. It was easy to do that without much risk. What you have to understand is that when Rachel locks somebody, that person has no idea it's happening. If she makes you take off your glasses and clean them, you think it was your decision to do that. If she makes you get a cup of water from the cooler, same thing. She doesn't make your limbs disobey you. She makes you *want* to do whatever she's pushing you to do.' Gaul was quiet a beat, then said, 'These days, she can do a lot more than make you clean your glasses.'

'Like what?' Dryden asked.

'She can sit in a hotel room in lower Manhattan, lock a portfolio manager from two blocks away, and make him wire ten million dollars to an account on the other side of the world. Then she can make him drink vodka until he passes out, and by the time he wakes up the money's been bounced through a dozen stops and there's no way to trace it.'

Dryden shut his eyes and tried to appreciate the power of an ability like that. The subtlety of it.

'Locking is entirely different from the short-range ability to hear thoughts,' Gaul said. 'That's important to understand. It's a separate phenomenon altogether, stemming from different genes, different development. For one thing, the range is far greater. Rachel can lock you from as much as a mile away. And you don't feel it – you don't get the chill at your temples. When she locks in, she can see and hear with your senses, *and* read your thoughts . . . and she can make you do anything she wants. Anything.'

Thinking about that, Dryden felt certain dots begin to connect. Not all of them, but some.

He said, 'Audrey and Sandra wouldn't tell Rachel about the scary thing, because . . .'

'Because Rachel *is* the scary thing,' Gaul said. 'In a sense, at least. She's the first living example of it.'

'The first?' Dryden asked.

Gaul nodded. 'Western Dynamics has its own generation of operatives whose development is based on Rachel's. Subjects treated in utero. They dosed the first group not quite five years ago. Those subjects are four years old now, and all appear to have Rachel's capabilities. Early trial runs with them, using the antennas, could start any day now. They might not be made to do very much at first, but in a few years' time . . .' Gaul's mouth seemed to have gone dry. He licked his lips. 'In a few years' time, I think we're going to find ourselves in a very different world.'

Dryden felt as if the room had suddenly cooled by five degrees. The skin on his arms seemed to tighten. Before he could say anything, a heavy engine approached and stopped outside the building. Two of Gaul's men left the room, and Dryden heard them speaking to someone down the hall. Footsteps followed – hard soles tapping lightly. When the door opened again, Holly Ferrel stepped through it.

Chapter Thirty-six

Gaul introduced her to Dryden. He'd seen her at a distance outside her town house in Amarillo; up close she looked like someone who'd been getting by on reduced sleep for a while. The skin was dark under her eyes, pale everywhere else. When she shook Dryden's hand, her grip seemed almost powerless. He'd been right about her age: forty, give or take.

'Were you one of the researchers who worked on Rachel?' Dryden asked.

She spoke without meeting his eyes. 'I wasn't part of the project at first. I worked at NCI-Frederick, a branch of the National Cancer Institute, based there at Detrick. I'd been there for about a year when I was approached to get involved in . . . the other stuff. I was told that certain research grants I had pending at Frederick could be approved quickly if I helped with—'

She stopped. She shook her head. 'That's all bullshit. It's true, but it's still bullshit. I knew what I was saying yes to. I was scared to turn them down, and part of me really wanted to get involved. It was bleeding-edge stuff. It was fascinating. So I did it.'

She left it at that. Her gaze stayed on the floor.

Gaul spoke. 'I'm going to tell you how Rachel and the other two managed to get free from Detrick, Mr Dryden. It's the last part of the story. But you should understand something about Audrey and Sandra – and Rachel's mother. You knew all those subjects came from prison, felons with long-term sentences. In Rebecca Grant's case, the crimes were drug related. Mostly possession, some minor trafficking. She wasn't the best decision maker, but she was no monster. Audrey and Sandra were. Both had been convicted of murder. Both were almost certainly sociopaths.' He composed his thoughts, then said, 'There were *two* escape attempts from Fort Detrick, actually. One failed and the other succeeded, but the first attempt was . . . the nice version. That was the one Rachel and her mother preferred. Keep in mind that Rachel was seven when all this happened.'

Dryden waited for him to go on.

Gaul turned to Holly. 'Can you show him?'

Holly nodded. She reached into her pocket and withdrew a thick square of folded notepad paper. When she opened it, Dryden saw it comprised three sheets. The first was covered with writing. The penmanship looked like that of a child: messy and too careful at the same time. Holly separated it from the others and passed it to Dryden.

'What is this?' he asked.

Holly struggled for an answer.

'You'll see,' Gaul said.

Dryden turned the sheet around in his hands and read.

Holly it's me Rachel. I am afraid to ask you this when your here with us, because I know the people here are always watching, and my mom says there are probably machines recording sound in this place, day and night. This is the only way I know how to send you this message, and ask you for help. My mom thinks if you tell a reporter at a newspaper or on tv what is happening here, all the things you know, then it would make it so they have to let us go, my mom says it is illegal that they are keeping us here forever. Holly, please talk to a reporter and get them to let us out of here. I know you mean it when your nice to me, and you care. Please help us.

Dryden finished reading it and looked up.

'Rachel slipped you this note?' he asked. That was hard to believe, given the level of security there must've been in a facility like that.

Holly shook her head. 'Not exactly. I was in my office at the other place, at NCI-Frederick, a few hundred yards from where Rachel and the others were kept. It was late at night. I was looking at lab work and then I just pushed it aside and picked up a pen and started writing that message myself. It didn't feel like I was being forced to do it. I just . . . wanted to. It was like I'd had an idea for some kind of short story. The kind that are made up of people's journals or letters – what do

314

they call that, epistolary fiction? That's what it felt like. Just some stream-of-consciousness thing I'd thought up, using Rachel and her mom as the basis for it, and I was jotting it down as it came to me. Bad handwriting and spelling and all, like it was part of the story.'

Dryden looked at the words again. He imagined Rachel in a cage, seven years old, every ounce of her hope tied to these words on Holly's notepad.

'I had no idea what else to think of it,' Holly said. 'I stared at it for five minutes and then put it aside. I had work to do.' She drew the second sheet from the stack. 'Half an hour later, I picked the pen back up and wrote this one.'

You are not making it up. My mom says there is a way to show you its real. Your boss in this building has this email address, EGraham@detrick.usabri.mil and it takes two passwords to open it, first is leanne424miami and second is murphyhatesthe-vet87. If you were making this up in your head, you would not know his email passwords, we know them because we hear him think when he types them. Open his email with the passwords and you will know this is real, it is really me asking you to help us. Holly, please help us get out of here.

Dryden looked up at Holly again.

'I assume the passwords worked,' he said.

She nodded, looking miserable.

'Did you consider really going to the press?' Dryden asked.

'Yes.'

'But you didn't.'

'I was scared,' Holly said. 'I'd had years to get used to them hearing my thoughts, as weird as that was, but this was different. Actually being controlled. It rattled the hell out of me.' She took a deep breath. 'And I didn't want to do it. That's the no-bullshit answer. I was afraid. You know what could have happened to me, going public against the military on something like that. I thought of Bradley Manning. I thought of people we've probably never even heard of. Maybe I could have gotten the whole thing shut down, but . . . I just didn't want to try. That's all it came down to.'

She sounded like she could cry. Then she said, 'What would you have done, if you were me? Honestly.'

Dryden thought about it. He gave her the only answer he could. 'I don't know.'

'I sat there for ten minutes getting more wound up,' Holly said, 'and then I went to my superior at NCI-Frederick. He was somebody I trusted, and . . . I don't know. I wanted someone's advice. I didn't want to be alone with all of it. It's all I could think of.'

'Shit,' Dryden whispered.

'I'd take it back,' Holly said. 'I'd give anything to take it back.'

'Your superior ran it further up the chain, I imagine,' Dryden said.

Another sharp little nod.

'What happened then?' Dryden asked.

Gaul went to the computer. 'This,' he said, and clicked the slideshow's PLAY button.

Holly turned away from it. She grabbed a chair and took it a few paces off and sat down, her hands balled tight in her lap.

Dryden watched the monitor.

A grainy color image appeared. It looked like it had been shot by a security camera inside the cell block of a prison. A viewpoint from up near the ceiling, looking out and down at a row of cells. Dryden could see women in black jumpsuits behind the bars. Nine of the cells had a single occupant each. A tenth held Rachel, seven years old, and her mother.

'These are frame grabs from inside the unit they were kept in,' Gaul said. 'Building Sixteen at Detrick.'

Dryden scanned the row of cells again and picked out Audrey and Sandra. Each had a different hair color than he'd seen in Chicago.

Finally he took in the screen's lower left corner, and the digital text stamp there: DETRICK 16 − 2008 06 08 23:30:52.07.

A moment later the slideshow skipped to the next image. Another angle on the same scene, time-stamped a few seconds later.

In the third image, seconds later still, everything changed. The women were suddenly alert in their cages. Some were on their feet. Rachel, already in her mother's lap in the first two shots, now clung tightly to her.

In the fourth frame, a team of five men in security

uniforms had just entered the room, moving toward Rebecca and Rachel's cell. Everyone in the cages was up and screaming, mouths contorted. Rachel had her face buried in Rebecca's shoulder.

Gaul began to narrate the progression, his voice flat and devoid of emotion. Dryden looked away from the slideshow and just listened.

'The security team is young and inexperienced. Unlike real prison guards, they've never actually encountered resistance from detainees. They have shotguns loaded with beanbag rounds, nonlethal at a distance but devastating at point-blank range. They enter the cell with their attention on Rachel and her mother. They pay almost no attention to the prisoners in adjoining units. Eleven thirty-one and nine seconds: The leftmost guard loses his weapon to prisoner seven through the bars. Within the next four seconds the situation falls completely apart; at the end of that time frame, two men are down and the rest are shooting. One man is still grabbing for Rachel. Eleven thirty-one and fifteen seconds: Rachel is being forcibly pulled from Rebecca's arms, while the officer's weapon is coming up to level on the woman's face. Rachel is looking directly into her mother's eyes at sixteen seconds, when the shotgun discharges into Rebecca's forehead from less than six inches away.'

In her chair, Holly seemed almost to have shrunk. Her hands gripped her forearms, everything drawn inward as if she were sitting somewhere very cold.

'The shooter is himself struck fatally in the next

frame,' Gaul said. 'The rest withdraw. Rachel stays with her mother's body while other prisoners use the dropped shotguns to compromise the locks on their cells. What happens next is crucial.'

Dryden looked at the screen again. Three security men were down. Rebecca was slumped forward, her face mercifully out of view to the camera. Both Audrey and Sandra had entered that cell by then and were holding Rachel, turning her away from Rebecca's body.

'The two of them sit with the girl for over three minutes,' Gaul said, 'while the other surviving prisoners – four in all – finish freeing themselves and gather the weapons. These four trade gunfire with security teams in the hallway, men who are now firing live ammo, and over the course of the three minutes, those women are dropped one by one. By eleven thirty-four and twenty-eight seconds, the only prisoners alive are Audrey and Sandra and Rachel. The two women make no move toward the remaining shotguns, though some still have shells in them. They continue to sit with Rachel, calming her and speaking continuously into her ear. They do this even as security advances in the corridor.'

The slideshow ended. It reset to the black-text-on-white frame it had begun with, and stayed there.

'What follows is later reported as a gas-line explosion on base,' Gaul said. 'Maybe you remember seeing it on the news. Sixty-seven dead, burned to the point of requiring dental ID. But there is no explosion. No one is burned. What happens instead is that, without warning, the man leading the security advance in the hallway suddenly turns and opens fire into his own ranks. As they fall back in confusion, he fires his last shell into his own head. Seconds later another officer appears to suffer the same inexplicable breakdown. Like the first man, he fires on his own people until he has only one shot left and then uses it on himself. By this point the chaos is absolute. No one is thinking about the prisoners in the containment room. Everyone's focus is on getting away. The violence spreads outside the building within the next minute. Footage from over a hundred cameras on base will later show how it unfolds. How the effect only ever touches one man at a time, jumping from one to the next at an interval of two to three seconds. It passes like a wave from Building Sixteen to the nearest gate out of the Fort Detrick campus, a quarter mile away. All sentries in its path are killed. All personnel at the outer gate are killed. This entire time, cameras in the holding block show Audrey and Sandra still sitting there with Rachel. Arms around her. Speaking into her ear. Talking her through it. Lip-reading analysis would later show them saying the word *shoot* several dozen times.'

Gaul had been staring at the text screen on the monitor. Now he turned back to Dryden.

'When it was over, four minutes later,' Gaul said, 'there was no one to stop the three of them from taking a vehicle and simply driving away. Footage shows

Rachel catatonic as Sandra carries her from the building. Brain-locked, I imagine, at what she'd seen in the cell, and what the two women had then made her do. Around the time they buzzed the gate open on their way out, Rachel did probably the only thing that was of her own free will. She made Holly write a third message, hiding in her office like everyone else on base.'

Dryden turned to Holly. The last sheet of notebook paper was just visible, crushed and twisted in one hand. She released it and handed it to him without looking up. Dryden saw what it said even before he'd smoothed the page.

Your fault.

Chapter Thirty-seven

Dryden thought of the conversation over lunch the day before, in the Chicago apartment. Rachel asking the others about Holly, terrified for her safety.

Sandra had tried to calm the girl's fears. *For the time being, this week for sure, nobody's going to hurt her.*

Dryden understood.

This week for sure.

The time it would take for Rachel's memory to come back.

Because Rachel was the threat to Holly's life.

The notion of it made the edges of Dryden's vision darken.

'In the days that followed,' Gaul said, 'a number of people closely involved with the research, living in and around D.C., committed suicide – appeared to, anyway. They were the very people the military needed alive, to advise them on what the hell was going on. From Audrey and Sandra's point of view, it was tactically brilliant: Take out the key players as fast as possible, leave the government scratching its ass trying to piece it all together. It would be months and months before the military, and companies like mine and Western Dynamics, came up with any means of protecting against the threat Rachel posed.'

The computer was still on. Gaul reached under the monitor and switched off the display.

'You can never really stop them from spying on you,' he said, 'but you can mostly keep your people safe. You need the right organizational structure; no one person can know too much, especially in the rank and file, in case their thoughts get compromised. And your research sites need to be in remote places, like islands far offshore, or little compounds in the middle of arctic wilderness. Places someone like Rachel couldn't get close to without being spotted. You need to be paranoid, really. And in that sense, Holly was way ahead of us.'

Dryden glanced at her, sitting there with her arms around herself.

'Holly left D.C. within an hour of the violence at Detrick,' Gaul said. 'She felt irrational doing it, at the time, but it probably saved her life.'

'A friend of mine had a vacation home in the Florida Keys,' Holly said. 'I dropped off the planet for over six months, just trying to get my head back together. No one I'd worked with at Detrick knew where I was. I guess if they had, Rachel and the other two would've found me. By then, they wouldn't have had any real logical reason to kill me. They'd done enough of that damage. But I think . . .' She shook her head. Whatever she had to say, it hurt.

'I understand that Rachel hated me,' she said, 'but I don't believe she meant to kill me, early on. She *could* have, when she sent that third message. She could've buried the pen in my throat instead. I think the real hate came later, over months and years. Audrey and Sandra made sure of that; they worked to fan whatever Rachel initially felt. Do you see the reason? They were always going to need Rachel, for what she could do. They needed her as a weapon, which meant they needed her to be cold, without remorse. They achieved that by keeping her focused on me. On the idea of finding me and killing me. Everything we now know supports that.'

'In time,' Gaul said, 'once the military had set up special groups to hunt for Rachel and the others, and to protect people in danger from them, Holly was relocated to Amarillo with her new name.'

Dryden looked at the dark skin under Holly's eyes. The hollows beneath her cheekbones. A face shaped by half a decade of living in fear.

He pictured Rachel standing in her bedroom doorway with her stuffed dinosaur. A scared little girl who just wanted her life to make sense. He saw her on the ledge, in that final moment, her eyes looking past him to the abyss.

It's not too late. You can let me go.

He tried to reconcile that girl with the specter that had stalked Holly Ferrel's nightmares, and all at once he felt like he wanted to throw up. He looked around but saw no door to a bathroom. He muscled the feeling down.

'How did you get Rachel?' he asked Gaul. 'Two months ago.'

For the first time, a hint of shame edged into Gaul's expression. Then he seemed to set it aside, as if he had some tried-and-true way of exorcising those kinds of feelings.

'I used Holly as bait,' he said. 'Without her knowledge. A contact of mine in the military learned where Holly had been relocated to, and I saw the chance to benefit from that information. To get control of Rachel.'

Holly set her jaw and looked away. It was clear she'd known this already.

'There were certain government databases we believed Rachel and the other two had compromised at some point,' Gaul said. 'We allowed Holly's location to end up stored on one of those, like it was an accident, so Rachel would find it.' He shrugged with his eyebrows. 'She found it.'

Dryden considered the logistics of the trap itself. It didn't add up. How could Holly have been kept safe, if Rachel could kill her from anywhere in a one-mile radius? How would Gaul and his people pin down Rachel's location within that radius, to catch her?

Holly seemed to recognize the confusion in his expression.

'They didn't care if I got killed,' she said, 'and they

knew the odds of capturing Rachel were small, even if she got me. They risked my life just for a tiny chance of getting her.'

The little ghost of shame flickered through Gaul's eyes again, though only briefly.

'It worked,' he said. 'We had cameras hidden in Holly's home and car and workplace. If we saw her kill herself, we would know with certainty that Rachel was within a mile of that location, in that moment. We had half a dozen drones on station above Amarillo for weeks, and the Miranda satellites tasked on the city 24/7. In the end, we just got lucky. One of the drones identified Rachel in a city park, two blocks from where Holly lived. The drones were armed with low-powered, nonfragmenting warheads. We targeted a spot five meters from where Rachel was standing. The blast wave broke three of her ribs and gave her a concussion. She was still unconscious when my people got to her and subdued her with narcotics.'

'Weren't the other two with her?' Dryden asked.

Gaul shook his head. 'If they were in Amarillo, they weren't close by when the missile hit. It wasn't ideal.'

'No, it really wasn't ideal,' Holly said. 'I've had armed security for the last two months, wondering every minute if those two women were watching me. Did you know they can gauge their distance just right, so you don't feel the chill at your temples? Yeah, they're old hands.'

Dryden considered telling her they *had* been watching. It made sense that they'd done that, after Rachel's capture. Audrey and Sandra would've been desperate to learn where the girl had been taken. By monitoring Holly, they could eventually learn the names of the military people who'd changed her identity and hidden her in Amarillo. Those same people would have played some role in setting the trap for Rachel – or would know people who had. The daisy chain could've plausibly led to El Sedero someday.

Dryden kept it all to himself. Holly was rattled enough already.

'You're really on board with trying to save Rachel's life?' Dryden asked.

Holly nodded. 'None of this is her fault. She's a kid. She didn't choose any of it.'

'She's dangerous,' Gaul said. 'Not just to you. To plenty of people.'

'That issue can be dealt with,' Holly said.

Gaul seemed to be already weary of whatever Holly was referring to.

Dryden looked back and forth between the two of them. 'What do you mean?' he asked. 'How can it be dealt with?'

'The same way it got started,' Holly said. 'Genetic manipulation. We've got twelve years' worth of progress over the drug that was used on Rachel. We know how to reverse it now.'

Chapter Thirty-eight

Dryden stared. Holly held his gaze, unblinking.

'It would take months,' she said, 'but it would work. If she could be taken alive again, and drugged like she was in El Sedero, it could be done.'

'You don't know for certain it would work,' Gaul said. 'Just because it's worked in animal trials, that doesn't—'

'It would work,' Holly said. 'Afterward, she'd be a very screwed-up kid who needed years of therapy . . . but she'd be no more dangerous than anyone else. She could have a chance at some kind of life, anyway. Some kind of happiness, after all this.'

Gaul was shaking his head, looking off.

'So what's the plan?' Dryden asked. 'Assuming there is one.'

'There is one,' Harris said.

'Let's hear it.'

A look passed between Harris and Gaul.

'What?' Dryden asked.

'It's another bait trap,' Gaul said. 'Using both you and Holly this time. You can opt out, if you like. If so, you're free to go. The manhunt for the suspect with your face, the guy with the dirty bomb, will be resolved either way; we'll make up a name for him and announce we've killed him. You can go home free and clear.'

'You already know I'm staying in this thing,' Dryden said. 'How does the plan work?'

'Don't you see?' Harris asked softly. 'You can't know that. If you two are the bait, you can't have the details in your heads. Or Rachel will have them, too.'

Dryden laced his fingers behind his neck and shut his eyes. It was Rachel's bedroom in Chicago all over again.

'I can tell you this much,' Gaul said. 'The two of you will be in a house. It's on farm land in eastern Kansas, half a mile from a busy street, where there are restaurants and twenty-four-hour stores.'

Dryden saw the point. 'You want Rachel to be confident she can get within a mile of us and still be hidden in a crowd.'

Gaul nodded. 'But I expect her to get closer, in the end. A lot closer.'

'What makes you say that?' Dryden asked.

Holly answered before Gaul could. 'Under questioning in El Sedero, Rachel made her intentions toward me very clear. She has no interest in making me commit suicide. Remember how locking works: I would actually *want* to kill myself, in that final moment. That's no good, for her.' Holly's voice almost cracked on the next part. 'Rachel wants to kill me. *Really* kill me. She wants to be looking me right in the eyes at the end.'

A silence fell over the huge room.

'I'm not naive, you know,' Holly said. 'I know what I'm volunteering for.'

She went quiet again.

'That's it for the briefing,' Gaul said. 'We put you two in the farmhouse and you stay there. Holly's employer in Amarillo will be given the address and a fake explanation for her departure. Rachel will easily get that information once she's ... herself again. Once her memory comes back. Beyond that, we wait.'

'Rachel's going to see through that set-up like it's cling wrap,' Dryden said. 'She's going to know the farmhouse is a trap.'

'Yes,' Gaul said. 'She was always going to find out anyway. When she's close enough to lock the two of you, she'll hear your thoughts. It would be impossible for you to hide why you're really there.'

'So why the hell would she go for it?' Dryden asked.

'Maybe she won't,' Gaul said, 'but I expect her to. This time around she'll *know* it's a trap. She can watch for its teeth. Drones, for example – you can spot them with the right equipment, which she and Audrey can probably get. So those are out. Knowing it's a trap may give Rachel confidence. She might think she can outsmart us.'

'She might be right,' Dryden said.

Gaul simply nodded.

'And Audrey's going to just let her take this risk?' Dryden asked.

'Do you really suppose Audrey's in charge of her?'

Gaul said. 'That she and Sandra were still calling the shots, after all these years? Here are three people: Two of them can hear thoughts across a room; the third can make anyone in the nearest mile do anything she can imagine. Over time, who do you think would emerge as the alpha?'

Dryden thought about that. It clashed so vividly with his own understanding of Rachel that it hadn't even occurred to him.

'Don't assume you really know her,' Gaul said. 'We know what the real Rachel wants with Holly. As far as how she'll feel about you, don't even try to guess.'

The real Rachel.

Seeing the effect of that notion on him, Holly stood from her chair. 'I'm like you,' she said. 'I know what she would've been, if none of these things had ever happened to her. I believe she can be that way again.'

'Then let's go,' Dryden said.

Chapter Thirty-nine

Marcus Till rolled his old hatchback to the end of his driveway, stopped at the turnout, and stared back at the trailer he had called home for all his adult life. The place wasn't much to look at, but it was his. He watched it and wondered if he would ever see it again, and then he pulled onto the county two-lane and headed east toward town, and didn't look back.

He was forty-one years old. He had lived all of those forty-one years right here in the little backwater of Clover, Wyoming, ten miles from the somewhat larger backwater of Red City. For much of the early part of his life, he had struggled to stay out of trouble. The trouble had been brawling, mostly, always a result of drink or bad manners – the one led to the other, of course. Around thirty he'd left all that behind; you could only wake up in so many jail cells before you started to do some thinking. He had gone to work for his uncle in the woodshop, making custom cabinets and furniture for building contractors over in Cheyenne. Something in the work had appealed to Marcus at once. He liked putting in a day's effort and having a new thing to show for it at the end, a desk or maybe a bookshelf. He liked to stay alone in the shop after hours, turn on this light or that one, and see how a newly finished piece gleamed from different angles. He had expected the rest of his life to play out on this clean, simple track he'd gotten it onto. He wasn't going to be rich, but he also wasn't going to wake up in jail ever again, and that was fine with him. Everything had been fine, really, until just shy of a year ago when the Ghost had gotten into his head. All these rotten months later – months of denying and resisting and finally giving in like a beaten dog with his snout turned down – here he was, following his orders. What else could he do?

They were strange, the orders he'd gotten today. They were always strange – and now and again they were as god-awful as anything Marcus could imagine – but these were especially unusual. Until today, the Ghost's commands had always involved doing things right here in town, give or take a few miles. Now, out of the blue, the voice had commanded him to get in his car, get on the freeway, and head for Kansas. The instructions had specified a particular motel in a particular town, where he was to check in and stay and await further orders.

What those orders would be, he couldn't guess. They'd be nothing good – he knew that much. Still, he would follow them. God help him, he would follow them.

Chapter Forty

Just before midnight Dryden put aside the book he'd been reading and stepped out onto the farmhouse's porch. The breeze coming in off the fields was warm and humid. He went to the top of the steps and looked out at the night. In front of the house, the land fell away in a long slope to the road, two hundred yards south. The driveway cut straight down the middle, the fields on either side lying fallow and choked with short grass. The same held for the land on all sides of the place: a vast zone of open visibility stretching at least six hundred feet in each direction, without so much as a tree growing in it. No doubt this geometry had been part of Gaul's reason for choosing the site.

The house itself was probably a hundred years old, biding the decades out here in the sticks while Topeka grew north to meet it. It wasn't far off – the busy street Gaul had spoken of lay directly south, running east-west across the near horizon like a scar of neon and sodium-lit parking lots. Rachel could be there right now; Dryden and Holly had been in the farmhouse for ten days.

In the darkness to Dryden's right, the porch swing creaked in the wind. The swing was a big rough-beam construction, maybe as old as the house itself. He stood listening to it and watching the fields a while longer, then went back inside.

Holly was in her room, asleep. For the sake of staying vigilant, they'd staggered their schedules so they were never both sleeping at the same time. Gaul had given them very few instructions when they'd said good-bye to him, but among them were *Stay close to each other* and *Stay alert*. He'd given them each a cell phone, with his own number on the contact list. *The first sign of anything happening, you call me*, he'd said. That'd been it.

Dryden went to the kitchen. The big pantry leading off of it was stocked with easily two months' worth of nonperishable food. In the attached garage were three giant chest freezers, also chock-full. There were two vehicles in the garage as well, a Ford Escape and a Chevy Malibu. Keys had been left in both ignitions, though Gaul had said nothing about leaving the place. Dryden had started both vehicles to make sure they ran and had found each to have a full tank of gas.

Holly's laptop was on the counter, plugged in and charging. Gaul hadn't objected to her bringing it, or even using it to stay in touch with friends and colleagues; it was a way of maintaining some semblance of normalcy, for what it was worth.

Earlier in the evening Holly had used the laptop to check e-mail. Afterward she'd closed it and gone out to sit on the porch swing, and through the screen door Dryden thought he'd heard her crying. She'd stayed out there for over an hour and gone to bed soon after coming back in.

Dryden slid the laptop aside and started making a sandwich. He got a brick of cheese from the fridge, took a chef's knife from a block on the counter, and cut two slices. He held the knife a moment longer, studying its edge, its point. What would it be like if Rachel locked him right now? How would it feel to suddenly, inexplicably want this knife in his throat? To want it badly enough to put the tip under his Adam's apple and shove. He set it in the sink and went back to making the sandwich.

Holly woke four hours later. Dryden went to his room and lay down. He had the window open to the screen, and lay listening to the sounds of crickets and katydids and the wind sliding over the grass. He began to drift, and in the vague space near sleep Rachel came to him. They were sitting in the dark town house again, and she was leaning against him, warm and shapeless and fragile. He tried not to move. Tried to keep the moment from changing as long as he could.

'That's Arcturus,' Holly said.

It was two nights later. They were sitting side by side on the porch steps, looking at the stars. Even with the city's outskirts so close, the night sky here was almost ink black.

'You can't tell, but Arcturus is a giant star,' Holly

said. 'If you put our sun next to it, it would look like a cherry beside a beach ball.'

'You've studied astronomy?' Dryden asked.

Holly shook her head. 'I knew someone who wanted to study it. She told me a lot of these little facts.'

She was quiet for a long time.

'What was Rachel like when you were with her?' she asked.

He considered his answer for a while. 'Like a reminder that it's worth it to be alive.'

Holly pulled her feet up to the step beneath the one she sat on. She hugged her knees. 'It's a hell of a thing to be truly sorry for something. Sorry with every part of yourself. Do you think she could ever accept that from me?'

Dryden heard needfulness in her voice. He wanted to tell her it was possible. Instead he pictured that last moment between Rachel and her mother, and said nothing.

The wind picked up. Holly shuddered and pulled her knees closer. Dryden looked at her. Her bangs hung past her temples. Her eyes were almost shut. Something in her vulnerability commanded his attention.

She looked up and met his eyes. For a few seconds she seemed almost afraid of him, the way he was looking at her. She was caught off guard, at least. Then she took a deep breath, and her eyes changed. Not afraid – intense. And still needful.

A second later they were kissing. Hands on each

other's backs, grabbing, clinging. Her knees dropping out of the way, her body turning, mashing against his as hard as she could manage. Her mouth alive with her excitement, her breathing accelerating to match his. They were moving, then. Pushing up past the steps, sprawling on the old wood planking of the porch, hands going to shirt buttons, fumbling, pulling. He found her bra clasp and got it undone. She pulled her mouth back from his just long enough to speak.

'I haven't done this in a long time. If I seem—'

Dryden shook his head. 'Same here. You don't even want to know.'

Kissing again. Shirts coming off. Skin against skin with nothing in the way. Jesus, how had he waited this long to do this with someone again?

She pulled back once more, their foreheads still touching. 'Is this a good idea?'

'It's a great idea.'

'It's not really staying alert.'

'It's really staying close to each other.'

She breathed a laugh. Pushed in again. Kissed him. Her hands traced the contours of his ribcage. His sides. Moving downward—

Dryden opened his eyes. He pulled his face back six inches. All his excitement receded like hot water down a tub drain. His thoughts focused.

Holly reacted. 'What?'

'Twelve days, and there hasn't been any kind of spark between us. Not a thing.'

She looked confused. 'It seems like there's one now.'

'You're not even close to my type,' Dryden said.

'Well – okay, thanks. Jesus Christ—'

'Think about what I'm saying,' Dryden said.

For another half second she remained baffled. Then it hit her like a shove.

'Oh shit,' she whispered.

Dryden nodded. 'It's not us. It's her. She's here.'

Dryden got out his phone even as they pulled their shirts back on. He brought up the contact list and tapped Gaul's number. As it began to ring, he turned and scanned the grassy field south of the house. Holly was already doing the same thing.

It was almost pointless, though. In the near-total lack of moonlight, the terrain lay deep in darkness.

The call rang a second time. Then a third.

Sensing the delay, Holly turned and looked at him.

Four rings.

Five.

'What if she already got to Gaul?' Holly asked. Her eyes were wide at the implications. 'What if he's dead and there's no plan anymore? No help coming?'

Six rings.

Seven.

Dryden turned and crossed to the front door, keeping the phone at his ear. Holly followed him into the house.

Eight rings.

Dryden hung up and pocketed the phone; Gaul could call back as easily as he could answer.

They stood in the middle of the living room, all indoor lights doused, the night visible through the windows of every room that surrounded it.

'She locked you and then me,' Holly said. 'Right? The way you looked at me on the steps – you felt it first, and I didn't. And then I did.'

Dryden nodded. 'She can only lock one person at a time, but – I guess with something like that, you give people a push and they'll probably keep going.'

'It worked.'

'Yeah.'

She went to the screen door and looked out again. 'She wanted us distracted for a long time. Long enough for her to cross the open space to this house.'

Holly turned and faced him.

She wants to be looking me right in the eyes at the end.

Dryden nodded, seeing her point.

All the same, something about the situation didn't add up. Rachel had locked them each just long enough to turn them on to each other, but she wasn't locking them now. Why not? If she wanted them preoccupied while she herself approached the farmhouse, she could've just *kept* locking them, alternating from one to the other, and made them sit on the floor helplessly. That would've been the surest move. So why hadn't Rachel done it? Dryden had no answer to that. Which put him on edge.

He took out his phone again. Stared at the blank display.

'What the hell are we going to do?' Holly asked.

Two thousand thirty-one miles above the southern Great Plains, Miranda Twenty-six trained its instruments on the countryside north of Topeka, Kansas. Its lens platform made microscopic adjustments, keeping its viewing frame on the target it had been commanded to cover whenever it was in range. The target was a house centered in a broad square of uniform surface vegetation, a grass 97.441 percent likely to be Bouteloua gracilis, given the region and time of year. There were two human beings outdoors within the target frame, just entering the broad square of grass from the southern edge and moving north toward the house at walking speed. Their shapes suggested an adult and an adolescent, both female. Miranda Twenty-six relayed the image stream to the secure downlink designated 0814–13151, as instructed 12 days, 4 hours, 27 minutes, 41 seconds earlier. Since that time, there had been no further contact from the human operator.

Chapter Forty-one

Three minutes since Dryden had tried calling Gaul. No response. Holly had tried, too, with the same result. Then she'd called Dryden's phone to make sure the damn things worked at all. She'd gotten through immediately.

They moved from window to window, staying on opposite sides of the house from one another, watching the dark fields for any sign of approach.

'This is stupid,' Dryden said. He came out of the kitchen and met Holly in the living room. 'Even if we spot her, so what? What good would it do?'

'What *are* we supposed to do?'

Dryden turned and looked back toward the kitchen – then past it to the door leading to the garage.

'What if we just get the hell out?' he asked. 'Get in one of the cars, leave the headlights off, and make a run for it across the fields.' He looked through the screen door, toward the porch and the south field. 'If they're coming from the edge of town, we'd want to go north. We could be out of her range in less than a minute.'

'Unless she hears the engine and locks us again.'

'We stay here, it's going to happen anyway.'

Holly shut her eyes hard, thinking. 'Even if Gaul's

dead, we don't know the plan is off. We can't even be sure he *is* dead. If it's still on, and we leave, we're going to screw it up. We may not get another chance at this.'

Dryden started to respond but stopped. Out in the dark beyond the porch, two hundred feet from the house: movement. Two silhouettes. He didn't need detail to recognize their size and shape.

Holly turned and followed his gaze. Dryden heard her breathing go shallow.

Her hand found his and took hold of it. He squeezed back.

The silhouettes came on, still deep in the darkness beyond the house's glow. As Dryden watched, something in their movement struck him, but he couldn't place what it was. He didn't get the chance. A second later the night flashed blinding white, and then a blast front of sound slammed down over the house, blowing in the windowpanes on the south side. Holly screamed and threw her arms around Dryden. A second flash followed, and over Holly's shoulder Dryden saw the two silhouettes turn to run. A moment later the flashes were coming one after another like strobe pulses at a light show, and the sky sounded like the inside of a machine-gun barrel.

'*What is it?*' Holly screamed.

'*The plan,*' Dryden said.

In the wild flickers of light, he saw Rachel and Audrey still running away. Running south, back the way they'd come from. They covered sixty feet and made it no farther. Thick white streamers of powder were raining down over the field, as if a giant were slinging handfuls of flour into the wind. Where the stuff hit the ground it billowed out in all directions. Rachel and Audrey were right in the middle of it. In the last of the flashes, Dryden saw them both double over and fall.

Darkness. Silence.

Dryden's ears were keening. He almost missed the ringtone of the phone in his pocket. He took it out; Gaul's number showed on the display. He answered.

'Where the hell were you?' Dryden asked.

'Sorry about that,' Gaul said. 'I wanted you both panicking, in case Rachel was reading you. Better to keep her confident.'

There was a noise in Gaul's background. It sounded like chopper turbines powering up.

'Go to the couch and tear the middle cushion off,' Gaul said. 'There are two gas masks underneath.'

Dryden turned and crossed to it. The cushion came off as if it had been held by fewer than a dozen threads. He reached into the space below and took out the masks.

'I'm ten miles south,' Gaul said. 'I'll be on-site in three or four minutes. Rachel and Audrey should be unconscious a lot longer than that, but as a precaution I want Holly to leave right now. Have her take either vehicle and just go anywhere, any route. Best if she doesn't tell you where she's going. Again, as a precaution.'

'Good enough,' Dryden said.

'See you when I get there.' Gaul hung up.

The gas was already swirling into the house through the empty window frames. Smoky clumps of it, twisting and snaking. Holly had her mask on; in the last of the clear air, Dryden picked up his own and secured it to his face.

He nodded out through the screen door. 'Gas mortar shells.' His voice sounded filtered and mechanical in his own ears. 'The launchers can be remote operated. Firing range can be several miles.'

They went out through the screen door and stood atop the porch steps. Against the backdrop of lights at the edge of town, the gas cloud hovered like a fog over the field.

Dryden relayed Gaul's last instruction. Holly stared off into the cloud a moment longer, considering it.

'I'll stay with her,' Dryden said. 'I'll make sure she's okay. Go.'

Holly nodded at the gas. 'Could that much of it kill someone? Especially a kid?'

'I don't think so.' He said it confidently, though he wasn't sure at all. He'd been wondering the same thing since almost the first detonation.

'Go,' he said again. 'I'll call you when it's safe to come back.'

She hesitated a few seconds longer, then nodded. She went past him, back into the house. Thirty seconds later he heard one of the vehicles start. The garage door opened, and the Malibu rolled out into the haze. At the end of the driveway it turned right; Dryden watched its taillights disappear to the west. He descended the steps and started into the field.

Gaul made another phone call, even as he strapped into the chopper. He connected the phone to his headset, and over the rotors he heard the call begin to ring.

A man answered. 'This is Hager.'

'Everything's set,' Gaul said. 'Rachel's neutralized on-site, and Dryden's with her. I sent Holly away, but I can call her back when the time comes. She and Dryden are fully in the dark.'

Gaul pictured Hager on his end of the line. The little compound in the Canadian Rockies. It was tough to keep his envy in check, thinking of the place – like imagining your enemy's trophy on its pedestal. It made this uneasy cooperation all the harder.

You had to do what you had to do, though. Whatever it took to bloom.

'Understood,' Hager said. 'Control asset will be airborne in five; expect it on-station above the target area in thirty minutes. We'll go live as soon as we're in range.'

Gaul had seen an example of the control asset before, bolted to its cell tower at the test site in Cold Spring, Utah. The one coming into play tonight wasn't attached to a tower; it was strapped down in the cargo hold of a C-5 Galaxy.

We can't guarantee we'll tie off every loose end you're worried about, Hager had told him, days before. *Marsh, Harris, Dryden's other friends. It's not on me if they still go public against you.*

Would they, though? After what happened at the farmhouse in the next hour, would people like Dennis Marsh really have the nerve to stand up and make waves?

We'll see about that, Gaul thought.

Just over a thousand miles away, in his office in Washington, D.C., Dennis Marsh stared at his computer, his mouth going dry.

On-screen, the phone-intercept program read TRANS-LINK INIT. — CALL STATUS LIVE — 0 MIN, 24 SEC.

At twenty-five seconds he heard Gaul say, 'Copy that. We'll talk after.'

The call went dead with a click.

It occurred to Marsh to wonder what his own expression looked like right now. Not quite one of surprise, he guessed. Maybe just that of a man bitten by a snake he'd been handling.

He reached for his own phone; he already knew the numbers for the phones Sam Dryden and Holly Ferrel had with them. He brought up the on-screen number pad and then stopped.

Gaul had given them those phones. There was no question Gaul's people could monitor voice traffic on them.

347

Shit.

How to warn Dryden and Holly without tipping off anyone else?

Marsh leaned forward in his chair and shut his eyes hard.

Think. Think.

Down in the field, the gas was thicker than it had been on the porch, but it would be gone in a matter of minutes; the wind was moderate but moving steadily, shoving the whole cloud mass slowly east.

Dryden was a hundred feet out from the house now. Watching his step. The gas was visibly thinning already.

Over the ringing that still throbbed in his ears, he heard the chopper coming in. Far south yet, not even visible.

He picked up his speed.

One hundred fifty feet from the house. The cloud was slipping away by the second.

He saw Audrey and Rachel. Straight ahead, a few dozen yards. Lying facedown in the grass. He broke into a run, his feet kicking up swirls of chalky gas residue.

It came to him even before he reached them that something was wrong. Something was missing. He realized what it was in the last five yards: no chill at his temples.

Their minds should've generated that sensation even if they were asleep.

What did it mean? That they were more than asleep? Comatose?

Worse than that?

'Goddammit.' Through the mask, the mutter sounded almost animal.

The chopper was louder now. He looked up and saw it coming north over the city lights, less than two miles out.

He got to Rachel and knelt down beside her. Her hair lay in a tangle around her neck. He reached through it, to her jawline, and pressed his finger to the carotid artery pulse point.

Her pulse was strong.

Still no chill touching him. Not even a trace.

Understanding hit him a second before he rolled her over. He thought of the silhouettes' movements in the field, before the barrage started. Something strange in the way they were walking. All at once he knew what it had been.

They had only been moving one at a time.

He let go of the pulse point, grabbed the shoulder, and shoved hard. The unconscious body rolled onto its back, the hair cascading away from its face.

Which wasn't Rachel's.

He was on his feet in half a second, tearing off the mask, pulling his phone from his pocket as he sprinted into the wind – into the thinnest reaches of the gas. He pulled up the recent call list, stabbing Gaul's number even as the sound of the rotors swelled.

One ring. Two. It connected.

'*Turn the chopper around!*' He screamed it without even listening for a reply. '*Turn around! She sprung the trap! Turn the fucking chopper around!*'

He saw it happen even as he shouted, the aircraft passing over a point maybe a mile south of the farmhouse – well within Rachel's reach, wherever the hell she was. The chopper's pitch and attitude changed abruptly, and as they did Dryden heard men screaming over the phone's earpiece. He pictured the pilot or copilot – it really didn't matter which – taking his hands off the controls and attacking the man beside him. Either way, there was suddenly no one flying the aircraft. It tipped steeply to one side, the tail whipping around like a boom, and a second later the chopper simply plunged. It dropped three hundred feet and exploded in the city sprawl like a percussion bomb. Orange flame and thick black smoke rolled up and away.

Dryden stared. He still had the phone at his ear, but the call had gone dead. He watched the flames seethe and curl.

Five seconds passed.

He had no idea what to do.

What *was* there to do, under the circumstances?

He thought about it a few seconds longer and found he had an answer. He turned off the phone and slipped it back into his pocket and let the gas mask fall at his feet. He glanced at the crash site one last time, then turned and faced east across the field. Around him the gas haze had thinned to nothing, but fifty yards east it was as thick as ever. Thick enough to put him to sleep, if he simply walked into it.

He couldn't say why it made sense to do that – only that he wanted to. It was *all* he wanted.

He got moving, each stride putting him deeper into the cloud, sucking in breath after breath as the air thickened around him.

Chapter Forty-two

He woke with his heart pounding, his body spasming under a surge of ice water. A bucket clattered to the floor. He opened his eyes and found himself hand-cuffed to a chair in the farmhouse's dining room. The table had been shoved aside. The room was clear, and he was sitting in the middle of it.

Rachel stood before him, watching him.

For a second Dryden couldn't understand how he'd gotten here. He remembered seeing the chopper crash, with Gaul on board, and he remembered walking into the gas cloud afterward because—

Because why? Why the hell had he done that?

The answer settled over him. He shut his eyes for a long beat, getting his head around it. When he opened them again Rachel was still watching him, her eyes large, maybe curious.

Was she in there somewhere? The girl who'd fallen asleep on his shoulder? The hope felt like a blade twist-ing in his chest.

Rachel blinked, and the curiosity was gone. In its place Dryden saw only cool appraisal.

'Had to let Holly drive away,' she said. Her voice was

soft, but there was no emotion in it. 'If I'd stopped her, you would've had time to warn off the chopper.'

She went to a chair near the wall and picked up a cell phone; Dryden realized it was his own. She turned it on and opened the call list and showed it to him.

'One of those is Holly's number,' she said. 'I want you to call her and tell her it's okay to come back.'

'I'm not doing that. Force me if you want. I'm not doing it on my own.'

She stared at him, impassive. For a second he expected her to simply lock him again. He waited for the change of mind to come over him – the desire, out of nowhere, to make the call.

Seconds passed. Nothing happened.

Rachel turned aside. She stared off at empty space as if considering options.

'It comes out better if I don't have to make you say it,' she said.

'What?'

'Did Holly show you the notes? I bet she did.'

Dryden nodded.

'Her hand,' Rachel said. 'My handwriting.'

Dryden started to ask what the point was, but stopped. He thought he saw it.

'It's the same with talking,' Rachel said. 'I can force you if it comes to it, but—' She stopped. She turned to him. 'It won't be as convincing as I'd like. I'd rather you did it yourself.'

353

'I'm not going to. You're wasting your time asking.'

'I think you will,' she said. There was something almost like sadness in her voice.

She set the phone back down on the chair. As she did, Dryden glimpsed a surgical scalpel next to it.

'You've tortured people before,' Rachel said. 'You've been there, at least. You've stood and watched it happen.'

Dryden said nothing.

'You've also been trained to resist torture,' Rachel continued. 'But I have to think this is one of those areas where training is different than the real thing.'

'I'm not calling her,' Dryden said. 'Nothing you do to me is going to change that.'

'It's not what I'm going to do to you. It's what you're going to do to me.'

She came forward and sat astride his knees, facing him with her arms draped behind his neck. Her face hovered six inches from his own.

'You were very good to me,' she said. 'Even I can appreciate that. I don't really want to see you hurting. I think you should call her, before this gets bad.'

She waited for a response.

He offered none.

'Okay,' she said.

Her arms slipped down behind him, to the handcuffs binding him to the back of the chair. He heard the lock disengage, and then his arms were free.

Rachel stood and stepped back from him. She

reached behind her and picked up the scalpel, studying its blade in the light.

Dryden considered the distance between himself and her. Five or six feet. He could cross it in far less than a second and knock her unconscious with a blow to the head. Audrey, wherever she was, would be armed, but he'd deal with that problem in its own—

The will to do any of that simply left him. Blew away like a piece of lint in the wind.

'Not even worth thinking about,' Rachel said. 'Any plan you come up with, I can stop you from even wanting to try it.'

He looked up at her. What he'd heard in her voice earlier – that edge of sadness – was in her eyes now. Just barely, but it was there.

'In a few seconds you're going to take this scalpel out of my hand and attack me with it,' she said. 'You won't be able to help yourself.'

Dryden stared. There was no point pleading out loud.

'All you have to do is call her,' Rachel said.

'You can hear what I'm thinking. Can't you already tell I'm not going to do this?'

'I know what you're thinking right now. I have no idea what you'll be thinking in thirty seconds. Neither do you.'

'I'm not going to call her.'

'We'll see.'

It happened before he could say anything more. The

change came over him so quickly it altered the color saturation of his vision, as if the blood vessels in his eyes had distended. Then contemplation itself was gone and there was only the girl, standing before him, flinching back as he exploded from the chair and grabbed the scalpel from her hand. Her eyes were huge and terrified, her breath rushing in. He grabbed her and pivoted and threw her across the table, slamming her onto it, feeling it buckle and snap beneath the two of them. Her arms came up, fighting him, both of her hands grappling for one of his – the one that held the scalpel. He broke the grip and slashed the top of one of her forearms, shirt fabric and skin opening up, blood spilling fast. He could hardly think of it as blood, though. It seemed more like nectar, her whole body a vessel full of it, pulsing with it, intense as her desperation to live. He grabbed a fistful of her hair and wrenched her head back, baring her throat, and his teeth had just touched her skin there when—

As quickly as it had come, the mindset vanished. As if she'd pushed a button and released him from it. Dryden threw himself off of her and fell backward, propelling his body across the floor until his back hit the wall. Not stopping even then; pushing away until he'd reached the corner, the farthest he could physically get from her.

He could remember it all: the intensity of the compulsion, the almost erotic craving to put his teeth into her skin, to feel her blood gush inside his mouth.

Tears now, stinging his eyes, the first tears he'd cried since the day he buried his family. Within seconds he could see nothing but the swimming colors of the room.

Rachel sat up. She turned sharply toward the sound of footsteps crossing the house, stopping just out of sight.

'I'm fine,' Rachel said. 'Go back to your watch. Now.'

The footsteps retreated. The screen door opened and banged shut.

Rachel stood. She pulled back her shirt sleeve and studied the slash wound. It was bleeding steadily, but she seemed unfazed. She went to the chair in the middle of the room. She spun it around and sat in it, leaning forward and staring down on him.

'Call Holly,' she said.

'I can't.'

'Of course you can.'

Dryden shook his head and looked down, still trying to get control of the tears.

For a long time Rachel didn't speak. When she finally did, her voice was softer than before.

'Ever heard of a place called Lucero, Colorado?'

Dryden shook his head again.

'My mom told me about it, in Building Sixteen. In our cell. She talked about it all the time. Her own mom and dad took her camping there when she was a little girl. It's up in the mountains, and there are horses you can ride, and trails you can walk on. But what my mom really liked was that you could rent canoes at the lake above town. You could rent them even at night, and that was the best thing, because at night all this cold air would come spilling down out of the mountains higher up, and the lake water would still be warm, so this little fog layer would rise up off the surface, just about as high as the canoe. It would cover the whole lake, and in the moonlight it looked like you were riding on a cloud. The last thing my mom said to me, before I sent Holly those messages, was that we were going to go there, to Lucero. Soon as we got out we were going there, and we were going to rent a canoe and go out on the lake the very first night.'

Her voice had changed pitch, just noticeably. Her throat was constricting.

'That's all she wanted,' Rachel said. 'A regular life, with her little girl, where she could take her to see a place like that when she felt like it.'

'Holly didn't know what would happen to your mom, Rachel. How could she have—'

'All she had to do was what I begged her to do. Just talk to someone, any reporter in the world. That e-mail address, the things they would've seen in it—'

'She was scared out of her mind. Anyone else would've been, too.'

'I didn't ask anyone else. I asked her.'

'She regrets what she did. She'd take it back if—'

'I finally went there, you know. To Lucero. About a year ago. They still rent out canoes. Even at night.'

'Holly Ferrel didn't kill your mom. The people who made all that happen are dead. You got them. It's over.'

Rachel swallowed and forced resolve back into her voice. Her eyes hardened again.

'Call her,' she said.

'You know I'm not going to.'

'You might change your mind. There are other things I can make you do to me. Some of them, you'd rather die than do.'

Dryden understood. At the thought of it, his insides seemed to contract. Like filthy rags being twisted.

'You better call her,' Rachel said.

'Please don't do this—'

'It's up to you—'

'*I'm not going to fucking betray her!*'

Rachel took a deep breath. Steadied herself.

'Don't,' Dryden said.

'Sorry.'

Dryden fixed in his mind the image of Rachel in the first moment he'd met her, pleading with him to trust her, to protect her. Maybe if he could hold on to that picture, maybe—

'Headlights!'

Audrey's voice, out at the screen door.

Dryden felt the change of mind brush past him like a wing. There and gone. Rachel had already let it go. She rose from the chair.

'Chevy Malibu,' Audrey said. 'Coming up the driveway.'

Rachel crossed toward the doorway to the living room.

'This isn't you,' Dryden said.

She stopped. Looked down at him.

'This is only what those two trained you to be,' he said. 'You wouldn't be this person if your mom had raised you.'

If it stung her, she didn't show it. She held his gaze and spoke evenly. 'She didn't, though.'

Headlights washed through the house as the car pulled up in front. Rachel turned back to the doorway, and a second later she was gone.

Chapter Forty-three

Dryden got to his feet and followed. He entered the living room in time to see Rachel reach the screen door. Audrey was holding it open with her shoulder; in her hands she had a 12-gauge shotgun. Looking past Rachel, she saw Dryden start across the room.

'We're done with him, right?' Audrey said. She was already turning, raising the weapon toward him.

'Leave him alone,' Rachel said.

Audrey looked at her. 'Why?'

'Because I told you to.'

Rachel said it like she was used to giving orders. Audrey reacted like she was used to taking them. After Rachel went through the doorway, Audrey turned to face Dryden again, the gun falling away to her side.

'Keep your distance,' she said, then followed Rachel.

Dryden crossed to the door as it banged shut. He pushed it open and stepped out into the darkness and the cool air of the porch. A mile south, several blocks of the town had become a sea of police and fire response flashers. Tendrils of smoke still rose from the crash site. Closer, the field had cleared entirely of the gas. There was no sign of the two decoys where they'd been lying. There'd been more than enough time for them to wake up and leave, no doubt confused as all hell.

The Malibu was parked and idling in the dooryard, its lights stabbing through the dust it'd kicked up.

Rachel stood at the top of the porch steps. Audrey had descended them and stood five feet out from their base, training the shotgun on the car.

The headlights cut out.

The engine died.

Holly Ferrel shoved open the driver's door and stood. She ignored Audrey and stared up at Rachel.

Seconds passed.

Holly stood there, saying nothing. Her arms were low at her sides, her posture the embodiment of defenselessness.

Dryden couldn't read Holly's thoughts, but he knew what she had to be thinking. It occurred to him that he was watching the most honest apology a person could offer. Words could be bullshit. Thoughts and feelings couldn't. Holly was just standing there, letting Rachel take it all in. *Here's what's in my head. Take it for what it is.*

Down in front of the steps, Audrey was looking back and forth from Holly to Rachel. She seemed unnerved, and Dryden thought he knew why: Though Audrey could hear everything coming out of Holly's mind, she could only guess what Rachel might be thinking in response.

To Rachel, Audrey said, 'What are you waiting for?'

Rachel didn't answer.

362

Dryden moved to the porch rail near the old swing, putting himself ten feet to Rachel's right. He could see her in profile. Could see her eyes reflecting the distant city light.

They were filmed with tears.

Audrey crossed to the foot of the steps and looked up at the girl. 'This is what you wanted. It doesn't matter if she feels bad. It doesn't even matter if she means it – that doesn't undo what she did.'

Rachel made no reply. She didn't even look down at Audrey. She was staring at Holly, and Holly was staring back.

'*Hey,*' Audrey said.

Rachel flinched. She blinked away the moisture and looked at Audrey.

'It has to happen,' Audrey said. 'You know it. There's no reason to keep listening to all this.'

For a moment Rachel didn't respond. Then she took a hard breath and nodded.

Audrey looked relieved. 'How do you want to do it?'

Rachel pointed to the shotgun. 'Put it in her hands.'

Audrey smiled at the idea. She turned, crossed the dooryard, and shoved the weapon at Holly.

Holly made no move to take it. She continued staring at Rachel, her eyes searching. Begging.

Then they simply went slack.

She turned and took the shotgun from Audrey.

Dryden doubted Holly had ever touched a firearm in her life, but she cradled this one with casual ease. She turned it in the light spill from the house and clicked off the safety, pressed the slide release, and opened the action just enough to see that there was a shell in the chamber. She racked it back shut with authority.

Then she shouldered the weapon, swung it to the side, and blew the top half of Audrey's head off.

She'd cycled another shell into the chamber by the time the body dropped. She turned toward the steps then and leveled the weapon straight at Rachel.

'No!' Dryden shouted.

Rachel spoke just above a whisper. 'It has to end.'

The girl had her eyes closed. She sank to a sitting position on the top step. Drew her knees against herself. Bowed her head.

Holly advanced with the shotgun shouldered and aimed at her.

Dryden crossed to Rachel in two long steps. He dropped himself in front of her, shielding her from the gun's firing angle.

Holly changed her position in response. She ascended the broad steps along the opposite handrail, keeping the gun out of Dryden's reach. Its barrel stayed centered on Rachel's head as she climbed.

It was impossible to keep Rachel shielded from all sides. Dryden settled for simply pulling her against himself, her head to his chest, so that any shot pattern that hit her would also hit him.

'It has to end,' Rachel whispered again. It came out high and cracked, and Dryden felt her body begin shaking with quiet sobs. 'I want it to end. I'm sick of it all.'

The shotgun trembled in Holly's hands but remained leveled.

'Let Holly go, Rachel,' Dryden said softly. 'You're going to be okay now. Audrey and Sandra are both gone.'

Holly was on the plank surface of the porch, the shotgun aimed down at Rachel's face from three feet away. Dryden saw her snug it tightly into her shoulder.

'Let her go,' he whispered to Rachel. He kissed the top of her head. 'It's already over. Let her go.'

He felt her tears soaking through his shirt. She was shaking harder. Losing control.

'It's over,' he said.

Holly gripped the shotgun tighter – then faltered.

Rachel took her arms from around her knees, turned, and hugged Dryden. She held on with what must've been all her strength.

A second later Holly exhaled deeply and lowered the gun. Her body sagged as if she'd just been cut from restraints. She went to the rail and pitched the weapon into the grass, then turned and stared at Rachel. For a moment she hesitated, unsure what to do – maybe unsure what to feel. Then she crossed to the top of the steps and sat down against the two of them. Sensing her, Rachel turned in place and put her arms around her. Holly pulled the girl close and held her as she cried.

*

For the next minute none of them spoke or moved. Dryden heard Rachel's breathing become rhythmic, regular, as if she'd fallen asleep. He guessed it was something more than that, though. He thought of the surveillance video from outside Building 16: Rachel being carried out to the car, in the first moments after the nightmare part of her life had begun. *Brain-locked*, Gaul had said. Maybe this moment was the other end of the tunnel she'd entered that night. Maybe she would sleep for a day and a half. She had every right to.

Somewhere inside the house, a ringtone sounded. Dryden's phone, in the dining room where Rachel had left it.

It rang a second time, the sound filtering out through the screen door and into the night.

'I've got her,' Holly whispered.

Dryden nodded, separated from the two of them, and got to his feet. He crossed the porch and entered the house and got the phone on its fifth ring.

'This is Dryden.'

Cole Harris's voice came over the line. 'Sam.'

'Cole. Where are you—'

'Please just listen,' Harris said. 'I've heard from Dennis Marsh, and I need to tell you something. No matter what happens, you have to sit tight there at the farmhouse. Don't leave. Okay?'

Dryden had made his way back across the house to the front door. He pushed it open and stepped out onto the porch planking. Holly was staring at him. Rachel was still unconscious in her arms.

'Sam?' Harris said. 'Did you hear me?'

'Don't leave the farmhouse,' Dryden said. 'That's the whole message?'

'That's the whole message.'

'I understand,' Dryden said.

He ended the call, pocketed the phone, and went to the porch rail. He looked at the road to the south. He turned left and right to study where it led to the horizon in each direction.

The glow of headlights appeared beyond a low rise, a mile west. To the east was a more diffuse light, farther out, but definitely there – another vehicle or more coming in.

'We need to get out of here,' Dryden said. 'Right now.'

He was already moving, crossing to where Holly sat with Rachel.

'What is it?' Holly asked.

Dryden crouched and got Rachel in his arms, lifting her and cradling her as Holly stood. The girl remained unresponsive.

'Get the shotgun,' Dryden said. 'And get in the car.'

He descended the steps to the dooryard, jogging for the Malibu. Holly, coming down right behind him, picked up the 12-gauge as she followed.

'Passenger side,' Dryden said.

Holly went past him, rounding the front of the car.

She opened the door and got in and rested the shotgun across the console and the backseat. Dryden hunched down and eased Rachel into her arms.

'Tell me what's going on,' Holly said.

'That was Harris on the phone.'

'And?'

'And he didn't say goldenrod.'

Chapter Forty-four

They were halfway down the long gravel drive when the twin pinprick of headlights finally crested the rise to the west. It was clear at a glance the vehicle was approaching fast, from a distance of maybe a quarter mile. A second later another set appeared just behind them.

Dryden looked east in time to see the lights in that direction break into view. Half a mile away, give or take.

In both directions, the incoming vehicles were closer than any available cross street.

Dryden pictured the road as he'd seen it when he and Holly had first arrived here. It was like a million others out in farm country: two-lane blacktop with waist-deep runoff ditches on either side. If he pulled out onto that road, they would be trapped on it as if it were a suspension bridge.

'Hold on to her,' Dryden said.

He jammed his foot hard on the brake. The Malibu skidded to a halt in a cloud of dust, swirling gray in the moonlight – Dryden had kept the car's headlights off.

Now he dropped it into reverse and stepped on the gas. The vehicle shot backward. When it was doing twenty, he took his foot off the accelerator, jerked the wheel counterclockwise, and shoved the selector to neutral. The front end went sideways and the night-time fields spun 180 degrees around them. When the world stabilized, the car was pointed back toward the farmhouse. Dryden put it in drive and accelerated again, as fast as the vehicle could go. He veered to the right at the top of the drive, passing the garage on its east side and heading north into the grassland behind the farmhouse.

He considered the viewpoints of the approaching drivers; at their distance they couldn't have seen the Malibu yet – a dark shape against dark terrain – but they would see the dust above the driveway when they turned in, and the tire tracks denting the grass beyond. They would follow. No question of that.

'Who are they?' Holly asked.

In her arms, Rachel still had her eyes closed.

Dryden glanced in the mirror; the nearest of the vehicles braked and slowed before the foot of the driveway.

He had only a hunch as to who they were. He hoped he was wrong about it.

Hager was in his favorite spot again. The big window in his office, overlooking the work floor with its glass-walled stations.

The place was hopping tonight. All twelve stations were occupied. Within each of them, in the deep bloody light, lay a controller, eyes closed and focused on the work. Each was connected to a human subject – a mark, to use the popular term – down there in rural Kansas.

More than a week ago, after Martin Gaul had gotten in touch to lay out his proposal, each controller had chosen a mark from one of the three test areas – the unlucky little towns hosting the antennas. The controllers had given their marks special instructions, sending them on road trips to the boondocks north of Topeka, to hole up in run-down motels or to pitch tents in campgrounds, and to await further instructions.

Hager had been more than a little nervous about the whole thing. Once the marks actually left their hometowns and got out of range of their respective towers, there would be no way to get into their heads again until Gaul called with the go-ahead.

Until the airborne asset got into position.

More than a few nights, Hager had lain awake wondering if the marks would really be there when the controllers tried to reach them again. Maybe they would all slip away into the ether, after a week or more of freedom from the voices in their heads. Time and again, he'd found his mind full of Yeats's falcon in its widening gyre.

Watching the controllers now, Hager felt the deepest kind of relief – and a little amusement. Every last one of the marks had turned up where they were supposed to. Any dog trainer would've been proud.

*

Dryden turned on the headlights a hundred yards beyond the farmhouse. There was no advantage in leaving them off any longer – the pursuers couldn't miss the Malibu's trail through the grass – and there was plenty of risk in going without them.

The moment the beams came on, a distant line of trees appeared out of the dark, a quarter mile ahead.

Ahead was north. They were driving toward the back of the property the farmhouse sat on. Presumably there was someone else's property butted up against it – some other plot of farmland stretching farther north, until it tied into the next blacktop two-lane.

By the time they'd covered half the distance to the trees, it was clear they would never reach the next road north. The dense tree line ran unbroken across the landscape ahead of them. A perfect barricade marking the back of the property. Dryden veered left and right, sweeping the headlights like search beams. There was no gap visible anywhere in the woods.

Behind them, the first pair of lights rounded the farmhouse and came on straight toward them. A second and third set followed.

Dryden swung the Malibu left, toward the west edge of the property. Another farm bordered it there, and beyond it should be a road running north to south. There would be a ditch before the road, but with any luck there would be a break in it somewhere – a place meant for tractors and other vehicles to come and go. The trick would be finding one of those points before the pursuers caught up with them.

Dryden checked the mirror. Four sets of lights back there now, strung out in a line, snaking their way up the field.

He turned his attention forward again—

Something was wrong.

He couldn't place it, but the grass straight ahead was different in some way that made his scalp prickle. Something in how it caught the headlights.

'What is that?' Holly asked.

Dryden knew the answer half a second later. Which was too late.

The Malibu's front end dropped sickeningly, and water surged up over the hood onto the windshield. Holly screamed as she and Rachel were thrown forward by the instant deceleration. Dryden reached for them; he caught some of their momentum with his arm as his own body was slammed against the steering wheel.

Then everything was still – or almost still. The car was bobbing in place, rocking side to side and front to back.

All around it were the tops of the weeds that fully choked the shallow pond, their height just about perfect to match the ankle-high grass in the surrounding field. There was no open water at all. In the headlights, the pond had been all but invisible.

The car settled another six inches and touched

bottom; the water level was midway up the side windows. The engine stuttered and then died; its intake ports were underwater. The beams from the headlamps shone out through the murk beneath the surface.

But already there was other light playing over the tops of the weeds. Brightening by the second as the pursuing cars closed in.

'What do we do?' Holly asked. She pulled the handle and tried to shove open the door on her side. It wouldn't budge. There were thousands of pounds of water pressure working against it.

Rachel's breathing remained steady and slow. She clung to Holly unconsciously, like a sleeping infant.

Dryden twisted in his seat and got hold of the shotgun. In the tight space of the car it was almost impossible to maneuver the thing; before he'd even gotten it past the seatback, he heard the first of the other vehicles come to a stop somewhere close behind them. Its engine went idle, and a door opened and closed.

Both he and Holly went quiet. They turned and looked at each other, listening.

A rifle cracked like a stick of dynamite going off almost on top of them. The bullet whined off the car's roof and hit the water twenty feet ahead.

'Down!' Dryden said. 'Flat as you can get.'

Holly was already moving, shoving Rachel even lower than herself, down into the footwell on the passenger side. She lay her own body flat on the seat, curled fetal.

The rifle fired again. The bullet punched through the back window near the top, went through the seatback above Holly, and smashed into the glove box. In the same moment Dryden heard another vehicle brake and slide to a stop. Another door opened and shut, and the sound that followed was unmistakable: a pump shotgun being cycled. A second later the passenger window exploded, and water surged down into the space where Rachel lay.

Rachel had been hovering somewhere warm inside herself. She had a vague memory of a feeling she associated with fireplaces. A feeling that rolled off somebody and pressed comfortably around her, like a hot bath. Was it Sam? Yes — Sam had sent out that feeling from almost the moment she'd met him. Now there was someone else doing that. Someone holding her, protecting her.

Holly. It was Holly.

Coming from her, the feeling had a different flavor. It took Rachel back to a time when someone else had held her this way. It felt wonderful, and for minutes on end she'd simply clung to the sensation of it. She'd let the rest of the world fade out to nothing. This was all she wanted, for now. This was—

Freezing cold.

Rachel blinked. Her eyes stung.

What was happening?

She was underwater, and hands were grasping for her, pulling at her while voices screamed.

Something boomed, like a sharp drumbeat, though she knew that wasn't it.

She blinked again and shook her head, and the world came all the way back to her, crisp and hard and clear.

She was with Sam and Holly in the car. The car was stuck in deep water, which was flooding in through a broken-out window. Another gunshot sounded – a high-powered rifle, she thought. She turned toward the sound of the weapon, and felt her mind automatically running the complex formulas for locking.

Marcus Till worked the bolt action of his Winchester 70. He heard the spent casing land in the grass to his right, not far from the man with the Mossberg 500, who'd just arrived.

That there might be other people working in the service of the Ghost had never crossed Marcus's mind until ten minutes ago, when he'd found he wasn't alone on the back country roads leading to this place. He wasn't sure how to feel about that development, though in some deep part of himself he seemed to be relieved at it. It meant there were other hands to help carry the weight of guilt. He supposed it might even mean he could let himself off the hook entirely, looking back on a night like this: He would never know for sure that his bullets had killed the people in this car, whoever they were. It was possible the Mossberg's shots would actually do the killing. It would be something to tell himself, anyway.

Marcus shouldered the Winchester. He just had to buckle down and do this, that was all. He lowered his eye to the sights and took a steadying breath – then cocked his head.

He turned to the man with the shotgun. The guy had it braced on his thigh for reloading. He hadn't so much as glanced in Marcus's direction, and yet—

There was something grating about the man.

Something in the way he carried himself, or maybe in the look on his face. He seemed like a smug little son of a whore, the kind that'd lipped off to Marcus in bars, back in the day, and gotten his blood up. Marcus stared. He couldn't say why he suddenly felt so riled, only that he did, and that he had a mind to do something about it.

Sensing eyes on him, the guy turned. 'What?'

Marcus stepped forward, drew his arm back, and brought one fist looping down into the guy's face like a ten-pound sledge.

He felt the bridge of the man's nose crunch like a walnut shell. The guy screamed, but only briefly – he blacked out and flopped on his back in the short grass. Still pissed at him, Marcus swiped up his shotgun, turned, and heaved it out into the pond. Even as he did so, the headlights of the next two arrivals swept the ground around him. He turned to them, the glare of their high beams only fanning his anger.

He shouldered the rifle again and took aim high on the windshield of the nearest of the two cars – no need to kill anyone, he just wanted them to bug the fuck off.

He fired. The top of the windshield cratered and pulled loose from its frame. From inside the car someone screamed.

'Get out of here!' Marcus shouted. He racked the rifle's bolt again, and past the glare of the car's headlights he saw the driver fumbling for his gear selector. A second later the vehicle lurched backward, turned clumsily around, and then sped away across the field. The second car had come to a stop thirty yards shy of the pond. Marcus swung the rifle toward it and simply waited. He could almost sense the driver struggling against himself in there. Or struggling against the Ghost, maybe. Which Marcus could sympathize with. He meant to send the jackass away all the same. He kept the rifle leveled, watching for a response.

Rachel had only the smallest part of her attention on her surroundings inside the car. She knew her head was above water now. Sam and Holly had pulled her up. They were asking if she was okay, and she was nodding, but she was only barely aware of doing so. All the rest of her attention was outside the vehicle, locking the big man with the rifle. Through his eyes she watched the last car suddenly reverse itself, its tires briefly spinning in the grass before they dug in. The vehicle backed around in a half circle and lumbered away toward the farmhouse. Rachel watched it go, then turned the big man toward the pond again. She regripped the rifle, holding it like a spear, and chucked it far out into the weed-filled pond. She heard the splash with her own ears as well as his.

There wasn't much left to do. This man, and the one who'd brought the shotgun, could be sent away without any more trouble—

Rachel cut herself off in the middle of the thought.

The big man had something strange going on in his head. The effect was hard to notice; Rachel had missed it at first, but it was there. It seemed almost that his mind had a second doorway leading away from it, different than the one she'd entered through. This second doorway was open. She had no real sense of what lay on the other side of it, but—

She'd encountered something like it before. Only it hadn't been in a person's head. She'd felt it . . . at the tower. In Utah. That day in the desert, with Sam.

The thing beyond the door was a kind of tunnel. The one in the desert had seemed to plunge away beneath her, deep into the ground. This one went up. It stretched up like a kite string, toward something high in the night above the dark farm fields.

Rachel followed it, her mind climbing through it like a bullet along a gun barrel. She caught a mental glimpse of some sort of airplane, and then she was shooting away down another tunnel, which connected the plane to some distant place – this second tunnel was very long.

She had done this in the desert, too. She had found a man's mind at the far end of the long tunnel, but—

But that day, she'd had no idea what any of it meant. This time was different. She had her memory back. She knew who the people at the other end of the tunnel were. She knew the sorts of things they did – how they treated the people they took control of.

Most important of all, this time she had her old tricks handy.

Hager had just turned from the window to pick up his phone from his desk – Gaul should've long since gotten back to him – when he heard someone yelling down on the work floor.

He spun to face the window again.

The shouting was coming from one of the stations; it belonged to a controller named Leonard Bell. But it was an assistant who was making the noise – a young woman standing in the station's doorway.

Leonard Bell was no longer lying down with electrodes pasted to his forehead. He was up on his feet, and his face was covered with blood; it looked black in the red light of the workroom. Hager wondered for only a moment where the blood had come from – it was obvious a second later. Calmly, even methodically, Bell was digging his own fingernails into his face and raking deep gouges into the skin. Hager could see the muscles in his forearms strain under the force he was using – like a man applying steady but immense pressure to a wrench handle. Tearing open his own face as if it were a simple chore to be done.

All at once Bell seemed to notice the assistant. He pivoted and lurched toward her, and the girl turned and ran, screaming.

Hager was already moving. He shoved open his office door, crossed the landing, and took the stairs down to floor level, three at a time. He saw the assistant coming more or less in his direction; he dodged past her and crashed head-on into Bell, bear-hugging the guy and bringing him down onto the concrete floor. Christ, the man's face was a shredded mess. He strained and bucked against Hager's hold, little red droplets flying as he shook his head.

'What the fuck's wrong with him?'

Hager looked up. The question had come from Seth Cobb, standing in the doorway of his own station, nearby.

Before Hager could answer, Bell went slack in his arms. In almost the same instant, the man seemed to become aware of the damage to his face – aware of the pain. He took a hissing breath, worked a hand free, and put it delicately to one ripped-up cheek. He made a low moaning sound, full of fear and confusion.

Cobb stepped out of his doorway. He seemed to be coming to help, but then he stopped. He turned in place and surveyed his surroundings. His eyes settled on a steel support column that came up out of the floor and rose to the ceiling, forty feet above. The column was an I beam standing upright, each of its flat faces about twelve inches wide. Cobb took two long strides to the beam and grabbed the edges of the nearest side, like a karate student holding a pine board he meant to break with his head.

Hager saw what he planned to do, absurd as it was.

'No!' Hager shouted.

Cobb reared back and swung his whole upper body forward, like an upside-down pendulum. He didn't take the impact with his forehead; he took it with his face. His nose and chin and cheekbones hit the steel with a sickening crack. To Hager it sounded like ceramic coffee mugs being crunched under a tire.

Cobb's grip on the steel didn't so much as falter. He leaned back – there was blood coming out of his mouth and nose like a trickle from a tap – steadied himself, and rammed his face once more into the steel, harder than before. Hager saw a tooth skitter onto the concrete at Cobb's feet, and a second later the man blacked out and dropped in a heap where he'd stood.

All the controllers were watching now, along with the assistants and the few technicians present. Everyone stood frozen, unable to process what they were seeing.

Hager, still lying on top of Bell, looked around and found all eyes turning to him for answers. Never in his life had he felt so unable to offer any.

Except—

Well, there were a *few* things he could do, he

supposed, now that he thought about it. Yes, he did have the answers. They were all coming to him, just like that.

He let go of Bell, pushed himself up, and got on his feet.

'Everybody out!' he shouted. 'Right now. That's a direct order.'

Thirty seconds later he had the building to himself; the others had even carried Cobb and Bell away. Hager went to the metal staircase that led to his office and climbed halfway up – just high enough that he could see out above the tops of the glass-walled workstations. He swept his gaze over the vast chamber and found it drawn to something in the far corner, in the shadows near the restrooms and the supply closet.

It was the fuel tank for the furnace and the generator. The thing was massive – it was, in fact, simply the trailer of an 18-wheel tanker truck, flown up here aboard a C-5 and rolled into position. Various hoses now connected it to the building's heating and power systems. Hager descended the stairs again and sprinted across the huge room toward it.

The hoses were secured to the tank's outflow ports with heavy-duty clamps, and though Hager had no expertise working with any of this hardware, he could see at a glance what it would take to unfasten them. There were bolts securing the clamps. The tools to loosen them – no doubt the same tools that had been used to tighten them – lay on utility shelves twenty feet away. Hager went to the shelves, grabbed the only three wrenches he could see, and took them to the nearest port sticking out of the tank. The first wrench he tried fit snugly and turned the bolt with no effort at all.

A dozen turns later, the clamp gave way. Fuel erupted from the port like a sideways geyser, blasting the hose and clamp away and spraying in a gush toward the open space of the work floor. The stink of it filled Hager's sinuses and lungs. It made his eyes water. Some kind of alarm began sounding at the front end of the tank. It was like the beeping of a forklift backing up, only deeper and maybe a bit faster. It sounded frantic.

None of it was any cause for concern. Hager had never felt so confident of purpose before.

He dropped the wrenches and walked away from the tank, back the way he'd come from. The shower of fuel soaked his back as he crossed through it. He paid the sensation no mind. He sloshed through the puddles that were filling every concavity in the concrete floor. The first glass-walled workstations went by on his left. He ignored them. He was headed for one station in particular, the one where he was sure to find what he needed.

Cobb's station.

Hager reached it and passed through the open doorway. Even this far from the tank, a film of the spreading fuel had begun seeping under the walls.

Hager went to the desk on the far side of the station.

He opened the shallow tray drawer at the top, and saw immediately what he was after.

A Bic cigarette lighter.

Dryden watched Rachel. It was clear her attention was directed somewhere far away, though who or what she was focusing on, he couldn't guess.

The shooting had stopped more than a minute ago. Since then, there'd been no more sounds from outside the submerged car. Dryden and Holly had simply waited, keeping Rachel above the water and letting her do whatever she was doing.

All at once the girl blinked. She looked around, meeting Holly's eyes and then Dryden's.

'That's the end of that problem,' Rachel said.

Before either of them could ask what she meant, she turned her focus away again. After a moment, Dryden heard movement out at the edge of the pond. Little grunts of exertion and words of encouragement. One man helping another to his feet.

In succession, two car doors opened and closed. Engines, already running, revved and slipped into gear. Less than a minute later the vehicles were gone, and there was nothing to hear but the chirping of night insects in the field.

Chapter Forty-five

The Ford Escape was still in the farmhouse's garage. They changed into dry clothes in the house. Holly's shirts and pants, though too big for Rachel, worked well enough with the cuffs and sleeves rolled. Before they left, Dryden took his phone from his soaked pants and dried it out the best he could. It still worked. He pulled up the recent call list and tapped Harris's number at the top.

'Remember the cop that was going to nail you for public intoxication,' Dryden said, 'and she let you go because you sang her Stevie Wonder's "Isn't She Lovely?"'

'Sure.'

'You remember the exact place it happened?'

'Yes.'

'Meet us there Wednesday at two in the afternoon. And bring Marsh.'

'Is that the whole message?' Harris asked.

'Goldenrod,' Dryden said.

He ended the call and tossed the phone in the trash. Holly left hers behind, too; the phones were a type that had built-in GPS and could be tracked by the phone company.

It was plausible enough that the Escape had some kind of tracking on board, too. They left it in a parking lot in downtown Topeka and paid cash for three bus tickets.

The meeting place was a café on the waterfront in Galveston, Texas. The day was hot, and the Gulf of Mexico lay sharp and blue under a clear sky.

The five of them took a table on the patio, far from any other diners. Rachel seemed shy around Harris and Marsh; she sat between Dryden and Holly and leaned on one or the other in turn.

There was an idea circling at the edges of Dryden's thoughts. An unwelcome stray, scratching to be let in. It had been there since around the time they'd left Kansas. He was sure Rachel had picked up on it by now, though he'd done his best to keep it at the margins. But there was no holding it back forever. In the next few minutes, the door would open wide for it.

'A couple of nights ago,' Marsh said, 'Western Dynamics suffered a major setback with its program. Maybe the three of you already knew that.'

'No great loss for the world,' Dryden said.

'The tower sites are shut down indefinitely,' Marsh said. 'We don't know the status of any of the company's operatives, including the next-gen group – the children who were given the drug in utero. Presumably they're all sequestered away somewhere. The people in charge won't want to plug anyone into the towers again while Rachel's still an existing threat.' Marsh glanced at the girl, then continued. 'The three of you need to understand, this is *only* a setback for these people. Not the end of the road. Even if it were the end for this company, someone else would pick up the ball. The technology in play here is like drone aircraft; it's never going back in the box. The kinds of powerful interests that want to see it developed – they always get their way, eventually. In this case, those people will always want Rachel out of the equation. The deal Gaul pretended to make with you – allowing Rachel's genetic changes to be reversed – would probably have been impossible to implement, even if he'd honored it. Not that the treatment wouldn't work, but someone would've had her killed before it was over.'

Harris said, 'She needs to hide for the rest of her life. There's no place she'd ever be safe in the open. Foreign countries with nonextradition policies – nothing like that would be good enough.'

Dryden didn't bother nodding. All of those things were obvious. He imagined they were obvious to Rachel, too.

'For starters,' Marsh said, 'my guess is they'll relaunch the manhunt for the guy with the dirty bomb, who happens to look just like you, Mr Dryden.'

'How can they do that?' Holly asked. 'They went on TV and said the suspect was dead.'

Marsh shrugged. 'They'll say they got it wrong. The government screwing up – it's not a hard thing to convince people of. And that's only one of the means they'll use to hunt you. In time they'll whip up a reason to put *your* face on the news, Miss Ferrel. My point is that you three need to go deep under, if you want to stay alive. If you're thinking of some little village in the Ivory Coast where you can help dig wells or teach English, you better pick some place where Western newspapers never show up. Some place where there's no Peace Corps presence. No tourism. The three of you need to do more than get off the grid. You need to vanish off the earth. I'll be honest: I'm not sure it's possible.'

Dryden could almost hear the hinges creaking inside his mind. The scrape of claws scrabbling through.

Rachel took hold of his arm and shook her head. She knew. Of course she knew.

'You're right,' Dryden said to Marsh. 'But it won't be the three of us vanishing. Just two.'

He saw Holly turn to him, at the edge of his vision. 'What are you talking about?'

Dryden kept his eyes on Marsh. 'You know some of these people, don't you. The people at the tops of these companies, and the people in government who serve them.'

Marsh nodded. 'I know a few.'

'You know other kinds of people in government, too,' Dryden said. 'The kind who aren't corrupted all the way. Who aren't so cozy with these interests. You can't be the only Boy Scout left.'

'Not quite.'

'Then here's what's going to happen,' Dryden said.

He spent two minutes laying out the idea. By the time he'd finished, Marsh's expression had gone slack. For the longest time, the man only sat there, thinking.

At last Marsh said, 'If I help you do that, it'll be the end of my career.'

'It will be,' Dryden said.

'Even setting that aside, it's a tall order.'

'You're the secretary of Homeland Security,' Dryden said. 'You answer to the president of the United States. Don't tell me you can't make the phone calls to get these people together in a room.'

'I can do it, one way or another. What I can't do is ensure your safety, if you go through with this.'

'It's not my safety I'm trying to ensure,' Dryden said. He nodded to Rachel and Holly. 'It's theirs.'

Marsh shrugged with his eyebrows. 'Them, it would help. You . . . you could end up dead. Or detained at Guantanamo Bay. They'd probably make me sign the transfer forms. I've sent people there before.'

'So have I,' Dryden said, 'but I don't think I'll be there when this is over. I don't think I'll be dead, either.'

Beside him, Rachel was holding it together, though it was a struggle. Then he felt her hand tighten on his arm – a reaction to what he would say next.

'What do you expect to be?' Marsh said.

'Bait,' Dryden said. 'What else? Maybe they'll rough me up for a while at first. Maybe they'll use enhanced interrogation techniques, and have a mind reader from Western Dynamics present, for good measure. They might get a lot out of me that way, but they won't find out where Rachel and Holly have gone, because I won't know. Once these people figure that out, I'll be of no more value to them. At which point they'll probably kill me, if they're stupid – but they're not stupid. So what I expect them to do is send me home, and watch me for the rest of my life, in the hope Rachel shows up at my door someday.' He paused. Now that it came to saying the last part, he found he had to force the words. 'For her sake, she can never do that.'

Rachel started to shake her head, but stopped herself, and a moment later she was simply crying, saying nothing at all. Dryden realized why: She couldn't even have a bit of denial to comfort herself with. Not with the thoughts of every adult at the table washing over her. Their awful agreement with what Dryden had said. There was nothing for her to do but sit there and take it. Dryden pulled her against himself, and she held on as if the patio were going to drop out from under her.

For more than a minute, no one spoke. Then, by silent agreement, Holly and Marsh and Harris stood from the table. They wandered off to leave the two of them alone.

Dryden found himself focusing on taking in the moment: Rachel in his arms, her face against his shoulder. The details he would come back to for the rest of his life – he had to experience them as much as he could, this last time they would ever be real.

'You know there's another way this could go,' Rachel whispered. There was more in her voice than the strain of tears. There was an edge there – a trace of the other Rachel.

'Yes, I know,' Dryden said.

'I could take it to these people, instead of hiding. I could hole up in D.C., a mile from the Capitol, and get into the heads of everyone who helps these companies. I wouldn't need to kill anyone. There are lots of ways I could end their careers. Make them buy drugs and get caught. Make them say the wrong word near an open microphone. Make them tear off their clothes on a street corner and scream at the traffic. I could rip their lives to pieces without hurting a hair on their heads. If their replacements are no better, I could get rid of them, too. I could do it forever.'

'It wouldn't be wrong, either,' Dryden said. 'It's exactly what they deserve. But it's not what you deserve – that life.' He eased her away from his shoulder and tilted her face up to his own. The edge was in her gaze, too. The ghost of what she'd been, all those lost years. 'What you deserve is a childhood,' Dryden said. 'And I mean for you to have one.'

Rachel nodded, blinking as new tears formed. They seemed to clear her eyes of everything that didn't belong there.

Chapter Forty-six

The plan unfolded two days later, at the Hart Senate Office Building in Washington, D.C. Marsh booked a small hearing room on the fifth floor, for three in the afternoon. He accompanied Dryden into the building an hour beforehand, ushering him through the security checkpoint.

'Thanks for this,' Dryden said. 'You really will lose your job over it.'

'If I'm losing it for finally doing the right thing, I guess that should give me a moment of pause.'

'Thanks, all the same. I'll owe you one. That's not just a figure of speech, coming from me. If there's something I can help you with, someday, get in touch.'

'I'll keep it in mind.'

At 2:58 Dryden stood alone in a small hallway behind the dais of the hearing room. He listened to the murmur of the crowd in the seats; Marsh had invited more than forty people, the most powerful he could get. Among them were six senators, nine representatives, four cabinet officials, and staffers for all of them. They'd been told only that the event was a presentation related to intelligence-gathering technology, which was true in a roundabout way.

2:59.

Close enough.

Dryden stepped through the doorway into the chamber, and the buzz of voices died away. He crossed to the podium at the center of the dais and faced the crowd. Behind and above him, a projector screen showed a bright white expanse – the empty first slide of a PowerPoint presentation.

For a long moment Dryden said nothing. He kept his expression blank and stood there, letting the crowd get a good look at his face.

The expected reaction kicked in at three seconds. A woman near the front narrowed her eyes, then turned and spoke quietly to the man beside her. The man, still staring at Dryden, suddenly flinched.

By ten seconds everyone had picked up on it, either on their own or by way of being told. Everywhere in the crowd, heads swiveled, looking for the exits, or maybe an authority figure of some kind.

'You recognize me,' Dryden said.

The whisper of voices died again. All eyes settled on him.

'I'm the guy with the dirty bomb,' Dryden continued. 'I'm also dead. Two good reasons I shouldn't be standing here.'

The remote for the projector lay atop the podium. Dryden picked it up and pressed the SLIDE ADVANCE button. His own face filled the screen above him – the so-called composite image that had gone out on the airwaves back when the manhunt began.

'My name is Sam Dryden,' he said. He pressed the ADVANCE button again, and the composite was replaced by the original version of the photo. Bright colors instead of grayscale. A smile instead of a deadpan. Trish beside him, and the Embarcadero and San Francisco Bay behind him, instead of empty space.

Confusion filtered through the crowd.

'Here's a few more, for the hell of it,' Dryden said.

He pressed the button five times in slow succession, cycling through the other snapshots that had captured that moment. Trish was blinking in one of them, Dryden in another.

'You and the rest of the world were lied to about this,' Dryden said. 'In the coming weeks or months, it may happen again.'

Another press of the button. A photo of Holly and Rachel came up, taken with a disposable camera in Galveston after they'd left the café.

The next photo was a closer shot of their faces.

'Get a good look,' Dryden said. 'Somewhere down the road, if CNN says there's a woman running around with weaponized smallpox, you might see one or both of these faces in the coverage.'

In the crowd, Dryden began to see the second reaction he'd expected. The split. In almost every set of eyes there was only confusion, but in a few he saw other things: concern, tension, calculation. The eyes of people who weren't confused at all. As Dryden watched, those people traded looks with one another. Two or three of them took out cell phones.

Not much time left now.

'I don't expect most of you to believe the next thing I'm going to tell you,' Dryden said. 'I wouldn't believe it, in your place. But if this woman or this girl become the subject of a manhunt next month, or next year, you'll have to wonder, won't you? You might even sit down with a friend from *The New York Times* and have a long chat about it.'

He saw the calls begin to connect. Men cupped their hands over their phones and spoke urgently.

How long did he have? Two minutes? One?

Well, that would do. He'd rehearsed the bullet points with a stopwatch. He had the spiel down to thirty-five seconds – time enough to rattle off names and places and locations, and repeat them so that no one would forget.

He got all the way through it twice before the Capitol Police stormed the room.

Chapter Forty-seven

Sam Dryden's house in El Sedero stood empty for more than seven weeks. The lawn grew out of control. The entry floor beneath the mail slot piled up with flyers and credit card offers and bills. Neighbors knocked on the doors and tried to see in through the windows, but all the shades were drawn. In seven weeks, no relatives showed up to see about him. No friends.

It was foggy the night he came back. He stepped out of the taxicab with nothing in his hands, and walked up the concrete path to his front door. The key was behind the cedar shake next to the light, where he'd left it.

As soon as he stepped inside, the smell hit him. Flies buzzed in a cloud above the kitchen wastebasket, and all the drain traps had evaporated, letting in air from the sewer.

Dryden tied off the trash bag and hauled it out, ran the taps, and then opened every window in the place. Moist night air pressed through the house, scented with evergreens and sea salt.

In the master bath he disrobed and studied himself in the mirror. He'd lost ten or fifteen pounds, and there were faint red marks where the shock paddles had touched his skin. He stared at the beard he'd grown, ragged and unkempt beneath the hollows of his eyes, then opened the vanity drawer where he kept his razors and shaving cream.

An hour later, showered and dressed in clean clothes, he walked the rooms of his home. The smell of decay was gone, but he kept the windows open. He tried to remember the last time he'd opened any of them, in all the years he'd lived here, but couldn't recall a single time. How often had he even bothered to pull up the shades?

When he finally closed all the sashes again, the house's silence surprised him. Had it always been like this? So dead that every metal tick of the air ducts stood out?

He went to his bedroom and stretched out on the sheets. Exhausted as he was, it took forever for sleep to find him.

He stood on the wet sand margin of the beach, watching the sunset. The day had been hazy, and the sun was deep red by the time it touched the horizon.

Behind him was the boardwalk, and up and down the shore, campfires burned. There was a dog barking, a couple hundred yards up the beach. Little kids were throwing a Frisbee for it to catch.

'Hey.'

A woman's voice. Dryden turned. She was standing

there, twenty feet away, next to the fire he'd started a few minutes before.

Her name was Riley. She worked at an art gallery in town. Dryden had met her there three months ago, a few days after he'd come home and shaved his beard.

He crossed the sand to her, and she sank into him; they stood that way a long time, arms around each other, listening to the firewood popping and the kids laughing and the dog barking. He wasn't sure how it was shaking out with the two of them, but he liked being with her. She seemed to like being around him, too. For now, that was enough.

They sat on a blanket and watched the twilight melt away. As the first stars showed through, Dryden's neighbors from two houses down came onto the beach with their nine-year-old son. Dryden waved them over, and the five of them sat talking as the night darkened and cooled beyond the halo of the fire.

It was a quarter to four in the morning. Dryden lay awake, Riley breathing softly against him. He slipped her arm off of his chest, eased out from under the covers, and stood.

In the den off the kitchen he found a notepad. He sat down at the desk with it, opened the tray drawer, and looked for something to write with, but all he could find was a Sharpie. He popped off the cap and began to print in rough-scrawled penmanship. The words bled dark into the paper.

Hi Sam. Don't say anything out loud. There are laser
microphones aimed at your windows most of the time, but
there's nothing hidden inside the house. No bugs. No cameras.

By the time he'd finished writing it, his pulse was
slamming in his ears.

You shouldn't be anywhere near me, he thought. *You should
be halfway around the world.*

He put the marker to the page again.

I've been that far away, most of these months. I will be again,
soon. I had to check on you, though. I had to find out if the
people watching you had any other plans in mind. I had to know
if you were in danger. But I think you were right — they're
just watching you in case I show up. Sooner or later I think
they'll even give up on that. They seem bored with it.

You can never risk meeting me in person, Dryden thought.
*Even if you think it's safe. I'd give anything to see you, but you
can't take the chance.*

I know, promise.

Are you and Holly safe?

Yes. That's the other part of why I'm here — to tell you
we're okay. We're more than okay. It's warm where we live.
Holly works as a doctor for the local people, and we're both

400

learning the language. There are so many kids my age. My life has never been like this before. Never this happy.

Dryden stared at the words on the pad. They warmed him every bit as much as the fire on the beach had. Their meaning sank deep into his skin.

You seem happier, too, Sam. I haven't been watching you for long, but I can tell. I'm glad you met someone. Are you going to take my advice? Are you going to be somebody's father again?

He laughed under his breath. *Slow down*, he thought. *She and I have toothbrushes at each other's places. That's all the further along we are.*

He drew a smiley face on the page, and next to it he wrote,

I know, I know, none of my business.

For the longest time he found he couldn't form a thought in reply. His mind was simply full of feelings, a whole storm of them. The reality of the moment suddenly hit him: Rachel was here. She was right here, within a mile of where he was sitting. They could sprint to each other in a matter of minutes—

Except they couldn't. Ever.

His eyes stung. He blinked and pushed the feeling away; Rachel could probably pick up on it.

He found himself writing again.

I miss you too, Sam. I keep waiting for it to not hurt so much, but part of me doesn't want the pain to go away, because it's ours. It's only ours, yours and mine, and I don't want to lose it. If that makes any sense.

It makes perfect sense, Dryden thought.
The Sharpie was still for a few seconds. Then:

There's something I need to tell you about.

What?

Have you ever heard people say to each other, it wasn't an accident we met?

Yes.

You and me, it wasn't an accident.

Dryden waited for more.

All the things I can do, that I didn't know about when my memory was gone — deep down, I could still do them without knowing it.

The roadblock in Fresno, Dryden thought. *The cop who let us go.*

Yes. But there was another time I did it.

Seconds passed. Dryden imagined Rachel, some-where out there, working out what she wanted to say. Then he started writing.

The two months they had me in that little room, here in El Sedero, I had a game I'd play in my head. I did it whenever I got scared or felt too alone. The game was, I'd imagine I could feel other people, far away outside the building. A whole town full of them. I told myself I could feel their emotions — little kids were like puppies, old people were like deep water without any waves. But there was one person in town I liked focusing on more than all the rest. Someone who seemed strong. Someone hard, like the soldiers who watched over me in that place, but not cold like them. Everything about that person seemed good, and at the worst times, that's who I kept my mind on, to make myself feel less afraid. I never knew if I was making it all up or not.

Another pause.

So many times, I thought about trying to get away from that place. I even knew where I'd run if I did it. I'd seen the boardwalk in the soldiers' thoughts, all the time. But the idea of it was scary, being alone out in the dark, being chased. So I had this fantasy, almost every night. I imagined myself running away, and I pictured that spot where one boardwalk meets the other. In my fantasy, that person in town, the one who made me feel safe, would be waiting for me when I got there.

Dryden smiled, in spite of the pain.
The night jogs.
Compulsions that came on like fits.
Drawing him out to the boardwalk at all hours of the night. Out to the junction, to stand for minutes on end, for reasons he could never quite place.

All at once he was sure Rachel was smiling, too. Even laughing. Through tears.

Sorry about all that.

'I'm not sorry,' Dryden whispered in the silence.

I know.

Acknowledgments

Here's one of the best – and most humbling – things about being a writer: you see firsthand all the work other people do to bring your book to life, and you know it would have never made it without them. These people I can't thank enough:

My agent, Janet Reid, for motivating me with the perfect combination of encouragement, swearing, and various threats of bodily harm – and for being the funnest person to hang out with at any writing conference. My editor, Keith Kahla, who saw this book through several revisions, and pushed it to be better every time. Hannah Braaten, and so many others who make the world turn at St. Martin's Press and Minotaur: Sally Richardson, Matthew Shear, Andy Martin, Paul Hochman, Hector DeJean, Cassandra Galante, Amelie Littell, Bob Berkel, India Cooper – I'm sure I'm leaving a hundred names out. Thank you to Pouya Shahbazian at New Leaf Literary & Media, and Steve Younger at Myman, Greenspan, Fineman, Fox, Rosenberg & Light. Great thanks to Michael De Luca, Justin Lin, Elaine Chin, and Adam Cozad, as well as Lynn Harris and everyone at Warner Brothers.

He just wanted a decent book to read ...

Not too much to ask, is it? It was in 1935 when Allen Lane, Managing Director of Bodley Head Publishers, stood on a platform at Exeter railway station looking for something good to read on his journey back to London. His choice was limited to popular magazines and poor-quality paperbacks – the same choice faced every day by the vast majority of readers, few of whom could afford hardbacks. Lane's disappointment and subsequent anger at the range of books generally available led him to found a company – and change the world.

'We believed in the existence in this country of a vast reading public for intelligent books at a low price, and staked everything on it'
Sir Allen Lane, 1902–1970, founder of Penguin Books

The quality paperback had arrived – and not just in bookshops. Lane was adamant that his Penguins should appear in chain stores and tobacconists, and should cost no more than a packet of cigarettes.

Reading habits (and cigarette prices) have changed since 1935, but Penguin still believes in publishing the best books for everybody to enjoy. We still believe that good design costs no more than bad design, and we still believe that quality books published passionately and responsibly make the world a better place.

So wherever you see the little bird – whether it's on a piece of prize-winning literary fiction or a celebrity autobiography, political tour de force or historical masterpiece, a serial-killer thriller, reference book, world classic or a piece of pure escapism – you can bet that it represents the very best that the genre has to offer.

Whatever you like to read – trust Penguin.